The Treasure of the Lake

H. RIDER HAGGARD

The Treasure of the Lake

HUTCHINSON OF LONDON

HUTCHINSON & CO (*Publishers*) LTD
178–202 Great Portland Street, London W1

London Melbourne Sydney
Auckland Johannesburg Cape Town
and agencies throughout the world

First published 1926
This edition 1971

Printed in Great Britain by litho on antique wove paper
by Anchor Press, and bound by Wm. Brendon,
both of Tiptree, Essex

ISBN 0 09 107190 9

PREFACE

By Allan Quatermain

I CANNOT remember that anywhere in this book I have stated what it was that first gave me the idea of attempting to visit Mone, the Holy Lake, and the Dabanda who live upon, or, to be precise, at some distance from its shores. Therefore I will do so now.

There is a certain monastery in Natal where I have been made welcome from time to time, among whose brethren was a very learned monk, now "gone down", as the Zulus say, who, although our faiths were different, honoured me with his confidence upon many matters, and I think I may add with his friendship. Brother Ambrose, as he was called in religion—what his real name may have been I do not know—a Swede by birth, would have been an archæologist, also an anthropologist pure and simple, had he not chanced to be a saint. As it was he managed to combine much knowledge of these sciences with his noted and singular holiness. For example, he was the greatest authority upon Bushmen's paintings that I have ever met, and knew more of the history, religions, customs, and habits of the inhabitants of Southern, Eastern, and South-central Africa—well, than I did myself. Thus is came about, our tastes being so similar on these and other subjects, that when we could not meet and talk, often we corresponded.

One of his learned letters, which I still preserve, was written to me many years ago from Mozambique, whither he had gone upon a journey connected with the missionary enterprises of his order. From it, for the sake of accuracy, I will quote some passages.

Brother Ambrose says :

"In this island I have come into touch with a man, a rescued slave whom it was my privilege to baptize and to attend through his last illness, during which he made many confidences to me. Peter, as he was called because he was received into the Church upon the feast day of that saint, was a man of unusual appearance. His general cast of countenance and physique were Arab, and his native language was a somewhat archaic dialect of Arabic. His eyes, however, were large and round, almost owl-like, indeed—by the way, he had a singular faculty of seeing in the dark—and his handsome features were remarkable for a melancholy, which I think must have been inherited and not due to his experiences of life.

"He told me that he belonged to a small tribe dwelling in the neighbourhood of mountains called Ruga, far beyond a great lake—I am not sure what lake—which mountains I gathered are not far distant from some branch of the Congo River in the remote interior. The home of his tribe, if I understood him aright, was a large hollow of land enclosed by cliffs. In the centre of this hollow lies a big sheet of water surrounded by forest which, he said, is considered holy. When I asked him why it was holy, he replied because on an island in this water dwelt a priestess who is a Shadow of God, or of the gods, a beautiful woman with many magical powers, who utters oracles and bestows blessings on her worshippers (which, being interpreted, means, I take it, a fetish or rather the head servant of a fetish credited with the power of making rain and of averting misfortunes). About this person he told me many legends too absurd to record, amongst others that she and her husband, who is the chief of the tribe—for she has a husband—are sacrificed at a certain age, when her place is taken by another 'Shadow', who is reputed to be her daughter.

"One other thing he told me which I am sure will interest you very much ; indeed, although I am very busy, I write this letter chiefly in order to pass on the superstition, or legend, or whatever it may be, before I forget exactly what he said. You and I have often discussed the mysteries of the African forms of taboo. Well, Peter described a variety of it that was quite new to me. He declared that to his tribe *all* wild game are taboo and may not be killed or eaten by any member of the tribe, who, it seems, are largely vegetarians, but supplement this diet with the flesh of goats and cattle, of which they possess many herds. Nor is this all, for he assured me further that his people exercised great power over these untamed beasts, living with them on the same terms of familiarity as we do with dogs and horses and other domestic animals. Thus he asserted positively that they can send them away to or call them back from any given spot, and make them do their bidding in various other fashions, even to the extent of being able to cause them to attack anyone they choose.

"I tried to extract from him what he believed to be the reason for this alleged remarkable authority over the wild fauna of his country, but all I could make out was that the priests taught some form of the old Pythagorean doctrine of metempsychosis (as you know, not uncommon in Africa, especially when tyrannical chiefs are concerned) ; I mean that the souls of men, particularly of those who had led evil lives, are reborn in the bodies of beasts, which beasts are therefore, in a sense, their kin, and on this account feared and venerated.

"It was extremely curious to hear these pre-Christian delusions from the mouth of a modern African native, and I wonder very much if his story has any faint foundation in fact. Probably not, but, my dear friend, if ever you get the chance in the course of your explorations, *do* try to find out. You know that, like you, I hold that scattered here and there through the vast expanse of Africa are the remains of peoples who still preserve fragments of ancient systems and religions, such as the Babylonian star-worship or that of the gods of old Egypt."

Then the letter goes on to tell of the decease of Peter, before Brother Ambrose could further pursue his inquiries about a carving that he had discovered somewhere on the East Coast, which he thought must have been executed by Bushmen in the remote past ; although there is, or was, no other evidence that they ever lived so far north.

This incident of the strange story told to Father Ambrose by the dying native, Peter, remained fixed in my mind, and in the end was the real cause of the journey described in the following pages.

I should like to take this opportunity to say that on re-reading this record, which is an expanded version of a diary I kept at the time, I am not sure that I have succeeded in conveying an adequate sense of the eeriness that pervaded the Dabanda people and their country. No wonder that added to the various humiliations which I suffered in their land, this unearthly atmosphere, whereof dwellers in the fetish-ridden districts of Africa have often had experience, at last got upon my nerves to such an extent that if I had stopped there much longer I believe I should have gone crazy.

Another thing that I wish to state is that on weighing the evidence, whatever reasons old Kumpana and others may have given, I am now convinced that Hans was right and that the real cause which led them to procure the return of Kaneke to Moneland, was that they might execute him in punishment for his crime of sacrilege in earlier life. On this I believe they were determined both from vindictiveness and because, under their iron law, while he lived it was impossible for the mysterious "Treasure of the Lake" to take another man to husband, as for their own secret reasons they desired that she should do.

Lastly, it might be asked why I do not more accurately indicate the exact geographic position of Mone-land and its holy hidden lake. I will face ridicule—especially as I shall never live to feel its shafts—and make a confession. Before I left his country, as Arkle had done in his letter, Kumpana assured me with much quiet emphasis that if I revealed its exact locality and explained how it could be reached by any other white man, the results to them, also to myself and Hans in this or later lives, would be most unpleasant. I did not and do not believe him ; still, in view of my experience of the uncanny powers of the Dabanda priests, I thought it wise—well, to keep on the safe side and on this point to remain a little indefinite.

ALLAN QUATERMAIN.

CONTENTS

The Treasure of the Lake

CHAPTER I

Now when I grow old it becomes every day more clear to me, Allan Quatermain, that each of us is a mystery living in the midst of mysteries, bringing these with us when we are born and taking them away with us when we die ; doubtless into a land of other and yet deeper mysteries. At first, while we are quite young, everything seems very clear and simple. There is a male individual called Father and a female called Mother who, between them, have made us a present to the world, or of the world to us, whichever way you like to put it, apparently by arrangement with the kingdom of heaven ; at least that is what we are taught. There are the sun, the moon, and the stars above us and the solid earth beneath, there are lessons and dinner and a time to get up and a time to go to bed—in short there are a multitude of things, all quite obvious and commonplace, which may be summed up in three words, *the established order*, in which, by the decree of Papa and Mamma and the heavens above, we live and move and have our being.

Then the years go by, the terrible, remorseless years that bear us as steadily from the cradle to the grave as a creeping glacier bears a stone. With every one of them, after the first fifteen or so when we become adult, or in some instances earlier if we chance to be what is called "rather unusual", a little piece of the curtain is rolled up or a little hole is widened in the veil, and beneath that curtain, or through that enlarging hole, we see the mysteries moving in the dusk beyond. So swiftly do they come and go, and so dark is the background, that we never discern them clearly. There, if time is given to us to fix them in our minds, they appear ; for a moment they are seen, then they are gone, to be succeeded by others even yet more wondrous, or perhaps more awful.

But why go on talking of what is endless and unfathomable ? Amidst this wondrous multitude of enigmas we poor, purblind, slow-witted creatures must make our choice of those we wish to study. Long ago I made mine, one local and terrestrial, namely the land with which I have been connected all my life—Africa—and the other universal and spiritual, namely human nature. What! some may ask, do you call human nature spiritual? The very words belie you. What is there spiritual about that which is human?

My friend, I answer, in my opinion, my most humble and fallible opinion, almost everything. More and more do I become convinced that we are nearly all spirit, notwithstanding our gross apparent bodies with their deeds and longings. You have seen those coloured globes that pedlars sell—I mean the floating things tinted to this hue or that, that are the delight of children. The children buy these balls and toss them into the air, where they travel one way or the other, blown by winds we cannot see, till in the end they burst and of each there remains nothing but a little shrivelled skin, a shred of substance, which they are told is made from the gum of a tree. Well, to my fancy that expanded skin or shred is a good symbol of the human body, so large and obvious to the sight, yet driven here and there by the breath of circumstance and in the end destroyed. But what was within it which escapes at last and is no more seen? To my mind the gas with which the globe was filled represents the spirit of man, imprisoned for a while; then to all appearance lost.

I dare say that the example is faulty; still, I use it because it conveys something of my idea. So, good or bad, I let it stand and pass on to an easier theme, or at any rate one easier to handle, namely that of the mysteries of the great continent of Africa.

Now all the world is wonderful, but surely among its countries there is none more so than Africa; no, not even China the unchanging, or India the ancient. For this reason, I think: those great lands have always been more or less known to their own inhabitants, whereas Africa, as a whole, from the beginning was and still remains unknown.

To this day great sections of its denizens are quite ignorant of other sections, as much so as was mighty Egypt of the millions of the neighbouring peoples in the time when a voyage to the Land of Punt, which I take to have been the country that we now know as Uganda, was looked upon as a marvellous adventure. Again, there is the instance of Solomon, or rather Hiram and his gold traffic with Ophir, the dim and undefined, that doubtless was the district lying at the back of Sofala. But why multiply such examples, of which there are many? And if this is true of Africa, the Libya of the early world, as a country, is it not still more true of its inhabitants, divided as these are into countless races, peoples, and tribes, each of them with its own gods or ancestral spirits, language, customs, traditions, and mental outlook established in the passage of innumerable ages?

So far as my small experience goes, for though many might think it large it is still small, these are my opinions which I venture to state as an opening to what I have always considered a very curious history, in which it was my fortune to play some small and humble part. For let it be understood at once that I was by no means the chief actor in this business. Indeed, I was never more than an agent, a kind of connecting wire between the parties concerned, an insignificant bridge over which their feet travelled to certain ends that I presume to have been appointed by Fate. Still, I saw much of the play and now, when the curtain has been long rung down, by help of the diary I kept at the time and have preserved, I will try to record such memories of it as remain to me—well, because rightly or wrongly I think that they are worth recording.

Years ago, accompanied by my servant Hans, the old and faithful Hottentot with whom I have experienced so many adventures, I made a great journey to what I may almost call Central Africa, starting in from the East Coast. It was a hazardous adventure into which I had been led by tales that had reached me of the enormous herds of elephants to be found in what I suppose must now be the north of the Belgian Congo. Or perhaps it is still No Man's Land as it was in those days—really, I do not know. Nor is this wonderful, seeing that with a single exception I believe that I was the first white man to set foot in that particular district which lies beyond the Lado mountains north of Jissa and of the Denbo River.

To be truthful, however, it was not only the elephants that took me to these parts, guessing, as I did, that if I found them it might be of little avail, since probably ivory in bulk would prove impossible to carry. No, it was rather the desire to look upon new things, to discover the Unknown which is so strong a part of my nature, that at times it half reconciles me to the prospect of death which I, who believe that we do not go out, believe also must be a land or a state full of all that is strange and wonderful.

I had heard from natives in the neighbourhood of the great lake Victoria Nyanza that there was a marvellous country between two rivers known as M'bomu and Balo, where dwelt strange tribes who were said to dress like Arabs and to talk a

sort of Arabic ; also that somewhere in this country was a holy
lake, a big sheet of water that none was allowed to approach.
Further, that in this lake, which was called Mone (pronounced
like groan), a word of unknown meaning, was an island "where
dwelt the gods", or the spirits, for the term used was capable of
either interpretation.

Now, when I heard of this Holy Lake called Mone, "where
dwelt the gods", at once my mind went back to the letter of
which I have spoken in the preface of this book, that long years
before I had received from my late friend, Brother Ambrose,
telling me what he had learned from a slave whom he had
christened.

Could it be the same, I wondered, as that of which the slave
had told Brother Ambrose ? Instantly, and with much suppressed excitement, I set to work to make further inquiries,
and was informed that a certain Kaneke, a stranger who had
been a slave and was now the chief or captain of an Arab settle-
ment some fifty miles away from where I met these natives,
could give me information about the lake, inasmuch as he was
reported to be born of the people who dwelt upon its borders.

Then and there I changed my plans, as indeed was convenient
to me because of the suddenly developed hostility of a chief
through whose territory I had intended to pass, and in order to
seek out this Kaneke, took a road running in another direction
to that which I had designed to travel.   Little did I guess at the
time that Kaneke was seeking *me* out and that the natives who
told me the legend of the lake were, in fact, his emissaries sent
to tempt me to visit him, or that it was he who had incited the
chief against me in order to block my path.

Well, in due course I reached Kaneke-town, as it was called,
without accident, for although between me and it dwelt a very
dangerous tribe whom at first I had purposed to avoid, all at once
their chief and headman became friendly and helped me in every
way upon my journey.   Kaneke, a remarkable person whom I
will describe later, received me well, giving me a place to camp
outside his village and all the food that we required.   Also he
proved extraordinarily communicative, telling me directly that
he belonged to a tribe called Dabanda, which had its home in
the wild parts whereof I have spoken.   He added that he was
the "high-born" son of a great doctor or medicine-man, a calling
which all his family had followed for generations.   In some
curious way, of which I did not at first learn the details, while
undergoing his novitiate as a doctor or magician, this man had

been seized by a rival tribe, the Abanda, and ultimately sold as a slave to an Arab trader, one Hassan, who brought him down to the neighbourhood of the great lake.

Here also, according to his own story, it seemed that one night this Kaneke succeeded in murdering Hassan.

"I crept on him in the night. I got him by the throat. I choked the life out of him," he said, twitching his big hands, "and as he died I whispered in his ear of all the cruel things he had done to me. He made signs to me, praying for mercy, but I went on till I had killed him, whispering to him all the while. When he was dead I took his body and threw it out into the bush, having first stripped him. There a lion found it and bore it away, for in the morning it was gone. Then, Macumazahn" (that is the native name by which I, Allan Quatermain, am known in Africa, and which had come with me to these parts), "I played a great game, such as you might have done, O Watcher-by-Night. I returned to the tent of Hassan and sat there thinking.

"I heard the lion, or lions come, for I think there was more than one of them, as I was sure that they would come who had called them by a charm, and guessed that they had eaten or carried away Hassan the evil. When all was quiet I dressed myself in the robes of Hassan. I found his gun, which on the journey he had taught me to use, that I might shoot the slaves who could travel no farther for him ; his pistol also, and saw that they were loaded. Then I sat myself upon his stool and waited for the light.

"At the dawn one of his women crept into the tent to visit him. I seized her. She stared at me, saying :

" 'You are not my master. You are not Hassan.'

"I answered, 'I am your master. I am Hassan, whose face the spirits have changed in the night.'

"She opened her mouth to cry out. I said :

" 'Woman, if you try to scream, I will kill you. If you are quiet I will take you. Look on me. I am young. Hassan was old. I am a finer man, you will be happier with me. Choose now. Will you die, or live ?'

" 'I will live,' she said, she who was no fool.

" 'Then I am Hassan, am I not ?' I asked.

" 'Yes,' she said, 'you are Hassan and my lord. I am sure of it now.'

"For I tell you, that woman had wit, Macumazahn, and I was sorry when, two years afterwards, she died.

" 'Good,' I said. 'Now, when the servants of Hassan come you will swear that I am he and no other, remembering that if you do not swear you die.'

" 'I will swear,' she answered.

"Presently the headman of Hassan came, a big fat fellow who was half an Arab, to bring him his morning drink. I took it and drank. The light of the rising sun struck into the tent. He saw and started back.

" 'You are not Hassan,' he said. 'You are the slave Kaneke, whom we bought.'

" 'I am Hassan,' I answered. 'Ask my wife here, whom you know, if I am not Hassan. Also, if I am not, where is Hassan?'

" 'Yes, he is Hassan, my husband,' broke in the woman.

" 'This is witchcraft!' he cried, and ran away.

" 'Now he is gone to fetch the others,' I said to the woman. 'Fasten back the sides of the tent that I may see, and give me the guns.'

"She obeyed, though then she sat exposed, and I took the double-barrelled gun and held it ready.

"Presently, they all came, five or six Arabs, or half Arabs, and a score or so of black soldiers. Even the slaves came, dragging their yokes, fifty or more of them of whom perhaps thirty were men, all known to me, for had we not shared the yoke? There they stood huddled together behind the Arabs, staring.

" 'Take a knife,' I whispered to the woman; 'slip out, get among the slaves and cut the thongs of the yokes.'

"She nodded—have I not told you that girl had wits, Macumazahn?—and slipped away.

"Cried the fat one, the captain:

" 'This fellow, whom we all know for Kaneke, the slave whom we bought, says that he is Hassan our lord. Yes, there he sits in Hassan's robes and says that he is Hassan. Dog, where is Hassan?'

" 'Inside this garment,' I answered. 'Listen. I made a bargain with Hassan, I who am a wizard. I forgave him his sins against me, and in return he gave me his soul while his body flew away to Paradise.'

" 'The liar!' shouted the captain. 'Kill him!' and he brandished a spear.

" 'Admit that I am Hassan or I will send you to where you will learn that I am no liar,' I said quietly.

"In answer he lifted the spear to stab me. Then I shot him dead.

" 'Now am I Hassan?' I asked, while the rest stared at him.

"One or two who were frightened said 'Yes'. Others stood silent, and a big fellow began to put a cap upon his gun. I shot him with the other barrel, then, rising, roared in a great voice :

" 'On to them, slaves, if you would be free !' for by now I saw that the woman had cut many of the thongs.

"Those men were brave, they came of good stock. They heard, and leapt on to the Arabs with a shout, knocking them down with the yokes and throttling them with their hands. Soon it was over. Most of them were killed, but two or three crawled before me crying that I was certainly Hassan.

" 'Very well,' I said. 'Take away these'—here I pointed to the dead men—'and throw them into yonder ravine, and bid the women prepare food while I make prayer according to my custom.'

"Then I took Hassan's beautiful prayer-rug, spread it and made obeisance in the proper fashion, muttering with my lips as I had often watched him do ; after which everything went smoothly. That is all the story, Macumazahn."

When he had finished this tale, which, true or false, of its sort was remarkable even in equatorial Africa, where such things happen, or happened, by the score without anybody hearing of them, I sat awhile considering Kaneke.

To tell the truth he was worth study. A giant of a man in size, he was not a negro by any means, for his features had a somewhat Semitic cast and he was yellow-hued rather than black. Moreover, he had hair, not wool, wavy hair that he wore rather long. His eyes were so prominent, round, and lustrous that they gave an owl-like cast to his countenance, his features well cut, although the lips were somewhat coarse and the nose was hooked like a hawk's beak, while his hands and feet were thin and shapely, and in curious contrast to his great athletic frame and swelling muscles. His age might have been anything between thirty-five and forty, and he carried his years well, moving with the swing and vigour of youth.

It was his face, however, that commanded my attention as a student of character. It was extraordinarily strong and yet dreamy, almost mystical, indeed, when in repose, the face of a thinker, or even of a priest. Contemplating him I could almost believe the strange tale he had told me, which in the case of most natives I should have set down as an outrageous lie.

For here, without doubt, was a man who could conceive a plot of the sort and execute it without hesitation. Yet he was one to whom I took a dislike from the moment I set eyes upon him. Instinctively, however attractive he might be in some ways, I felt that at bottom he was dangerous and not to be trusted. Still, he interested me very much, as did his story, especially that part of it in which he said that he called the lions "by a charm".

"What happened afterwards, Kaneke?" I asked at last.

"Oh, very little, Macumazahn. I became Hassan, though they called me 'the Changeling'; that is all. I did not travel on towards the coast because I thought it safer to stop where I was, not daring to go either forward or back. So I gathered people about me and founded the town in which you are. Once some Arabs came to kill me, but I killed them, and after that I was no more molested, because, you see, I was looked upon as a ghost-man, one who had a great *ju-ju*, one not to be touched; and all were afraid of me."

"You mean you became a witch-doctor again, Kaneke."

"Yes, Macumazahn. Or, rather, I was that already, a diviner and a master of spells, like my fathers before me. So here I set up as a sort of wise man as well as a warrior, and soon gained a great repute, which caused all the people round about to send to me to give them medicines and charms, or to make rain. Thus, and with the help of trade, I became rich and powerful as I am today."

"Then you are a happy man, Kaneke."

He rolled his big round eyes and looked at me earnestly, asking:

"Is any man happy, Macumazahn, or at least any man who thinks? The beasts are happy; can man be happy like the beasts who never look to tomorrow or to the hour of death?"

"Now that you mention it, Kaneke, I do not suppose that any man is happy, except sometimes for an hour when he forgets himself in drink, or love, or war."

"Or when he talks with the heavens," added Kaneke, which I thought a strange remark. "Yes, then and in sleep he is sometimes happy till he wakes to the sorrow of the day."

He paused a little and went on:

"If this be so with all men, how much more is it so with those who have known the yoke and who must grow old far from their homes, as I do? For such there is no joy, for even

their dreams are haunted. In these they see the village where
they were born and the distant mountains and the face of their
mother, and hear the voices of their playmates and of those
they loved, that now are still."

I sighed as the truth of his words came home to me.

"If you feel thus," I answered presently, "why do you not
return to your home?"

"I will tell you, Macumazahn. There are many reasons,
among them these. Here I rule over people who would not wish
to go with me and who, if I forced them, would run away, or
perhaps poison me. Indeed, they would not let me go because
I am necessary to them, protecting them from their enemies
and from wild beasts, and giving them rain, as I can do. Again,
the road is long and dangerous, and maybe I should not live to
come to its end. Also, if I did, what should I find? I was my
father's eldest son, born of his chief wife, and to me he told the
secrets of his wisdom that have come down to us through the
generations. But I have been absent for years and mayhap
another has taken my place. My people would not welcome me,
Macumazahn. They might kill me, especially if they who know
all, have learned that I have betrayed my own goddess by bending
the knee to the Prophet, even though I never bent my heart.
Still, it is true that I wish to risk all and return, even if it be
to die."

Now I grew deeply interested, for always I have loved to
discover the mysteries of these strange African faiths.

"Your own goddess?" I asked. "What goddess?"

All this time we were seated in the shade of a flat-topped,
thick-leaved tree of the banyan species, the Tree of Council
it was called, that grew upon a little knoll at a distance from
Kaneke's town. He rose and walked all round this place, as
though to make sure that no one was near us. Then he stared
up into its branches, where he discovered a monkey sitting. I
knew that it was there, but he did not seem to have noticed it.
At this monkey he began to shout out something, as though he
were giving it orders, till at last the little beast ran along the
boughs of the tree, dropped to the ground and bolted for the bush
in the distance.

"Why do you hunt it away?" I asked.

"A monkey can hear and is very like a man. Perhaps a
monkey can tell tales, Macumazahn."

I laughed, for of course I understood that this was an African
way of indicating that the matter to be discussed was most

solemn and private.   By driving away that monkey Kaneke was swearing me to the strictest secrecy—or so I thought.

He came back and moved his stool, I noted, into such a position that the light of the westering sun striking through the lower boughs of the tree flickered on my face and left his in shadow.   I lit my pipe leisurely, so that for some time there was silence between us.   The fact is I was determined that he should be the first to speak.   It is a good rule with any native when a subject of importance is concerned.

"You asked me of my goddess, Macumazahn."

"Did I, Kaneke?" I replied, puffing at my pipe to make it burn.   "Oh yes, I remember.   Well, who is she and where does she live?   On earth or in heaven—which is the home of goddesses?"

"Yesterday, Macumazahn, you—or perhaps it was that little yellow man, your servant Hans—asked me if I had ever heard of a lake called Mone which lies in the hidden land where dwell my people, the Dabanda, beyond the Ruga-Ruga Mountains."

"I dare say.   I remember having heard of this lake, which interested me because of legends connected with it, though I forget what they were.   What about it?"

"Only that it is there my goddess dwells, Macumazahn."

"Indeed.   Then I suppose that she is a water-spirit."

"I cannot say, Macumazahn.   I only know that she dwells with her women on the island in the lake, and at night, when it is very dark, sometimes she and her companions are heard upon the water, or passing through the forests, singing and laughing.

"Did you ever see her, Kaneke?"

He hesitated like one who seeks time to make up a plausible story, or so I thought, then answered:

"Yes.   Once when I was young.   I had been sent to look for some goats of ours that had strayed, and following them into the forest which slopes down to the lake, I lost myself there. Night came on and I lay down to sleep under a tree, or rather to watch for the dawn, so that with the light I might escape from that darksome, haunted place, of which I was afraid."

"Well, and what happened?"

"So much that I cannot remember all, Macumazahn.   Spirits went by me; I heard them in the tree-tops and above; I heard them pass through the forest, laughing; I felt them gather about me and knew that they were mocking me.   At length all those Wood-Dwellers went away, leaving me as terrified as though a lion had come and eaten out of my bowl. The moon rose and her light pierced down through the boughs, a shaft of it here, a shaft of it there, with breadths of blackness between. I shut my eyes, trying to sleep, then hearing sounds, I opened them again. I looked up. There in the heart of one of the pools of light stood a woman, a fair-skinned woman like to one of your people, Macumazahn. She seemed to be young and slender, also beautiful, as I perceived when she turned her head and the moon shone upon her face and showed her soft, dark eyes, which were like those of a buck. For the rest she was clad in grey garments that glimmered like a spider's web filled with dew at dawn. There was a cap upon her head and from beneath it her black hair flowed down upon her shoulders. Oh, she was beautiful—so beautiful . . ." and he paused.

"That what, Kaneke?" I asked curiously.

"Lord, that I committed a great crime, the greatest in the whole world, the crime of sacrilege against her who is called the Shadow."

"Shadow! Whose shadow?"

"The Shadow of the Engoi, the goddess who dwells in heaven and is shone upon by the star we worship above all other stars." (This, I found afterwards, was the planet Venus.) "Or perhaps she dwells in the star and is shone upon by the moon—I do not know. At least, she who lives upon the island in the lake is the shadow of the Engoi upon earth, and that is why she is called Engoi and Shadow."

"Very interesting," I said, though I understood little of what he said, except that it was a piece of African occultism to which as yet I had not the key. "But what crime did you commit?"

"Lord, I was young and my blood was hot and the beauty of this wanderer in the forest made me mad. Lord, I threw my arms about her and embraced her. Or, rather, I tried to embrace her, but before my lips touched hers all my strength left me, my arms fell down and I became as a man of stone, though I could still see and hear. . . ."

"What did you see and hear, Kaneke?" I asked, for again he paused in his story.

"I saw her lovely face grow terrible and I heard her say, 'Do you know who I am, O man Kaneke, who are not afraid to do me violence in my holy, secret grove where none may set his foot?' Lord, I tried to lie, but I could not who must answer,

'I know that you are the Engoi; I know that your name is Shadow. I pray you to pardon me, O Shadow.'

" 'For what you have done there is no pardon. Still, your life is spared, if only for a while. Get you gone and let the Council of the Engoi deal with you as it will.' "

"And what happened then?"

"Then, Lord, she departed, vanishing away, and I too departed, flying through the forest terribly afraid and pursued by voices that proclaimed my crime and threatened vengeance. Next day the Council seized me and passed judgment on me, driving me from the land so that I fell into the hands of our enemies, the Abanda, who dwell upon the slopes of the mountains, and in the end was sold as a slave."

"And how did this Council know what you had done, Kaneke?"

"What is known to the Shadow is known to her Council, and what is known to her Council is known to the Shadow, Lord."

Now I considered Kaneke and his story, and came to the conclusion, a perfectly correct one, as I think, that he was lying to me. What his exact offence against this priestess may have been I don't know and never learned in detail, though I believe that it was much worse than what he described. All that was certain is that he had committed some sacrilegious crime of such a character that, notwithstanding his rank, he was forced to fly out of his country in order to save his life, and to become an exile, which he remained.

Leaving that subject without further comment, I asked him who were these Abanda who delivered him into slavery.

"Lord," he replied, "they are a branch of a people from whom we separated ages ago and who live on the plains beyond the mountains. They hate us and are jealous of us because the Engoi gives us rain and fruitful season, whereas often they suffer from drought and scarcity. Therefore they wish to take the land and Lake Mone, so that the Engoi may once more be their goddess also. More, they are a mighty people, whereas we are very few, for from generation to generation our numbers dwindle."

"Then why do they not invade and defeat you, Kaneke?"

"Because they dare not, Lord; because if they set foot within the land of Mone a curse will fall upon them, seeing that it and we who dwell there are protected by the Stars of Heaven. Yet always they hope that the day will come when they can defy the curse and conquer us, who hold them back by wisdom and not by spears. And now, Macumazahn, I must go to make my prayer before the people to that prophet in whom I do not believe. Yet come to me again when the evening star has risen, for I have more to say to you, Macumazahn."

I got up, then said :

"One more question before I go, Kaneke. Is this Engoi of whom you speak, who lives in a lake, a woman or—something more ?"

"Lord, how can I answer ? Certainly she is a woman, for she is born and dies, leaving behind her a daughter to take her place. Also she is something more, or so we are taught."

"What do you mean ?"

"I mean that the same flesh or Shadow dwells in every Engoi, although the flesh which holds it changes from generation to generation. There is a legend that she is an angel who sinned and fell from heaven."

"What is the legend and how did she sin ?"

A cunning look came over the face of Kaneke as he answered :

"The priests' tale runs, Lord, that an Engoi of long ago loved a white man and that when he was forbidden to her, she killed him to take him to heaven with her. Therefore she must return to the world again and again till she finds that white man" (here he glanced at me) "and makes amends to him for her crime. She is looking for him now, and the Stars declare that the time is at hand when she will find him again."

"Do they really ?" I remarked. "Well, I hope she won't be disappointed," I added, reflecting to myself that Kaneke was a first-class imaginative liar, for though the idea of the sinful spirit returning to inhabit mortal flesh is as old as the world, his adaptation of it was ingenious.

What, I wondered, as I walked away, did that specious but false-hearted ruffian Kaneke want to get out of me ? Whatever his object, certainly the man could not be trusted. According to his own account he was a fugitive outcast who had committed murder, one also who for his personal advantage pretended to profess a faith in which he admitted that he had no belief, showing thereby that he was of a traitorous and contemptible character. So sure was I of this, that but for one thing I would have put an end to my acquaintance with him then and there. He knew the way to Lake Mone and declared that it was his country. And I—well, I burned to find out the truth about this holy lake and the mysterious priestess who dwelt in the midst of its waters, she, without doubt, of whom Brother Ambrose had written to me so many years ago.

CHAPTER II

ALLAN'S BUSINESS INSTINCTS

I WENT to my camp, which was situated upon the outskirts of Kaneke's village in a deserted garden where bananas, oranges, papaws, and other semi-tropical products fought for existence in a neglected confusion, working out the problem of the survival of the fittest. Here I found Hans the Hottentot, who had been my servant and in his own way friend from my youth up, as he was that of my father before me. He was seated in front of the palm-leaf shelter watching a pot upon the fire made of mealie-cobs from which the corn had been stripped, looking very hot and cross.

"So you have come at last, Baas," he said volubly. "An hour ago that coast cook-boy, Aru, went off, leaving me to watch this stew which he said must be kept upon the simmer, neither boiling nor going cold, or it would be spoiled. He swore that he was going to pray to Allah, for he is a Prophet-worshipper, Baas. But I know what his prophet is like, for I found him kissing her last night ; great fat girl with a mouth as wide as that plate and a bold eye that frightens me, Baas, who have always been timid of women."

"Have you ?" I said. "Then I wish you would be timid of other things too, gin-bottles, for instance."

"Ah, Baas, a gin-bottle, I mean one that is full, is better than a woman, for of a gin-bottle you know the worst. You swallow the gin, you get drunk and it is very sad, and next morning your head aches and you think of all the sins you ever did. Yes, Baas, and if the gin was at all bad, their number is endless, and their colour so black that you feel that they can never be forgiven, however hard your reverend father, the Predikant, may pray for you up there. But, Baas, as the morning goes on, especially if you have the sense to drink a pint of milk and the luck to get it, and the sun shines, you grow better. Your sins roll away, you feel, or at least I do, that the prayers of your reverend father may have prevailed there in the Place of Fires, and that the slip is overlooked because Life's road is so full of greasy mud, Baas, that few can travel it without sometimes sitting down to think. Now with women, as the Baas knows better perhaps than anyone, the matter is not so simple. You can't wash *her* away with a pint of milk and a little sunshine, Baas. She is always waiting round the corner ; yes, even if she is dead—in your mind you know, Baas."

"Be silent, Hans," I said, "and give me my supper."

"Yes, Baas ; that is what I am trying to do, Baas, but something has gone wrong after all, for the stuff is sticking to the pot and I can't get it out even with this iron spoon. I think that if the Baas would not mind taking the pot and helping himself, it would be much easier," and he thrust that blackened article towards me.

"Hans," I said, "if this place were not Mahommedan where there is no liquor, I should think that you had been drinking."

"Baas, if you believe that Prophet-worshippers do not drink, your head is even softer than I imagined. It is true that they have no gin here, at least at present, because they have finished the last lot and cannot get any more till the traders come. But they make a kind of wine of their own out of palm trees which answers quite well if you can swallow enough of it without being sick, which I am sorry to say I can't, Baas, and therefore this afternoon I have only had two pannikins full. If the Baas would like to try some——"

Here I lifted the first thing that came to hand—it was a three-legged stool—and hurled it at Hans, who slipped cleverly round the corner of the hut, probably because he was expecting its advent.

A while later, after I had tackled the stew—which had stuck to the pot—with unsatisfactory results, and lit my pipe, he returned to clear up, in such a chastened frame of mind that I gathered the palm-wine—well, let that be.

"What has the Baas been doing all the afternoon in this dull place ?" he asked humbly, watching me with a furtive eye, for there was another stool within reach, also the pot. "Talking to that giant rain-maker, who looks like an owl in sunlight— I mean Kaneke—or perhaps to one of his wives ; she who is so pretty," he added, by an after-thought.

"Yes," I said, "I have—to Kaneke, I mean, not to the wife, whom I do not know ; indeed, I never heard that he had any wives."

Then I added suddenly, for now that he had recovered from the palm-wine I wished to surprise the truth out of his keen mind :

"What do you think of Kaneke, Hans ?"

Hans twiddled his dirty hat and fixed his little yellow eyes upon the evening sky, then he took the pot and, finding a remaining leg of fowl, ate it reflectively, after which he produced his corn-cob pipe and asked me for some tobacco.   This, by the way, I was glad to see, for when Hans could smoke I knew that he was quite sober.

These preliminaries finished, he remarked.

"As to what was it that the Baas wished me to instruct him ? Oh, I remember. About that big village headman, Kaneke. Well, Baas, I have made inquiries concerning him from his wife, who says she is jealous of him and therefore in a mood to speak the truth. First of all he is a great liar, Baas, though that is nothing for all these people are liars—not like me and you, Baas, who often speak the truth, or at least I do."

"Stop fooling, and answer my question," I said.

"Yes, Baas. Well, I said that he was a liar, did I not ? For instance, I dare say he has told the Baas a fine tale about how he came to settle here, by killing the head of the slave-gang, after which all the other slavers acknowledged him as their chief. The truth is that he and the other slaves murdered the lot of them because he said he was a good Mahommedan and could not bear to see them drinking gin against the law, which for my part I think was clever of him.   They surprised them in their sleep, Baas, and dragged them to the top of that cliff over the stream, where they threw them one by one into the water, except two who had beaten Kaneke.   These he flogged to death, which I dare say they deserved. After this the people here, who hated the slavers because they robbed them, made Kaneke their chief because he was such a holy man who could not bear to see followers of the Prophet drink gin, also because they were afraid lest he should throw them over the cliff too.   That is why he must be so strict about his prayers, because, you see, he must keep his fame for holiness and show that he is as good as he wishes others to be."

Hans stopped to re-light his pipe with an ember, and I asked him impatiently if he had any more to say.

"Yes, Baas, lots.   This Kaneke is not one man, he is two. The first Kaneke is a tyrant, one full of plots who would like to rule the world, a lover of liquor too, which he drinks in secret ; fierce, cunning, cruel.   The second Kaneke is one who dreams, who hears voices and sees things in the sky, who follows after visions, a true witch-doctor, a man who would seek what is afar, but who, living in this soft place, is like a lion in a cage. His mother must have made a mistake, and instead of bearing twins, got two spirits into one body where they must fight together till he dies."

"I dare say. Many men have two spirits in one body. Is that all, Hans?"

"Yes—that is, no, Baas. You know this Kaneke brought you here, don't you, Baas, and that all those troubles which we met with, so that we could not go the road we wanted because that tribe sent to say they would kill us if we did, were made by him so that you might come to his village."

"I know nothing of the sort."

"Well, it was so, Baas. The jealous woman told me all about it."

"Why? What for? There is no big game here that I can shoot, and I am not rich to give him presents. Indeed, he has asked for nothing and feeds us without payment."

"I am not sure, Baas, but I think that he wishes you to go somewhere with him; that the lion wants to come out of the cage and to kill for himself, instead of living on dead meat of which he is tired. Has he spoken to you about that holy lake of which we have heard, Baas? If not, I think he will."

"Yes, Hans. It seems that it is in his country where he was born and that he had an adventure there in his youth, because of which his people drove him away."

"Just so, Baas, and presently you will find that he desires to go back to his country and have more adventures or to pay off old scores, or both. Do you wish to go with him, Baas?"

"Do you, Hans?"

"I think not, Baas. This Kaneke is a spook man, and I am afraid of spooks who always make me feel cold down the back."

Here Hans stared at the sky again, then added:

"And yet, Baas, I'd rather go to the lake or anywhere than stop in this place where there is nothing to do and the palm-wine makes one sick, especially as after all, a good Christian like Hans has nothing to fear from spooks, whom he can tell to go to hell, as your reverend father did, Baas. Lastly, as your reverend father used to say, too, when he stood in the box in a nightshirt, it doesn't matter what I wish to do, or what you wish to do, since we shall go where we must, yes, where it pleases the Great One in the sky to send us, Baas, even if He uses Kaneke to drag us there by the hair of the head. And now, Baas, I must wash up those things before it gets dark, after which I have to meet that

B

jealous wife of Kaneke's yonder in a quiet place, and learn a little more from her, for as you know, Baas, Hans is always a seeker after wisdom."

"Mind that you don't find folly," I remarked sententiously. Then remembering my promise and noting that the evening star was showing brightly in the quiet sky, I rose and went through the gate of the town, for my camp was outside the fence of prickly pears which was planted round the palisade, thinking as I walked that in his ridiculous way Hans had spoken a great truth.   It was useless to bother about plans, seeing that we should go where it was fated that we should go, and nowhere else. Doubtless man has free will, but the path of circumstance upon which he is called to exercise it is but narrow.

At the gate I found a white-robed man waiting to guide me to Kaneke's abode, "to keep off the dogs and see that I did not step upon a thorn", as he said.

So I was conducted through the village, a tidy place in its way, to the north end, where outside the fence was that cliff with a stream, now nearly dry, running at the bottom of it over which Hans said Kaneke had thrown the slave-traders.

Round Kaneke's house, that was square, thatched, and built of whitewashed clay, was a strong palisade through which the only entrance was by a double gate, for evidently this chief was one who took no risks.   At the inner gate my guide bowed and left me.   As he departed it was opened by Kaneke himself, who, I noted, made it fast behind me with a bar and some kind of primitive lock.   Then he bowed before me in almost reverential fashion, saying :

"Enter, my lord Macumazahn, White Lord whose fame has travelled far.   Yes, whose fame has reached me even in this dead place where no news comes."

Now I looked at him, thinking to myself for the second time, "I do wonder what it is you want to get out of me, my friend." Then I said :

"Has it indeed ?   That is very strange, seeing that I am no great one, no Queen's man who wears ribbons and bright stars, nor even rich, but only a humble hunter who shoots and trades for his living."

"It is not at all strange, O Macumazahn.   Do you not know that every man of account has two values ?—one his public value in the market-place, which may be much or little ; and the other his private value, which is written in all minds that have judgment.   Nor is it strange that I should be acquainted with this second and higher value of yours that stands apart from wealth, or honours cried by heralds. Have I not told you that I am one of the fraternity of witch-doctors, and do you not know that throughout Africa such doctors communicate with one another by curious and secret ways? I say that before ever you set foot upon our shores I knew that you were coming in a ship, also much concerning you. Amongst others a certain Zikali who dwells in the land of the Zulus, a chief of our brotherhood, sent me a message."

"Oh, did he?" I said. "Well, Zikali's ways are dark and strange, so I can almost believe it. But, friend Kaneke, is it wise to talk thus openly here? Doubtless you have women in your house, and women's ears are long."

"Women," he answered. "Do you suppose that I keep such trash about me in my private place? Not so. Here my servants are men who are sworn to me, and even these leave me at sundown, save for the guard without my gates."

"So you are a hermit, Kaneke."

"At night I am a hermit, for then I commune with heaven. In the day I am as other men are, better than some and worse than others."

Now I bethought me of Hans' definition of this strange fellow whom he described as having two natures and not for the first time marvelled at the little Hottentot's acumen and deductive powers.

Kaneke led me across the courtyard of beaten polished earth to the *stoep* or verandah of his house, which was more or less square in shape, consisting apparently of two rooms that had doors and windows after the Arab fashion, or rather window-places closed with mats, for there was no glass. On this *stoep* were two chairs, large string-seated chairs of ebony with high backs, such as are sometimes still to be found upon the East Coast. The view from the place was fine, for beneath at the foot of a precipice lay the river bed, and beyond it stretched a great plain. When I was seated Kaneke went into the house where a lamp was burning, and returned with a bottle of brandy, two glasses, curious old glasses, by the way, and an earthen vessel of water. At his invitation I helped myself, moderately enough ; then he did the same—not quite so moderately.

"I thought that you were a Mahommedan," I said, with an affectation of mild surprise.

"Then, Macumazahn, you have a bad memory. Did I not tell you a few hours ago that I am nothing of the sort. In the daytime out yonder I worship the Prophet. Here at night, when I am alone, I worship, not the Moslem crescent, but yonder star," and he pointed to Venus now shining brightly in the sky, lifted his glass, bowed as though to her, and drank.

"You play a risky game," I said.

"Not very," he said, shrugging his shoulders. "There are few zealots in this place, and I think no one who from time to time will not drink a tot. Moreover, am I not a witch-doctor, and although such arts are forbidden, have they not all consulted me and are they not afraid of me ?"

"I dare say, Kaneke, but the question is, are you not also afraid of them ?"

"Yes, Macumazahn, at times I am," he answered frankly, "for even a 'heaven-herd'" (he meant a rain-maker) "has a stomach, and some of these Great Lake people understand poisons very well, especially the women. You see, Macumazahn, I am a slave who has become a master, and they do not forget it."

"What do you want with me ?" I asked suddenly.

"Your help, Lord. Although I am rich here, I wish to get out of this place and to return to my own country."

"Well, what is there to prevent you from doing so ?"

"Much, Lord, without an excuse, as I told you before sundown. Indeed, it is impossible. If I tried to go I should be murdered as a traitor and a renegade. That is the tree of Truth ; ask me not to count the leaves upon it and tell you why or how they grow."

"Good. I see your tree and that it is large. But what do you want with me, Kaneke ?"

"Lord, have I not told you that your repute has reached me and the rest ? Now I add something which you will not believe, but yet is another tree of Truth. I am not all a cheat, Lord. Visions come to me, as they did to my fathers ; moreover, I have looked upon the face of Engoi, and he who has seen the Engoi partakes of her wisdom. Lord, in a vision, I have been warned to seek your help."

"Is that why you blocked my road by raising that Lake tribe against me, and otherwise, Kaneke, so that I was forced to come to your town ?"

"Yes, Lord, though I do not know who betrayed me to you. Some of the women, perhaps, or that little yellow man of yours, who hears in his sleep like a mere-cat—yes, even when he seems to be drunk—and is quick as a snake at pairing-time. Because of the vision, I did bring you here."

"What do you want me to do?" I repeated, growing impatient. "I am tired of talk. Out with it that I may hear and judge, Kaneke."

He rose from his seat, and, stepping to the edge of the verandah, stared at the evening star as though he sought an omen. Then he returned and answered:

"You are a wanderer, athirst for knowledge, a seeker for new things, Lord Macumazahn. You have heard of the holy hidden lake called Mone, on which no white man has looked, and desire to solve its mysteries, and what I have told you of it has whetted your appetite. Without a guide you can never reach that lake. I, who am of the people of its guardians, alone can guide you. Will you take me with you on your journey?"

"Hold hard, my friend," I said. "You are putting the tail of the ox before the horns. I may wish to find that place, or I may not, but it seems that you *must* find it, I don't know why, and that you cannot do so without me."

"It is so," he answered with something like a groan. "I will open the doors of my heart to you. I must seek that lake, for those upon whom the Shadow has fallen must follow the Shadow even though its shape be changed; and it has come to me in a dream, thrice repeated, that if I try to do so without your help, Lord, I shall be killed. Therefore, I pray you, give me that help."

Now my business instincts awoke, for though some do not think so, I am really a very sharp business man, even hard at times, I fear.

"Look here, friend Kaneke," I said, "I came to this country because I have heard that beyond it is a land full of elephants and other game, and you know I am a hunter by trade. I did not come to search for a mysterious lake, though I should be glad enough to see one if it lay in my path. So the point is this: if I were to consent to undertake a journey which according to your own account is most dangerous and difficult, I should require to be paid for it. Yes, to be largely paid," and I looked at him as fiercely as I suppose a usurer does at a minor who requires a loan."

"I understand. Indeed, it is natural. Listen, Lord, I have a hundred sovereigns in English gold that I have saved up coin by coin. When we get to the lake they shall be yours."

I sprang from my chair.

"A hundred sovereigns! When we get to the lake, which probably we shall never do! Man, I see that you wish to insult me. Good night, indeed good-bye, for tomorrow I leave this place," and I lifted my foot to step off the verandah.

"Lord," he said, catching at my coat, "be not offended with your slave. Everything I have is yours."

"That's better," I said. "What have you ?"

"Lord, I deal in ivory, of which I have a good store buried."

"How much ?"

"Lord, I think about a hundred bull-tusks, which I proposed to send away at next new moon. If you would accept some of them——"

"Some ?" I said. "You mean all of them, with the one hundred pounds for immediate expenses."

He rolled his eyes and sighed, then answered :

"Well, if it must be so, so be it. Tomorrow you shall see the ivory."

Next he went into the house and returned presently with a canvas bag, of which he opened the mouth to show me that it was full of gold.

"Take this on account, Lord," he said.

Again my business instincts came to my help. Remembering that if I touched a single coin I should be striking a bargain, whatever the ivory might prove to be worth, I waved the bag away.

"When I have seen the tusks, we will talk," I said ; "not before. And now good night."

Next morning a messenger arrived, again inviting me to Kaneke's house.

I went, accompanied this time by Hans to whom I had explained the situation, whereon that worthy gave me some excellent advice.

"Be stiff, Baas," he said ; "be very stiff, and get everything you can. It is unfortunate that you do not sell women like these Arabs, for this Kaneke has a nice lot of young girls whom he would give you for the asking, were you not too good a Christian. Listen, Baas, I have learned that you can't ask too much, for yonder Kaneke must get out of this place, and soon, if he wants to go on living. I am sure of it, and without your help he is afraid to move."

"Cease your foolish talk," I answered, though in my heart I had come to the same conclusion.

On reaching the house, as before the gate was opened by Kaneke, who looked rather doubtfully at Hans, but said nothing.

Within, for the most part arranged against the fence, was the ivory. My eyes gleamed at the sight of it, for it was a splendid lot, though in some cases rather black with age as if it had been hidden away for a long time, and among it were three or four tusks as large as any that I ever shot. Hans, who was a fine judge of ivory, went over it piece by piece, which took a long time. I made a calculation of its value and from market rates then prevailing, allowing twenty-five per cent for transport and other costs, I reckoned that it was worth at least £700, and Hans, I found, put it somewhat higher.

Then we bargained for a long time, and in the end came to the following agreement, which I reduced to writing : I undertook to accompany Kaneke to his own country of the Dabanda tribe, unless, indeed, sickness or disaster of any sort made this impossible, after which I was to be at liberty to return or to go where I would. He, on his part, was to pay me the ivory as a fee, also to deliver it free to my agent at Zanzibar, a man whom I trusted, who was to sell it to the best advantage and to remit the proceeds to my bank at Durban.

Further, the bag which proved to contain one hundred and three sovereigns was handed over to me. At this I rejoiced at the time, though afterwards I regretted it, for what is the use of dragging about gold in wild places where it has no value? Kaneke undertook also to guide me to his country, to arrange that I should be welcome there and generally to protect me in every way in his power.

Such, roughly, was our contract which I concluded with secret exultation while that ivory was before my eyes. I signed it in my large, bold handwriting ; Kaneke signed it in crabbed Arabic characters of which he had acquired some knowledge ; and Hans signed it as a witness with a mark, or rather a blot, for in making it he split the pen. Thus all was finished and I went away exultant, as I have said, promising to return in the afternoon to make arrangements about the despatch of the ivory and as to our journey.

"Hans," I said, for there was no one else to talk to, "I did that business very well, did I not ? Take a lesson from me and learn always to strike when the iron is hot. Tomorrow Kaneke might have changed his mind and offered much less."

"Yes, Baas, very well indeed, though sometimes if the iron is too hot the sparks blind one, Baas. Only I think that to-morrow Kaneke would have offered you double, for I know that he has much more ivory buried. If you had taken a lesson from *me*, you would have waited, Baas. Did I not tell you that he *must* get out of this place and would pay all he had for your help ?"

"At any rate, Hans," I replied, somewhat staggered, "the pay is good, as much as I could ask."

"That depends upon what price the Baas puts upon his life," said Hans reflectively. "For my part I do not see that all the tusks of all the elephants in the world are of any use when one is dead, for they won't even make a coffin, Baas."

"What do you mean ?" I asked angrily.

"Oh, nothing, Baas, except that I believe that we shall both be dead long before this business is finished. Also have you thought, Baas, that probably this ivory will never get to the coast at all ? Because you see Kaneke, who, I think, is also good at business, will arrange for it to be stolen on the road and returned to him later, just as you or I would have done, Baas, had we been in his place. However, the Baas has the hundred sovereigns which no doubt will be very useful to eat when we are starving in some wilderness, or as a bribe to Kaneke's fetish, whatever it may be. Or——"

Here, unable to bear any more, I turned upon Hans with intent to do him personal injury, whereon he bolted, grinning, leaving me to wait upon myself at dinner. It was not a cheerful meal, for, as I reflected, the little wretch was probably right. To secure very doubtful advantages I had to let myself in for unknown difficulties and dangers, in company with a native of whom I knew little or nothing, except that he was an odd fish, and whose servant I had practically become in consideration for value received. For even if I never saw that ivory again, or its proceeds, there were the hundred sovereigns weighing down my pocket—and my conscience—like a lump of lead.

Most heartily did I wish that I had never touched the business. I thought of sending back the gold to Kaneke by Hans, but for various reasons dismissed the idea. Of these the chief was that probably it would never reach him, not because Hans was dishonest where money was concerned, but for the reason that it would go against what he called *his* conscience, to return anything to a person of the sort from whom it had been extracted. He might bury it ; he might even give it to that jealous wife from whom he acquired so much backstair information ; but Kaneke, I was sure, would never see its colour unless I took it myself, which I was too proud to do.

Then suddenly my mood changed, transformed, perhaps,

by some semi-spiritual influence, or as is more likely, by that of a good meal, for it is a humiliating fact that our outlook upon life and its affairs depends largely upon our stomach. What a rabbit of a man was I that I should be scared from a great project by the idle chatter and prognostications of Hans, uttered probably to exercise his mischievous mind at my expense. If I were, and on that account turned my face towards the coast again, Hans, who loved adventure even more than I do, would be the first to reproach me, not openly, but by means of the casual arrows of his barbed wit. Moreover, it was useless to run away from anything, for as he himself had said but yesterday, we must go where Fate drives us. Well, Fate had driven me to pocket Kaneke's sovereigns and a kind of note of hand in ivory, so there was an end of the matter. I would start for the home of the Dabanda people, and for the unvisited shores of the Lake Mone, and if I never got there, what did it matter? All our journeyings must end some day, be it next month, or next year, or a decade hence.

I sent for Hans, who came looking pious and aggrieved, perhaps the most aggravating of his many moods.

"Hans," I said, "I have made up my mind to go with Kaneke to the Dabanda country, and if you try to prevent me any more, I shall be angry with you and send you down to the coast with the ivory."

"Yes, Baas," he answered in a meek voice. "The Bass could scarcely do less, could he, after taking that fellow's money, which no doubt he made by selling girls; that is, unless he wished to be called a thief. Moreover, I never tried to stop the Baas. Why should I when I shall be glad to go anywhere out of this place, where, to tell the truth, that jealous little wife of Kaneke who tells me so much, is beginning to think me too handsome and to roll her eyes and to press her hand upon her middle whenever she sees me, which makes me feel ill, Baas."

"You mean you make her feel ill, you little humbug," I suggested.

"No, Baas. I wish it were so, for then I could think better of her. For the rest, Baas, if I pointed out the dangers of this journey, it was not for my own self, but only because the Baas's reverend father left him in my charge and therefore I must do my best to guide him when I see him going astray."

At this I jumped up and Hans went on in a hurry.

"The Baas will not send me away to the coast with the ivory as he threatened to do, will he? He knows that in one way

I am weak and perhaps if I was separated from him, grief might cause me to drink too much of that palm-wine and make myself ill." Then, reading in my face that I had no such intention, Hans took my hand, kissed it, and departed.

At the corner of the cook-house he turned and said :

"The Baas has made his will, has he not ? So I need only remind him that if he wishes to write any good-bye-we-shall-meet-in-heaven letters, he had better do so at once, so that they can be sent down to the coast with the ivory."

CHAPTER III

THE TRIAL OF KANEKE

I WILL pass over all the details concerning the dispatch of the ivory on its long road to Zanzibar and our other preparations for departure. Suffice it to say that the stuff went off all right on the shoulders of porters, together with a lot more, for Hans guessed well when he said that Kaneke had plenty of other tusks hidden away, although he declared that these belonged to some-one else. What is more, here I will state that, strange as it may seem, in due course the ivory reached Zanzibar in safety and was delivered to my agent, who sold it according to instructions and, minus his commission, remitted the proceeds, which were more than I had expected, to my bank in Durban. So in this matter Kaneke dealt honestly.

What happened to the remainder of the ivory, which I presume to have been his, I do not know, nor can it have interested him, as he never returned to receive its price. Nor do I know what other goods went with that caravan which was led by Arabs, for I was careful not to inquire.

Notwithstanding the insinuations of Hans, I saw no girl slaves, and imagine them to have been apocryphal. Indeed, I believe that what Kaneke really dealt in was guns and powder. Once a year a caravan came up from Zanzibar laden with these and other goods, such as cloth, calico, and beads, returning with the ivory that Kaneke had collected in the interval. The money which he made on these transactions was large and kept in an English bank at Zanzibar, as I learned in after years. I wonder what became of it.

Well, the string of porters, headed by Arabs mounted upon donkeys, departed and were no more seen. We, too, prepared to depart. Here I should explain that my following was limited. I had with me two gun-bearers, skilled hunters both of them, who had been strongly recommended to me in Zanzibar and who, having learned my repute as a professional big-game shot, which had followed me from the South, were very glad to enter my service. One of these men was, it appeared, an Abyssinian by birth with a name so unpronounceable that I christened him Tom, though the natives called him "Little Holes", because his face was marked with small-pox.

The other was born of a Somali woman and an Arab, or perhaps a European father. To tell the truth he was remarkably British in his appearance with a round, open face and almost straight, reddish hair, although of course—except in certain lights—his skin was dark. His name, he informed me proudly, speaking in excellent English, for he had been educated at one of the first Mission schools and served as gun-bearer to several English sportsmen, was Jeremiah Jackson. Who his father might have been he had no idea, and as his mother died before he was five, she had never told him.

This man I called Jerry, because of the natural association of the name with that of Tom, for who has not heard of Tom and Jerry, the typical "gay dogs" of the Georgian days of whom my father used to tell me? Both of them were of about the same age, somewhere between thirty and forty. Both were Christians of a sort, for Tom belonged to the Abyssinian section of that faith, and both were brave and competent men. Of the two Tom had the more dash, but perhaps owing to a European strain of blood Jerry was the cooler and the more dogged. Soon I became very friendly with them, but Hans looked upon them suspiciously, at any rate at first, I think because he was jealous.

These gun-bearers were well paid, according to the rate of that day ; still, as they had come with me to hunt elephants and not to make long journeys of exploration, I thought it right to explain to them my change of plans and to give them the opportunity of returning to the coast with the ivory if they wished.

Tom said at once that he would go on with me to the end of the journey, whatever it might be, for he was a born adventurer with that touch of a mystic in him which I have observed to be not uncommon among such Abyssinians as I have met. Jerry, more cautious, began to talk about his wife, from whom it appeared he was separated, and his little daughter who was at a Mission school, which caused Hans, who was present, to make some sarcastic remark about "family men", who, he said, should stop at home and nurse the babies. This caused Jerry to fire up and say that he would come too and that Hans would see which of them wished to nurse babies before all was done.

When the matter was settled I thanked them both and told them that Kaneke had given me a hundred pounds in gold, a sum that, in view of the dangers of the trip, I proposed to divide into three parts, one for each of them and one for Hans. Now they thanked me warmly, only Jerry remarked that he thought it probable he would never live to earn his third, for which he was sorry as it would have been an endowment for his little daughter.

"You are mistaken," I said. "I propose to give you this money now, trusting to the honour of you both to stick to me to the end, so that if there is anyone in whom you put sufficient faith, among those who are going to the coast with the ivory," —for this was before the caravan had started—"you can send it to your friends in his charge." They were much astonished and, I could see, touched, swearing, both of them, Tom who was a Protestant by God, and Jerry by the Virgin Mary, that they would never desert me, but would see the business through to the end, whatever it might be. When they had finished their pro- testations I turned to Hans, who all this while had stood by twirling his hat with a superior smile upon his ugly little face, and asked him if he did not thank me for his share.

"No, Bass. I am not going to take the money, so why should I thank you for nothing ? I am not a hired man like these two hunters. I am the Baas's guardian appointed to look after him by his reverend father, and when I want anything of the Baas, I take it as a guardian has a right to do."

Then as he marched off I called after him in Dutch, which the others did not understand :

"You are a jealous, ill-conditioned little begger, and I shall keep your share for myself." This I did until eventually he drew it a long while afterwards. I should add that besides Tom and Jerry I had about twenty native bearers, who agreed, though very doubtfully, to go on with me and carry the loads.

As the date fixed for our departure drew near, I observed that Kaneke grew more and more nervous, though exactly of what he was afraid I could not understand. He summoned a meeting of the headmen of his village, at which I was present, and explained that he proposed to accompany me upon an elephant-shooting trip whence we should return in due course. This intimation was very ill received, although he had added that they could elect one of their number to act as father of the village during his absence. They said that the time was coming when they expected him to pray for rain, and if he were not there to do so they would get none.

Here I should explain that the religion of these people was a strange mixture between that of Mahomet and the superstitions of the East Coast savages. Indeed a man called Gaika, a truculent, fierce-eyed fellow, not quite an Arab, for he had a dash of negroid blood, leapt up and denounced him venomously, ostensibly because of this proposed journey.

Kaneke, to my astonishment, remained very meek and calm, saying that he would think the matter over and speak with them again, after which the meeting broke up.

"What is at the back of all this?" I asked of Hans, who had been present with me, when we were in our camp again.

"The Baas is very blind," he said. "Does he not see that this Gaika wishes to kill Kaneke and take his place?"

I pointed out that if it were so he ought to be glad to get rid of him out of the town.

"Not so," answered Hans, "for they think he is really going to gather men from other tribes where his name as a witch-doctor is great, with whom he will return and put them all to death. Baas," he added in a whisper, "they have a plan to kill Kaneke, whom they both hate and fear, but they are not quite ready with their plan, which is why they do not want him to go away."

"How do you know all this—through that woman?" I asked.

Hans nodded.

"Some of it, Baas. The rest I picked up here and there when I seemed to be asleep, or when I am asking that old fellow who is called a Mullah to teach me the religion of Mahomet, which he thinks I am going to adopt. Yet, Baas, I sit in that mosque-hut of his listening to his nonsense and telling him that my soul is growing oh! so happy, and all the while I keep my ears open and pick up lots of things. For they think me very wise, Baas, and tell me plenty which they would not trust to you."

I looked at Hans with disgust, mixed with admiration, reflecting that without doubt he had got the hang of the business. But I said no more, for that place was a nest of spies.

That afternoon I had sent our porters on to a certain spot about three miles away, together with the loads. This I did because I was afraid lest they should be corrupted and the goods stolen. So now only Hans, Tom, and Jerry remained with me in the town.

Next morning Hans brought me my coffee as usual and said in a casual fashion :

"Baas, there is trouble. Kaneke was seized while he was asleep last night. They broke into his house and tied him with ropes. It seems that yesterday afternoon he had a quarrel with one of them and killed him with a blow of his fist, or with a stone that he held in his hand, for he is strong as an ox."

I whistled and asked what was going to happen.

"They are going to try him for murder this morning, Baas, according to their law, and they have sent to ask if you will be present at the trial. What shall I say, Baas ?"

At first I was inclined to answer that I would have nothing to do with the business, but on reflection I remembered that if I did so it would be set down to fear ; also that I had taken Kaneke's ivory and gold and that it would be mean to desert him in his trouble. So I sent an answer to say I would attend the trial with my servants.

At the appointed hour we went accordingly, armed, all four of us, and at the gate of the town were informed that the trial was to take place at the Tree of Council, which, it will be remembered, stood outside the village. So thither we marched and on arrival found all the population of the place, numbering perhaps three or four hundred people, assembled around the tree but outside of its shadow. In that shadow sat about a dozen white-robed men, elders, I suppose, whom I took to be the judges, some of them on the ground and some on stools.

As we advanced through the crowd towards them they stared doubtfully at our rifles, but in the end I was given a seat on the right of the Court, if so it may be called, but at a little distance, while my three retainers stood behind me. We were not spoken to, nor did we speak. Presently the crowd parted, leaving an open lane up which marched Kaneke with his hands bound behind his back, guarded by six men armed with spears. I noted that all looked upon him coldly as he went by. To judge by their faces he had not a friend among them.

Finally he was placed in such a position that he had the judges, who sat with their backs to the trunk of the tree, in front of him, with myself on his right, and the audience on his left. There he stood quietly, a fine and striking figure notwithstanding his bonds, taller by a head than any of that company. Somehow he reminded me of Samson bound and being led in to be mocked by the Philistines, so much so that I wondered where Delilah might be. Then I remembered Han's tale of the jealous wife and thought that I knew—which I didn't. He rolled his big eyes about him, taking in everything. Presently they fell upon me, to whom he bowed. Of his judges he took no notice at all, or, for the matter of that, of the people either.

The "Mullah man", as Hans called the priest, opened the proceedings with some kind of prayer and many genuflexions. Then Gaika, who appeared to act as Attorney General and Chief Justice rolled into one, set out the case at considerable length and with much venom. He narrated that Kaneke was a slave belonging to some strange people, who by murder many years before, and cunning, had acquired authority over them. Then he proceeded to detail all his crimes as a ruler which, if he could be believed, were black indeed. Among them were cruelty, oppression, theft, robbery of women, and I know not what besides.

These were followed by a string of offences of another class : necromancy which was against the law of the Prophet, bewitchments, raising of spirits, breaches of the law of Ramadan, betrayal of the Faith by one who was its secret enemy, worship of strange gods or devils, drinking of spirituous liquors, plottings with their enemies against the people, midnight sacrifice of lambs and infants to the stars, and so forth. Lastly came the immediate charge, that of the murder of an elder on the previous day.   For all of these crimes Gaika declared the slave and usurper Kaneke to be worthy of death.

Having settled his hash in this fashion, he sat down and called upon the prisoner to plead.

Kaneke answered in a resonant voice that struck me, and I think all present, as powerful and impressive.

"To what purpose is it that I should plead," he said, "seeing that my chief judge and enemy has already declared me guilty of more crimes than anyone could commit if he lived for a hundred years ?   Still, letting the rest be, I will say that I am guilty of one thing, namely of killing a man yesterday in a quarrel, in order to prevent him from stabbing me, though it is true that I did not mean to kill him, but only to fell him to the ground ; so that it was Allah who killed him, not I.   Now I will tell you, O people, why I am put upon my trial here before you, I who have lifted you up from nothingness into a state of wealth and power.

"It is that yonder Gaika may take my place as your headman. Good.   He is welcome to my place.   Know that I weary of ruling over you and protecting you. What more need I say? It is enough. For a long while you have plotted to kill me. Now let me go my way, and go you yours."

"It is not enough," shouted Gaika. "You, O Kaneke, say that you would accompany the white hunter, Macumazahn yonder, to shoot elephants. It is a lie. You go to raise against us the tribes to the north who have a quarrel with us from our father's time, saying that these seized their young people and sold them as slaves. We know that it is your plan and it is for that reason that for years we have never allowed you to leave our town. Nor shall you leave it now. Nay, you shall stay here for ever while your spirit dwells in hell, where wizards go."

He ceased, and from the audience rose a murmur of applause. Whatever his good qualities might be—if he had any—evidently Kaneke was not popular among his flock. As the prisoner made no answer, Gaika went on, addressing the other judges thus:

"My brothers, you have heard. To call witnesses is needless, since some of you saw this Kaneke murder our brother yesterday. Is he guilty of this and other crimes?"

"He is guilty," they answered, speaking all together.

"Then what should be his punishment?"

"Death," they answered, again speaking all together, while the audience echoed the word "Death".

"Kaneke," shouted Gaika in triumph, "you are doomed to die. Not one among these hundreds asks for mercy on you; no, not even the women. Nor have you any children to plead for you, since doubtless, being a magician, you slew them unborn lest they should grow up to kill you. Yet according to the law it is not lawful that you should be despatched at once. Therefore we send you back to your own house under guard, that there you may pray to Allah and His Prophet for forgiveness of your sins. Tomorrow at the dawn you shall be brought back here and beaten to death with clubs, that we may not shed your blood. Have you heard and do you understand?"

Then at length Kaneke spoke again. Showing no fear, he spoke quietly, almost indifferently, yet in so clear a voice that none could miss a word, saying in the midst of a deep silence:

"O Gaika, son of a dog, and all the rest of you, sons and daughters of dogs, I hear and I understand. So tomorrow you would beat me to death with clubs. It may happen or it may not, but if I know I shall not tell you. Still, listen to the last wisdom that you shall hear from my lips. You are right when you say that I am a magician. It is so, and as such I have foreknowledge of the future. I call down a curse on you all. Let Allah defend you if he can, and will, and Mahomet make prayer for you. This is the curse : a great sickness shall fall on you ; I think it will begin tonight. I think that some who are already sick are seated yonder," and he nodded towards the crowd, "although they know it not. Yes, they began to be sick a minute ago, when the words of cursing left my lips" (here there was a sensation among the audience, every one of them staring at his neighbour). "Most of you will die of this sickness because after I am gone there will be none to doctor you. The rest will flee away. They will scatter like goats without a herd. They will be taken by those whose sons and daughters you used to steal, and become slaves and die as slaves."

Then he turned towards me and added, "Farewell, Lord Macumazahn. If it is fated that in flesh I cannot guide you on your journey to the place whither you would go, yet fear not, for my spirit will guide you and when you are come there safely, then give a message from me to one of whom I have spoken to you, which message shall be delivered to you, perhaps in the night hours when you are asleep. I do not ask you to lift your gun and shoot this rogue," and he nodded towards Gaika, "because you are but one and would be overwhelmed with your servants. Nay, I only ask you to hearken to the message when it comes and to do what it bids you."

Not knowing what to say I made no answer to this peculiar appeal, although Hans, to judge by his mumblings and fidgets, appeared to wish me to say something. As I still declined, with his usual impertinence he took it upon himself to act as my spokesmen, saying in his debased Arabic :

"The great lord, my master, bids me inform you, Kaneke, that he is sorry you are going to be killed. He tells me to say also that, if you are killed and become a spook, he begs that you will keep away from him, as spooks, especially of those who are magicians and have been put to death for their evil deeds, are not nice company for anyone."

When I heard this, indignation took away my breath, but before I could speak a word Gaika addressed me fiercely, crying out :

"White Wanderer, we believe that you are in league with this evil-doer and plot mischief against us. Get out of our town at once, lest you share his fate."

Now this unprovoked assault made me furious, and I answered in the first words that came to my tongue :

"Who are you that tell lies and dare to talk to me of Fate ? Let my fate be, fellow, and have a care for your own, which perhaps is nearer than you think."

Little did I guess when I spoke thus, at hazard as it seemed, that very soon doom would overtake this ruffian, and by my hand. Are we sometimes filled with the spirit of prophecy, I wonder ? Or do we, perhaps, know everything on our inmost souls whence now and again bursts a rush of buried truth ?

After this the company broke up in confusion. Kaneke was hustled away by his guards ; men who waved their spears in a threatening fashion advanced upon us and were so insolent that at last I looked round and lifted the rifle I carried—I remember that it was one of the first Winchester repeaters of a sort that carried five cartridges. Thereon they fell back and we were allowed to regain our huts in peace.

I did not stop there long. Nearly all our gear had been sent forward with the bearers ; indeed, no more of it remained than the four of us could carry ourselves, although the arrangement was that some of Kaneke's men should do us this sevice on the morrow. As this was now out of the question we loaded ourselves, also a donkey that I possessed, with blankets, guns, cooking-pots, ammunition, and I know not what besides, and started, I riding on the donkey and looking, as I have since reflected, like the White Knight in *Alice in Wonderland.*

Then, keeping clear of the town, we trekked for the place where our bearers were encamped, reaching it unmolested about an hour later. This spot, chosen by myself, was on the lowest slope of a steep hill covered with thorn trees, through which ran a little stream from a spring higher up the slope. The first thing I did was to cut down a number of these thorns and drag them together into a fence, making what is called a *boma* in that part of Africa, behind which we could protect ourselves if necessary. By the time that this was done and my tent was pitched, it was late in the afternoon. Feeling tired, more, I think, from anxiety than exertion, I lay down and after musing for a while upon the fate of the unfortunate Kaneke and wishing, much as I disliked the man, that I could save him from a doom I believed to be unjust, which seemed impossible, I feel asleep, as I can do at any time. In my sleep a curious dream came to me, which after all was not wonderful, seeing how my mind was occupied.

I dreamed that Kaneke spoke to me, though I could not see him, but distinctly I heard, or seemed to hear, his voice saying :

"Follow the woman. Do what the woman tells you, and you will save me."

Twice I heard this, and then I do not know how long afterwards, I woke up, or rather was awakened by Hans setting some food upon the camp table near the rent. On going out I saw that it was night, for the full moon was just rising and already giving so clear a light in a cloudless sky, that I could see to eat without the aid of a lamp.

"Hans," I said presently, "what did Kaneke mean when he talked of a great sickness that was about to smite the town?"

"The Baas observes little," answered Hans. "Did he notice nothing among the people of that caravan which took away the ivory?"

"Yes, I noticed that they were a dirty lot and smelt so much that I kept clear of them."

"If the Baas had come a little closer, he would have seen that two or three of them had pimples coming all over their faces."

"Small-pox?" I suggested.

"Yes, Baas, small-pox, for I have seen it before. Also, they had been mixing with the people of the town who have not had small-pox for many years, for Kaneke kept it away by his charms, or stopped it when it broke out. Baas, this time he did not keep it away, and quite a number of the townspeople, as I heard this morning, are feeling bad, with sore throats and headaches, Bass. Kaneke knew all this as well as I do and that is why he talked about a pestilence. It is easy to prophesy when one knows, Bass."

"Is it easy to send dreams, Hans?" I asked; then before he could answer I told him of the words I had seemed to hear in my sleep.

For a moment I caught sight of a look of astonishment upon Hans' wrinkled and impassive countenance. Then he answered in an unconcerned fashion:

"I dare say, Baas, if one knows how. Or perhaps Kaneke sent no dream. Perhaps the Baas heard me and the woman talking together, for she is here and waiting to see the Baas after he has eaten."

CHAPTER IV

WHITE-MOUSE

"A woman !" I said, springing up.   "What woman ?"

"Kaneke's jealous wife who likes me so much, she whom they call White-Mouse because she is so quick and silent, I suppose. She has a plan to save that bull of a man, just as the dream said, or you overheard."

"Then she must be fond of him after all, Hans."

"I suppose so, Baas.   Or perhaps she thinks she will get him back again now, because some other woman, of whom she is jealous, has got small-pox, of which she hopes that she will die, or become very ugly.   At least that is her tale, Baas."

"I will see her at once," I said.

"Best eat your supper first, Baas ; it is always wise to keep women waiting a while, for that makes them think more of you."

Knowing that Hans always had a reason for what he said, even when he seemed to be talking the most arrant nonsense, I took his advice.

When I had finished my food he led me to a patch of bush that grew round a pool at the foot of the slope about two hundred yards from the camp.   We entered and presently from beneath a tree a little woman glided out so silently that she might have been a ghost, and stood still with the moonlight falling on her white robes.   She threw back a hood that covered her head, revealing her face, which was refined and in its way very pretty ; also so fair for an Arab that I thought she must have European blood in her.   She looked at me a little while, searching my face with her dark, appealing eyes, then suddenly threw herself on her knees, took my hand, and kissed it.

"That will do," I said, lifting her up.   "What do you want with me ?"

"Lord," she said in Arabic, speaking in a low, impassioned voice, "I am that slave of Kaneke whom here they call White-Mouse, though elsewhere I have another name.   Although he has treated me badly, for he who loves a Shadow cares for no woman, his spell is still upon me.   Therefore I would pray you to save him if you can."

"Me !"

"Yes, Lord, you." Then as I said nothing she went on quickly, "I know that you white men do not work without pay, and I have nothing to give you, except myself. I will be a good servant to you and Kaneke will not mind. He has told me to go where I will."

"Don't be frightened, Baas," whispered Hans into my ear in Dutch. "When she says you—she must mean me."

I hit him in the middle with the point of my elbow, which stopped his breath. Then I said:

"Set out your plan, White-Mouse, if you have one. But please understand that I do not want you as a servant."

"Then you can drive me away, Lord, for if you do my will, your slave I shall be till death. Only one thing do I ask, that you do not give me to that little yellow monkey, or to either of your hunters."

"How well she acts!" grunted the unconquered Hans behind me.

"The plan, the plan," I said.

"Lord, it is this: there is a path up the cliff on the crest of which is the house of Kaneke, wherein he lies bound awaiting death at the rising of the morrow's sun. It is known to few; indeed only to Kaneke and myself. I will lead you with your two hunters and this yellow one up that path and into Kaneke's house. There, if it be needful, you can deal with those who guard him—there are but three of them, for the rest watch without the fence—and get him away down the cliff."

"This is nonsense," I said. "I examined that cliff when I visited Kaneke. There is no fence upon its edge because it overhangs in such a fashion that without long ropes, such as we have not got, made fast above, it cannot be climbed or decended."

"It seems to do so, Lord, but beneath its overhanging crest there is a hole, which hole leads into a tunnel. This tunnel ends beneath the pavement of Kaneke's house just in front of where he sits to watch the stars. Do you understand, Lord?"

I nodded, for I knew that she meant the *stoep* where Kaneke and I had drunk brandy and water together.

"The pavement is solid," I said. "How does one pass through it?"

"A block of the hard floor, which is made of lime and other things so that it is like stone, can be moved from beneath. I have its secret, Lord. That is all. Will you come with me now? The beginning of the gorge is not very far from this place which, as your know, by any other road is a long way from the town.

Therefore we need not start yet because I do not wish to reach the house until two hours after midnight, when all men are asleep, except those who watch the sick in the town, where a pestilence has broken out, as Kaneke foretold, and these will take little heed if they hear a noise."

"No, I won't," I answered firmly. "This is a mad business. Why should I give my life and those of my servants to try to save Kaneke, whom I have only known for a week or two and who may be all that his enemies say ?"

She considered the point, then answered :

"Because he alone can guide you to that hidden place whither you wish to go."

"I don't wish to go anywhere in particular," I replied testily ; "unless it is back to Zanzibar."

Again she considered, and said :

"Because you have taken Kaneke's ivory and gold, Lord."

At this I winced a little and then replied :

"I took the ivory and gold in payment for services to be rendered to Kaneke, if he could accompany me upon a certain journey, and he paid, asking nothing in return if he could not do so. Through no fault of mine he is unable to come, and therefore the bargain is at an end."

"That is well said, Lord, in the white man's merchant-fashion. Now I have another reason to which I think any man will listen. You should help Kaneke because I, your slave, who am a woman young and fair, pray you to do so."

"Ah ! she is clever ; she knows the Baas," I heard Hans mutter reflectively, words that hardened my heart and caused me to reply :

"Not for the sake of any woman in Africa, nor of all of them put together, would I do what you ask, White-Mouse. Do you take me for a madman ?"

She laughed a little in a dreary fashion and answered :

"Indeed I do not, who see that it is I who am mad. Hearken, Lord : like others I have heard tales of Macumazahn. I have heard that he is generous and great-hearted ; one who never goes back upon his word, a staff to lean on in the hour of trouble, a man who does not refuse the prayer of those in distress ; brave too, and a lover of adventure if a good cause may be served, a great one whom it pleases to pretend to be small. All these things I have heard from that yellow man, and others ; yes, and from Kaneke himself, and watching from afar, although you never knew I did so, I have judged these stories to be true. Now

I see that I am mistaken. This lord Macumazahn is as are other white traders, neither better nor worse. So it is finished. Unaided I am not able to save Kaneke, as by my spirit I have sworn that I would. Therefore I pray your pardon, Lord, who have put you to trouble, and here before your eyes will end all, that I may go to make report of this business to those I serve far away."

While I stared at her, wondering what she meant, also how much truth there was in all this mysterious tale, suddenly she drew a knife from her girdle, and tearing open her robe, lifted it above her bared breast. I sprang and seized her wrist.

"You must love this man very much!" I exclaimed, more, I think, to myself than to her.

"You are mistaken, Lord," she answered, with her strange little laugh. "I do not love him ; indeed I think I hate him who have never found one whom I could love—as yet. Still, for a while he is my master, also I have sworn to hold him safe by certain oaths that may not be broken and—I keep my word, as I must do or perish everlastingly."

For a little while there was silence between us. Never can I forget the strangeness of that scene. The patch of bush by the edge of the pool, the little open space where the bright moonlight fell, and standing full in that moonlight which shone upon the whiteness of her rounded breast, this small, elfin-faced woman with the dark eyes and curling hair, a knife in her raised right hand.

Then myself, much perplexed and agitated, rather a ridiculous figure, as I suspect, clasping her wrist to prevent that knife from falling ; and in the background upon the edge of the shadow, sardonic, his face alight with the age-old wisdom of the wild man who had eaten of the tree of Knowledge, interested and yet indifferent, hideous and yet lovable—the Hottentot, Hans. And the look upon that beautiful woman's face, for in its way it was beautiful, or at any rate most attractive, the inscrutable look, suggestive of secrets, of mysteries even—oh ! I say I shall never forget it all.

As we stood thus facing each other like people in a scene of a play, a thought came to me, this thought—if that woman was prepared to die because she had failed in an effort to save from death the man whom she declared she hated (why was she prepared to die and why did she hate him ? I wondered), ought I not to try to save her even at some personal risk to myself ? Also if I could, ought I not to help Kaneke, whose goods I had taken ? Certainly it was impossible to allow her to immolate herself in this fashion before my eyes. I might take away her knife, but if I did she could find a second ; also there were many other roads to self-destruction by which she might travel.

"Give me that dagger," I said, "and let us talk."

She unclasped her hand and it fell to the ground. I set my foot upon it and loosed her.

"Listen," I went on. "I am minded to do what you wish if I can."

"Yes, Lord, already I have read that in your face," she replied, smiling faintly.

"But, White-Mouse," I continued, "I am not the only one concerned. I cannot undertake this business alone. Others must risk their lives as well. Hans here, for instance, and I suppose the two hunters. I cannot lay any commands upon them in such a matter and I do not know if they will come of their own will."

She turned and looked at the Hottentot, a question in her eyes. Hans fidgeted under her gaze, then he spat upon the ground and said :

"If the Baas goes I think that the Baas will be a fool. Still, where the Baas goes, there I must go also, not to pull Kaneke out of a trap, but because I promised the Baas's reverend father that I would do so. As for those other men I cannot say. I think they will answer, 'No, thank you', but if they reply, 'Oh yes', then I believe that we should be better without them, because they are so stupid and think so much about their souls that they would be sure to grow frightened at the wrong time, or to make a noise and bring us all to trouble. In a hole such as White-Mouse talks of, two men are better than four. Also it would be wiser to send Tom and Jerry on with the porters, for should we drag Kaneke out of this hole, those Arabs will try to follow and drag him back, and the farther off we are with the stores the safer we shall be. Porters go slowly, so we can catch them up, Baas."

"You hear," I said to the woman. "What is your word ?"

"This yellow one, whom I thought but a vain fool, is wise— for once, Lord. What has to be done I cannot do alone, for there must be some to deal with the guards and hold the mouth of the hole while I cut Kaneke's bonds. Yet for this business two will serve as well as four ; indeed better, for they can get back into the tunnel more quickly. Therefore I say do as the yellow man says. Order your hunters to march on with the porters and the stores as long before the break of day as the men

will move. If you escape with Kaneke, you can run upon their
spoor and join them much faster than will the Arabs who must go
round. Then if the Arabs overtake you, they will be tired and
you can beat them off with your guns."

"And what will you do ?" I asked curiously, for I noticed
that she left herself out of the plan.

"Oh ! I do not know," she answered, with another of her
strange smiles. "Lord, have I not said that I am your slave ?
Doubtless in this fashion or in that I shall follow my master as a
slave should, or perhaps I shall go before him."

Now I remembered that she had spoken of Kaneke as her
"master", and presumed that she alluded to him, although in the
hyperbole of her people she spoke of herself as my slave. However, I did not pursue the subject, which at the time interested
me little, who had more important matters to consider. Indeed, I set myself to extract details from her which I need not
enumerate, and to examine her scheme of rescue.

When I had learned all I could, bidding the woman, White-
Mouse, to remain hidden, I went back to the camp with Hans and
sent for Tom and Jerry. In as careless a fashion as I could,
I told them that with Hans I must return towards the town to
speak with a man who had promised to meet me secretly upon
a matter of importance. Then I ordered them to rouse the
porters two hours before dawn and to march on with them towards a certain hill which we had all visited together upon a little
shooting-expedition I had made while we were at Kaneke's town,
to kill duiker buck and *pauw*, as we called bustards, for a change
of food.

Although I could see that they were troubled, Tom and
Jerry said that they would obey my instructions and, that
there should be no mistake, fetched the headman of the porters,
that I might repeat them to him, which I did. This done, they
went away to sleep, Tom saying, as he bade me good night, that
he would have preferred to accompany me back to the town where
he thought I might come into danger. I thanked him, remarking that I was quite safe. So we parted ; I wondering whether
I should ever see them again and what they would do if I returned
no more. Travel back to the coast, probably, and become rich
according to their ideas by selling the guns and goods.

Then I lay down to rest for a while, making Hans do likewise.

At the appointed time I woke from my doze, as I can always
do, and left the tent to find Hans awaiting me without and

checking such things as we must carry. These were few—a water-bottle filled with cold tea, a small flask of spirits, a strip or two of *biltong* or dried meat in case we should need food, and a few yards of thin cord. For arms I took a Winchester repeater and a pocketful of cartridges, also a revolver and a sharp butcher's knife in a sheath. Hans had no rifle, but carried two revolvers and a knife, also a couple of candles and a box of matches.

Having made sure that we had collected everything and packed our other belongings to be cared for by Tom and Jerry as arranged, we slipped away to the patch of bush by the pool, taking with us extra food, for we remembered that White-Mouse must be hungry. We did not find her at once, whereon Hans explained to me that having made fools of us, doubtless she had run away. While he was still talking I saw her leaning against the trunk of a tree. Or rather I saw her eyes, which at first I took for those of some animal, for she was no longer a white figure, but a black, having covered her white robe with a thin dark garment she had brought with her in a bundle. I offered her the food, but she shook her head, saying :

"Nay, I eat no more"—words which frightened me a little.

Indeed, altogether there was something fateful and alarming about this woman. She glanced at the moon, then whispered :

"Lord, it is time to depart. Be pleased to follow me and do not smoke, or make fire, or talk too loud."

So off she went, gliding ahead like a shadow, while we marched after, I with a doubting heart. Our road ran along the bank of a little stream, of which the spring I have spoken of seemed to be the source, that wended its way through thin bush to the mouth of the gorge, which here sloped up to the high lands. Doubtless it was this stream, once a primeval torrent, that in the course of thousands of years dug out this cleft in the bosom of the earth. As we went Hans murmured his reflections into my ear.

"This is a strange journey, Baas, made at night, when we ought to be asleep. I wonder that the Baas should have undertaken it. I think, although he does not know it, he would never have done so had not White-Mouse been so pretty. Perhaps the Baas has noted that when a woman asks for anything of a a man, generally he finds it impossible to give it her if she be old and ugly, and quite possible if she is young and very pretty."

"Rubbish !" I answered. "I gave way because, if I had not, White-Mouse would have killed herself, and for no other reason."

"Yes, but if she had been a hideous old grandmother, with a black face wrinkled like that of the Baas, he would not have cared whether she killed herself or not. For who wants a slave with a skin like the hide of a buck that has lain for three months in the sun and rain?"

"As I have told you, I want no slave, Hans," I answered indignantly.

"Ah! so the Baas says now, but sometimes he changes his mind. Thus a little while ago the Baas swore that never, never would he go up the hole to try to save Kaneke. And yet we are taking this long walk with lions about and God knows what at the end of it, to do what the Baas said could not be done. Why, then, did he change his mind, unless it is because that woman is such a pretty mouse with big eyes and a queer smile and not an ugly old yellow-toothed rat? Also, is he sure that all this story of hers is true? For my part I don't believe it, and even doubt whether she is Kaneke's wife as she pretended to me."

At this moment we began to enter the gorge, and our guide turned and laid her finger on her lips in token that we must be silent. Of this I was very glad, for really Hans' jeers were intolerable.

Very soon we descended into the cleft itself, which proved to be a huge donga with sheer sides quite two hundred feet high where it was deepest. The bottom along which the shrunken river ran was strewn with boulders washed from the cliffs above, that made progress slow and difficult. Especially was this so as we scrambled down the deeps, where often little of the moonlight reached us, and sometimes even the sky was hidden by tropical shrubs and tall palms and grasses which grew along the edge of the torrent bed.

Fortunately the journey was not very long, for after about half an hour of this break-back work White-Mouse halted.

"Here is the place," she whispered. "Listen. You can hear the dogs in the town above."

It was true; I could, and the sound of those brutes howling at the moon, as they do at night in Africa, was eerie enough in our depressing circumstances.

"This is the place," she repeated, then after studying the sky a while, added: "Presently will be the time. Meanwhile let us rest, for we shall need all our strength."

Motioning to Hans to remain where he was, she led me to a flat stone out of his hearing, on which I sat down, while she crouched on the ground at my feet, native fashion, a little black ball in the shadow with the faint light gleaming upon a white patch that I knew to be her face.

"Lord," she said, "you go upon a dangerous business, yet I say to you, fear nothing for yourself or the yellow man."

"Why ? I fear much."

"Lord, those who have to do with Kaneke's people, as I have from a child, catch something of their wisdom and mind ; also I too have been taught to read the stars he worships."

"So our friend is an astrologer," thought I to myself. That is new to me in Africa, but aloud I said :

"Well, what wisdom have you caught or read in the stars ?"

"Only that you are both safe, Lord, now and on the journey you will make with Kaneke ; yes, and for many years after."

"I am glad to hear it," I remarked somewhat sarcastically, though in my heart I was cheered, as even the most instructed and civilized of us are when anyone speaks words of good omen. Also in that darksome place at the dead of night, on the edge of a desperate adventure, a little comfort went a long way, for when the bread is dry some butter is better than none at all, as Hans used to observe.

"Lord, a word more and I cease to trouble you. Do you believe in blessings, Lord ?"

"Oh yes, White-Mouse, though I don't see any about me just now."

"You are wrong, Lord ; I see them. They are thick upon your head, they shall be with you through life, and afterwards thousands shall love you. Among them is that blessing which I lay upon you."

"You are very kind, I am sure, White-Mouse. But as you say you hate this Kaneke I don't understand why you should bless me for what I am trying to do."

"No, Lord, and perhaps while you live you never will. Yet I would have you know one thing. I am not Kaneke's jealous wife as I made yonder yellow one believe, or his wife at all, or any man's, any more than my name is White-Mouse. Lord, you go to seek a wonderful one whom I serve, and I think that you will find her far away. Perhaps I shall be there in her company, and in helping her you will again help me. Now it is time to be at our work."

Then she took my hand and kissed it. I remember that her kiss felt like a butterfly alighting on my flesh, and that her breath was wonderfully sweet. Next she beckoned to Hans, who, devoured by curiosity, was glowering at us from a distance, and led the pair of us a little way up the cliff which sloped at its bottom because of debris washed up by the torrent in ancient days, or perhaps fallen from above. We came to some bushes, in the midst of which lay a large boulder. Here she halted and spoke to us in a whisper, saying :

"On the farther side of that stone is the mouth of the cleft. If you look you will see that the crest of the cliff overhangs its topmost part by many feet, so that it is impossible for it to be ascended or descended, even with any rope the Arabs have, because the height is too great. As I have told you, this tunnel, or waterway, runs to the top for the most part underground, though here and there it is open to the sky. After it reaches that sheer face of the cliff which the stone lip overhangs, the passage pierces the solid rock and is very steep. Here two lamps are hid which I will light with the little fire sticks that your servant has given to me. One lamp must be left as a guide in the descent when you return ; the other I, who go first, will carry to show you where to set your feet. Do you understand, Lord ?"

"Yes, but what I want to know is, what happens when we reach the top of the tunnel ?"

"Lord, as I have said, at its head the hole is closed with a moving block that seems to be part of the floor of the courtyard of Kaneke's house. I have its secret and can cause it to open, which I will do after I have hidden the lamp. Then we must creep into the courtyard. Kaneke, as I believe, is on the *stoep* of the house with his hands tied behind him, and bound with a rope round his middle to a post that supports the roof of the *stoep*. It may be, however, that he is in one of the rooms of the house, in which case our task will be difficult——"

"Very difficult," I interrupted with a groan.

"My hope is," she went on, taking no heed of my words, "that those who guard him will be asleep, or perhaps drunk, for doubtless they will have found the white man's drink that Kaneke keeps in the house, which they love, all of them, although it is forbidden by their law. Or Kaneke himself may have told them where it is and begged them to get him some of it. If so, I shall cut his bonds so that he may come to the mouth of the hole and climb into it and thus escape."

"And if they are awake and sober—as they ought to be ?" I said.

"Then, Lord, you and the yellow man must play your part ; it is not for me to tell you what it is," she answered dryly. "There will not be many of these men set to keep one who is bound, and the most of the guard watch outside the fence, thinking that if any rescue is attempted, it will be from the town. Now I have told you all, so let us start."

Well, start we did; White-Mouse, going first, went round the boulder and pulled aside some loose stones, revealing an orifice, into which we crept after her, Hans nipping in before me. For some way we crawled in the dark up a slope of rock. Then, as she had said would be the case, light reached us from the sky because here the cleft was open. Indeed, there were two or three of these alternating lengths of darkness and light.

After ten minutes or so of this climbing White-Mouse halted and whispered:

"Now the real tunnel begins. Rest a while, for it is steep."

I obeyed with gratitude. Presently there was the sound of a match being struck. She had found the lamp, an earthenware affair filled with palm-oil such as the Arabs used in those days, and lit it. After the darkness its light seemed dazzling. By it I saw a round hole running upwards almost perpendicularly; it was the tunnel which she had told us pierced the lip of solid cliff that overhung the gorge. To all appearance it had been made by man, though a long while ago. Perhaps it was a mine-shaft, hollowed by primeval metal-workers; after all, these are common in Africa, where I have seen many of them in Matabele Land.

At any rate, on its walls I noted gleaming specks that I took to be ore of some sort, but of course this guess may be quite wrong. Up this shaft ran a kind of ladder with little landing-places at intervals, made by niches cut in the rock to give foot- and hand-holds. There was a rope also that must have been fastened to something above, which, I may add, looked to me rather rotten, as though it had been there a long while. My heart sank as I contemplated it and the niches, and most heartily did I wish myself anywhere else than in that beastly hole. However, it was no use showing fear; there was nothing to be done except go through with the business, so I held my tongue, though I heard Hans praying, or cursing, or both, in front of me.

"Forward now. Have no fear," whispered our guide. "Set your hands and feet in the niches as I do; they will not break away, and the rope is stronger than it looks."

Then she slung or strapped to her back the second lamp, which I forgot to say she had lit also and placed in a kind of basket so made that it could be used in this fashion without setting fire to its bearer, thus giving us light whereby to climb, and sprang at the face of the rock.   Up she went with an extraordinary nimbleness, which caused me to reflect in an inconsequent fashion that she was well named Mouse, a creature that can run up a wall.

We followed as best we could, clasping the rotten-looking rope, which seemed to be made of twisted buffalo-hide, with our right hands and the niches in which we must afterwards set our feet with our left.   I think that rope was the greatest terror of this horrible journey ; though, as we were destined to prove, White-Mouse was right when she said that it was stronger than it looked —very strong, in truth, though this we did not know at the time.

No, not the greatest, for even worse than the rope, that is when we had ascended a long way, was the lamp which we had left burning at the bottom of the hole, because the spark of light it gave showed what a terrible distance there was to fall if one made a mistake.   I only looked at it once, or at most twice ; it frightened me too much.   Another minor trouble in my case was my Winchester repeater that was slung upon my back, of which the strap cut my shoulder and the lock rubbed my spine. Much did I regret that I had not followed the example of Hans and left it behind.

We reached the first landing-place and rested.   After eyeing me with some anxiety, for doubtless my face showed trepidation, Hans, I imagine to divert my mind, took the chance to deliver a little homily.

"The Baas," he said, wiping the sweat from his face with the back of his hand, "is very fond of helping people in trouble, a bad habit of which I hope the Baas will break himself in future. For see what happens to those who are such fools.   Not even to help my own father would I come into this hole again, especially as I don't know who he was.   However, Baas," he added more cheerfully—for secretly agreeing with Hans, I made no reply— "if this is an old mine-shaft as I suppose, think how much worse it must have been for the miners to climb up it with a hundred-pound bag of ore on their backs, than it is for us ; especially as they weren't Christians, like you and me, Baas, and didn't know that they would go to heaven if they tumbled off, like we do.   When one is fording a bad river safely, Baas, as we are, it is always nice to remember that lots of other people have been drowned in it."

Will it be believed that even then and there that little beast Hans made me laugh, or at any rate smile, especially as I knew that his cynicism was assumed and therefore could bring no ill luck on us? For really Hans had the warmest of hearts.

Presently, off we went again for another spell of niches and apparently rotten rope, and in due course came safely to the second landing-place. Here White-Mouse bade us wait a little.

Saying that she would return presently, she went up a third flight of niches at great speed, and reaching yet another landing-place, did something—we could not see what.

Then she returned, and her descent was strange to see. Taking the rope in both hands (afterwards we discovered that it was made fast to a point or hook of stone on the third landing-place in such fashion that it hung well clear of the face of the rock below), she came down it hand over—or rather under—hand, sometimes setting her foot into one of the niches, but more often swinging quite clear. She was wonderful to look on ; her slight figure illumined by the lantern on her back and surrounded by darkness, appeared more like a spirit floating in mid-air than that of a woman. Presently she stood beside us.

"Lord," she said, when she had rested a minute, "I have been to see whether the catch of the stone which covers the mouth of the hole is in order. It works well and I have loosed it. Now at a push this stone, that like the rest of the courtyard is faced with lime plaster, will swing upwards, for it is hung upon a bar of iron, and remain on edge, leaving a space large enough for any man to climb into the courtyard by the little ladder that is set upon the landing-place. Be careful, however, not to touch the stone when you have passed the opening into the courtyard, for if so much as a finger is laid upon it, it will swing to again and make itself fast, cutting off retreat."

"Cannot it be opened from above?" I asked anxiously.

"Yes, Lord, if one knows how, which it is impossible to explain to you except in the courtyard itself, as perhaps I shall have no time or chance to do. Still, do not be afraid, for I will fix it with a wedge so that it cannot shut unless the wedge is pulled away. Nay, ask no more questions, for I have not time to answer them," she went on impatiently, as I opened my mouth to speak. "Have I not told you that all will be well? Follow me with a bold heart."

Then, as though to prevent the possibility of further conversation, she went to the edge of the resting-place and began to climb, Hans and I scrambling after her as before. Of this ascent I remember little, for my mind was so fixed upon what was to happen when we reached the top that, dreadful as it was, it made small impression on me. Also by now I was growing more or less used to this steeplejack work, and since I had seen the woman hanging on to it, gained confidence in the rope. The end of it was that we reached the third landing-place in safety, being now, as I reckoned, quite two hundred feet above the spot where the actual tunnel sprang from the cleft which sometimes went underground and sometimes was open to the sky.

CHAPTER V

THE RESCUE

WHEN we had recovered breath White-Mouse unfastened the lantern from her back and showed us a stout wooden ladder with broad rungs almost resembling steps, which ran from the edge of the resting-place to what looked like a solid roof, but really was the bottom of the movable stone.

"Examine it well," she said, "and note that this resting-place is not beneath the stone, but to the right of it. There-fore I can leave the lamp burning here that it may be ready for use in the descent ; for if the basket is set in front of the flame the light will not show in the courtyard above."

This she proceeded to do, and it was then that I noted how the hide rope was fastened to a hook-shaped point of rock at the edge of the platform, also—which I did not like—that it was somewhat frayed by this edge, although originally that length of it had been bound round with grass and a piece of cloth.

Now we were in semi-darkness and my spirits sank propor-tionately.

"What are we to do, White-Mouse ?" I asked.

"This, Lord. I will go up the ladder and push open the stone, as I told you. Then I will climb into the courtyard and creep to the *stoep* where I am sure Kaneke lies bound, hoping that there I may be able to cut his cords without awakening those who guard him, who, I trust, will be asleep, or drunk, or both. You and Hans will follow me through the hole and stand or kneel on either side of it with your weapons ready. If there is

C

trouble you will use those weapons, Lord, and kill any who strive to prevent the escape of Kaneke."

Now my patience was exhausted, and I asked her :

"Why should I do this thing ? Why should I take the lives of men with whom I have no quarrel in order to rescue Kaneke, and very probably lose my own in the attempt ?"

"First, because that is what you came here to do, Lord," she answered quietly. "Secondly, because it is necessary that Kaneke should be saved in order that he may guide you, which he alone can do, to a place where you will save others, and thus serve a certain holy one against whom he has sinned in the past."

Now I remembered the story that this Kaneke had told me about a mysterious woman who lived on an island in a lake whom he had affronted, and answered :

"Oh yes, I have heard of her and believe nothing of the tale."

"Doubtless you are right not to believe the tale as Kaneke told it to you, Lord. Learn that once he tried to work bitter wrong to that holy one, being bewitched by her beauty ; yes, to do sacrilege to our goddess." (I remembered that "our" afterwards, though at the time I made no comment.) "Being merciful, she spared him, but because of his crime misfortune overtook him, and for years he must dwell afar. Now the hour has come when for certain reasons he is bidden to return and expiate his evil deeds, and not here must his fate find him, Lord——"

"Baas," broke in Hans, "it is no use talking to this White-Mouse, who stuffs our brains with spiders' webs and talks nonsense. She wants us to save Kaneke for her own ends or those of others of whom she is the voice, and we have said that we will try. Now either we must keep our word or break it and climb down this hole again, if we can—which would be much better. Indeed, Baas, I think we should start——"

Here White-Mouse looked at Hans with remarkable effect, for he stopped suddenly and began to fan himself with his hat.

"Which advice does the Lord Macumazahn desire to take ?" she asked of me in a cold and quiet voice.

"Go on," I said, nodding towards the ladder, "we follow you."

Next instant she was running up it with Hans at her heels, for as before, he slipped in before me. I may add that it was quite dark on that ladder, which was very unpleasant.

Soon something above me swung back. I felt a breath of

fresh air on my face, and looking upwards, saw a star shining in the sky, for at that moment a cloud had passed over the moon, which star gave me comfort, though I did not know why it should.

I reached the top of the ladder and saw that White-Mouse had vanished and that Hans was scrambling into the courtyard. Then he gave me his hand and dragged me after him. The place was quite quiet and because of the cloud I could only see the house as a dark mass and trace the outlines of the *stoep*, which I remembered very well. Presently I heard a faint stir upon this *stoep* and got my rifle ready ; Hans, on the other side of the mouth of the pit, already had his revolver in his hand.

A while went by, perhaps a minute—it seemed an hour—and looking upwards, to my dismay, I perceived the edge of the moon appearing beyond the curtain of cloud. Swiftly she emerged and flooded the place with light, as an African moon can do. Now I saw all. Coming down the steps of the *stoep*, very slowly as though he were cramped by his bonds, was the great form of Kaneke leaning on the shoulder of the frail girl, as a man might upon a stick. Pieces of rope still hung to his arms and legs, and she had a bared knife in her hand. In the shadow of the *stoep* I made out the dim figures of men, two I saw, but in fact there were three, who appeared to be asleep.

As he reached the courtyard Kaneke stumbled and fell on to his hands and knees with a crash, but recovering himself, plunged towards us. The men on the *stoep* sat up—then it was that I counted three. White-Mouse flung off her dark cloak and stood there in shining white, looking like a ghost in the moonlight ; indeed, I believe her object was to personate a ghost. If so it was successful as far as two of the men were concerned, for they howled aloud with terror, crying out something about *Afreets*. The third, however, who was bolder or perhaps guessed the truth, rushed at her. I saw the knife flash and down he went, yelling in fear and pain. The others vanished, I think into the house, for I heard them shouting there. Kaneke reached us. The woman flitted after him, saying :

"Into the pit ! Into the pit ! Help him, Lord !"

We did so and he scrambled down the ladder.

At this moment a terrific hubbub arose. The guard outside the fence were rushing through the gate, a number of them, I do not know how many.

Hans snatched the rifle from my hand and pushed me to the edge of the hole—I noticed that the gallant fellow did not wish to go first this time ! I clambered down the ladder with great rapidity, calling to Hans to follow, which he did so fast that he trod upon my fingers.

"Where's White-Mouse ?" I said.

"I don't know, Baas. Talking with those fellows up there, I think."

"Out of the way !" I cried. "She can't be left. They will kill her !"

I climbed past him up the ladder again until I could look over the edge of the hole.

This is what I saw and heard : White-Mouse, the knife in her hand, was haranguing the oncoming Arabs so fiercely that they shrank together before her, invoking curses on them as I imagine, which frightened them very much, and pointing now at one and now at another with the knife. As she called down her maledictions she retreated slowly backwards towards the mouth of the pit, whence she must have rushed to meet the men as they burst through the gateway, I presume in order to give us time to get down the ladder. Suddenly the crowd of them seemed to recover courage. One shouted :

"It is White-Mouse, not a ghost !" Another invoked Allah ; a third called out : "Kill the foreign sorceress who has brought the spotted sickness on us and snatched away the star-worshipper."

They came forward—doubtfully lifting their spears, for they did not seem to have any firearms.

"Give me my rifle," I called to Hans, for in my hurry I forgot that I had a pistol in my pocket, my purpose being to get on the top step of the ladder, and thence open fire on them, so as to hold them back till White-Mouse could join us.

"Yes, Baas," called Hans from below as he began to climb the ladder again with the rifle in his hand, a slow job, because it cumbered him. I bent down as far as I could to grasp it, thus lowering my head, although I still managed to watch what was going on in the courtyard.

Just as my fingers touched the barrel of the Winchester, White-Mouse hurled her knife at the first of her attackers. Then she turned, followed by the whole crowd of them, and ran for the pit. One caught hold of her, but she slipped from his grasp and, although another gripped her garment, reached the stone which stood up edgeways some three feet above the level of the pavement of the courtyard.

In a flash I divined her purpose. It was not escape she sought, indeed, now that was impossible, but to let fall the block of rock or cement, and thus make pursuit of us also impossible. Horror filled me and my blood seemed to freeze, for I understood that this meant that she would be left in the hands of her enemies.

It was too late to do anything; indeed, as the thought passed my mind she hurled her weight against the stone (if she had ever wedged it open, as she said she would, which I doubt, she must have knocked away the prop with her foot). I saw it begin to swing downwards, and ducked instinctively, which was fortunate for me, for otherwise it would have struck my head and killed me. As it was it crushed in the top of the soft hat I was wearing. Down it came with a clang, leaving us in the dark.

"Hans," I cried, "bring that lantern and help me to try to push up this stone!"

He obeyed, although it took a long while, for he had to go back to the resting-place to fetch it. Then, standing side by side upon the ladder, we pushed at the stone, but it would not stir a hair's breadth. We saw something that looked like a bolt, and worked away at it, but utterly without result. We did not know the trick of the thing, if there was one. Then I bethought me of Kaneke who all this while was on the landing-place beneath, and sent Hans to ask him how to raise the stone. Presently he returned and reported that Kaneke said that if once it had been slammed down in this fashion, it could only be opened from above with much labour, if, indeed, this could be done at all.

I ran down the ladder in a fury and found Kaneke seated on the landing-place, a man bemused.

I reviled him, saying that he must come and move the stone, of which doubtless he knew the secret, so as to enable us to try to rescue the woman who had saved him. He listened with a kind of dull patience, then answered:

"Lord, you ask what cannot be done. Believe me I would help White-Mouse if I could, if indeed she needs help, but the catches that loose this mass of rock are very delicate and doubtless were destroyed by its violent closing. Moreover by this time of a certainty she is killed, if death can touch her, and even were it possible to lift it, you would be killed also, for those sons of Satan will wait there hoping that this may happen."

Still I was not satisfied, and made the man come up the ladder with me, which he did very stiffly, threatening to shoot him if he did not. This, to tell the truth, at that moment I would have done without compunction, so enraged and horrified was I at what had happened which, perhaps unjustly, I half attributed to him.

Well, he came and explained certain things to me about the catches whereof I forget the details, after which we pushed with all our might, till the stave of the ladder on which we stood began to crack, in fact; but nothing happened. Evidently in some way the block was jammed on its upper side, or perhaps the pin or hinges upon which it was balanced had broken. I do not know and it matters nothing.

All was finished. We were helpless. And that poor woman— oh, that poor woman!—what of her?

I returned to the landing-place and sat down to rest, almost weeping. Hans, I observed, was in much the same state, without a gibe or an impertinence left in him.

"Baas," he said, "if we had got out of the hole too, it would have been no better; worse, indeed, for we should have been killed as well as White-Mouse, even if we had managed to shoot some of those Prophet-worshipping dogs before they spotted us. Alas, Baas, I think that White-Mouse meant to get herself killed from the first. Perhaps she had had enough of that man," and he nodded towards Kaneke, who sat brooding and taking no heed, "or perhaps her job was done and she knew it. Or perhaps she can't be killed, as this Kaneke seems to think."

Listening to him, I reflected that he must be right, for now I remembered that White-Mouse had spoken several times of the escape of Hans, Kaneke, and myself, and never of her own, though when she did so I had not quite caught her drift. The woman meant to die, or knew that she would die, it did not matter which, seeing that the end was the same. Or she meant something else that was dark to me.

Presently, Hans spoke again:

"Baas," he said, "this place is a good grave, but I do not want to be buried in it, and oil in these Arab lamps does not last for ever; they are not like those of the widow, which the old prophet kept burning for years and years to cook meal on, as your reverend father used to tell us. Don't you think we had better be moving, Baas?"

"I suppose so," I answered, "but what about Kaneke? He seems in a bad way."

"Oh, Baas, let him come or let him stay behind. I don't care which. Now I will strap the basket with the lantern on to my back as White-Mouse did, and go first, and you must follow me, and Kaneke can come when he likes, or stop here and repent of his sins."

He paused, then added (he was speaking in Dutch all this time) :

"No, Baas, I have changed my mind. Kaneke had better go first. He is very heavy, also stiff, and if he came last and fell on to our heads, where should we be, Baas ? It is better that we should fall on Kaneke rather than that Kaneke should fall on us."

Being puzzled what to do, I turned to speak to the man. Hans, who was fixing the basket on his back, had set down the lamp which was to be placed in such a position that its light fell full upon Kaneke. By it I saw that his face had changed. While I was questioning him about the bolts of the stone, it had been that of a man bemused, of one who awakes from a drunken sleep, or has been drugged, or is in the last stage of terror and exhaustion. Now it was very much alive and grown almost spiritual, like to the face of one who is rapt in prayer. The large round eyes were turned upwards as though they saw a vision, the lips were moving as if in speech, yet no word came from them, and from time to time they ceased to move, as though the ears listened for an answer.

I stared at him, then said politely in Arabic :

"Might I ask what you are doing, friend Kaneke ?"

He started and a kind of veil seemed to fall over his face ; I mean that it changed again and became normal.

"Lord," he answered, "I was returning thanks for my escape."

"You take time by the nose, for you haven't escaped yet," I replied, adding rather bitterly, "and were you returning thanks for the great deed of another who has not escaped, of the woman who is called White-Mouse ?"

"How do you know that she has not escaped ?"

"Because you yourself said that she must be dead—if she could die, which of course she can."

"Yes, I said some such words, but now I think that she has been speaking to me, although it may have been her spirit that was speaking."

"Look here !" I said, exasperated. "Who and what is, or was, White-Mouse ? Your wife, or your daughter ?"

"No, Lord, neither," he answered, with a little shiver.

"Then who ? Tell me the truth or I have done with you."

"Lord, she is a messenger from my own country who came a while ago to command me to return thither. It is because of her that these Arabs hate me so much, for they think she is my familiar through whom I work magic and bring evil upon them."

"And is she, Kaneke?"

"Baas," broke in Hans, "have you finished chatting, for the oil in that lamp burns low and I have only two candles. Those niches will not be nice in the dark, Baas."

"True," I said.

Then I bid Kaneke go first, suggesting that he knew the road, with Hans following him and I coming last.

"My legs are stiff, Lord," he said, "but my arms are recovered. I go."

He went; he went with the most amazing swiftness. In a few seconds he was over the edge of the pit and descending rapidly, hand over hand, as it seemed to me only occasionally touching the niches with his feet. Not that I had much time to judge of this, for presently he was out of sight and only by the jerking of the hide rope could we tell that he was there at all.

"Will it break, Baas?" asked Hans doubtfully. "That brute Kaneke weighs a lot."

"I don't know and I don't much care," I answered. "White-Mouse said we should get through safely, and I am beginning to believe in White-Mouse. So say your prayers and start."

He obeyed, and I followed.

I will omit the details of that horrible descent. Hans and I reached the second platform and rested. Unfortunately in starting again I looked down, and far, far below saw the lamp we had left burning at the bottom, which gave me such an idea of precipitious death that I grew dizzy. My strength left me and I almost fell, especially as just then my foot slipped in one of the niches, leaving all my weight upon my arms. I think I should have fallen, had not a voice, doubtless that of my subconscious self at work, seemed to say to me:

"Remember, if you fall, you will kill Hans as well as yourself."

Then my brain cleared, I recovered control of my faculties, and slipping down the rope a little way I found the next niche with my left foot. Doubtless this return was even more fearsome than the ascent, perhaps owing to physical weariness, or perhaps because the object of the effort was achieved and there was now nothing left to hope for except personal safety, the thought of which is always the father of fear. I am not sure; all I know is that my spine crept and my brain sickened much more than had been the case on the upward adventure.

At length, thank God, the worst of it was over and we reached the sloping passage or gulley, or whatever it may have been, that in places was open to the sky. By help of the lamps that now were almost spent, we scrambled down this declivity with comparative ease, and so came out of the mouth of the hole into the little clump of bush that concealed it.

I sat down trembling like a jelly ; the perspiration pouring off me, for the heat of that place had been awful. Hans, who although so tough, was in little better case than myself, found the water-bottle full of cold tea which, to save weight, we had left hidden with everything else we could spare, including our jackets, and passed it to me. I drank, and the insipid stuff tasted like nectar ; then gave it to Hans, although I could gladly have swallowed the whole bottleful.

When he had taken a pull I stopped him, remembering Kaneke, who must also be athirst. But where was Kaneke ? We could not see him anywhere. Hans opined that he had bolted into some hiding-place of his own, and being too weary to argue or even to speculate upon the matter, I accepted the explanation.

After this we finished the cold tea and topped it up with a nip of brandy apiece, carefully measured in a little cup. The flask itself, to which the cup was screwed, I did not dare to give to Hans, knowing that temptation would overcome him and he would empty it to the last drop.

Much refreshed and more thankful than I can say at having escaped the perils of that darksome climb, I put the extinguished lamps into poor White-Mouse's basket, thinking that they might come in useful afterwards (or perhaps I wished to keep them as a souvenir, I don't remember which). Then by common consent we started for the bottom of the great gulley, proposing to trek up it back towards the camp. On reaching the stream we stopped to drink water—for our thirst was still unsatisfied—and to wash the sweat from our faces, also to cool our feet bruised by those endless niches of the shaft.

Whilst I was thus engaged, hearing a sound, I peeped round a stone and perceived the lost Kaneke kneeling upon the rock like a man at prayer, and groaning. My first thought was that he must be hurt, perhaps in the course of his remarkably rapid descent, and my second that he was grieving over the death of White-Mouse, or mayhap because of his separation from his wives whom he would see no more. Afterwards, however, I reflected that the latter was improbable, seeing that he was so ready to leave them. Indeed, I doubted whether he had really any wives, or children either. Certainly I never saw any about the house in which he dwelt like a hermit ; there was nothing to show that these ever existed. If they did, I was sure that Hans would have discovered them.

However, this might be, not wishing to spy upon the man's private sorrows, I coughed, whereon he rose and came round the rock.

"So you are here before us," I said.

"Yes, Lord," he answered, "and waiting for you. The descent of the shaft is easy to those who know the road."

"Indeed. We found it difficult, also dangerous. However, like the woman called White-Mouse"—here he winced and bowed his head—"that is done with. Might I ask what your plans are now, Kaneke ?"

"What they have always been, Lord. To guide you to my people, the Dabanda, who live in the land of the Holy Lake. Only, Lord, I think that we had better leave this place as quickly as we can, seeing it is certain that, thinking we have escaped, the Arabs, my enemies, will follow to your camp to attack you there."

"I agree," I answered. "Let us go at once."

So off we went on our long tramp up the darksome gorge, I, to tell the truth, full of indignation and in the worst of tempers. At length I could control myself no longer.

"Kaneke," I said, for he was walking at my side, Hans being a little ahead engaged in picking our way through the gloom and watching for possible attacks—"Kaneke, it seems that I and my servant are suffering many things on your behalf. This night we have run great risks to save you from death, as has another who is gone, and now you tell me that because of you we are to be attacked by those who hate you. I think it would be better if I repaid to you what I have received, together with whatever money the ivory you gave me may bring, and you went your way, leaving me to go mine."

"It cannot be," he answered vehemently. "Lord, although you do not know it, we are bound together until all is accomplished as may be fated. Yes, it is decreed in the stars, and destiny binds us together. You think that I am ungrateful, but it is not so ; my heart is full of thankfulness towards you and I am your slave. Ask me no more, I pray you, for if I told you all you would not believe me."

"Already you have told me a good deal that I do not believe,"

I replied sharply, "so perhaps you had better keep your stories and promises to yourself. At any rate, I cannot desert you at present, for if I did, I suppose those Arab blackguards would cut your throat."

"Yes, Lord, and yours too. Together we shall best them, as you will see, but separated they will kill us both, and your servants and porters also."

After this we went on in silence and in the end, without molestation except from a lion, emerged from the gorge and came to the knoll where I had camped. We struck this beast in the open bushy country just outside the mouth of the gorge, or rather it struck us and followed us very persistently, which made me think that it must have been in great want of food. Occasionally it growled, but for the most part slunk along not more than thirty or forty paces to our right, taking cover in the high grass or behind bushes. Also twice it went ahead to clumps of thorn trees as though to waylay us. I think I could have shot it then, but Hans begged me not to fire for fear of letting our where-abouts be known to Arabs who might be searching for us. So instead we made detours and avoided those clumps of trees.

This seemed to irritate the lion, which for the third time crept forward and, as I saw clearly by the light of the sinking moon, crouched down on our path about fifty paces in front of us in such a spot that, owing to the nature of the land, it was difficult to circumvent it without going a long way round.

Now I thought that I must accept the challenge of this savage or starving animal, but Hans, who was most anxious that I should not shoot, remarked sarcastically that since the "owl-man", as he called Kaneke, was such a wonderful wizard, perhaps he would exert his powers and send it away.

Kaneke, who had been marching moodily along as fast as his legs, still stiff from the bonds, would allow, paying little or no attention to the matter of the lion, heard him and seemed to wake up.

"Yes," he said, "if you are afraid of the beast I can do that. Bide here, I pray you, Lord, till I call you."

Then, quite unarmed, without so much as a stick in his hand indeed, he walked forward quietly to where the lion, a large one with a somewhat scrubby mane, lay upon a rock between the bank of the stream and a little cliff. I watched him amazed, holding my rifle ready and feeling sure that unless I could shoot it first, which was improbable because he was in my line of fire, there would soon be an end of Kaneke. This, however, did not happen, for the man trudged on and presently was so close to the lion that his body hid it from my sight.

After this I heard a growl which degenerated into a yelp like to that of a beast in pain. The next thing I saw was Kaneke standing on the rock where the lion had been, outlined very clearly against the sky, and beckoning to us to come forward. So we went, not without doubt, and found Kaneke seated on the rock with his face towards us as though to rest his legs, and as it seemed once more lost in reverie.

"The lion has gone," he said shortly, "or rather the lions, for there were two of them, and will return no more to trouble you. Let us walk on, I will go first."

"He is a very good wizard, Baas," said Hans reflectively in Dutch, as we followed. "Or perhaps," he added, "that lion is one of his familiars which he calls and sends away as he likes."

"Bosh !" I grunted. "The brute bolted, that is all."

"Yes, Baas. Still, I think that if you or I had gone forward without a gun it would have bolted us, for as you know, when a lion follows a man like that, its belly has been empty for days. This Kaneke's other name must be Daniel, Baas, who used to like to sleep with lions."

I did not argue with Hans ; indeed, I was too tired to talk, but stumped along till presently we came to the site of the camp which we had left early on that eventful night—days ago it seemed to be. Here I found that my orders had been obeyed and that Tom and Jerry had gone forward with the porters, as I judged from various indications, such as the state of the cooking-fire, not much more than an hour before. Therefore there was nothing to do but follow their trail, which was broad and easy, even in the low moonlight.

On we marched accordingly, always uphill, which made our weary progress slow. At length came the dawn, a hot, still dawn, and after it the sunrise. By its bright light we saw two things : our porters camping at the appointed spot about half a mile away among some rocks just above a pool of water that remained in a dry river-bed ; and behind us, perhaps two miles off, tracking our spoor up the slope that we had travelled, a party of white-robed Arabs, twenty of them or more.

"Now we are in for it," I said. "Come on, Hans, there is no time to spare."

CHAPTER VI

KANEKE'S FRIENDS

I KNOW of no greater pick-me-up for a tired man than the sight of a body of enemies running on his spoor with the clear and definite object of putting an end to his mortal existence. On this occasion, for instance, suddenly I felt quite fresh again and covered that half-mile which lay between us and the camp in almost record time. So did the other two, for the three of us arrived there nearly neck and neck.

As we scrambled into the place I observed with joy that Tom and Jerry had taken in the situation, for already the porters were engaged in piling stones into a wall, or in hacking down thorn trees and dragging their prickly boughs together so as to form a *boma*. More, those excellent men had breakfast cooking for us upon a fire, and coffee ready.

Having given such orders as were necessary, though in truth there was little to be done, I fell upon that breakfast and devoured it, for we were starving. Hot coffee and food are great stimulants, and in ten minutes I felt a new man. Then the four of us, namely, Tom, Jerry, Hans, and I, took counsel together, for at the moment I could not see Kaneke who, having bolted some meat, had gone, as I presumed, to help with the *boma*-building. It was needful, for the position seemed fairly desperate.

By now the Arabs, who advanced slowly, were about half a mile away, and with the aid of my glasses I saw that there were more of them than I had thought, forty or fifty indeed, of whom quite half carried guns of one sort or another. I surveyed the position and found that it was good for defence. The camp was on the slope of a little koppie, round-topped and thickly strewn with boulders. To our right at the foot of the koppie was the long, broad pool I have mentioned.

Behind lay the river-bed half encircling the koppie, or rather a swamp through which the river ran when it was full, which swamp was so deep with sticky mud that advance over it would be difficult, if not impossible. To our left, however, was a dry *vlei* overgrown with tall grass and thorn trees, through which wended the native path that we had been following. In front the veld over which we had advanced, was open, but gave no cover, for here the grass had been burned leaving the soil bare. Therefore the Arabs could only advance upon us from this direction, or possibly through the thick grass and trees to our left.

But here came the rub. With a dozen decent shots I should have feared nothing. We, however, had but four upon whom we could rely, and Kaneke, who was an unknown quantity. If these Arabs meant business our case was hopeless, for of course no reliance could be placed on the porters, or at any rate upon most of them, who moreover had no guns. In short there was nothing to be done except trust in Providence and fight our hardest.

We got out the guns, Winchester repeaters all of them, of which I had six with me, and opened a couple of boxes of ammunition. The heavy game rifles we loaded and kept in reserve, also a couple of shot-guns charged with loopers, as we called slugs, for these are very effective in meeting a rush. Then I told Hans to find Kaneke, that I might explain matters and give him a rifle. He went and returned presently saying that Kaneke was not working at the walls or cutting down thorns.

"Baas," he added, "I think that skunk has run away or turned into a snake and slid into the reeds."

"Nonsense," I answered. "Where could he run to? I will look for him myself; those Arabs won't be here yet awhile."

So off I went and climbed to the top of the koppie to get a better view. Presently I thought I heard a sound beneath me, and looking over the edge of the boulder, saw Kaneke standing in a little bay of rock, waving his arms in a most peculiar fashion and talking in a low voice as though he were carrying on a conversation with some unseen person.

"Hi!" I said, exasperated. "Perhaps you are not aware that those friends of yours will be here presently and that you had better come to help to keep them off. Might I ask what you are doing?"

"That will be seen later, Lord," he answered quietly. Then, with a final wave of the hand and a nod of the head, such as a man gives in assent, he turned and climbed up to where I was.

Not one word did he say until we reached the others, nor did I question him. Indeed, I thought it useless as I had made up my mind that the fellow was mad. Still; as he was an able-bodied man who said that he could shoot, I gave him one of the rifles and a supply of cartridges, and hoped for the best.

By now the Arabs had come within four hundred yards,

whereon a new trouble developed, for the porters grew frightened and threatened to bolt. I sent Hans to tell them that I would shoot the first man who stirred, and when, notwithstanding this, one of them did begin to run, I fired a shot which purposely missed him by a few inches and flattened on a rock in front of his face. This frightened him so much that he fell down and lay still, which caused me to fear that I had made a mistake and hit him through the head. The effect upon the others was marked, for they squatted on the ground and began to pray to whatever gods or idols they worshipped, or to talk about their mothers, nor did any of them attempt to stir again.

At the sound of this shot the Arabs halted, thinking that it had been fired at them, and began to consult together. After they had talked for some time one man came forward waving a flag of truce made of a white turban cloth tied to a spear. In reply I shook a pocket handkerchief which was far from white, whereon he walked forward to within twenty yards of the *boma*. Here I shouted to him to stop, suspecting that he wished to spy upon us, and went out to meet him with Hans, who would not allow me to go alone.

"What do you and your people want?" I said, in a loud voice to the man, whom I recognized as one of the judges who had tried Kaneke.

"White Master," he answered, "we want the wizard Kaneke, whom you have stolen away from us, and whom we have doomed to die. Give him to us, dead or alive, and we will let you and your people go in peace, for against you we have no other quarrel. If you do not, we will kill you, every one."

"That remains to be seen," I answered boldly. "As for the rest, hand over to me the woman called White-Mouse and I will talk with you."

"I cannot," he answered.

"Why not? Have you killed her?"

"By Allah, no!" he exclaimed earnestly. "We have not killed that witch, though it is true we wished to do so. Somehow in the confusion she slipped from our hands, and we cannot find her. We think that she has turned into an owl and flown to Satan, her master."

"Do you? Well, I think that you lie. Now tell me why you wish to kill Kaneke after he has run away from you, leaving you to walk your own road?"

"Because," answered the Arab in a fury, "he has left his curse upon us, which can only be loosed with his blood. Did you not hear him swear to bring a plague upon us, and has not the spotted sickness broken out in the town so that already many are ill and doubtless will die ?   Also has he not murdered our brother and bewitched us in many other ways, and will he not utterly destroy us by bringing our enemies upon us, as two moons ago he swore that he would do unless we let him go ?"

"So you were keeping him a prisoner ?"

"Of course, White Man.   He has been a prisoner ever since he came among us, though at times it is true that he has been seen outside the town, and now we know how he came there."

"Why did you keep him a prisoner ?"

"That in protecting himself he might protect us also by his magic, for we knew that if he should escape he would bring destruction upon us.   And now, will you give him up to us, or will you not ?"

There was a certain insolence about the way in which the man asked this question that put my back up at once, and I answered on the impulse of the moment :

"I will not.   First, I will see all of you in hell.   What business have you and your fellow half-breed Arabs to threaten to attack me, a subject of the Queen of England, because I give shelter to a fugitive whom you wish to murder ?   And what have you done with the woman called White-Mouse who, you say, has changed into an owl ?   Produce her, lest I hold you all to account for her life.   Oh, you think that I am weak because I have but few men with me here.   Yet I tell you that before the sun has set, I, Macumazahn, will teach you a lesson, if, indeed, any of you live to learn it."

The man stared at me, frightened by my bold talk.   Then, without a word, he turned and ran back towards his people, zigzagging as he went, doubtless because he feared that I would shoot him.   I too, turned, and strolled unconcernedly up the slope to the *boma*, just to show them that I was not afraid.

"Baas," said Hans, as we went, "as usual you are wrong. Why do you not surrender that big-eyed wizard who is putting us to so much trouble ?"

"Because, Hans, I should be ashamed of myself if I did, and what is more, you would be ashamed of me."

"Yes, Baas, that is quite true.   I should never think the same of you again.   But, Baas, when a man's throat's going to be cut, he doesn't remember what he would think afterwards if it wasn't cut.   Well, we are all going to be killed, for what we can do against those men I can't see, and when we meet your reverend father presently in the Place of Fires, I shall tell him that I did my best to keep you from coming there so soon. And now Baas, I will bet you that monkey-skin tobacco pouch of mine of which you are so jealous, against a bottle of gin, to be paid when we get back to the coast, that before the day is over I put a bullet through that Arab villain who talked to you so insolently."

We reached the *boma*, where I told Tom and Jerry, also Kaneke, the gist of what had passed. The dashing Tom seemed not displeased at the prospect of a fight, while Jerry the phlegmatic, shook his head and shrugged his shoulders, after which they both retired behind a rock for a few moments, as Hans informed me, to say their prayers and confess their sins to each other. Kaneke listened and made but one remark.

"You are behaving well to me, Lord Macumazahn, and now I will behave well to you."

"Thank you," I answered. "I shall remind you of that if we meet on the other side of the sun, or in that star you worship. Now please go to your post, shoot as straight as you can, and don't waste cartridges."

Then, when the hunters had returned from their religious exercises, we took our places, each in a little shelter of rocks, so arranged that we could fire over the fence of the *boma*. I was in the middle, with Hans and Kaneke on either side of me, while Tom and Jerry were at the ends of the line. There we crouched, expecting a frontal attack, but this did not develop. After a long talk the Arabs fired a few shots from a distance of about four hundred yards, which either fell short or went I know not where. Then suddenly they began to run over the open land where, as I have said, the veld was burned, towards the tall grass with thorn trees growing in it that lay upon our left, evidently with the design of outflanking us.

At the head of their scattered band was a tall man in whom, by the aid of my glasses, I recognized the venomous and evil-tempered Gaika, who had acted as chief-justice at Kaneke's trial, a person who had threatened me and of whom I had conceived an intense dislike. Hans, whose sight was as keen as a vulture's, recognized him also, for he said :

"There goes that hyena Gaika."

"Give me my express," I said, laying down the Winchester, and he handed it to me cocked.

"Let no man fire !" I cried as I took it, and lifted the flap-sight that was marked five hundred yards. Then I stood up, set my left elbow upon a stone, and waited my chance.

It came a few moments later, when Gaika must cross a little ridge of ground where he was outlined against the sky. The shot was a long one for an express, but I knew my rifle and determined to risk it. I got on to him, aiming at his middle, and swung the barrel the merest fraction in front to allow time for the bullet to travel. Then, drawing a long breath to steady myself, I pressed the trigger, of which the pull was very light.

The rifle rang out and I waited anxiously, for, although the best of shots need not have been ashamed to do so, I feared to miss, knowing that if this happened it would be taken as an omen. Well, I did not miss, for two seconds later I saw Gaika plunge to the ground, roll over and over and lie still.

"Oh !" said my people simultaneously, looking at me with admiration and pride. But I was not proud, except a little perhaps at my marksmanship, for I was sorry to have to shoot this disagreeable and to us most dangerous man, so much so that I did not fire the other barrel of the express.

For a moment his nearest companions stopped and stared at Gaika ; then they fled on towards the high grass and reeds, leaving him on the ground, which showed me that he must be dead. I hoped that they were merely taking cover and that the sudden end of Gaika would have caused them to change their minds about attacking us, which was why I shot him. This, however, was not the case, for a while later fire was opened on us from a score of places in these reeds. Here and there in the centre of clumps of them and behind the trunks of thorns the Arabs had hidden themselves, singly or in pairs, and the trouble was that we could not see one of them. This made it quite useless to attempt to return their fire because our bullets would only have been wasted, and I had no ammunition to throw away in such a fashion. So there we must lie, doing nothing.

It was true that for the present we were not in any great danger, because we could take shelter behind stones upon which the missiles of the Arabs flattened themselves, if they hit at all, for the shooting being erratic, most of them sang over us harmlessly. The sound of these bullets, which sometimes I think were only pebbles coated with lead, or fragments of iron, terrified our bearers, however, especially after one of them had been slightly wounded by a lead splinter, or a fragment of rock. The wretched men began to jabber and now and again to cry out with fear, nor could all my orders and threats keep them quiet.

At length, after this bombardment had continued for nearly

two hours, there came a climax.   Suddenly, as though at a word of command, the bearers rose and rushed down the slope like a bunch of startled buck.   They ran to the bank of the pool which I have mentioned, following it eastwards towards Kaneke's town, till they came to the bed of the river of which the pool formed a part in the wet season, where they vanished.

Of course we could have shot some of them as they went, as Hans, who was feeling spiteful, wanted to do, but this I would not allow, for what was the use of trying to stop a pack of cowards who, as likely as not, would attack us from behind if a rush came, hoped thus to propitiate the Arabs?   What happened to those men I do not know, for they vanished completely, nor did I ever hear of them again.   Perhaps some of them escaped back to the coast, but being without arms or food, this I think more than doubtful.   The poor wretches must have wandered till they starved or were killed by wild beasts, unless indeed they were captured and enslaved.

Now our position was very serious.   Here we were, five men and one donkey ; for I think I have said that I possessed this beast, a particularly intelligent creature called Donna after a half-breed Portuguese woman the rest of whose name I forget, who had sold it to me with two others that died on the road. Beneath us, completely hidden, were forty or fifty determined enemies who probably were waiting for nightfall to creep up the koppie and cut our throats.   What could we do ?

Hans, whose imagination was fertile, suggested various expedients.   His first was that we should try to fire the reeds and long grass in which the Arabs had taken cover, which was quite impracticable, because first we had to get there without being shot ; also they were still too green to burn and the wind was blowing the wrong way.   His next idea was that we should follow the example of the porters and bolt.   This, I pointed out, was foolish, for we should only be run down and killed.   Even if we waited till dark, almost certainly the end would be disaster ; moreover we should be obliged to leave most of our gear and ammunition behind.   Then he made a third proposal in a mixture of Dutch and English, which was but an old one in a new form, namely, that we should try to buy off the Arabs by surrendering Kaneke.

"I have already told you that I will do nothing of the sort. I promised White-Mouse to try to save this man, and there's an end."

"Yes, Baas, I know you did.   Oh, what bad luck it is that

White-Mouse was so pretty. If only her face had been like a squashed pumpkin, or if she had been dirty, with creatures in her hair, we shouldn't be looking at our last sun, Baas. Well, no doubt soon we shall be talking over the business with her in the Place of Fires, where I am sure she has gone, whatever that liar of a messenger may have said. Now I have finished who can think of nothing more, except to pray to your reverend father, who doubtless can help us if he chooses, which perhaps he doesn't, because he is so anxious to see me again."

Having delivered himself thus, Hans squatted a little more closely beneath his stone, over which a bullet had just passed with a most vicious whiz, and lit a pipe.

Next I tried the two hunters, only to find that they were quite barren of ideas, for they shook their heads and went on murmuring prayers. There remained Kaneke, at whom I glanced in despair. There he sat silent, with a face like a brickbat so impassive was it, giving me the idea of a man who is listening intently for something. For what ? I wondered.

"Kaneke," I said, "by you, or on your behalf by another whom I think is dead, we have been led into a deep hole. Here we are who can be counted on the fingers of one hand, under fire from those who hate you, but against whom we have no quarrel, except on your account. The porters have fled away and our enemies, whom we cannot shoot because they are invisible in the reeds and grass of that *pan*, only await darkness to attack and make an end of us. Now if you have any word of comfort, speak, for it is needed, remembering that if we die, you die also."

"Comfort !" he answered in his dreamy fashion. "Oh yes, it is at hand. I am waiting for it now, my Lord Macumazahn," and he went on listening like one who has been interrupted in a serious matter by some babbler of trivialities.

This was too much for me ; my patience gave way, and I addressed Kaneke in language which I will not record, saying amongst other forcible things that I was sorry I had not followed Hans' advice and abandoned him or surrendered him to the Arabs.

"You could not do that, my Lord Macumazahn," he answered mildly, "seeing that you had promised White-Mouse to save me. No one could break his word to White-Mouse, could he ?"

"White-Mouse !" I ejaculated. "Where is she ? Poor woman, she is dead, and for you, as the rest of us soon will be. And now you talk to me about my promises to her. How do you know what I promised her, you anathema'd bag of mysteries ?"

"I do know, Lord," he replied, still more vaguely and gently. Then suddenly he added, "Hark! I hear the comfort coming," and lifted his hand in an impressive manner, only to drop it again in haste, because a passing bullet had scraped the skin off his finger.

Something caught my ear and I listened. From far away came a sound which reminded me of that made by a pack of wild dogs hunting a buck at night, a kind of surging, barbarous music.

"What is it?" I asked.

Kaneke, who was sucking the scraped finger, removed it from his mouth and replied that it was "the comfort", and that if I would look perhaps I should see.

So I did look through a crack between two stones towards the direction from which the sound seemed to come, namely eastward beyond the dry swamp where the veld was formed of great waves of land spotted with a sparse growth of thorn trees, swelling undulations like to those of the deep ocean, only on a larger scale. Presently, coming over the crest of one of these waves, now seen and now lost among the thorns, appeared a vast number of men, savage-looking fellows who wore feathers in their hair and very little else, and carried broad, long-handled spears.

"Who the deuce are these?" I asked, but Kaneke made no answer.

There he sat behind his stone, pointing towards the reeds in which the Arabs were hidden with his bleeding finger and muttering to himself.

Hans who, wild with curiosity, had thrust his sticky face against mine in order to share the view through the chink, whispered into my ear:

"Don't disturb him, Baas. These are his friends and he is telling them where those Arabs are."

"How can he tell people half a mile away anything, you idiot?" I asked.

"Oh, quite easily, Baas. You see, he is a magician, and magicians talk with their minds. It is their way of sending telegrams, as you do in Natal, Baas. Well, things look better now. As your reverend father used to say, if only you wait long enough the devil always helps you at last."

"Rot!" I ejaculated, though I agreed that things did look better, that is, unless these black scoundrels intended to attack us and not the Arabs. Then I set myself to watch events with the greatest interest.

The horde of savages, advancing at a great pace—there must have been two or three hundred of them—made for the dry *pan* like bees for their hive. Whether Kaneke instructed them or not, evidently their intelligence department was excellent, for they knew exactly what they had to do. Reaching the edge of it, they halted for a while and ceased their weird song, I suppose to get their breath and to form up. Then at some signal the song began again and they plunged into those reeds like dogs after an otter.

Up to this moment the Arabs hidden there did not seem to be aware of their approach, I suppose because their attention was too firmly fixed upon us, for they kept on firing at the koppie in a desultory fashion. Now of a sudden this firing ceased, and from the thicket below arose yells of fear, surprise, and anger. Next at its further end, that which lay towards Kaneke's town, appeared the Arabs running for all they were worth, and presently, after them, their savage attackers.

Heavens, what a race was that ! Never have I seen men go faster than did those Arabs across the plain with the wild pursuers at their heels. Some were caught and killed, but when at last they vanished out of sight, most of them were still well ahead. Hans wanted to shoot at them, but I would not allow it, for what was the use of trying to kill the poor wretches while others were fighting our battle ? So it came about that the only shot we fired that day, I mean in earnest, was that which I had aimed at Gaika, which was strange when I had prepared for a desperate battle against overwhelming odds.

All having vanished behind the irregularities of the ground, except a few who had been caught and speared, in the silence which followed the war-song and the shoutings, I turned to Kaneke and asked for explanations. He replied quite pleasantly and briefly, that these black men were some of his "friends" whom the Arabs had always feared he would bring upon them, which was why they kept him prisoner and wished to kill him.

"I had no intention of doing anything of the sort, Lord," he added, "until it became necessary in order to save our lives. Then, of course I asked them for help, whereon they came at once and did what was wanted, as you have seen."

"And pray how did you ask them, Kaneke ?"

"Oh, Lord, by messengers as one always asks people at a distance, though they were so long coming I feared lest the messengers might not have reached them."

"He lies, Baas," said Hans, in Dutch. "It is no good trying

to pump the truth out of his heart, for you will only tire yourself bringing up more lies."

As I agreed, I dropped the subject and inquired of Kaneke whether his friends were coming back again. He said he thought so and before very long, as he had told them not to attack the town in which dwelt many innocent women and children.

"But, Lord," he went on, with unusual emphasis, "when they do return I think it will be well that you should not go to speak to them. To tell the truth, they are savage people, and being very naked, might take a fancy to your clothes, also to your guns and ammunition. I will just go down to give them a word of thanks and bring back some porters to take the place of those who have run away, whom, by the way, I hope they have not met. Foreseeing something of the sort, I asked them to bring a number of suitable men."

"Did you?" I gasped. "You are indeed a provident person. And now may I ask you whether you intend to return to your town, or what you mean to do?"

"Certainly I do not intend to return, Lord, in order to care for people who have been so ungrateful. Also, that spotted sickness is most unpleasant to see. No, Lord, I intend to accompany you to the country of the Lake Mone."

"The Lake Mone!" I said. "I have had enough of that lake, or rather of the journey to it, and I have made up my mind not to go there."

He looked at me, and under the assumed mildness of that look I read intense determination as he answered:

"I think you will go to the Lake Mone, Lord Macumazahn."

"And I think I will not, Kaneke."

"Indeed. In that case, Lord, I must talk to my friends when they return, and make certain arrangements with them."

We stared at each other for what seemed quite a long time, though I dare say it was only a few seconds. I don't know what Kaneke read of my mind, but what I read of his was a full intention that I should accompany him to the Lake Mone, or be left to the tender mercies of his "friends", at present engaged in Arab-hunting who, it seemed, had so great a passion for European guns and garments.

Now there are times when it is well to give way, and the knowledge of those times, to my mind, often marks the difference between a wise man and a fool. As we all know, wisdom and folly are contiguous states, and the line dividing them is very thin and crooked, which makes it difficult not to blunder across its borders, I mean from the land of wisdom into that of folly, for the other step is rarely taken, save by one inspired by the best of angels.

In this instance, although I do not pretend to any exceptional sagacity, I felt strongly that it would be well to stick on my own side of the line and not defy the Fates as represented by that queer person Kaneke, and his black "friends" whom he seemed to have summoned from nowhere in particular. After all, I was in a tight place. To travel back without porters, even if I escaped the "friends" and the Arabs who now had a quarrel against me, was almost impossible, and the same might be said of a journey in any other direction. It seemed, therefore, that it would be best to continue to suffer those ills I knew of, namely the fellowship of Kaneke on an expedition into the unknown.

"Very well," I remarked casually, after a swift weighing of these matters and a still swifter remembrance of the prophecy of White-Mouse that I should come safely through the business. (Why this should have struck me at that moment I could not say.)—"Very well, it does not much matter to me whether I turn east or west. So let us go to Lake Mone, if there be such a place, though I wonder what will be the end of that journey."

"So do I," replied Kaneke dryly.

CHAPTER VII

THE JOURNEY

Now, for sundry reasons, I am going to follow the example of a lady of my acquaintance who makes it a rule to read two three-volume novels a week, and skip, by which I mean that I will compress the tale of our journey to the land of the mysterious Lake Mone into the smallest possible compass. If set out in full the details of such a trek as this through country that at the time was practically unknown to white men—it took between two and three months—would suffice to fill a volume. It might be an interesting volume in its way, to a few who care for descriptions of African races and scenery, but to the many I fear that its chapters would present a certain sameness. So I shall leave the untold and practise the art of précis-writing until I come to the heart of the story.

After the conversation of which I have spoken, we cooked and ate food, which all of us needed badly. Then, being very tired and worn with many emotions, Hans and I went to sleep in the shade of some rocks, leaving Tom and Jerry to keep watch. About three o'clock in the afternoon one of them woke us up, or rather woke me up, for Hans, who could do with very little sleep, was already astir and engaged in overhauling the rifles. They told me that the black men were returning. I asked where Kaneke was, and learned that he had gone to meet them. Then I took my glasses and from a point of vantage kept watch upon what happened.

The savages, impressive-looking fellows in their plume-crowned nakedness, came streaming across the veld, some of them carrying in their hands objects which I believe to have been the heads of Arabs, though of this I cannot be sure because they were so far away. They were no longer singing or in haste but walked quietly, with the contented air of men filled with a sense of duty done. Appeared Kaneke marching towards them, whereon they halted and saluted by raising their spears, thus showing me that in their opinion he was a man of great position and dignity. They formed a ring round Kaneke, from the centre of which he seemed to address them. When this ring opened out again, which it did after a while, I observed that a fire had been lit, how, or fed with what fuel, I do not know, and that on it the savages were laying the objects which I took to be the heads of Arabs.

"Kaneke is their great devil, and they are sacrificing to him, Baas," whispered Hans.

"At any rate, on this occasion he has been a useful devil," I answered, "or, rather, his worshippers have been useful."

A while later, when the rite, or sacrifice, or whatever it may have been, was completed, the savages started forward again, leaving the fire still burning on the veld, and marched almost to the foot of the koppie, which caused me some alarm, as I thought they might be coming to the camp. This was not so, however, for when they were within a few hundred yards, of a sudden they broke into a chant, not the same which they had used when advancing, but one which had in it a kind of note of farewell, and departing at a run past the outer edge of the dry *vlei* from which they had driven the Arabs, soon were lost to sight. Yes, their song grew fainter and fainter, till at length it was swallowed up in silence and the singers vanished into the vast depths of distance whence they came.

Where did they come from and who were they ? I know not, for on this matter Kaneke preserved a silence so impenetrable that at length the mystery of their appearance and disappearance began, to my mind, to take the character of an episode in a dream. Or, rather, it would have done so had it not been for the circumstance that they did not all go. On the contrary, about twenty were left, who stood before Kaneke with folded arms and bent heads, their spears thrust into the ground in front of them, blade upwards, by means of the iron spikes that were fixed to the handles. Also at the feet of each man was a bundle wrapped round with a mat.

"Hullo !" I said. "What do those men want ? Do they mean mischief ?"

"Oh no, Baas," answered Hans. "The Baas will remember that Kaneke promised us some more porters, and these are the men. Doubtless he is a great wizard, and for aught I know, may have made them and all the rest out of mud ; like Adam and Eve, Baas. Still, I am beginning to think better of Kaneke, who is not just a humbug, as I thought, but one who can do things."

Meanwhile at some sign the men picked up the bundles and slung them over their shoulders, drew their spears from the ground and followed Kaneke towards the camp, where we waited for them with our rifles ready in case of accidents.

"Baas," said Hans, as they approached, "I do not think that these men are the brothers of those who attacked the Arabs just now ; I think that they are different."

I studied them and came to the same conclusion. To begin with, so far as I could judge who had only seen our wild rescuers from a distance, these were lighter in colour, brown rather than black, indeed, also they were taller and their hair was much less woolly, only curling up at the ends which hung down upon their shoulders. For the rest, they were magnificently built, with large brown eyes not unlike those of Kaneke, and well-cut features with nothing negroid about them. Nor, in truth, were they of Arab type who seemed rather to belong to some race that was new to me, and yet of very ancient and unmixed blood.

Could they, I wondered, belong to the same people as Kaneke himself ? No ; although so like him, it seemed impossible, for how would they have got here ?

Very quietly and solemnly the men approached to where I was sitting on a stone, walking in as good a double line as the nature of the ground would allow, as though they had been accustomed to discipline, and laying their right hands upon their hearts, bowed to me in a courtly fashion that was almost European ; so courtly, indeed, that I felt bound to stand up, take off my hat, and return the bow. To Hans they did not bow, but only regarded him with a mild curiosity, or to the hunters either, for these they seemed to recognize were servants.

The sight of the donkey, Donna, however, appeared to astonish them, and when at that moment she broke into her loudest bray, intimating that she wished to be fed, they looked downright frightened, thinking, I suppose, that she was some strange wild beast.

Kaneke spoke a word or two to them in a tongue I did not know, whereon they smiled as though in apology. Then he said :

"Lord Macumazahn, you, and still more your servant Hans, have mistrusted me, thinking either that I was mad or leading you into some trap. Nor do I wonder at this, seeing that much has happened since yesterday which you must find it hard to understand. Still, Lord, as you will admit, all has gone well. Those whom I summoned to aid us have done their work and departed, to be seen of you no more ; the Arabs over whom I ruled and who went near to murdering me, and would have murdered you because you refused to deliver me to them, as Hans wished that you should do, have learned their lesson and will not trouble you again. These men"—and he pointed to his companions—"you will find brave and trustworthy, nor will they be a burden to you in any way ; nay, rather they will bear your burdens. Only, I pray you, do not question them as to who they are or whence they come, for they are under a vow of silence. Have I your promise ?"

"Oh, certainly," I answered, adding with inward doubt, "and that of Hans and the hunters also. And now as I understand nothing of all this business, which I do not consider has gone as well as you say, seeing that White-Mouse, the woman who saved your life, although, as she told me, she was not your wife——"

"That is true, as I have said already," interrupted Kaneke, bowing his head in a way that struck me as almost reverential.

"——Seeing that White-Mouse," I repeated, "doubtless is dead at the hands of those Arabs of yours who hated you, which blackens everything, perhaps you will be so good as to tell me, Kaneke, what is to happen next."

"Our journey, Lord," he replied, with a stare of surprise. "What else? Moreover, Lord, be sure that about this journey you need not trouble any more. Henceforward, until we reach the land of my people I will take command and arrange for everything. All that you need do is to follow where I lead and amuse yourself, resting or stopping to shoot when you will, and giving me your orders as to every matter of the sort, which shall be obeyed. This you can do without fear seeing that, as White-Mouse told you, all shall go well with you."

Now once more I was tempted to question him as to the source of his information about what passed between me and White-Mouse, but refrained, remarking only that he was very good at guessing.

"Yes, Lord," he replied. "I have always had a gift that way, as you may have noticed when I guessed that those savages would come to help us, and bring with them men to take the place of the porters who have fled. Well, I notice that you do not contradict my guess and again I assure you that White-Mouse spoke true words."

Now for a minute I was indignant at Kaneke's impudence. It seemed outrageous that he, or any native African, should presume to put me, Allan Quatermain, under his orders, to go where *he* liked and to do what *he* chose. Indeed, I was about to refuse such a position with the greatest emphasis when suddenly it occurred to me that there was another side to the question.

Although I had never travelled there, I had heard from friends how people touring in the East place themselves in charge of a dragoman, a splendid but obsequious individual who dry-nurses them day and night, arranges, commands, feeds, masters difficulties, wrangles with extortioners or obstructionists, and finally gently leads his employers whither they would go and back again. It is true I had heard, too, that these skilled and professional persons are rather apt to melt away in times of real danger or trouble, leaving their masters to do the fighting, also that their bills are invariably large. For every system has its drawbacks and these are chances which must be faced.

Still, this idea of being dragomanned, personally conducted like a Cook's tourist, through untrodden parts of Africa, had charms. It would be such a thorough change—at any rate to me. Then and there I determined to accept the offer, reflecting that if the worst came to the worst, I could always take com-

mand again. It was obvious that I must accompany Kaneke
or run the risk of strange things happening to me at his hands
and those of his followers whom he had collected out of nowhere.
Therefore the responsibilities of the expedition might as well be
his as mine.

So I answered mildly :

"Agreed, Kaneke. You shall lead and I will follow. I
place myself and my servants in your hands, trusting to you to
guide us safely and to protect us against every danger. Though,"
I added in a sterner voice, "I warn you that at the first sign of
treachery I will shoot you dead. And now tell me, when are we
to start ?"

"At moonrise, I think, Lord, for then it will be cooler.
Meanwhile you and your servants can sleep who need rest
after so many labours. Fear nothing ; I and my men will
watch."

"Baas," said Hans as we went away to act upon this advice,
"I never thought you and I, who are getting old, would live to
find a new mammy, and such a one with eye and beak of an owl
who, like an owl, loves to stare at the stars and to fly at night.
However, if the Baas does not mind, I don't."

I made no answer, though I thought to myself that Kaneke's
great sleepy eyes were really not unlike those of an owl, that
mysterious bird which in the native mind is always connected
with omens and magic. Yes, in calling him an owl Hans showed
his usual aptitude, especially as he believed that he was the
destroyer of that strange and beautiful woman, White-Mouse.

Well, we rested, and ate on waking, and at moonrise departed
upon our journey, heading nor'-west. Everything was prepared, even the loads were apportioned among the new porters.
Indeed, there was nothing left for us to do except roll up the
little tent and tie it, together with my personal belongings, on to
the back of Donna, whom Hans fed and Tom and Jerry led
alternately. We met with no adventures. The lion or lions, on
whom, according to Hans, Kaneke had thrown a charm, did not
trouble us ; we saw nothing of the Arabs or the savages whom
that strange person called his "friends". In short, we just walked
forward where Kaneke guided as safely as though we had been
upon an English road, till we came to the place where he said we
were to halt.

Such was our first march which in the weeks that followed was
typical of scores of others. Nothing happened to us upon that

prolonged trek ; at least, nothing out of the way. It was as though a charm had been laid upon us, protecting us from all evils and difficulties. A great deal of the country through which we passed was practically uninhabited. I suppose that the slave-traders had desolated in it bygone years, for often we saw ruined villages with no one in them. When they were inhabited, however, Kaneke would go in advance and speak to their headman. What he said to them I do not know, but in the issue we always found the people friendly and ready to supply us with such provisions as they had, generally without payment.

One thing I noted : that they looked on me with awe. At first I put this down to the fact that most of them had never before seen a real white man, but by degrees I came to the conclusion that there was more behind, namely that for some reason or another I was regarded as a most powerful fetish, or even as a kind of god. Thus they would abase themselves upon their faces before me and even make offerings to me of whatever they had, generally grain or fruits.

While they confined themselves to these I took no notice, but when at one village the chief, who could talk a little Arabic, having mixed with slave-traders in his youth, brought a white cock and proceeded to cut its throat and sprinkle my feet with the blood, I thought it time to draw the line. Snatching the dead bird from his hand, I threw it away and asked him why he had done this thing. At first he was too terrified to answer, imagining that his offering was rejected because I was angry with him.

Presently, however, he fell upon his knees and mumbled something to the effect that he was only doing me honour, as the "messenger", or "my messenger", had commended him. For the life of me I could not understand what he meant, unless he alluded to Kaneke. While I was trying to find out, that worthy arrived and gave the chief one look which caused him to rise and run away.

Then I cross-examined Kaneke without result, for he only shrugged his shoulders and said that all these people were very simple and wished to do honour to a white man.

Hans took a different view.

"How is it, Baas," he asked, "that they are always prepared to receive us at these places and waiting with gifts ? None of those men of the Owl's" (he often called Kaneke the "Owl") "go forward to warn them, for I count them continually, especially at night and in the morning, to find if one is missing. Nor when we are travelling through bush can they see us coming from far away. How, then, do they know?"

"I can't tell you."

"Then I will tell the Baas. The owl-man sends his spirit ahead to give them notice." He paused, then added, "Or perhaps——" Here he stopped, saying that he had left his pipe on the ground, or something of the sort, and departed.

So this mystery remained unsolved, like others.

In every way our good luck was so phenomenal that with the superstition of a hunter, which infects all of our trade, I began to fear that we must have some awful time ahead of us. When we came to rivers they were invariably fordable. When we wanted meat, there was always game at hand that could be shot without trouble by Tom and Jerry—Kaneke, I observed, would never fire at any beast even when I offered to lend him my rifle. The weather was most propitious, or if a bad storm came up we were under shelter. No one fell sick of fever or any other complaint ; no one met with an accident. No lion troubled us, no snake bit us, and so forth. At last this unnatural state of affairs began to get upon our nerves, especially upon those of Tom and Jerry, who came to me one evening almost weeping, and declared that we were bewitched and going to our deaths.

"Nonsense," I answered, "you ought to be glad that we have so much good luck."

"Sugar is good," replied Tom, who loved sweet things, "but one cannot live on nothing but sugar ; it makes one sick, and I have had bad dreams at night."

"I never expect to see my little daughter again, but if it is the will of Heaven that cannot be helped," remarked the more phlegmatic Jerry, adding, "Master, we do not like this Kaneke whom Hans calls the Owl, and we wish that you would take command, as we do not know where he is leading us."

"Nor do I, so I should be of no use as a guide. But be at ease, for I am making a map of the road for our return journey."

"When we return we shall need no map," said Tom in a hollow voice. "We have heard from Hans that the lady or the witch called White-Mouse promised safety and good fortune to him, and to you, Lord, but it seems that about us she said nothing——"

"Look here," I broke in, exasperated, "if you two men are so frightened for no cause that I can see, except that everything goes well with us, you had better follow the example of the porters at our first camp, and run away. I will give you your rifles and as many cartridges as you want, also the donkey Donna to carry them. I can see no reason why you should not get back to the coast safely, especially as you have money in you pockets."

Tom shook his head, remarking that he thought it probable that they would be murdered before they had completed the first day's journey. Then Jerry, the phlegmatic, showed his real quality, or perhaps the English blood, which I am sure ran in his veins, manifested itself.

"Listen, Little Holes," he said to Tom. "If we go on like this, our master Macumazahn will learn to despise us, and we shall be the laughing stock of the yellow man Hans, and perhaps of Kaneke and his people also. We undertook this journey ; let us play the man and go through with it to the end. We can only die once, and because we are Christians, should we also be cowards ? You have none to mourn for you, and I have but one daughter, who has seen little of me and who will be well looked after if I return no more. Therefore I say let us put aside our fears, which after all are built on water, and cease to trouble the master with them."

"That is well said," replied Tom, alias Little Holes, "and if it were not for the accursed wizard, one of those who is spoken against in the Holy Book, I should be quite happy. But while he is our guide, he who with his people, as I have seen at night, makes incantations to the stars——"

Here Tom chanced to look up and to perceive Kaneke standing at a distance, apparently out of hearing, with his large eyes fixed upon us. The effect was wonderful. "Be careful. Here is the wizard himself," he whispered to Jerry, whereon they both turned and went away.

Kaneke came up to me.

"Those hunters are afraid of something, Lord," he said quietly. "For days past I have read it in their faces. What is it that they fear ?"

"You," I answered bluntly—"you and the future."

"All men should hold the future in awe, Lord, so there they are wise. But why should they dread me ?"

"Because they think you are a wizard, Kaneke."

He smiled in his slow fashion, and answered :

"As others have done and do. If a man has more foresight or sees deeper into hearts, or turns from women, or worships that which most men do not worship, or is different from the rest in other ways, then he is always called a wizard, as I am. Lord,

what your servants need is that which will change their minds so
that they cease to think about themselves.   I have come to tell
you that tomorrow we enter into forest lands, which at this
season are haunted by vast herds of elephants that travel from
different quarters and meet here for the purposes of which we men
know nothing.   It might please you and those brave hunters
of yours to see this meeting and to shoot one or two of those
elephants, for among them are their kings, mighty bulls."

"I should like to see such a sight," I answered, "but there is
little use in shooting the beasts when one cannot carry the ivory."

"It might be buried till you return, Lord ; at any rate it will
give the hunters occupation for a while."

"Very well," I answered indifferently, for to tell the truth I
did not believe in Kaneke's tale of vast herds of elephants that
held a kind of parliament in a particular forest.

Next night we camped on the outskirts of this forest of which
Kaneke had spoken.   It was a very strange place, different from
any other that I have seen.   In it grew great and solemn trees of
a species that was new to me ; huge, clean-bolled trees with leafy
tops that met together and shut out the sun, so that where they
were thickest there was twilight even at midday, nor could any
undergrowth live beneath them.   But the trees did not grow
everywhere, for here and there were wide open spaces in which,
for some unknown reason, they refused to flourish.   These
spaces, that sometimes were as much as a mile across, were
covered with scanty bush and grasses.

All that night we heard elephants trumpeting around us, and
when morning came found that a great herd of them must have
passed within a quarter of a mile of our camp.   The sight of their
spoor excited the professional instincts of Tom and Jerry, who,
forgetting their gloom, prayed me to follow the herd.   I objected,
for the reason I have given, namely that if we killed any of them
it would be difficult to deal with the ivory.   Kaneke, however,
hearing our talk, declared that the porters needed rest and that
he would be very glad if it could be given to them for a day or
two, while we amused ourselves with hunting.

Then I gave way, being anxious to learn if there was any
truth in Kaneke's story about the meeting-place of elephants that
was supposed to exist in this forest.   Also I was desirous that the
two hunters should find something to do which would take their
thoughts into a more cheerful channel.   Personally, too, I felt
that I should be glad of a change from this continuous marching,
unmarked by any incident.

D

So, after we had eaten and made our preparations, the four of us, that is Tom, Jerry, Hans, and I, started—Kaneke would not come—carrying large-bore rifles, a good supply of cartridges and some food and water. All the rest of that day we followed the spoor of the elephants, that had not stopped to feed in the glades I have described, as I had hoped that they would do, but appeared to be pushing forward at a great rate towards some definite objective. With one halt we marched on steadily in the shadow of those huge trees, noticing that the elephant-spoor seemed to follow a kind of road which wound in and out between their trunks or struck in a straight line across the stretches of thin bushes and grass.

More than once I wished to return, as did Hans who, like myself saw no use in this adventure. Always, however, Tom and Jerry prayed to be allowed to proceed, so on we went. Towards sunset we lost the spoor in a thick patch of forest. Pushing on to find it again while there was still light, we came suddenly to one of the open spaces that I have mentioned which seemed to be much larger than any other we had seen, also more bare of vegetation. It must have covered at least a thousand acres of ground, and perfectly flat ; indeed, I thought that at some far-away epoch it had formed the bottom of a lake.

Near the centre of this oasis in the forest was a mound which, if I may judge from pictures I have seen of them, resembled one of those great tumuli that in a certain parts of Europe the wild tribes of thousands of years ago reared over the bones of their chieftains. Or, as I afterwards discovered, more probably it was the natural foundation of some lake-town where a tribe dwelt for safety when all this place was under water. At any rate there it stood, a low, round eminence covered with a scanty growth of flowering bushes and small trees.

Thinking that from this mound we might be able to see the elephants, or at least which way they had gone, we marched thither, I reflecting that at the worst it would be a better place for camping than the gloomy and depressing forest. Having climbed its sloping side, we found that on the top it was flat except for a large depression in the centre, where perhaps once had stood the huts of its primeval inhabitants. What was of more interest to us, however, than the past history of the place, was that at the bottom of this depression lay a pool of water supplied by some spring, or by rain that had fallen recently.

Seeing this water, which we needed who had drunk all our own, I determined that we would pass the night on the mound, although the most careful search from its top failed to show any sign of the elephants we had been spooring.

"Yes, Baas," said Hans, when I gave my orders, "but, all the same, I don't like this place, Baas, and should prefer to get back to the forest after we have drunk and filled our bottles."

I inquired why.

"I don't know, Baas. Perhaps the spooks of those who once lived here are all about, though we can't see them.   Or—but tell me, Bass, why did that Owl-man, Kaneke, send us after those elephants ?"

"To give Tom and Jerry something to think about, Hans."

He grinned and answered :

"Kaneke does not care whether those fellows have anything to think about or not.   I should believe that he did it to give us the slip, only I am sure that he does not want to go on alone. So, Baas, it must be to teach us some lesson and show us how powerful he is, so powerful that he makes the Baas do what he wants, which no one has done before."

I reflected that Hans was right.   I had not desired to come upon this absurd hunt, yet somehow Kaneke had pushed me into it.

"I don't believe there are any elephants," went on Hans with conviction.   "The spoor ?   Oh, a magician like Kaneke can make spoor, Baas.   Or if there seem to be elephants, then I believe that they are really ghosts that put on that shape.   Let us go back to the forest, Baas—if the Owl-man will give you leave."

Now I felt that the time had come for me to put my foot down, and I did so with firmness.

"Stop talking nonsense, Hans," I said.   "I don't know what's the matter with all you fellows.   Is your brain going soft as a rotten coconut, like those of Tom and Jerry ?   We will sleep here tonight and return tomorrow to the camp."

"Oh, the Baas thinks he is going to sleep tonight.   Yes, he thinks he is going to sleep," sniggered Hans.   "Well, we shall see," and he bolted, still sniggering, before my wrath could descend upon him.

The sun set and presently the big moon came up.   We ate of the food we had with us ; as we had nothing to cook it was needless to light a fire, nor indeed did I wish to do so, for in such a spot a fire was a dangerous advertisement. So, as it seemed foolish to set a watch in the middle of that open space, where there being no buck there would be no lions—for lions do not hunt elephants— we just lay down and went to sleep, as tired men should do. I remember thinking, as I dropped off, how extraordinarily quiet the place was. No beast called, no night-bird cried, nothing stirred on that dead and windless calm. Indeed, the silence was so oppressive that for once I should have welcomed the familiar *ping !* of a mosquito, but here there were none.

So off I went and at some time unknown, to judge by the moon it was towards the middle of the night, was awakened by a sense of oppression. I dreamed that a great vampire bat was hanging over me and sucking my toe. Now I was lying on my face, as I often do when camping out to avoid the risk of moon blindness, just at the edge of that hole where, as I have told, water had collected, in such a position that I could look down into the pool. This water was very still and clear and thus formed a perfect mirror.

As it happened there was something remarkable for it to reflect, namely the head, trunk, and tusks of one of the hugest elephants I ever saw—not Jana* himself could have been much bigger ! As my mirror showed, he was standing over me ; yes, I lay between his fore-legs, while he was engaged in sniffing at the back of my head with the tip of his trunk which, however, never actually touched me.

Talk of a nightmare, or of a night-elephant for the matter of that, never did I know of one to touch it. Of course I thought it was a dream of a particularly vivid order arising from undigested *biltong*, or something of the sort. But that did not make it any better, for although I had wakened the vision did not go away, as every decent nightmare does. Moreover, if it were a dream, what was the hideous stabbing pain in my leg ? (Afterwards this was explained : Hans was trying to arouse me without calling the elephant's attention to himself by driving into my thigh the point of a "wait-a-bit" thorn which he used to pin up his trousers.) Also was it possible that in a dream an elephant could blow so hard upon the back of one's neck that it sent dust and bits of dry grass up one's nostrils, inducing a terrible desire to sneeze ?

While I was pondering the question in a perfect agony and staring at the alarming picture in the water, the gigantic beast ceased its investigation of my person and stepping over me with

* For the history of *the* huge elephant Jana, see *The Ivory Child.*—Editor.

calculated gentleness, went to where Tom and Jerry were lying at a little distance. Whether these worthies were awake or asleep I do not know, for what happened terrified them so much that it produced aphasia on this and some other points, so that they could never tell me. The beast sniffed, first at Tom and then at Jerry ; one sniff each was all it vouchsafed to them. Then with its trunk it seized, first Tom and next Jerry, and with an easy motion flung them one after the other into the pool of water. This done, avoiding Hans as though it disliked his odour, it walked away over the crest of the cup or depression in the mound, and vanished.

Instantly I sat up, boxed the ears of Hans, who was still stabbing at me idiotically with his wait-a-bit thorn and giving me great pain, for speak to him I dared not, and slipped down the slope to the lip of the pool to save Tom and Jerry from drowning, if indeed they were not already dead. As it happened, my attentions were needless, for the pool was quite shallow and this pair, whom the elephant had not hurt at all, were seated on its bottom and indulging in suppressed hysterics, their heads appearing above the surface of the water.

A more ridiculous sight than they presented, even in the terror of that occurrence, cannot be imagined. In all my life I never saw its like. Think of two men of whom nothing was visible except the heads, seated in the water and gibbering at each other in a dumb paroxysm of fear.

I whispered to them to come out, also that if they made a noise I would kill them both, whereupon somewhat reassured at my appearance, they crawled to the bank of the pool, which proved that none of their bones were broken, and emerged wreathed in water-cresses. Then leaving them to recover as best they could, followed by Hans and carrying my heavy rifle, I crept to the edge of the depression and peeped over.

There, as the bright moonlight showed me, not twenty yards away stood the enormous bull upon a little promontory or platform which projected from the side of the mound, reminding one of a rostrum erected for the convenience of the speaker at an open-air meeting. Yes, there it stood as though it were carved in stone.

CHAPTER VIII

THE ELEPHANT DANCE

NEVER shall I forget that amazing scene, bitten as it is into the tablets of my mind by the acids of fear and wonder.   Imagine it ! The wide plain or lake bottom surrounded upon all sides by the black ring of the forest and plunged in a silence so complete that it seemed almost audible.   Then there, just beneath us, the gigantic and ancient elephant—for it was ancient, as I could see by various signs, standing motionless and in an attitude which gave a strange impression of melancholy, such melancholy as might possess an aged man who, revisiting the home of his youth, finds it a desolation.

"Baas," whispered Hans, "if you shift a little more to the left you might get him behind the ear and shoot him dead."

"I don't want to shoot him," I replied, "and if you fire I will break your neck."

Hans, I know, thought I made this answer because my nerve was shaken and I feared lest I should bungle the job.   But as a matter of fact, it was nothing of the sort.   For some unexplained reason I would as soon have committed a murder as shoot that elephant, which had just spared my life when I lay at its mercy.

Low as we spoke, I suppose that the bull must have heard us.   At any rate it turned its head and looked in our direction, which caused me to fear lest I should be obliged to fire after all. It was not so, however, for having apparently satisfied itself that we were harmless, once more it fell into contemplation, which must have lasted for another two minutes.

Then suddenly it lifted its trunk and emitted a call or cry louder and more piercing than that of any trumpet.   Thrice it repeated this call, and for the third time as its echoes died the silence of the night was broken by a terrifying response.   From every part of the surrounding ring of forest rose the sound of elephants trumpeting in unison, hundreds of elephants, or so it seemed.

"Allemagter !   Baas," whispered Hans in a shaky voice, "that old spook beast is sending for his friends to kill us.   Let us run, Baas."

"Where to, seeing that they are all round us ?" I asked

faintly, adding : "If he wanted to kill us he could do so for himself. Lie still. It is our only chance ; and tell those hunters behind to stop praying so loudly and to unload their rifles, lest they should be tempted to fire."

Hans crept away to the edge of the pool, where the dripping Tom and Jerry were putting up audible petitions in the extremity of their terror. Then watching, I saw the most marvellous sight in my hunting experience. As though they were the trained beasts of India or of the ancient kings, marching in endless lines and ordered ranks, appeared three vast herds of elephants. From the forest in front of us, from that to our right and that to our left, and from aught I know from behind also, though these I could not see, they came out into the moonlit open space, and marched towards the mound with their regulated tread, which shook the earth.

Perhaps I saw double. Perhaps my nerves were so shaken that I could not estimate numbers, but I should be prepared to swear that there were at least a thousand of them, and afterwards the others declared that there were many more. In each troop the bulls marched first, the moonlight shining on their white tusks. Then came the cows with calves running at their side, and last of all the half-grown beasts, sorted seemingly according to their size.

So Kaneke had not lied. This was the meeting of the elephants which he had prophesied we should see. Only how in Heaven's name did he know anything about it ? For a few moments I began to think that he was really what Hans and the hunters believed him to be—some kind of magician who perhaps had sent us hither that we might be torn to pieces or trampled to death.

Then I forgot all about Kaneke in the immediate interest of that wild and wonderous spectacle. The herds arrived. They arranged themselves in a semicircle, deep, curved lines of them, in front to the mound upon which stood the ancient bull. For a while they were still, then as though at a signal, they knelt down. Yes, even the calves knelt, with their trunks stretched out straight upon the ground in front of them.

"They do homage to their king, Baas," whispered Hans, and so in truth it seemed to be.

The giant bull trumpeted once, as though in acknowledgment of the salute. The herds rose, and there followed a marvellous performance that might have been taken for a dream. The bulls massed themselves together in squadrons, as it were, and charged past the mound from right to left, trumpeting as they charged. After them came the regiments of the cows, and lastly those of the partly grown beasts, all trumpeting ; even the little calves set up piercing squeals. They re-formed, but not as they were before. For now the bulls faced the cows and the rest. Then began a kind of dance, so swift and intricate that I could not follow it, a kind of unearthly quadrille it seemed to be, in which the males sought out the females, or it may have been the other way about, and they caressed each other with their trunks. Perhaps it was some kind of ceremony of betrothal, I do not know.

It ceased as suddenly as it had begun. The herds massed themselves as at first, then wheeled and marched off in their three divisions back to the forest whence they came. Soon all were gone except the old king-bull, who still stood silent just beneath us, majesty and loneliness personified.

"Do you think he is going to stop here always, Baas ?" whispered Hans. "Because if so, really it might be best to shoot him now that the others have gone away."

"Be silent," I answered ; "he may understand you."

Yes, my nerves were so upset by what I had seen that I was fool enough to talk thus.

"Yes, Baas," assented Hans in his hoarse whisper, "I forgot that ; he may, so I didn't really mean what I seemed to say about shooting him. It was only a joke. Also it might bring the others back."

At that moment, to my horror, the king-bull turned and walked straight up to us. I couldn't have shot him if I had wished, because as I had made the others do, I had unloaded my rifle to keep myself out of temptation. Also I did not wish ; I was too much afraid. He stood still, contemplating us, a giant of a creature with a mild and meditative eye. Then he lifted his trunk and I muttered a prayer, thinking that all was over. But no, he only placed the tip of it against the middle of Hans, who somehow had got to his knees, and let off one fearful scream accompanied by such a blast of air that it blew Hans backwards down the slope on to the recumbent forms of Tom and Jerry.

This done, the bull turned again, walked down the mound and out across the plain, a picture of stately solitude till at last he vanished in the dark shadow of the forest.

When he was lost to sight I went down to the pool and drank, for the perspiration induced by terror seemed to have dried me up. Then I looked at my three retainers, who were huddled in a heap on the edge of the pool.

"I am dead," muttered Hans, who was lying on the other two. "That Satan of an elephant has blown out my inside. It has gone; there is nothing left but my backbone."

"No wonder, as you cursed him and wanted Macumazahn to shoot him," muttered Tom. "For did not that *afreet* of a beast cast us into the pool for nothing at all?"

"Whether you have a stomach or not, be pleased to cease sitting on my face, yellow man, or I will make my teeth meet in you," gurgled Jerry.

Thus they went on, and so ridiculous were the aspect and the talk of the three of them, that at last I burst out laughing, which relieved my nerves and did me good. Then I lit my pipe, hoping that those elephants would not see the light or smell the tobacco down in that hole, and not caring much if they did, for I seemed to desire a smoke more than anything on earth.

"Let us talk," I said to the others. "What are we to do?"

"Get out of this, master, and at once," said Tom. "That beast is not an elephant, it is an evil spirit in the shape of one. Yes, I who am a Christian and have renounced all superstitions, say that it is an evil spirit."

"Little Holes is quite right," broke in Jerry. "If it had been an elephant, it would have killed us, but being an evil spirit it threw us into the water."

"Fool!" grunted Hans, rubbing his middle, "do you make an evil spirit better than an elephant? In truth, as the Baas knows, the bull is neither; it is a chief or a king who once lived in this place as a man, and now had turned into an elephant, and all those other beasts whom you did not see, being so much afraid, were once his people, but now also are elephants. That is quite clear to the Baas, and to me who am a better Christian than either of you. Still, I agree with you that the sooner we see the last of this haunted place, the better it will be."

Thus they wrangled on till they were tired. When they had finished I said:

"Here we stop till dawn breaks. Do you three climb to the top of this hole and keep watch. I am tired and am going to sleep. Wake me if you see the elephants coming back."

So I lay down and slept, or at any rate dozed, which, as I have said—thank Heaven!—I can do at any time after any experience. I am a fatalist, one who does not trouble as to what is to happen in the future, because I know it must happen and that worry is therefore useless. If the elephants were going to kill me, I could not help it; meanwhile I would get some rest.

So I slept, and dreamed that I saw this place standing in the middle of a lake and full of people. They were tall, dark men and women, and latter decently dressed in garments that were dyed with various colours. The mound was covered with huts that were thatched with reeds, and wooden jetties, to which canoes were tied, ran out into the surrounding shallow water. On the broad surface of the lake were other canoes, each containing one or two men who were engaged in fishing, while round this lake lay the dense forest, as it did today. In my dream the hollow in which now was the pool by which I lay, was thatched over, the roof being supported by carved posts of black wood. They were very curious carvings, but when I woke up I could not remember their details.

There was a meeting going on in this large public gathering place, and a man who wore a cloak and cap made of feathers, the chief, I take it, had risen from a chair fashioned of four tusks of ivory with a seat of twisted rushes, and was addressing the assembly, apparently upon some important subject, for his audience of old men seemed to be much impressed. He beat his breast and put some question to them. Then, while they debated in low tones as to their answer, I woke up to find that it was light.

Of course this dream was all nonsense born of imaginings as to what might have been the previous history of that place, and I paid no attention to it. Still, it fitted in well enough with the surroundings, so well that had I been mystically minded, I might have been inclined to believe that it did really portray come incident of past history that had happened when this mound was an island in a lake inhabited by a primeval people who dwelt there in order to be safe from the attacks of enemies.

Hans, like myself, had been asleep, but the hunters, who were far too frightened to think of shutting their eyes, reported that they had neither seen nor heard any elephants.

"Then let's go off home, before they come back," I said cheerfully.

So I took a drink of water, ate a handful of watercress, which I have always found a very sustaining herb, and away we started ; glad enough to see the last of that haunted mount, as Hans called it. While we were on the plain we felt quite merry, at least Hans and I did, although it was strange to look at that lonesome lake bottom and think of the scene that had been enacted within a few hours, so strange, indeed, that I was almost tempted to believe we had been the victims of a vision of the night, induced by Kaneke's tale as to the great herds of elephants which came together in this district.

When we entered the forest, however, our mood changed, for about this place with its endless giant trees that shut out the light of the sun, there was an air of gloom which was most depressing. On we marched into the depths, following our own trail backwards, for I had been careful to mark the trunk of a tree here and there, Red Indian fashion, so that we might make no mistake upon our return. To lose oneself in that forest would indeed be a dreadful fate. When we had tramped for a good while and reached the spot where we had missed the spoor on the previous day, I observed that Hans was growing anxious, for he kept glancing over his shoulder.

"What is the matter?" I asked.

"If the Baas will look back the Baas will see; that is, unless I have become drunk upon water and stream grasses," he replied in a weak voice.

I did look back and I did see. There, about a hundred yards behind, standing between two tree-trunks, exactly on our spoor, was our friend the king-elephant!

I halted, for I confess that for a moment my knees grew weak.

"Perhaps it is only a shadow—or a fancy," I said.

"Oh no, Baas. It's him right enough. I have felt him in the small of my back for the last half-mile, but did not dare to look. Still, if the Baas has any doubts, perhaps he would like to go and see."

At this moment, Tom and Jerry, who were well ahead, came tearing up to announce that they had caught sight of elephants to their right and left, and that we must go back.

"Oh yes," said Hans, "you are both very brave men, as you have always told me, so please go back," and he pointed with his finger at the apparition behind us, that seemed to have come nearer as we were talking, although, if so, it was once more standing still.

They saw it, and really I thought that one or both of them would collapse in a fit, for they were horribly frightened, as indeed I was myself. However, I pulled myself together and spoke to them severely, ending with an order to advance.

"Oh yes," repeated Hans who, in this extremity seemed to be moved to a kind of grim humour.

"Advance, you brave hunters, for that is your trade, isn't it? and please protect me, the poor little yellow man. No, don't look at those trees, because we are not lizards or woodpeckers and nothing else could run up them. And if we could, what would be the use, seeing that those spook elephants would only wait till we came down again. Advance, brave hunters, who told me only the other night that all elephants will run away from a man."

So we went on till at last I cut his drivel short.

"Come on," I said, "and keep together, for there is nothing else to be done. Remember that if anyone fires unless we are actually charged, probably it will mean the death of all of us. Now follow me."

They obeyed ; indeed they followed uncommonly close, so close that when I halted for a moment, the barrel of the rifle of one of them, which I observed was at full cock, poked me in the back.

Soon I became aware that we were absolutely surrounded by elephants. That is to say, the great bull was behind, while unnumbered other beasts were on our right and left, though in front I could detect none. It was as though they were seeing us off the premises and politely leaving a road by which we might depart as quickly as possible. They saw us, there was no doubt of that, for occasionally one of them would stretch out its trunk and sniff as we passed within twenty or thirty yards of it. Moreover there was another thing. All these elephants were standing at intervals head on to our trail, forcing us as it were to keep to a straight and narrow road.

But each of them, when we had passed it, fell in behind the big bull and marched after it.   Of this there could be no question, for when we were crossing one of the open glades that I have described, I looked back and saw an enormous number of them, hundreds there seemed to be, stretching along in a solemn and purposeful procession. Yet to right and left there were more ahead. It was as though all the elephants in Central Africa were gathered in that forest !

Well, it is useless to continue the description, because to do so would only be to say the same thing over and over again.   For hours this went on, till we got near the camp, indeed, towards which we were travelling much faster than when we left it   Here the forest thinned and the glades were more frequent. I counted them one by one until I knew that we were close to the last of them and about a mile from the *boma*, or perhaps a little more. Just then one of the hunters looked back and gasped out :

"Lord, the elephants are beginning to run."

I verified the statement. It was true. The king-bull was

breaking into a dignified trot, and all his subjects were following his example. Needless to say, we began to run too.

Oh, that last mile ! Seldom have I done such time since I was a boy in the long-distance race at school, and fast as I went, the others kept pace with me, or went faster. We streaked across that glade and after us thundered the elephants, the ground shaking beneath their ponderous footfall. They were gaining, they were quite close, I could hear their deep breathing just behind. There ahead was the camp, and there, standing on a great ant-hill just in front of it, conspicuous in his white robe, was Kaneke watching the chase.

Suddenly the elephants seemed to catch sight of him, or perhaps they saw the smoke from the fire. At any rate they stopped dead, turned, and without a sound melted away into the depths of the forest, the king-bull going last as though he were loth to leave us.

I staggered on to the camp, dishevelled, breathless, ridiculous in my humiliation, as I was well aware. For was I not supposed throughout much of Africa to be one of the greatest elephant-hunters of my day ?—and here I appeared running away from elephants with never a shot fired. It is true that the audience was small, a mysterious person called Kaneke, a very spider of a man that seemed to have got me into his web, and a score of porters, probably his tribesmen. But that made the matter no better ; indeed, if there had been no one at all to see my disgrace, I should have felt almost equally shamed. I was furious, especially with Kaneke, whom I suspected, I dare say unjustly, of being at the bottom of the business. Also I had lost my hat, and what is an Englishman without his hat ?

Kaneke descended from his ant-heap to meet me, all smiles and bows.

"I trust that your hunting has been good, Lord, for you seem to have found plenty of elephants," he said.

"You are laughing at me," I replied. "As you know, I have not been hunting ; I have been hunted. Well, perhaps one day you will be hunted and I shall laugh at you."

Then I waved him aside and went into my tent to recover breath and composure.

Throwing myself down on the little folding canvas stretcher-bed which, whenever it was possible, I carried with me upon my various expeditions, I watched the arrival of the others who, after the elephants turned, had come on more slowly. Tom and Jerry were almost speechless with rage. They shook their fists at Kaneke ; indeed, if their rifles had been at hand, which was not the case for these were dropped in their last desperate race for life (they were recovered afterwards, unhurt, together with my hat), I think it very likely that they would have shot him, or tried to do so.

"You have made us cowards before our master's eyes," gasped one of them, I forget which. Then they passed on out of my range of vision.

Lastly Hans arrived (*he* had not dropped his rifle), who squatted on the ground and began to fan himself with his hat.

"Why is everybody so angry with me, Hans ?" said Kaneke.

"I don't know," answered Hans, "but perhaps if you gave me a drop out of that bottle which you keep under your blanket I might be able to remember—I mean the one the Baas gave you when you had the toothache."

Kaneke went into the shelter made of boughs where he slept, and returning with a flask of square-face gin, poured a stiff tot of it in to a pannikin, which he gave to Hans, who gulped it down.

"Now I am beginning to remember," said Hans, licking the edge of the empty tin. "They are angry with you, Kaneke, because they think that you have played a great trick upon them who being a wizard, have clothed a lot of spooks that serve you in the shapes of elephants and caused them to hunt us that you might laugh."

"Yet I have done nothing of the sort, Hans," answered Kaneke indignantly. "Am I a god that I can make elephants ?"

"Oh no, Kaneke, certainly whatever you may be you are not a god. Nor indeed do I believe anything of this story, like those silly hunters. Yet for your own sake I hope that the next time you send us out hunting, nothing of this sort will happen, because, Kaneke, we can still shoot, and those hunters might be tempted to learn whether a wizard's skin can turn bullets. And now, as your toothache has gone, I will take that gin and give it back to the Baas, because he has not much of it, and even a wizard cannot make good gin."

Then Hans rose and snatched the bottle out of Kaneke's hand. I must add that to his credit he returned it to me undiminished, which—in Hans—was an act of great virtue.

Such was the end of that elephant-hunt, by means of which I had hoped to relieve the tedium of that strangely uneventful

journey and to restore the moral tone of Tom and Jerry, also, to a
lesser degree, that of Hans and myself.   Certainly the first end
was achieved, for whatever may be thought of our experiences
at the meeting-place of elephants, and afterwards, they were not
tedious.   But of the second as much could not be said.   Indeed,
it left the hunters thoroughly frightened, the more so because
they did not know exactly of what they were afraid.

All the circumstances of the business were unnatural.   None
of us had seen elephants behave as did those great herds, and
the very mercy that the beasts showed to us was beyond
experience.

Why did not the old king-bull either run away or kill us there
upon the ground ?   Why did it and the rest of them hunt us back
to the camp in that fashion, yet without doing us any actual
harm ?   No wonder that these uneducated men saw magic at
work and were scared.

Thrusting such nonsense from my mind, for nonsense I knew
it to be, I could not help remembering the odd coincidence that
on this prolonged adventure of our expedition, nothing seemed to
materialize.   So far it had the inconsequence of a dream.   Thus,
at the beginning of it, when we expected a desperats fight for
our lives, there was no fight, at least on our part.   Only one shot
was fired, that with which I killed the Arab Gaika, who, be it
noted, was Kaneke's particular foe, whose death he ardently
desired.   In the same way when we went out with much preparation to slay elephants and found them in enormous numbers
no shot was fired and the beasts chased us ignominiously back
to our camp.   Further, there were more incidents of the same
kind which I need not particularize.

I was sick of the whole job and longed to escape.   Indeed,
that night I went to Kaneke and told him so, pointing out that
the hunters were off their balance and that as I could not send
them back alone I thought it would be well if he parted company with me and my men, as I proposed to retrace my steps
towards the coast.   Kaneke was much disturbed and argued
with me, very politely at first, pointing out the many dangers of
such a course.   As I would not give way, he changed his tone,
and told me flatly that what I proposed would mean the death
of all four of us.

"At whose hands ?   Yours, Kaneke ?" I asked.

"Certainly not, Lord," he answered.   "However cruelly you
break your bargain with me, and this after taking my pay,"
(here he was alluding to the cash and ivory which, like a fool,

I had accepted), "I should not be base enough to lift a hand against one who saved my life at what he believed to be the risk of his own, although in truth no risk was run."

"What do you mean ?   How do you know that, Kaneke ?"

"I mean what I say, and I do know it, Lord.   Even in that pit which you thought so dangerous you were quite safe, as you were when the Arabs attacked you and the elephants chased you, and as you will be to the end of this adventure, if only you keep your promises.   For was this not vowed to you at the beginning ?"

"Yes, Kaneke, by an unhappy woman whom I see no more."

"Those who are not seen may still be present, Lord, or their strength may remain behind them.   But if you turn back before your mission is ended, it will depart.   Those tribes who have welcomed you upon your outward journey will one and all fight against you on your return, until in this way or in that you are brought to your deaths.   Never again will you look upon the sea, Lord."

"That's pleasant !" I exclaimed, controlling my temper as best I could.   "Listen.   You talk of my mission.   Be so good as to tell me what it is.   The only mission that I have, or had, was to visit a certain lake called Mone, if it exists, in order to satisfy my curiosity and love of seeing new things.   Well, I have changed my mind ; I no longer desire to travel to the Lake Mone."

"Yet I think you must go there, Lord, as I must, for that which is stronger than we are draws us both.   In this world, Lord, we do not serve ourselves, we serve something else ; I cannot tell what it is.   Everything we do or seem to do, good and bad together, is done to carry out the purpose of what we cannot see.   Like that beast Donna of yours, we travel our road, some-times willingly, sometimes to satisfy our appetites, sometimes driven forward with strokes.   Each of us has his powers, which are given to him, not that he may gain what he desires, but that he may fulfil an invisible purpose.   Thus you have yours and I have mine.   I know that your servants and others hold me to be a magician, and now and again you are tempted to believe them.   Well, perhaps in a certain way I am something of a magician, that is to say, strength works through me, though whence that strength comes I cannot say."

"All this does not leave me much wiser, Kaneke."

"How can we who have no wisdom at all ever grow wiser,

Lord? To do so, first we must be wise, and that will not happen to us until we are dead. All our lives we toil that we may grow wise—in death, when we may learn that wisdom is nothingness, or nothingness wisdom."

"Oh, have done!" I said in a rage. "Your talk goes round and round, and ends nowhere. You are fooling me with words, but I suppose that what you mean is, that we must go on with you."

"Yes, Lord, I mean that, amongst other things, unless indeed you wish to stop altogether and go to seek wisdom in the stars, or wherever she may dwell. Safety and good fortune have been promised to you and to the yellow man your servant, knowledge also such as you love. These lie in front of you, but behind lies that which all men shun, or so I read what is written."

"Where do you read it, Kaneke?"

"Yonder," he answered, pointing to the sky that was thick with stars, though the moon had not yet risen.

I stared at this solemn-faced, big-eyed man. Of all that he said I believed nothing, holding that if not merely a clever cheat, like others of his kind, he was a self-deluder. Yet of one thing I was sure, that if I tried to cross his will and deserted him, his prophecies would certainly be fulfilled, so far as we were concerned. Evidently this Kaneke was one who had authority among natives. It would be easy for him to pass a word back over the road that we had travelled, or in any direction that we might go, which word would mean what he foretold for us, four men only who must be at the mercy of a mob of savages, namely—death. On the other hand, if we went forward, his vanity would see to it that what he had asserted should come true, namely that we should be safe. Not till afterwards did I remember that only Hans and I were included in that assertion. Nothing was said about the two hunters.

On the whole, after this talk I hated Kaneke more than ever. Something told me that however plausible and smooth-tongued he might be, at heart the man was deceitful, one, too, whose ends were not good.

CHAPTER IX

EXPLANATIONS

NEXT morning early I laid all this matter before Tom and Jerry, telling them that I had made up my mind to go forward with Kaneke and that Hans would accompany me, as I considered on the whole that this would be the safer course. If, however, they wished to return, I would give them rifles with a fair share of our ammunition, also the donkey Donna to take the place of porters. In fact, only in more detail, I repeated the offer which I made before we went out to hunt, or rather to be hunted by, elephants, explaining that I did so because after that experience they might have changed their mind about its acceptance.

They consulted together, then Tom the Abyssinian, who was always the spokesman, said :

"Master, after what we went through on the mound in the midst of the plain and in the forest with those elephants, which we believe to have been creatures bewitched, it is true that we are much more frightened even than we were before. So frightened are we that were it not for one matter, we would now do what we said we would not do, and attempt to work our way towards the coast, even though we must go alone."

"What matter ?" I asked.

"This, Macumazahn. We are men disgraced ; not only did we show fear and run when on duty, we did worse, we threw away our guns that we might run more quickly, and therefore, although they have been found and brought back by Kaneke's people, I say that we are men disgraced."

"Oh !" I said, trying to soothe their pride. "Hans and I ran also. Who would not have run with all those elephants thundering after him ? It was the only thing to do."

"Yes, Macumazahn, you ran also, and it was the only thing to do. But, Lord, neither you nor Hans threw away your rifle against the hunter's law——"

"No, we should never do that," I said, trying to interrupt, but he went on rapidly :

"——So ashamed are we, Macumazahn, that I tell you, were it not that we are Christians, both of us, we should have hung

ourselves or otherwise have put an end to our lives. But being
Christians, this we cannot do, for then we should go to answer for
that crime to a greater Master than you are. For this reason,
Macumazahn, seeing that we may not wipe out our shame as
savages would do, we propose to redeem our honour in another
fashion. We hold that if we go forward with Kaneke we shall die,
for we believe ourselves to be men bewitched, yes, men doomed
by that wizard, whatever may be the fate of you, master, and of
Hans. If so, thus let it be, for we are determined that if we must
die, we will do so in some great fashion which will cause you to
forget that we are men who broke the hunter's law and threw
away our guns, with which it was our duty to defend you, and
to remember us only as two faithful servants who knew how to
give their lives to save that of their master."

I was so astonished at this solemn speech that I began to
wonder whether Tom, in order to console himself for the slur
upon his honour, the breach of the "hunter's law", as he called
it, had got at my scanty stock of spirits.

"What do you say?" I asked, looking hard at Jerry.

"Oh, Macumazahn," answered that phlegmatic person,
"I say that Little Holes is quite right. We two who have always
had a good name—as the writings about us told you—when trouble
came have shown ourselves to be not watch-dogs, but jackals.
Yes, we are fellows who in the hour of danger have thrown away
our rifles, which we should have kept to the last to protect the
white lord who paid us. Therefore we will not go back, although
we believe that we walk to our deaths, being under a curse. No,
we will go on hoping that before the end you may learn that we
are not really jackals but stout watch-dogs; yes, if God is good
to us, that we are more, that we are bull-buffaloes, that we are
lions."

"Stuff and rubbish!" I exclaimed. "You make trees of
grass stalks. I never thought you jackals, who know you to be
great-hearted. I dare say if I had remembered to do so when
those elephants were at my heels, I should have thrown away my
own rifle that I might run the faster. Still, I think that on the
whole you are wiser to come on than to try to return alone, for
reasons that I have told you. If there are dangers in front of us
there are worse behind, because, although he is no wizard, as you
think, Kaneke is better as a friend than as an enemy. So I pray
you to cease from dreams and quakings born of superstitions at
which Christians should mock, and to go on with bold hearts."
Then, as I thought we had talked enough, I shook them both

by the hand, to show that I was not angry with them, and sent them away.

Afterwards very diplomatically I began to tell Hans something of this conversation, hoping to learn from him of what these hunters really were afraid.

"Oh, Baas," he broke in, "it is no use to speak to me about what passed between you and those fellows with half your tongue and your head turned aside"—by which he meant telling only a part of the truth—"because I was on the other side of that bush and heard every word."

"You are a dirty little spy," I said indignantly.

"Yes, Baas, that's it, because if one wants to know the truth, one must sometimes be a spy. Well, there's nothing to be said. No doubt Little Holes and Jerry are quite right; they are bewitched, or at least the Owl-man while he is flitting about at night has read their deaths written in the stars, which they know. But they know also that, as they have got to die, it doesn't matter whether they go with us or by themselves. So, if coming on will make them depart to the place of Fires happy and singing instead of sad and ashamed, thinking themselves lions instead of jackals, as they said—why, Baas, let them come on and don't trouble your head any more about them. For my part, however much I love them, I am quite content that it should be they who have to die, and not you and me. So cheer up, Baas, and take things as they happen."

"Get out, you heartless little beast," I said, and Hans got out. But all the while I knew that he was not really heartless, and, what is more, he knew that I knew it. Hans in his own way was, on the outside, just a rather cynical and half-savage philosopher, but within, a very warm-natured person.

The end of it all was that we marched on as before, and, as before, nothing particular happened. Kaneke, our guide, for I had not the faintest idea where we were going, led us through every variety of African country. We forded rivers, or if they were too deep and wide, were conveyed across them by friendly natives on rafts or in canoes, for when Kaneke had spoken to their chiefs, all the natives became most helpful. On one occasion, it is true, as there were no natives, or such as there were had no boats or rafts, we were obliged to swim, which I did with trembling, being afraid of crocodiles. However, the crocodiles, if there were any, politely left us alone, so that as usual we came over safely.

After passing the last of these rivers our path ran through a dense forest for two days. On the afternoon of the second day the forest grew thinner and at length changed to a plain, or rather barren land that was covered with small timber, bush-veld in short. This place was intensely hot, filled with game of every kind and, as we soon discovered from numerous bites, infested with tsetse-fly which lived upon the game. As tsetse, except for the irritation of their bites, are harmless to man and we had no horses or cattle, they did not alarm us, for up to that time I shared the belief that donkeys were immune as men and buck to their poison. This, however, proved not to be the case, at any rate in the case of Donna that I was riding a good deal because the heat made walking a most laborious business.

One day I noticed that she seemed suddenly to have grown weak and stumbled so frequently that at length I dismounted. Relieved of my weight she came on well enough without being led, for the intelligent and affectionate beast would follow me or Hans, who fed her, like a dog. When we camped that night she would not eat and was seized with a fit of staggering.

At once I guessed what must be the matter. Probably she had been infected a long while before and the added doses of the poison in this fly-haunted plain had brought matters to a crisis, helped by a shower of rain, which often developes the illness. There was nothing to be done, for this venom has no known antidote. So we lay down and went to sleep as usual. In the middle of the night I was awakened by feeling something pushing at me. At first I was frightened, thinking it must be a lion or some other beast, until I discovered that poor Donna had managed to thrust her way through the thorn fence we had built and even into my tent, of which the flaps were open because of the heat, and by prodding at me with her nose, was calling attention to her state and asking my assistance.

Of course I could do nothing except lead her out of the tent and offer her water, which she would not drink. I tried to go away, but whenever I moved she made piteous efforts to follow me, for the poor thing was growing weaker every minute, till at last she tumbled down. I sat myself at her side and presently she rolled over, laying her head, whether by accident or design, upon my knee and died.

I have told of her end in some detail, because with the single exception, that of a dog named Stump which once I owned when I was young, it was the most touching and piteous that I have known where an animal is concerned. Surely if there is any other life for us men, there must be one also for creatures which are capable of so much affection ; at least I do not think I should care for a heaven where these were not.

When it was all over I went back to my tent and slept as best I could, to be awakened at the first dawn by a sound of lamentation. Rising, I peeped over the fence to discover its origin and in the faint light saw—what do you think ?—Hans, whom it pleased to seem so callous and hard-hearted, seated on the ground blubbering—there is no other word for it—and kissing poor Donna's nose. Then I went back to bed, where in due course he brought me my coffee, as was his custom at sunrise.

"Baas," he said in a cheerful voice, "there is good news this morning. Those tsetse-flies have finished off Donna."

"Why is that good news ?" I asked.

"Oh, Baas, because the Owl-man, Kaneke, says there are mountains ahead of us which she could not have climbed. He told me only the other day that we should have to shoot her there, or leave her to be eaten by lions, which would have been a pity. Also she was growing weak and really was of very little use, so I am glad that she is dead, as now I shall be saved the trouble of feeding her."

"Yes, Hans," I answered, "I saw how glad you were when I looked over the fence just as the light began to glint upon the spears of Kaneke's porters."

At this Hans put down the coffee in a hurry and departed, apparently much ashamed of himself, because, as he said after I had told him the story, he did not like being spied upon when his stomach was upset and made him behave like a fool. I should add that the hunters were depressed at this incident, not that they cared particularly for Donna, but because they said that now our luck had changed and that death was "a hungry lion". who, having tasted beast's flesh, would long for that of men.

They were right. Our luck had changed. The decease of poor Donna marked the end of our peaceful progress.

A few days later we came to mountains which for a long time past we had seen in the distance, bold hills upon which at night-fall a wonderful and mysterious blue light seemed to gather —the Ruga Mountains, I believe they were called. It was quite true that here we should have been obliged to leave Donna, dead or alive, for their ascent proved to be a most precipitous business. Indeed, had not Kaneke known the path, never could we have climbed them, because of certain precipices that rose in tiers of terraces and must be circumvented, since to scramble up the faces of them was impossible.

However he did know it, though to call it a path is a misnomer, because there was nothing to show that it was used by man. For three or four days we crept along the base of those great bare cliffs, always at length finding some crack by which their flanks could be turned. So it went on, an exhausting business, and as we mounted higher, very cold at night, for although there was no snow, the air grew thin and piercing.

At length we reached the summit of the mountains, which I found to be table-topped, a very common African formation. (What caused it? I wonder. Were the crests shorn off by ice in some remote era of the world's history, say, a few hundred million years ago?) As it was nightfall I could see no more, especially as a sort of blinding Scotch mist, the fog called the "table-cloth" which so often hangs about these flat-topped mountains, came up and obscured everything.

Next morning before the dawn Hans woke me up saying that Kaneke wished to speak with me. I went grumbling in all the clothes I had, with a blanket on the top of them and an old otterskin kaross, that I used above the thin cork mattress of my portable bedstead, thrown over that, for the cold was bitter, or seemed so, after those hot tsetse-haunted lowlands. I found Kaneke seated on a stone near to the edge of the tableland. He rose and greeted me in his ceremonious fashion, saying:

"Lord, you should not have slept so long, for after midnight the mist melted or was blown away, and the stars were more beautiful and brighter than I have seen them since last I stood upon this place a long while ago. Indeed, so clear were they that in them I read many things which hitherto had been hidden from me."

"Did you?" I exclaimed. "I hope that among them you read that we shall soon escape from this cold which is gnawing my bones."

"Yes, Lord, I can promise you that before long you will be hot enough. Hearken," he went on with a change of tone, "the time has come when I must tell you something of my country and of what lies before us. Look! The sun rises in the east. The sight is fine, is it not?"

I nodded. It was very fine. The rays of the morning light revealed a vast plain lying some thousands of feet beneath us, and far away, set apparently in the centre of this plain, other mountains shaped like a flattened ring. Or perhaps it was a single mountain ; at that distance I could not be sure.

"See," went on Kaneke, pointing to this mass, "yonder within that wall of cliff is the home of my people, the Dabanda, and there too is the holy lake, Mone. From here the place looks small, but it is not small. For a whole day a swift-footed man might run and not cross it from side to side."

"What is it ?" I asked. "A valley ?"

"I think not, Lord. I think that it is the cup of one or more of those great mountains that once vomited out fire ; a huge basin with steep walls that cannot be climbed, and slopes within that run down to the forest at its base, which forest surrounds the Holy Lake."

"How large is this lake, Kaneke ?"

"I do not know. Perhaps if a man could walk on water it would take him two hours to reach the island in its centre ; one hour to cross that island and another two hours to come to the farther shore."

"That is a big piece of water, Kaneke, which means that the whole space within the lip of the rock must be large. Are your people who dwell in it also large ?"

"Nay, Lord. Perhaps they can count five hundred men of an age to bear arms ; not more. Still, they are strong because they are holy, and for another reason."

"What other reason ?"

He dropped his voice as he answered :

"Did I not tell you the story of the goddess who dwells in my country, she whose title is Engoi the Divine, and whose name is Shadow ?"

"You told me a story of which I remember something, as I remember also that I did not believe a word of it."

"There you are both right and wrong, Lord Macumazahn, because some of that story was lies with which I filled your ears for my own purposes, and some was true. For instance, what I said about the Engoi waiting for a white man was a lie. It was a bait in my trap. Lord, it was necessary that you should come with me ; why, I do not quite know, but so I was commanded."

"Who commanded you ?"

"That is my secret, Lord."

Now I bethought me of the deceased White-Mouse, and did not pursue the matter, but asked :

"What do you mean by telling me that this lie was a bait ?"

"What I say, Lord. I have learned through your servant,

the yellow man, who told it not to me but to another, that you worship all that is beautiful, especially beautiful women, who when they see you, so you announce, fall in love with you at once. Now you will understand, Lord, why I baited my trap with this story of one who was very lovely and waited for a white man, namely because I knew that you would believe yourself to be that man and come with me upon that journey, being sure that she who is named Shadow would reward you by kissing your feet and redeeming you from your sins towards the other beautiful women, whom the yellow man says you throw aside one after another as soon as you are tired of them."

Now when I heard this preposterous and most shameless yarn, it is true that, cold as it was, I nearly burst with heat and rage. If that mischievous and romancing little Hans had been there, which he was not, I declare that it would have gone ill with him ; indeed, so angry was I with Kaneke for repeating his calumnies, that I nearly made a physical attack upon him. On second thoughts, however, I refrained—first, because he was a much larger and stronger man than myself, and, secondly, because I wished to get at the kernel of this mystery, for I felt that, divested of the trappings invented by Kaneke, there remained something most unusual to be elucidated. So I put the brake upon my temper and answered :

"I thought that in your way you were a wise man, Kaneke, but now I see that after all you are but a fool, who otherwise would have known that Hans is an even bigger liar than you announce yourself to be, and that the last thing I wish is to run after beautiful women, or any woman, which always ends like our adventures with the elephants, in the hunter being hunted. But let that be. Was any of your story true ?"

"Yes, Lord, much. We have a goddess who is called Shadow, and who, as we believe and not we alone, controls the gifts of heaven, sending rain or withholding it, causing women to bear children or making them barren, and doing many such things that brings happiness or misery to men, though this goddess I have never seen, except once, as I told you."

"A goddess ! Do you mean that she is immortal ?"

"No, Lord, but I mean that her power is immortal, or at least that it goes on from generation to generation. The goddess, as I think, when her office is fulfilled, dies or perhaps is killed."

"What office ?"

"Lord, the Chief of my tribe, the Dabanda, is her head-priest. When the goddess is of ripe age he is married to her, and in due time becomes the father of a daughter, of which she is the mother. Perhaps he is also the father of male children, but if so they are never heard of, so I suppose that they are killed. When this daughter, the Engoi-to-be, grows up, her mother, the Engoi-that-was, vanishes away."

"Vanishes ! How does she vanish ?"

"I do not know, Lord. Some say that she who is called Shadow is drawn up to heaven, some that she who is also called the Lake-dweller, or Treasure of the Lake, swims out into the lake and is lost beneath its waters, and some that the virgins who attend her, poison her with the scent of certain flowers that bloom upon the island. At least she departs, and her daughter, the new Engoi, reigns in her place and, like her mothers before her, is married to her high-priest, the Chief of the Dabanda."

"What !" I asked, horrified. "Do you mean to say that this chief marries his own daughter ?"

"Oh no, Lord. The chief never outlives the Shadow. He knows when she is going to fade, and he fades at the same time, or earlier."

"How does he 'fade', as you call it ?"

"That is a matter for him to choose, Lord. Generally, if he seeks honour, in fighting our enemies the Abanda, among whom he will rush alone until he is cut down. Or sometimes he chooses other roads to darkness. At least he must walk one of them, because if he does not he is seized and burnt alive ; as the end is the same it does not matter how it is reached."

"My word," I exclaimed, "it is strange that this goddess finds it easy to get a husband !"

"It is not at all strange, Lord," answered Kaneke haughtily, "seeing that to wed the Engoi is the greatest honour that can befall any man in the world. Moreover, he knows that when his life here is over he will dwell with her for ever in joy in heaven. Yes, they will be twin stars shining to all eternity. Therefore before the Chief marries the Shadow, he names some child he loves to be the husband of the Shadow which shall appear.

"Thus it came about, Lord, that when I was but little, I was named by the Chief, the half-brother of my mother, to wed the Engoi-to-be. But I committed the great crime. I entered the sacred forest, hoping to look upon the Engoi, of whose beauty I had heard, not her whom I should wed, for as yet she did not live, but one who went before her. It was for this crime that misfortunes fell upon me, as I have told you, and I was driven from the land to atone my sins. Now I have been called back again to become the husband of the new Engoi, for such is my glorious destiny."

"Oh," I said, "now at last I get the hang of the thing. Well, every man to his taste, but after what you have told me, I am glad that no one nominated me to marry an Engoi or Shadow, or whatever you call her."

"Strange are the varying ways of men! That which you, White Lord, think of small account, we hold to be the greatest honour which can befall one born of woman. It is true that death lies beyond the honour, but what of this, seeing that soon or late death must come ?   It is true also that he who is named and consecrated the spouse of the Engoi of days to come, must look upon no other woman."

Here I could not help remarking :

"But surely, Kaneke, you told me a story of a woman who helped you to become chief of the Arabs in your town yonder, saying that you grieved much when she died ; also I think you spoke to me of your wives who dwelt without your fence."

"Very likely, Lord, for have I not told you many things ? Also, did I say that the child that brought the woman to her death was mine, or show you the wives who dwelt without my fence ?   Learn that I had not, nor even had a wife, which is one of the reasons why those Arabs held me a magician.   What does a man want with wives who is sealed as the husband of the Engoi, yes, of the Shadow herself, if only for a year, or even for an hour ?"

"Nothing.   Of course, nothing," I answered with enthusiasm. Then a thought struck me, and I added, "But supposing that when at last he sees this Engoi, he does not like her, or that she does not like him, having met some other man whom she prefers ?"

"Lord Macumazahn, you speak in ignorance, therefore I forgive you what might otherwise be considered insult, or even blasphemy.   It is not possible that her appointed husband should not like the Engoi.   Even were she hideous he would adore her, seeing the soul within.   How much more, then, will he do so, since she is always the loveliest woman on the earth, filled with light like a star and crowned with wisdom from above."

"Indeed ! In that case there is nothing more to be said. Only then, Kaneke, why do her adoring people drown or otherwise make away with such divine beauty and wisdom as soon as her daughter begins to grow up ?"

"As regards your second question," went on Kaneke, taking no notice of an interruption which doubtless he considered irreverent and trivial, "still less is it possible that the Engoi should prefer any other man to him to whom she is vowed, for the reason that she never sees one."

"Oh," I said, "now I understand. That accounts for everything, including your banishment from your home. A woman who never sees any man except the one she must marry is of course easily pleased, even if she is called a goddess."

"Lord Macumazahn," replied Kaneke, much offended, "I see that you wish to make a mock of me and my faith."

"As you did of that of the Mahommedans," I suggested mildly.

"I see also," he went on, "that you think I tell you lies."

"As you have just admitted you did in the past."

He waved his hand, as though to thrust this trifle aside, and went on ;

"Yet you will learn that as to the Lady Shadow, Treasure of the Lake, and her husband, who is called 'Shield of the Shadow'. I speak the truth. Indeed, you should have learnt it already, for have I not told you that amongst other powers, he who is affianced to her whose title is Engoi, yes, even before he has married her, has command over wild beasts and men. What of the lion that I turned aside on that night when you climbed the pit ? What of those whom I called to rescue you when the Arabs came up against you ? What of the elephants which hunted you when you went out to hunt them, and ceased when they saw me ?"

"What indeed ?" I echoed. "Perhaps when you have time you will answer your own questions. Meanwhile I will put one more to you. Why have you plotted and planned and so brought it about that I should be your companion upon this very mysterious business ?"

"Because it was conveyed to me that I must do so, Lord Macumazahn, for reasons that as yet are not made clear to me. Doubtless you are appointed to be of service to the Engoi and therefore to me. Also I know that there will be a great war between my people, the Dabanda, and the Abanda, who dwell in their thousands upon the farther side of yonder mountain and who desire—as they have always done—that their chief should wed the Shadow and thus bring rain and prosperity upon them, and in this war you, who are a great general or so I have heard, and who are so skilled with a rifle as I have seen, may be of use to me."

"I see," I said. "As I was when I rescued you from your house and afterwards when I shot that fellow Gaika. Well, perhaps I may and perhaps I mayn't, since no one knows to whom he will be of use. Meanwhile I thank you for telling me many things, some of which may be true. And now I will go to breakfast, so good-bye for the present," and I departed, aware that if I had disliked Kaneke before, now I positively detested him.

To me the man seemed to be a mixture of a liar, a braggart, a self-seeker, and a mystic, a most unpleasant compound, or so I thought. Yet I had taken his money and was bound to serve him, or at any rate to serve this wonderful Engoi, whose personal name was Shadow, if such a woman existed. Possibly she might be better than Kaneke ; at any rate I hoped so.

CHAPTER X

THE WANDERER

By evening that day we had reached the plain at the foot of the mountain and advanced some little way into its desolation. I use this word advisedly, for when once we had got away from the foothills where there was water, we entered most unpromising country upon which it was evident rain fell but seldom.

The vegetation here was almost entirely of the cactus order, grey or green prickly growths that stored up moisture within themselves. Some of these were enormous, thick and tall as moderate-sized trees, and, as I should judge, of great antiquity, their form suggesting huge candelabra (for they had no proper leaves) or straight fingers pointing up to heaven from flat bases, shaped like to the palm of the hand. Others again were round green lumps, ranging from the size of a football down to that of a pin-cushion, all of them, big or little, being covered with sharp spikes, which made progress among them difficult and, indeed, dangerous, for the prick of some of the species is poisonous. These cacti, I should add, or a large proportion of them, bore the most beautiful but unnatural-looking flowers of every size and brilliant hue.

Another feature of this strange semi-desert area was the outcrop here and there of columns of stone that from a distance looked like obelisks, monoliths sometimes, but generally formed of round, water-worn rocks resting one upon another. How they came here I cannot imagine ; it is a matter for geologists, but I noticed that they seemed to be composed of hard rock left, perhaps, when millions of years ago the lava from the great extinct volcanic area towards which we were heading, was washed away by floods.

Through this curious country we travelled for three days, coming on the second day to a small oasis where there was a spring of water, which I was glad to see for our bottles were empty and we had begun to thirst. I must add that we went at a great rate. Two or three of the porters, relieved of their loads, which the others added to their own, marched ahead, quite five hundred yards ahead, which, as Hans remarked, showed that they knew the way and were scouts sent out to guard against surprise. Kaneke followed, in the midst of the remaining porters, who acted as his bodyguard. Then came Hans and I, the two hunters bringing up the rear.

"Now I begin to believe, Baas," said Hans to me, "that something of all that story which Kaneke has told is true, for though they will never say so, it is evident that these men who know the road so well belong to his people, also that they are afraid of being attacked. Otherwise they would not go so fast through this wilderness of thorns, or look so frightened."

"How do you know what tale Kaneke told me ? Were you listening behind a stone ?" I asked, but got no answer, for at that moment Hans pricked, or pretended to prick, his foot upon a cactus, and dropped behind to dig out the thorn.

I pass on to the evening of the third day. We were at length getting clear of the cactus scrub and reaching the foot of the westernmost slope of the huge and massive mountain, which Kaneke had told me was the shell of an extinct volcano within whose crater dwelt his people, the Dabanda. There was but an hour to sunset, and though much distressed by the heat and the lack of water, we were marching at a great rate to reach a point where Kaneke said we should find a spring. This he was anxious to do before dark, for now the nights were almost moonless. Presently as we trudged forward, begrimed with dust and gasping from the still heat, Hans, who was at my side, poked me in the ribs, exclaiming in Dutch :

"*Kek !*" (that is, "Look !")

I did look in the direction to which he pointed, and saw so strange a sight that at first I thought I must be suffering from delusions. There, running towards us down the slope of a low ridge of the mountain mass where it merged into the plain, appeared a man, a very exhausted man, who came or rather staggered forward in short rushes, halting after every few paces as though to get his breath. This much I could see with my eyes, but when I took my glasses, which I always carry with me, I saw more, namely that this man was white! Yes, there could be no mistake, for his garments, which seemed to have been torn from his shoulders, showed the white skin beneath. Moreover his beard and hair were red, or even golden, and his height and breadth were greater than are those of most natives.

Next moment I saw something else also, for on that ridge of ground which he had crossed, appeared a number of black spears-men, who evidently were hunting him. Dropping the glasses into my pocket, I sang out to Tom and Jerry to give me my Winchester, which one of them carried as well as his own, the heavy rifles and ammunition being in charge of the bearers. In a minute it was in my hands, with a bagful of cartridges.

"Now follow me," I said, and the four of us ran forward, passing through the bearers.

By this time the exhausted white man was within about fifty paces of us, while his pursuers, not more than six yards or so behind, were beginning to throw spears at him as though they were determined to kill him before he could reach us. As it chanced it was some of them who were killed, for at my word we opened fire, and being decent shots, all four of us, down they went. The man arrived, unhurt, and sank to the ground, gasp-ing out:

"My God! you are white! Give me a rifle."

I didn't, because I hadn't one at hand, nor, indeed, was he in a fit state to handle a gun. Also, next minute there began a general engagement on a small scale.

More spearsmen—tall, shapely fellows—appeared over the ridge, thirty of forty of them perhaps. Our bearers threw down their loads and came into action with great vigour, uttering a war-cry of "Engoi!—Engoi!" We fired away with the repeat-ing rifles.

It was all over in a few minutes, for a good many of the attackers were down and the rest had bolted back across the ridge, while our losses were nil, except for one man who had received a spear-cut in the shoulder. They had gone, pursued by the porters who, from peaceful bearers of baggage suddenly were turned into perfect tigers, furious fighting-men who, weary as they were, rushed into battle like the best of Zulu veterans. The transformation was so marked and instantaneous that it astonished me, as it did Hans, who said :

"Look at those fellows, Baas. They are fighting, not strangers, but old enemies whom they have hated from their mothers' breasts. And look at Kaneke. He bristles with rage like a porcupine." (This was quite true ; the man's hair and beard seemed to be standing on end and his eyes, usually so sleepy, flashed fire.)

"Did you see him tackle that tall one whom you missed," (this was a lie. I never shot at the man), "the warrior who threw a knife at you—snatching the spear from his hand and driving it through him ? I think they must be Abandas whom, as we have heard, the Dabandas hate."

"I dare say," I answered, "but if so they are uncommonly like Kaneke's crowd ; of the same blood perhaps."

Then I bethought me of the white man, whom I had forgotten in the excitement of the scrap, and went to look for him. I found him seated on the ground, having just emptied a water-bottle that Jerry had given him.

"There is something in horoscopes, after all," he panted out, for he had not yet recovered his breath.

"Horoscopes ! What the devil do you mean ?" I asked, thinking that he must be crazy.

"What I say," he answered. "My father was cracked on astrology and cast mine when I was born. I remember that it foretold that I should meet a white man in a desert and that he would save me from being killed by savages."

"Did it indeed ? To change the subject, might I ask your name ?"

"John Taurus Arkle," he murmured. "Taurus from the constellation under which I was born, or so I understand," he added with a little smile and in the voice of one whose mind wandered ; then shut his eyes and began to faint.

Faint he did ; so thoroughly that he had to be revived from my scanty store of spirits. While he was recovering I took stock of the man, who evidently was off his head from exhaustion. That he was an Englishman of good birth was clear from that unfailing guide, his voice and manner of speaking. Also he was well named John Taurus, *i.e.* John Bull, though perhaps if the constellation Leo had been in the ascendant or whatever it is called when he was born, that of Lion would have suited him even better.

To tell the truth his physical qualities partook of both a taurine and a leonine character. The wide breast, the strong limbs and the massive brow were distinctly bull-like, while the yellow beard and hair which, having been neglected, hung down on to his shoulders like a mane, also the eyes which, when the sun shone on them, gleamed with a sort of golden hue, as do those of lions, did suggest something leonine.

In short, although not handsome, he was a most striking person, like to no one else I had ever seen ; aged, as I guessed, anything between thirty and thirty-five years. Much did I wonder how he came to be in this strange place where, as I believe from what Kaneke had told me, at that time I was the first white man to set foot.

The gin did its work, and in due course John Taurus Arkle—a strange name enough—regained his wits. While he was still unconscious Kaneke, looking both disturbed and fierce, the spear with which he had killed its owner still in his hand, came up and stared at him.

"It's all right," I said ; "only a swoon. He will recover presently."

"Is it so, Lord ?" he answered, staring at Arkle with evident disapproval and, I thought, dislike. "I hoped that he was dead."

"And why, pray ?" I inquired shortly.

"Because this white man will bring trouble on us, as I always feared."

"As you feared ! What do you mean ?"

"Oh, only that the stars told me something about him ; as I read them, that we should find his body."

Stars, I thought to myself ; more stars. But aloud I said :

"Well, you read them wrongly—if at all, for he is alive, and please understand that I mean to keep him so. But what is this talk of trouble ?"

"Talk," said Kaneke, pointing with the spear to certain silent forms that lay around. "Is there not already trouble here ? Moreover I learned something from one of those Abanda fellows before he died, namely that this white man had forced his way over the mountain crest into my country of the Dabanda ; that he had been driven out into that of the Abanda ; that he was forced to fly before them who wished to kill him, as they do all strangers ; that he fled, and being very strong and swift of foot,

E

outran them, till at last, when he was being hunted down like a tired buck by wild dogs, he met us, and that happened which was decreed."

"Yes," I repeated after him, "that happened which was decreed, whether in your stars or elsewhere. But I want to know what is to happen next. It appears that neither the Dabanda nor the Abanda like this white lord, who henceforth must be our companion."

"Why must he be our companion, Macumazahn? See, he is senseless. One tap on the head and he so will remain for ever, who, if he comes on with us among peoples whom he has offended—I know not how—may cost us our lives."

In an absent-minded fashion I took the revolver from my belt and began to examine it as though to see whether it were loaded.

"Look here, Kaneke," I said, "let us come to an understanding. You have just been suggesting to me that to suit some purpose of your own I should murder, or allow you to murder, one of my own countrymen who has been attacked by your people and other savages, and escaped. Perhaps you do not understand what that means to a white man, so I am going to tell you."

Here suddenly I lifted the revolver and held it within a few inches of his eyes. Then I said in a quiet voice :

"Look here, my friend, in your country when you take an oath that may not be broken, by whom do you swear?"

"By the Engoi, Lord," he answered in a startled voice. "To break an oath sworn by the Engoi is death, and more than death."

"Good. Now swear to me by the Engoi that you will not harm this white lord or cause him to be harmed."

"And if I refuse?" he asked sullenly.

"If you refuse, Kaneke, then I will give you time to change your mind, while I count fifty between my teeth. If, after I have counted fifty, you still refuse, or are silent, then I will send a bullet through your head, because, friend Kaneke, it is time to settle which of us two is master."

"If you kill me, my people will kill you, Macumazahn."

"Oh no, they won't, Kaneke. Have you forgotten that a certain lady called White-Mouse, in whom I put much faith, promised me that I should come quite safe out of this journey. Don't trouble yourself about that matter, for I will settle with your people after you are dead. Now I am going to begin to count."

So I counted, pausing at ten and at twenty. At thirty I saw Kaneke's fingers tighten on the handle of the spear with which he had killed the Abanda man.

"Be pleased to drop that spear," I said, "or I shall stop counting."

He opened his hand and it fell to the ground.

Then I counted on to forty, and pausing once more, remarked that time was short, but that perhaps he was right to have done with it and to take his chance of what awaited him in or beyond the stars he worshipped, seeing that this world was full of sorrows.

I counted on to forty-five, at which number I aligned the pistol very carefully on a spot just above Kaneke's nose.

"Forty-six, forty-seven, forty-eight," I said, and began to press upon the trigger.

Then came the collapse, for Kaneke threw himself down and in truly Eastern fashion began to kiss the ground before my feet. As he did so I fired, the bullet of course passing over his head.

"Dear me!" I exclaimed, "how fortunate that you made up your mind. This pistol is much lighter triggered than I thought or perhaps the heat has affected the spring. Well, do you swear?"

"Yes, Lord," he said hoarsely. "I swear by the Engoi that I will not harm yonder white man, or cause him to be harmed. That was the oath you asked, but I know that in it lies one that is wider, namely that henceforth, instead of your serving me, I must serve you, who have conquered me."

"That's it. You have put it very well," I replied cheerfully. "And now—a gift for a gift. I am quite ready to renounce my new-won lordship over you, and taking this white wanderer with me if he will come, to leave you to go your own ways, while I and my servants go mine, you promising not to follow or molest me in any manner. Is that your wish?"

"No, Lord," he answered sullenly. "You must accompany me to the Lake Mone."

"Very good, Kaneke, so be it. Tell me how matters stand and I will give you my orders. But remember that if you disobey one of them or try to trick me, or to injure this white lord, I who have only counted forty-eight, shall count forty-nine and fifty. It is agreed?"

"It is agreed, Lord," he replied humbly. "Hearken. Yonder," and he pointed to some rocks upon a slope not more than a few hundred yards away, where grew trees of a different and more vigorous character from any about us—"yonder, I say, is the spring we seek. Lord, we must reach it at once, for our water is done, the white man has drunk the last, and very soon it will be quite dark and impossible to travel."

"Good," I said. "Go on with your men and prepare the camp. I will follow with the wanderer as soon as he can walk. Afterwards we can talk."

He looked at me doubtfully, wondering, I was sure, whether I had it in my mind to give him the slip. If so, probably he concluded that without water and with a sick man it would not be possible for me to do so. At least he went to collect his people, and presently I saw them march with the loads up to the rocks where grew the green trees. To make certain of his movements I sent Hans with them, telling him to return at once and report if there was a spring and if so whether Kaneke was preparing to camp.

To tell the truth I was by no means certain as to his intentions. Possibly he meant to melt away in the darkness, leaving us in the wilderness to our fate. This would not have troubled me very much had it not been for the fact that nearly all the ammunition and food, also some of my rifles, were among the loads. Otherwise, indeed, I should have been glad to see the last of Kaneke, for I was filled with doubts of him and of the business into which he was dragging me. However, I must take my chance ; amongst so many risks what was one more ?

When he had gone I went to where the stranger lay behind some stones, and to my joy found that he was coming out of his swoon, for he had sat up and was staring about him.

"Who are you and where am I ? Oh, wasn't there a fight ? Give me water."

"Keep quiet a little, Mr. Arkle," I said. "I hope to have some water presently." (I had given Hans a bottle to fill.) "There has been a fight. By God's mercy we managed to save you. You shall tell me about your adventures afterwards."

He nodded, fixing his attractive eyes, which reminded me of those of a retriever, on my face. Then, doubtless unaware that he was speaking out loud, he said something rather rude, namely :

"Queer-looking little chap ; hair like that of a half-clipped poodle ; skin like an old parchment, but tough as nails ; and straight. Yes, I am sure, straight. John Taurus, you are in luck. Well, it's time."

Of course I took no notice, but went to speak to Tom and Jerry, who were standing close by bewildered and whispering, asking them how many cartridges they had fired in the scrap, and answering their questions as best I could, till presently in the waning light I caught sight of Hans returning.

"It is all right, Baas," he said. "There's a good spring yonder, as the Owl-man said, and he is camping by it. Here's water."

I took the bottle and handed it to Arkle, who seized it eagerly. Then suddenly a thought struck him and he held it out to me, saying in his pleasant, cultivated voice :

"You too look thirsty, sir. Drink first," words that showed me that I had to deal with a gentleman.

To tell the truth I was dry, perished with thirst, indeed. But not to be outdone I made him take the first pull. Then I drank and gave some to Tom and Jerry. Between us those two quarts did not go far ; still, a pint apiece was something.

"Can you walk a little ?" I asked Arkle.

"Rather," he said. "I'm a new man, and thank God those scoundrels didn't get my boots. But where are we going ?"

"To the camp yonder first. Afterwards to the Lake Mone if we can."

A flash of joy passed across his face.

"That will suit me very well," he said. Then it fell, and he added : "You are very good to me, and it is my duty to warn you that the journey is dangerous, and if we get there, that the place and people are—well, not canny. Indeed, you would be wise to turn back, for I think that death is very fond of Lake Mone."

"I guessed as much," I said. "Have you been there, Mr. Arkle ?"

He nodded.

"Then take my advice and say nothing of your experiences to those with whom we are going to camp, for I suppose you talk Arabic. I will explain why afterwards."

He nodded again, then asked :

"What is your name, sir ?"

I told him.

"Allan Quatermain," he said. "Seems familiar to me somehow. Oh, I remember, a man I knew—Lord Ragnall— told me about you. Indeed, he gave me a letter of introduction in case I went south. But that's gone with the rest. Odd to have met you in this fashion, but so is everything in this place. Now, Mr. Quatermain, if I may put my hand on your shoulder, for my head still swims a bit, I am ready to walk."

"Right," I answered, "but again I beg you not to be ready

to talk, at any rate in any language but our own, for except Hans, who can be trusted on all important matters"—and I pointed to the Hottentot—"none of these people understand English."

"I see," he said, and we started, Arkle, who limped badly, towering above me, for he was a very big man, and leaning on me as though I were a stick.

We reached the camp without difficulty just as darkness fell. While the hunters pitched my tent which, although low, was large enough to cover two men, Arkle lay down by the stream and drank until I begged him to stop. Then he poured water over his head, and thrust his arms into it to the shoulders, as though to take up moisture like a dry sponge, after which he asked for food. Fortunately, we had still plenty to eat—of a kind, hard cakes made of crushed corn that we had obtained from the last natives we had met, and sliced *biltong*, that is buck's flesh dried in the sun. These he devoured ravenously, as though they were delicious, which showed me that he was almost starved. Then he lay down in the tent and fell at once into a profound sleep.

For a while I sat listening to his breathing, which sounded quite loud in the intense stillness of the place, and staring at the stars that in the clear sky shone with wonderful brilliance. By their light I saw Kaneke glide past me and, taking his stand upon a flat stone at a little distance, make strange motions with his arms, which he held up above his head.

"The Owl-Man is talking to his star, Baas; that bright one up there," whispered Hans at my side, pointing to the planet Venus. "He does that every night, Baas, and it tells him what to do next day."

"I am glad to hear it," I answered, "for I am sure I do not know what we are to do."

"Oh, just go on, Baas," said Hans. "If you only go on long enough you always come out the other side," a remark which I thought contained a deal of true philosophy, though it left the question of what one would find on the other side quite unsolved.

After this, having arranged that Hans and the two hunters were to keep watch alternately, which was unnecessary where Hans was concerned, seeing that he always slept with one eye open, I lay down in the tent, and having said a short prayer, as I am not ashamed to confess I have always done since boyhood, or at any rate nearly always, fell instantly into a profound slumber.

While it was still dark—although, as I could tell by the stars and the smell of the air, the night drew towards morning, I was awakened by Arkle creeping into the tent.

"Been to get a bathe in that spring," he said, when he found that I was awake. "Needed it when one hasn't washed for a week. I feel all right again now."

I remarked that I was glad to hear it, and that he seemed to have had a squeak for his life.

"Yes," he added thoughtfully, "it was a very close thing. Lucky that I am a good runner. I won the three-mile race two years in succession at the Oxford and Cambridge sports. Look here, Mr. Quatermain, you must be wondering who I am and how I came here. I will tell you while it's quiet, if you care to listen.

"The Arkles, though that isn't the name of the firm, for some generations have been in a big way of business in Manchester and London ; colonial merchants they call themselves. They deal all over the world, with West Africa among other places. My father, who has been dead some years, struck out a line of his own, however. He was a dreamy kind of a man, a crank his relatives called him, who studied all sorts of odd subjects, astrology among them, as I think I told you. Also he refused to have anything to do with trade, and insisted upon becoming a doctor, or rather a surgeon. He met with great success in his profession, for notwithstanding his fads, he was a wonderful operator. Being well-off he took little private practice, but worked almost entirely at hospitals for nothing.

"When I left college, by his wish I became a doctor too, but shortly after I qualified at Bart's my father, whose only child I was, died. Also my cousin, the only son of my uncle, Sir Thomas Arkle the baronet, was killed in an accident, and my uncle begged me to enter the business. In the end I did so, very unwillingly, to please my relations. To cut the story short, I did not care for business, and when there was so much property entailed upon me with the baronetcy, I could not see why it was necessary that I should remain in an office. On the other hand my uncle did not wish me to return to practice.

"So we compromised ; I agreed to travel for some years in the interests of the firm, specially in West Africa, where they wanted to develop their trade, and incidentally in my own interest, because I wanted as a physician to observe man in his primitive state and to study his indigenous diseases. When the tour was finished I was to return and put up for Parliament and in due course inherit the Arkle fortunes, which are large, and advance the

Arkle dignity, which is nothing in particular, by the judicious purchase of a peerage, for that is what it came to. That, more or less, was the arrangement."

"Quite so," I said, "or as much of it as you choose to tell me, though perhaps there is a good deal more behind which, quite properly, you prefer to keep to yourself."

"Perfectly true, Mr. Quatermain. By the way, as I am telling you about myself, would you mind telling me who and what you are ?"

"Not in the least. I was born in England of a good family, and received a decent education from my father, who was a scholar, a gentleman, and something of a saint. For the rest I am nobody and nothing in particular, only a hunter with some skill at his trade, an observer, like you, of mankind in the rough, and one cursed with a curiosity and a desire to learn new things which, in the end, will no doubt put a stop to all my foolishness."

"Oh no, it won't," he answered cheerfully, "that is, not until the time appointed. I'll cast your horoscope for you, if you like—my father taught me the trick—and tell you when it will happen."

"No, you won't," I answered firmly.

At this moment Hans arrived with the coffee and informed me that Kaneke was anxious that we should march at sunrise, as here we were in danger.

Then followed anxious consultations. Arkle had a coat, or rather a Norfolk jacket, but no shirt ; and one of my spares, a flannel garment that had cost me fifteen shillings at Durban and had never been used, must be provided for him. Luckily it was over-size, so he managed to drag it on to his great frame. Then a hat must be found, and so forth. Lastly it was necessary to provide him with one of the spare Winchester rifles and some cartridges.

Even before we were ready Kaneke arrived, not a little agitated, as I could see, and prayed us to hasten.

"Where to, Kaneke ?" I asked.

"Up the side of the mountain and over its lip, Lord, that we may take shelter among my people the Dabanda. For be sure that after what happened yesterday, the Abanda will kill us if they can. If this white wanderer whom your servants call Red-Bull cannot march, he must be left behind."

Here Arkle, who it seemed understood and could speak Arabic perfectly, looked Kaneke up and down and replied that this was unnecessary, as he believed that he could get along.

So, having swallowed some food, presently off we went, guided by Kaneke up the steep mountain side.

"Did you call that man, Kaneke?" Arkle inquired when that worthy was out of earshot.

"Yes," I answered; "but why do you ask?"

"Oh, only because of late I have heard a good deal of a person named Kaneke from a native I know. But perhaps there are two Kanekes. The one he spoke of was a young fellow who committed a great crime.

Then rather abruptly he changed the subject, leaving me wondering.

CHAPTER XI

ARKLE'S STORY

At first Arkle walked rather lamely, being troubled with stiffness and his sore heel, but soon these wore off for the time, and in the fresh air of the morning his vigour returned to him. Certainly he was a splendid-looking man, I reflected, as I marched at his side, a perfect specimen of the finest stamp of the Anglo-Saxon race.

While we went he continued his story.

"You were quite right in supposing that there were other reasons which induced me to come to Africa besides those I mentioned. I will tell them to you, if you care to hear them, for I may as well put my cards on the table. If not, please say so, for I do not wish to bore anybody with my affairs."

I replied that nothing would please me better, for to tell the truth my curiosity was much excited.

"Here goes, then," he said, "though I expect that the tale won't raise your opinion of me and my intelligence. As I have said, I am what is called a man with prospects or rather I was, for these seem far enough off today, and as such, having plenty of money to spend, I was exposed to many temptations. Mr. Quatermain, I cannot pretend that these were always resisted. I will pass over my follies, of which I am ashamed, with the remark that they were such as are common to impetuous young men.

"In short, I lived fast, so fast that my uncle and connections —my mother, by the way, died when I was young—being non-conformist of that puritanical stamp which often combines piety with a continual thirst for worldly advancement, were quite properly scandalized, and remonstrated. They said that I must change my mode of life, and as a first step, get married. This my uncle desired above all things, for there was no other heir, and as he often used to remark in a solemn voice, life is uncertain.

"At length I gave way and became engaged to a lady very well born indeed and very handsome, but without means, which, as I would have plenty, did not matter. To be honest, I did not greatly care for this lady, nor did she care for me, being, as I discovered afterwards, in love with somebody else. In fact the marriage would have been one of mutual convenience, nothing more. Now I am going to make you laugh.

"Although no one knew it and I scarcely expect you to believe it, I, a man who, as I have said, could and did plunge into dissipations, have another side to my nature. At times, Mr. Quatermain, I am a dreamer and what is called a mystic. I suppose I inherited it from my father, at any rate there it is."

"There is nothing wonderful in that," I remarked ; "the old story of the flesh and the spirit, nothing more."

"Perhaps. At least I put faith in queer and unprovable things, for instance in what are called 'soul affinities', and even in the theory that we have lived before. Would you believe that the great lump of British flesh and blood which you see before you developed a 'soul affinity', if that is the right term, with someone I had never met ?"

I looked at him doubtfully, reflecting that the hardships through which he had passed had probably touched his brain. He read my mind, for he went on :

"Sounds as though I were a bit cracked, doesn't it ? So I thought myself, and should still think, were it not for the fact that I have found this affinity in Africa."

"Where ?" I asked lightly. "At Lake Mone ?"

"Yes," he replied, "at Lake Mone, where I always expected that I should find her."

I gasped, and felt as though I should like to sit down, which, owing to our hurry, was impossible. Evidently the poor man was rather mad.

"As I have begun it I had better go on with my story, taking things as they happened," he continued in a matter-of-fact voice. "I tell you that in the midst of my wild and rather unedifying career I began to be haunted by visions which came upon me at night."

"Dreams ?" I suggested.

"No, always when I was awake and looking at the stars, and generally when I was in the open air. The first, I remember, developed in Trafalgar Square at three in the morning after I had been to a dance."

"The wine is not always very good at those dances, I have been told, or if it is, sometimes one drinks too much of it," I suggested again.

"Quite true, but as it happened this one was given by a relative of mine who is a strict teetotaller and never allows anything spirituous in her house. I had to go to meet my fiancée ; it was a terrible affair. When it was over I went for a walk and came to Trafalgar Square, which at that hour was very quiet and lonely. There I stood staring at the Nelson Column, or rather at the stars above it, for it was frosty and they were beautiful that night. Then the thing came. I saw a desolate sheet of water lit up by the moon, an eerie kind of a place. Presently a form, that of a woman draped in white, appeared gliding over the water towards me, floating, not walking. It reached the shore and advanced to where I stood, and I saw that this woman was young and very beautiful, with large, tender eyes.

"She stopped opposite to me, considering me, and a change came over her face as though after long search she had found that which she sought. Looking at her, I too seemed to have found that which I sought. She held out her arms, she spoke to me ; distinctly I heard her words, not with my ears but through some inner sense. What is more, I understood one or two of them, though they were in Arabic.

"I have always had a taste for studying out-of-the-way subjects, and it happened that in my medical reading I had become interested in the works of some of the old Arabian physicians, and in order to understand them had found it necessary to master something of the language in which they were written. This was some years before, and I had forgotten most of what I had learned, but not everything. So it came about that I caught the meaning of a sentence here and there—such as these :

"'At last, O long sought. At last upon the earth.' . . . 'Not in dreams.' . . . 'Follow, follow.' . . . 'Far away you will find and remember.' . . . 'Yes, there the gates will be opened, the gates of the past and the future.'

"At this point the vision, or whatever you like to call it, came to a prosaic end, for a policeman arrived, eyed me suspiciously, and said :

" 'Move on, young gentleman. This ain't no place for the likes of you on a cold night. Go home and sleep it off.'

"I remember that I burst out laughing ; the contrast was so ridiculous. Then because my heart was full of a strange joy, such as is described by the old mystics who think that they have been in communication with things Divine, I presented that policeman with half a sovereign, wished him good night, walked away quietly to my rooms in St. James's Place, and went to bed a changed man."

"What do you mean by 'a changed man' ?" I asked.

"Oh, only that I seemed different in every way. It was as though something had been torn, or a veil had been lifted from my eyes, so that now I saw all sorts of new things ; at least the old things took on new aspects. From that moment, for example, I hated the dissipations which had attracted me. I acquired different and higher objectives ; I came to know, what doubtless is true, that here in the world we are but wanderers lost in a fog which shuts off glorious prospects, divine realities, so that we can see little except dank weeds hanging from the rocks by which we feel our way, and pebbles shining in the wet beneath our feet. We make crowns of the weeds and fight for the bright pebbles, but the weeds wither, and the pebbles when they are dry prove to be but common slate. The dream woman that I had seen in Trafalgar Square showed me all this, and a great deal more. I was changed ! I who had been a greedy caterpillar, devouring all that I could find, in that half-hour in Trafalgar Square became a chrysalis, and then was transformed into a butterfly."

"Most interesting !" I exclaimed, and with sincerity, for notwithstanding Arkle's fine words and metaphors which I found rather difficult to follow, this story did interest me very much. I didn't believe in the Trafalgar Square vision, but, as an American would say, I did hitch on to that transformation which, in our degree, most of us have experienced at one time or another, however impermanent its results may have proved. In some private Trafalgar Square of their own, nearly all have met the Ideal, or the Divine, and in its unearthly light have seen things high and strange ; have seen also how petty and how foul are the objects of their temporal desire.

Half an hour later it is probable that they will have forgotten the former, and be hunting the latter even more fiercely than before. Still, they have had the vision, and those to whom such

visions came may always hope. They have learned that there
are gates in the gross wall that is built about their souls. . . .

"Most interesting," I repeated, "but how about the lady to
whom you were engaged ? Did you tell her what you had seen
and heard in Trafalgar Square ?"

"No, I didn't, at least not all of it. The only difference was
that whereas I had merely disliked her before, afterwards I
detested her, that is, as a prospective matrimonial partner.
However, I may add at once that this engagement affair cleared
itself up in a most satisfactory fashion. The lady's aversion to
me was even more real than mine to her. Also she was rude
enough to believe and to tell me she believed that I was mad."

"That was pretty straight, though if you talked to her—
well, as you are doing now, not altogether surprising," I said.

"Quite straight, but I respected her for it. Lastly, as I
have said, there was a gentleman in the case. Now can you
guess what happened ?"

"Of course. You broke it off, that's all."

"Not a bit. We didn't dare, for the row in both families
would have been too terrific. No, my hated rival was impecunious
like my beloved betrothed, whereas I had a good lump of cash
at call, which my father had left me. So I lent him £5000—it's
more polite to call it lent—and they bolted to Florida to start
orange-farming. I need not say that I proclaimed myself
broken-hearted and everyone sympathized with me to my face
and laughed at me behind my back, almost as heartily as I laughed
myself behind their backs. Meanwhile, I studied Arabic like
anything, which amused me, as I am rather quick at languages,
and took long midnight walks to develop my spiritual side."

"I say," I said doubtfully, "you are not making fun of me,
are you, Mr. Arkle ?"

"Certainly not. At least I think I am not, for those Abanda
have killed my sense of humour. But you shall judge by the
sequel. To cut it short, I did seem to come more and more in
touch with that lady of the lake. Yes, in those starlit midnight
hours she appeared to talk to me more and more as my Arabic
improved, and to tell me all sorts of curious things about the past,
the very distant past, I gathered, in which we had been intimately
connected and taken part in various adventures, some of them
tragic and all in their way striking and even beautiful. I will
skip these, for what is the use of repeating a lot of old love-affairs
that apparently took place in remote ages, only saying that in
the last of them at some indefinite date she brought about my

death and her own, that we might go to heaven together or rather to a certain star, a crime for which, according to the visions, she is most anxious to make amends. That is why, still according to the visions, she must live in the distant spot where it happened, for as I understand, the experiment did not succeed—I mean that we never got to that star."

"Look here," I said, "all this sounds rather like a nightmare, doesn't it ?"

Yet as the words passed my lips, I remembered Kaneke's yarn about his goddess in the lake who was supposed to have descended from heaven and fallen in love with a man. Surely he said that she had killed this man to take him back to heaven with her, which was not allowed. Therefore she waited in the lake until he appeared again, after which I did not gather what was to happen. The legend was of a sort that is not unknown in Central and West Africa, but really it was odd to hear another version of it from Arkle's lips.

"Very much like a nightmare," he assented cheerfully. "Being a doctor I came to the same conclusion, as did some of the most eminent of my profession whom I consulted. One of them asked me if I had spotted the *locale* if these strange happenings. I replied, yes, somewhere near some mountains in the central parts of Africa that were called Ruga, where, as I believed, no white man had ever been, though I had found them marked on an old map. 'Well,' he replied, with a twinkle in his eye, 'if I were you I should go and look for the lady there. At the worst you will get some good big-game shooting, and I have noticed that people with hallucinations never come to any harm.'

"I thought this an excellent idea, and shortly afterwards I began to work upon my uncle to send me out to Africa to advance the trade interests of the firm. In the end he and the other partners agreed ; you see they sympathized with me very much on my matrimonial fiasco and thought that a change would do me good.

" 'In such a case,' said my uncle, who has a gift for platitude, 'new countries, new customs, and new faces are most helpful.' I sighed and shook my head, but said that I hoped so."

"How long have you been here ?" I asked.

"Oh, I landed on the West Coast about three years ago. It took me a long while to find those confounded Ruga Mountains, and I met with many adventures on the way. However, at last I fetched up all right with about half a dozen coast servants, good men all of them, for the rest of the crowd had bolted at one time or another. And now I come to the interesting part of the story, if you care to hear it."

"Of course I do. Who wouldn't ?" I answered. "Go on."

"Well, I had heard of Lake Mone, the holy lake as it is called ; right away from the Congo and beyond it, indeed, rumours of this place had reached me. I have told you that I am not bad at languages, and during my first year in Africa, while I was attending to the business of the firm, I also studied local tongues and customs on every possible occasion. Thus I would get servants who could not talk a word of English, and learn from them. Then I began to work my way up country and at every tribe I came to, or rather at every village, I always made a friend of the chief witch-doctor, for the African witch-doctors know everything that is passing for hundreds of miles around them. Indeed often they seem to know more than this, how or why I can't tell."

"That's quite true," I said, thinking of Zikali, "Opener of Roads", the great wizard of Zululand of whom I have told some tales.

"Now," went on Arkle, "I must explain that I was not certain for what I was searching. The visions which I had experienced in England had shown me the desolate lake and a beautiful woman who spoke about the past and our relations together in that past. But beyond saying, or conveying, that it was in Central Africa she had never mentioned the name of the lake, or told me how to get there, and from the moment that I sailed from Liverpool the visions, or whatever they may have been, ceased. In short I was left without any guidance whatsoever.

"It was here that the witch-doctors came in. I explained my case to several of them, and when their mouths were opened by gifts, also by a belief that although my skin was white I was one of their fraternity, they became communicative. They had heard something of a sacred lake that was inhabited by a great fetish, they believed this fetish was a woman ; they would inquire. That was the burden of their song. What is more, they *did* inquire, once or twice by means of drum messages which, as you know, the natives can send over hundreds of miles, but generally in fashions that were dark to me. Also answers came, from which in the end I learned that the lake where the great rain-doctoress dwelt was named Mone, that her title was the Engoi, and that she was known among the people round her as Shadow, or The Shadow.

"Following these clues, such as they were, though of course all the while I understood that this Engoi, or Shadow, might be quite different from her of whom I had dreamed, I work my way slowly eastwards and southwards, till at last I came to certain mountains which I was told bordered the country where the Engoi lived. Indeed, from the crest of them I was shown this great volcano, or whatever it may be, that we are climbing now, which was declared to be her home. Also, I was informed that between it and me dwelt a fierce and numerous tribe called the Abanda, whose habit it was to kill anyone who set foot within their borders.

"It was here that the last six men who had clung to me struck. They were good fellows, faithful and brave ; I never had to do with better. Still, they came in a body and explained that although they feared no man, they did fear wizards and ghosts. The country of the Abanda, and more especially that of the Dabanda beyond it was, they had sure information, full of both, and the stranger who entered there never came out alive, 'even his spirit remained captive after he was dead'. For these reasons they would not go one step farther.

"I saw that it was quite useless to argue, and therefore I made a bargain. The village where this talk took place was inhabited by some very friendly and peaceful agriculturists in country that the Abanda never visited. This was my bargain : that those men should rest here for one year awaiting my return. If at the end of that time I did not appear again or send them further orders, they were to be at liberty to divide my goods and go wherever they liked. These goods, I should explain, are, or were, of some value, trade-stuff of all kinds for presents or barter, rifles, ammunition, clothes, etcetera."

"How did six men manage to carry all these things ?" I asked.

"They didn't. After most of my people deserted, by the help of the witch-doctors and chiefs I arranged for their transport from town to town or from tribe to tribe, letting the bearers go back and procuring others when I moved forward. So if I appear no more those six coast men, old soldiers most of them, will be rich, that is if they can get the stuff away."

"Unless they are more honest than most of their kind, I expect that they have done that already," I said, smiling.

"Possibly. I don't know, and to tell the truth I do not much care, because it is improbable that we shall ever meet again. I realized this when I made up my mind to continue the journey to Lake Mone alone."

"Do you mean to say that you tried to do that, Mr. Arkle?"

"Yes, and what is more, I succeeded. No, that isn't true; I did not go quite alone. At the last moment, when I was about to start, a sharp-eyed, wrinkled old fellow turned up, where from no one seemed to know, who said that he was one of the people who lived in the Land of the Holy Lake, whither he wished to return. He said that his name was Kumpana, and that he wanted no reward except my companionship upon the journey. That was all I could get out of him. Of course this sounded fishy enough, but as I was going on anyhow, it did not matter, although my hunters and the chief of the tribe—which, by the way was called Ruga-Ruga, I suppose after the mountains—implored me not to trust myself to such a guide. You see, I knew I should arrive and therefore I wasn't anxious."

"Now I understand what faith is," I said.

"Yes, faith is everything. We are taught that in the Bible, you remember. Well, I started; by the state of the moon it must be a month ago. I took a gun and as much ammunition as I could carry, also a pistol, a hunting-knife, and a few other necessaries, including an extra pair of boots, while the mysterious old fellow, Kumpana, carried the food. I say that he was old, for he looked so, but I should add that he was one of the finest walkers and the best guide that I ever knew.

"In three days, travelling down hill, we came to the country of the Abanda, or rather to its outskirts. They are a numerous people who live on a great plain upon the other side of this mountain, also on its western slope, in a number of unfortified villages, with one central town, which is much bigger than the rest. Their land, consisting chiefly of decomposed lava, is extremely fertile when there is rain, but just now it is suffering from a severe drought which, Kumpana said, though how he knew it I can't tell you, has endured for three years, so that they are almost starving, and consequently in a state of great excitement.

"This drought, he said also, they attribute to the magic of the Dabanda who live over the rim of the mountain, that is in the great crater of the extinct volcano or group of volcanoes. Therefore—if they dared—they would attack these Dabanda and destroy them, in order to occupy their country and become the subjects of their goddess the Engoi. But for some strange reason, which Kumpana could not or would not explain, they do not dare."

"I have heard something of that tale—with differences," I said. "Did you meet any of these Abanda?"

"No, not at that time, thanks to Kumpana. But you know

what they are like, for yesterday you saw some of them. In point of fact they almost exactly resemble those bearers of yours, who from the look of them might be either Abanda or Dabanda, for the two people are doubtless of one blood and even speak the same dialect of Arabic."

"How did you avoid them?" I asked, making no comment on this statement.

"By lying hidden during the day and travelling at night. As there was no moon visible we must journey by starlight, and even that failed sometimes when mist or cloud came up. But it seemed to make no difference to old Kumpana, who must know the country like a book. On he went up the steep mountain paths, seeing and climbing like a cat in the dark, and leading me by a string tied to his wrist, for we were afraid to speak except in the lowest whisper. Once or twice we passed quite close to villages, so close that we could see the people gathered round the fires. Here our danger was from the dogs, which smelt us and rushed out barking, but fortunately their masters took no notice, thinking, I suppose, that they smelt jackals or hyenas.

"On the third morning we came to the lip of the crater and had no more to fear from the Abanda. Now another danger arose, for the pass, which was nothing but a cleft in the rock, only large enough in places for one man to squeeze through at a time, was occupied by Dabanda watchmen, who of course challenged us, and were much astonished at my appearance, for I think they had never seen a white man. Kumpana they seemed to know (indeed, I believe that they were waiting for him there), for they talked with him in a friendly and deferential fashion, though I was not allowed to hear what they said. The end of it was that we were detained here for a day and a night while messengers were sent to a body of priests who are called 'The Council of the Engoi'.

"At dawn of the following day, that is twenty-four hours after our arrival, these messengers returned, saying that we were to proceed to the chief town upon the edge of the forest that surrounds the lake. So off we went, escorted by some of the Dabandas, through a lovely country, rich beyond imagining, for there had been plenty of rain here. It reminded me of some of the lands that border on the Rhine, and lower down, of those about Naples, and lower still of the South Sea Islands. That is until I came to the deep belt of forest which surrounds the Holy Lake where no man may set his foot."

"Did you see that lake?" I asked.

"Later I saw it and once or twice on the journey I caught a glimpse of it, a black and gloomy sheet of water with an island in its midst. In the evening we came to a large village where the huts or houses, some of them round and some square, were white and stood in gardens. I was taken to a large one of the square variety with a courtyard outside of it, where soon I found I was a prisoner.

"After dark a man visited me. As there was no light in the hut I could not see his face, but he told me that he was a priest of the Engoi. Then, in the presence of Kumpana, he cross-examined me sharply as to the reason of my visit, and affected surprise when I answered him in his own tongue—Arabic. I told him all sorts of lies ; that I wished to see his country ; that I was a white merchant and wanted to open trade ; that I desired to learn the wisdom of the Dabanda ; and I know not what besides. He replied that by rights I should be burnt alive for sacrilege, but as a white man was expected in the country and possibly I might be that man, the matter must be referred to the Engoi. Meanwhile I was to remain a prisoner. If I left the courtyard of the hut I should be seized and burned.

"A prisoner I did remain accordingly. For ten long days I sat about in that horrible hut and high-fenced courtyard, over-eating myself, for I was supplied with plenty of excellent food, and driven nearly frantic by doubts and anxieties. I felt that I was close to her whom I had come to see, and yet in a sense farther away than I had been in London years before. No more visitors reached me, nothing happened. At last I drew near to madness. I even thought of suicide—anything to get out of that intolerable hut and courtyard, for I saw, or thought I saw, that I had been the victim of delusions.

"One evening when I was at my worst, Kumpana, my old guide, who from something the priest said was, I discovered, a person of great importance, came to visit me for the first time for days. He asked me if I had a bold heart and was one who would dare much to satisfy the desire of his heart, and if so, what was that desire. I replied that it was to speak with a certain holy one whom already I had met in dreams, she who was called Shadow and dwelt in a lake. He did not seem in the least surprised, indeed he said he knew that this was so. Then he added :

" 'When the moon appears, walk out of the hut boldly to-wards the darkness of the forest. There you will find those who will guide you. Go with them to the borders of the lake, where perchance "one" will meet you.   After that I do not know what may happen.   It may be death—understand that it may be death.   If you fear this adventure I will guide you back out of the country of the Dabanda, but, then, know that never more, in dreams or otherwise, at least during this life, will you meet her whom you seek.   Now choose.'

" 'I have chosen,' I answered.   'I go into the forest.'

" 'A certain holy one has judged you well.   Speak with her if you will, yet beware that you touch her not.   Again I warn you to beware,' he said, and bowing left me.

"At the appointed time I walked out of the door of the hut, my rifle in my hand, for my arms had been left to me, perhaps because my captors did not understand their use.   The gate of the fence was open and the guards had gone.   I went through it and, following a path, came to the edge of the forest.   Here beneath the trees the darkness was intense and I stood still, not knowing which way to turn.   Shadows glided up to me.   Who or what they were I could not see, nor did they speak.   They did not touch me, so far as I could feel, yet they seemed to push me along.   Surrounded by them I walked forward.

"I confess that I was afraid.   It came into my mind that my companions were not human, that they were the spirits of the forest, or ghosts of those long dead returned to their earthly habitations.   Their company frightened me ; I spoke to them, but there was no answer, only I thought that cold hands were laid upon my lips as though to enjoin silence.   Whither was I going in pursuit of a dream that had haunted me for years ? Perhaps not to find the lovely woman of that dream, but in her place some blood-stained African fetish, some evil-haunted symbol to which I should be offered as a sacrifice.   My blood ran cold at the thought, and I tell you, Mr. Quatermain, that had I known which way to go, I would have turned and fled, for in this last trial my faith failed me.

"But it was too late, and now I must face that risk of death of which the old messenger had warned me.

"In dead silence I went on and on through the endless trees.   My hands brushed their trunks, I stumbled over their roots, but I never struck them and I never fell.   I could see nothing, could hear nothing except my own footfall.   Yes, by a pressure like to that of wind, I was guided and sustained for hour after hour.

"At length we were out of the forest, for I saw the stars and the faint effulgence of the hidden moon, also the gleam of water at my feet. My guides seemed to have left me as though their task was done. I was utterly alone, and the sense of that great solitude appalled my soul.

"What was that upon the waters, just discernible, or perhaps imagined? No, for it glided forward as a canoe glides that drifts in a current, since of oars I heard no sound. It drew near, a magic boat; a white veiled figure stepped upon the shore and stood before me. The veil was drawn, I saw the outline of a face, I saw the starlight mirrored in eyes that gleamed like stars.

" 'You have dared much to come, O friend of my heart,' said a sweet voice, speaking in Arabic, 'and I have dared much to bring you here that I might talk with you a little while.'

" 'Who and what are you, lady?' I asked.

" 'I am one whose soul spoke with you in your great city far away. Ay, and afterwards until I drew you to this land to find me in the flesh. For I know that from of old your destiny and mine have been intertwined, and so it must be till that end which is the real beginning.'

" 'Yes, perhaps. Indeed, I think I feel that this is so,' I answered. 'Yet what is your office here, you who live upon a lake surrounded by savages?'

" 'For my sins, O Friend, I must play the queen to these savages, and be their oracle.'

" 'Are you, then, divine?'

" 'Are we not all divine, spirits fallen from on high to expiate our sins and to draw upwards those against whom we have sinned?'

" 'I do not know, Lady Shadow—for I suppose that you are she who in this land is known as Shadow—since on this matter the different faiths teach differently. Yet it may well be so, seeing that this world is no happy home for man, but rather a place of bondage and of tears. But let such questions be and tell me first—are you woman?'

" 'I am woman,' she answered very softly.

" 'Then being woman, why have you called me—a man—to your side from half across the earth?'

" 'Because it was so fated, and for the sake of ancient love.'

" 'And now having heard your call and come and found you in the place of which I dreamed, what must I do to win you?' "

" 'Look on me,' she said, 'and having looked, say whether you still wish to win me, and if it is between us as it was in days you have forgotten.'

"She came a little nearer ; she loosened that enveloping veil and stood before me, perfect and entrancing. The starlight gathered upon her pure and lovely face ; to my fancy it was as though she herself radiated light. She was human and yet a mystery. She was a woman and yet half spirit.

" 'Of the past I know nothing,' I said, hiding my eyes with my hand, 'and of the present only that I desire you more than life and all it has to give.'

" 'I thank you, and I am glad,' she replied humbly. 'Yet know that I may not be lightly won. Great dangers threaten me and those over whom I rule and whom I must save before I satisfy my soul—and yours. How are you now named in the world ?'

" 'John Arkle,' I answered.

" 'Is it so ? Then, O Arkle, you must return over the lip of this mountain, and there find a white man who comes to help us and my people in the war that is at hand. When you have found him and that war is won, we will talk again. Go now. Your guides await you.'

" 'I do not wish to go,' I said. 'Let me return with you to where you dwell.'

"She became agitated. I saw her tremble as she answered hurriedly :

" 'It is not lawful ; first all must be accomplished ; that is the price. No, lay no hand upon me, for I tell you we are watched by those you cannot see, and if you touch me I shall find it hard to save you.

"I heard, but took no heed who was seized with a kind of madness, and forgot Kumpana's warning. I had found one whom I had sought for years. Was I to lose her thus, perhaps for ever ? I stretched out my arms and swept her to my breast. I kissed her brow.

"Then came a tumult ; it was as though some frightful tempest had broken over us. She was wrenched away and vanished. I was seized and shaken as though by the hands of giants ; my senses left me.

"When they returned again—it must have been long afterwards—I was running on the mountain side, hunted by those savages whom you met and drove away."

CHAPTER XII

KANEKE SWEARS AN OATH

ARKLE'S story came to an end, and I said nothing. Luckily, he did not appear to expect me to speak, for, glancing at him, I saw that he was limping on like one in a dream, his eyes set upon the mountain lip above us as though he were looking over, or rather through it at some vision beyond, and that on his face was a faint, fixed smile such as I have seen upon those of persons under hypnotic influence while they go about the behests of the master of their will.

Evidently the man was not with me. He, or rather his mind, was fixed upon that lake and its mysterious lady, if such a woman lived. Contemplating him I came to the conclusion that he was the victim of hallucination, or to put it bluntly—mad. For years he had been haunted by this dream of a spiritualized maiden who was his twin soul, a very ancient fantasy after all, and one still believed in by thousands.

For it is interesting to imagine that somewhere, in the universe or beyond it, is hidden a counterpart, or rather a complement, of the other sex who exists for us alone and thinks of us alone, he or she from whom Fate has separated us for a while and laid upon us the need to find again in life or death.

Such a dream is always popular because it flatters our human vanity to believe that however lonesome and unappreciated we may seem to be, always somewhere waits that adoring and desiring mate who burns to welcome and to hold us everlastingly.

Without doubt Arkle was subject to this common craze, only in his case, instead of keeping it to himself, as do the more modest, he proclaimed it aloud, as might be expected of one of his robust and sanguine temperament, streaked as it was with veins of inherited mysticism. He had followed his clues, such as they were ; he who had dreamed of a lake-goddess, had heard of a holy lake supposed to be presided over by some local and female spirit, and with wonderful courage and resistance he had fought his way half across Africa to the neighbourhood of this place.

Here he had fallen into the hands of a tribe hostile to those who worshipped the water-fetish, or witch-doctoress, or rain-maker (nearly all these African superstitions are connected with rain). Naturally, never having seen a white man before, they seized him and kept him prisoner. Ultimately they determined to kill him, but getting warning of their kind intentions, he made a run for it, and so blundered on to us with his would-be assassins at his heels.

This, I doubted not, was the whole story, all the rest about the visit to the lady who met him on the shores of the lake being pure imagination, or rather dementia. Still it was true that Kaneke told somewhat similar tales—a puzzling fact. Oh, how I wished to heaven that I had never tied myself to this Kaneke by accepting his ivory and cash! But there it was : I had, as it were, signed the note of hand, and must honour the bill.

As a matter of fact, at this very moment an instalment was ripe for discharge.

We had stopped for a few minutes to rest and drink some water from a mountain stream, and eat a few mouthfuls of food. Just as we had finished our hasty meal, Kaneke, who was seated on higher ground fifty yards ahead, turned and beckoned to me to come to him. I went, and when I reached him, without a word he pointed to our left.

I looked, and there, advancing along a fold of the mountain at a considerably higher level than ourselves, just at the foot of the precipitous crater cliff a mile and a half, or perhaps two miles away, I caught sight of glittering specks which I knew must be the points of spears shining in the sun.

"What is it ?" I said.

"The Abanda, Lord, coming to block our road, two or three hundred of them. Listen, now. There in that cliff far above us is the only pass on this side of the mountain which runs through the cleft to the crater. The Abanda know that if they can reach the cliff before us we shall be cut off and killed, every one. But if we can reach it before them, we shall win through in safety to my own country, for there they will not follow us. Now it is a race between us as to which of us will first gain the mouth of the pass. See, already I have sent on the bearers," and he pointed to the line of them scrambling up the mountain-side several hundred yards ahead of us. "Let us follow them if you would continue to live."

By this time Arkle, Hans, and the two hunters had joined me. A few words sufficed to explain the situation, and off we went. Then ensued a struggle that I can only describe as fearsome. We who had marched far with little rest were tired ;

moreover we must climb uphill, whereas the Abanda savages were comparatively fresh and their path though rough lay more or less upon the flat ; therefore they could cover twice the distance in the same time. Lastly, Arkle, although so strong, was still stiff and footsore after his race for life upon the yesterday, which delayed his progress. The bearers who, it will be remembered, had the start of us, made wonderful time, notwithstanding their loads ; doubtless too they knew the Abanda and what would happen to them if they were overtaken. As we clambered up the mountain-side—heavens ! how the sun-scorched lava burned my feet—Hans gasped out :

"A lot of those fellows who were hunting the Bull-Baas, whom I wish we had never met, got away yesterday evening, Baas, and told their brothers, who have come to make us pay for those who didn't get away."

"No doubt," I grunted, "and what's more, I think they will reach the mouth of the pass—if there is one—before us."

"Yes, Baas, I think so too, for the Bull-Baas has a sore heel and walks slowly and that cliff is still some way ahead. But, Baas, the ones who escaped yesterday have told these fellows about what happened to those who didn't escape and what bullets are like. Perhaps we can hold them back with the rifles, Baas."

"Perhaps. At any rate we'll try. Look how fast Kaneke is going."

"Yes, Baas, he climbs like a baboon or a rock-rabbit. *He* doesn't mean to be caught by the Abanda, Baas, or his porters either, whatever happens to us. Suppose I sent a bullet after him, Baas, before he is out of shot, aiming at his legs to make him go a bit slower."

"No," I answered. "Let the brute run. We must take our chance."

At this moment Arkle, who was growing lamer, called out :

"Quatermain, get on with your servants. I'll look after myself."

"No, you won't," I replied. "We will sink or swim together."

Then I looked at Tom and Jerry and saw that they were alarmed, as well they might be. Hans saw it too, and began to fire sarcasms at them.

"Why don't you run, you brave hunters ?" he asked. "Will you let yourselves be beaten by the Owl-man ? If the rifles are heavy, you might leave them behind, as you remember you did when the elephants were after us."

Such were his rather bitter jests, for Hans would crack

jokes at Death itself. I know that afterwards he regretted them earnestly enough, as we often regret unkind words which it is too late to recall. They stung Tom to fury, for I heard him mutter :

"I'll kill you for this afterwards, yellow man," a threat at which Hans grinned.

The more phlegmatic Jerry, however, only smiled in a sickly fashion and made no reply.

At length we were quite close to the face of the cliff, into which we saw the porters vanishing, showing us where the pass or cleft began. Unfortunately, too, the Abanda were quite close to us ; indeed, their leading spearsmen had emerged from the fold in the mountain-side about three hundred yards away on to the open slope of lava, and were racing to cut off Kaneke. That active person, however, was too quick for them, as before they came within spear-cast of him he bolted into the cliff-face like a meer-cat into its hole—perhaps a snake would be a better simile.

"Now we are done," I said. "We can't get there before those brutes and it's no use trying to run down the hill, for they would overtake us. So we had better stay where we are to get our breath and make the best end we can."

"No, Baas," puffed Hans, who had been searching the scene with his hawk-like eyes. "Look. The Abanda are halting. They want to kill us, Baas, but there is a donga between them and the hole in the cliff. See, one of them is beginning to climb down it."

I looked. Although I had not observed it before, because it curved away from us, on our left there was a donga, that is a gully or crack, formed no doubt when the hot lava contracted ages before, which crack the Abanda must cross to reach us.

"Push on !" I cried. "We may beat them yet."

Forward we went, the lame Arkle resting his hand upon my shoulder. Now at last we were near the face of the cliff and, not more than sixty or seventy yards ahead of us, could see the crevice into which Kaneke and his crowd had vanished. Could we reach it ? As I wondered an Abanda appeared on this side of the donga. I halted, lifted my rifle, fired, and, so blown was I, missed him. Yes, I missed him clean, for I saw the bullet strike the spear-blade three feet above his head and shatter it to pieces. This seemed to frighten him, however, for he dropped back into the donga, and we pressed on.

When we had all but reached the cleft in the precipice that once had been the lip of the extinct volcano, whence I trusted, quite vainly as it proved, that Kaneke and his people would sally forth to help us, out of the donga appeared six or seven men who rushed between us and the cliff face in which we hoped to refuge.

There they stood preparing to attack us with their spears. We opened fire on them and this time did not miss. They went down, but as they fell more appeared, brave and terrible-looking fellows, furious at the death of their companions. We fired rapidly, forcing our way forward all the while, but I saw that the game was almost hopeless, for every moment more of these Abanda crawled up some narrow ladder or pathway from the bottom of the donga.

Then it was that I heard the Abyssinian hunter Tom call out:

"Run on, Macumazahn, with the lame master. Run on. I see how to stop them."

Without waiting to reflect how he proposed to do this, for at such moments one has little time to think ; with Arkle leaning on my shoulder and Hans at my side, I charged forward to the mouth of the cleft. Certain of the Abanda were between us and it, but with this we managed to deal with the help of our revolvers before they could stab us. Thus we reached the cleft and plunged into it, for, to my relief, no more Abanda appeared. Once in the mouth of the place, which was very narrow, so narrow and twisted that a few men could have held it against a thousand, as Horatius and his two companions held the bridge in the old Roman days, I stopped, for I heard firing still going on outside.

"Who is shooting ?" I asked, peering about me in the gloom of that hole, and as I spoke the echoes of the last shot died away and were followed by a savage yell of triumph.

"Little Holes and Jerry, I believe, Baas," answered Hans, wiping his brow with his sleeve, "though I do not think they will shoot any more. You see, Baas, for once in their lives they behaved very nicely. Yes, they ran to the edge of that donga and stuffed themselves into the mouths of the two paths by which these Abanda are climbing up it, firing away until they were speared, thus giving you and the Bull-Baas time to get into this hole, for of course they did not care what happened to me who was their friend. So I suppose that they are now dead, although perhaps they may have been taken alive."

"Great heavens !" I exclaimed. Then after a moment's reflection, in spite of the remonstrances of Hans (at the moment Arkle was ahead of us), I crept back to the mouth of the cleft and looked out, taking the risk of being speared.

He was right. Yonder on the lava plateau lay the bodies of Tom and Jerry, dragged there by the Abanda, one of whom was engaged in cutting off poor Jerry's head with a spear.

Filled with grief and fury, I put a bullet through that savage, which caused them all to scuttle back into their donga. Then, before they could recover from their surprise, followed by Hans I rushed out, seized Tom's rifle which one of them had been carrying and let fall in his fright, and bolted back with it into the mouth of the cleft. That of Jerry unfortunately we could not recover. I suppose it was carried away.

That was the end of those two brave but ill-fated hunters who, from the first day of our journey, had seemed to walk in the shadow of approaching doom. It was a very gallant end, for without doubt they had given their lives to save us, or rather to save me.

This indeed they had done, for by blocking the two exits of the steep-sided donga for a few minutes, they had enabled us to fight our way through into the cleft. Whether their courage was spontaneous, or whether it was induced by a sense of their previous failure when they had thrown away their guns, a trivial incident that seemed to prey upon their minds, and by the gibes of Hans, I do not know. At least in this moment of trial it asserted itself, with the result that they died and we lived. All honour to their memory! One of my hopes is that in some place and time unknown I may be able to thank them face to face.

I returned into the cleft filled with sorrow and told the others what had happened. Hans, to do him justice, when he saw that his guess—it was nothing more—had come true and that Tom and Jerry were really dead, was also much distressed. He began to talk of their many virtues and to rejoice that they, like himself, were "good Christians", and therefore had nothing to fear in the "Place of Fires", his synonym for heaven, which doubtless they were now inhabiting. Perhaps also his conscience smote him a little for all the sharp things which jealousy had caused him to say about them while they remained upon earth.

Arkle's attitude was different.

"These hunters," he said, "have died doing their duty, and therefore are not to be pitied, for how can one make a better end? But what of that fellow Kaneke, who ran ahead with his men and deserted you, his companions? I say nothing of myself, for I am a stranger towards whom he had no obligations. Why did he bolt?"

"I don't know," I answered wearily, "to save his skin, I suppose. You had better ask him if we ever meet again."

"I will !" exclaimed Arkle, and as he spoke I noted that his face was white with rage.

Soon the opportunity came. We thought it unwise to remain so near to the mouth of the cleft, although none of the Abanda so far had attempted to follow us, why, I could not imagine at the time, though it is true Kaneke had said it would be so. Therefore I suggested that we had better go on and find out whither the road led.

On we went accordingly, a darksome journey at first, for little light reached us in that deep and narrow hole. Presently, however, it widened and we found ourselves upon a kind of plateau bordered by cliffs.

Here Kaneke was waiting for us seated on a rock, the bearers having gone on ; at any rate I could see nothing of them. He stared at us with his sombre eyes and said to me :

"Knowing that you would be safe, Lord, I entered this passage before you and have waited for you here, where the Abanda will not follow us."

"So I see," I said sarcastically, "but pray, how did you know that we should be safe ?"

"I knew it, Lord, because it is written in your stars, as I knew that the two hunters would die because I saw death in their stars ; and they are dead, are they not ? As for the fate of the strange white man," and he looked at Arkle—malevolently, I thought—"I knew nothing, for I have not yet had time to study it in the heavens."

Before I could answer Arkle broke in, speaking very quietly in a low, fierce voice.

"No, you knew nothing, dog that you are, but I think that you hoped much, for you believed that to save himself this white lord would desert me who am lame, as you did, and that I should be speared. Well, I can read stars better than you, and I tell you that you will die before I shall and that what you lose I shall gain. Do you understand me ?—you who hope to be Chief of the Dabanda and Lord of the Lake with its Treasure, as I learned before ever I set eyes on you."

How had he learned this ? I wondered. At the moment I could not guess, but it was quite obvious to me, watching him, that Kaneke understood these dark words better than I did, for their effect upon him was remarkable. First he turned pale, or rather a kind of dirty white, as though with fear, a mood that was followed at once by one of fury. His big eyes rolled, foam appeared at the corners of his mouth, the hair of his face seemed to bristle.

"I know you," he cried, pointing to Arkle, "and why you have come here. Long ago my spirit warned me concerning you and your purpose. You hope to rob me again, as once you robbed me in the past, though that you have forgotten. For this reason I bribed the white hunter Macumazahn to accompany me here, knowing that without his help I was doomed to perish. But Fate has played me an evil trick. It was revealed to me that I should reach the land before you and be ready to make an end of you; revealed falsely, for while I tarried you came—you, the white thief. Still there is time. Never again shall you look upon the Treasure of the Lake."

As he hissed out these last words, suddenly Kaneke drew knife, a hideous curved knife of the Somali sort, and sprang at Arkle. He sprang swiftly as a lion on a drinking buck, and it flashed through my mind that all was over. Standing at a little distance with Hans, I could do nothing; there was no time, not even to draw a pistol; nothing except watch the end. It came, but in a strange fashion.

Arkle must have been waiting and ready. He did not move; he only stretched out his arms. Next instant, with his left hand he gripped the right arm of Kaneke, which was raised for the blow, and twisted it with such a grasp of iron that the knife fell to the ground. With his right he seized him by the throat and shook him as a mongoose shakes a snake. Then, putting out all his strength which in truth was that of a bull, Arkle loosed Kaneke's throat, gripped him in his arms, lifted him from his feet, and hurled him away so that he fell to the rocky ground, striking it with his back, and lay there senseless.

At this moment a little withered, keen-eyed man whom I had never seen before appeared from round a corner and, running across the open space to Arkle, whispered rapidly into his ear after the fashion of one who gives instructions. For quite a long time, or so it seemed to me, he whispered thus, while now and again Arkle nodded, showing that he understood the meaning of what he heard. At last the old fellow uttered a warning exclamation and pointed to Kaneke who, I saw, was recovering from his swoon. Then he ran back across the open space towards the corner of the cleft whence he had appeared, and for a minute I lost sight of him in its shadow.

Arkle picked up the knife, and, springing forward, set his foot upon the breast of Kaneke, who was trying to rise.

"Now, dog," he said, "shall I treat you as you would have treated me? I think it would be wisest. Or will you swear an oath?"

"I will swear," muttered Kaneke, fixing his eyes upon the knife.

"Good. Kneel before me."

Kaneke scrambled stiffly to his knees, and at this moment Hans nudged me and pointed. I looked and saw that from the corner of the cleft where the old man had vanished on the farther side of the open space, were advancing a number of the Dabanda, led, I think, by some of our bearers who no doubt had summoned them. They were tall, big-eyed men of the same type as Kaneke and the Abanda who had attacked us; by no means naked savages, however, as every one of them wore a long garment, apparently of linen, for the most part white in colour, though in some instances these robes had been dyed blue.

"Keep your rifle ready," I said to Hans, and waited developments.

If these men had meant to attack us—which I do not think—the strange sight before them caused them to abandon the idea, for all their attention seemed to be concentrated upon Kaneke kneeling at the white man's feet.

Arkle saw them also and called out in his big, booming voice:

"Welcome, Kumpana, and you, men of the Dabanda, guardians of the Treasure of the Lake. You come in a good hour. Listen now, while this Kaneke who I hear is a great one among you swears an oath of allegiance to me, the white wanderer from beyond the seas. Learn that but now he tried to murder me, springing at me with this knife to take me unaware, and that I overthrew him and spared his life. I say listen to the oath—and do you, O Snake Kaneke, repeated in a loud voice the words that I shall speak, so that all may hear them and make them known to the people of the Dabanda, the guardians of the Treasure of the Lake. Repeat them, I say, for if you refuse, you die."

Then he began thus, doubtless as Kumpana had taught him, and sentence by sentence Kaneke echoed his words:

"I, Kaneke, of the people of the Dabanda, tried teacherously to murder you, the white man from beyond the seas, but, being strong, you overcame me and gave me my life. Therefore I, Kaneke, bow myself to you henceforth, as your servant. All my rights and place among the Dabanda I give over to you.   Where I stood, there you stand ; henceforward my blood is in your body and all that comes to me with this blood is yours.   So I swear by the Engoi, the Shadow that rests upon the holy lake, and if I break the oath in word or deed, may the curse of the Engoi fall upon me."

All of this Kaneke repeated readily enough until he came to the words "So I swear by the Engoi", at which he jibbed, and indeed stopped dead.

"Continue," said Arkle, but he would not.

"As you will," went on Arkle, "but understand that if you refuse, you die, as a murderer deserves to do," and, bending down, he seized Kaneke by the hair with his left hand, preparing to cut off his head with the curved Somali knife.

Now Kaneke, evidently in a great fright, appealed to me.

"O Lord Macumazahn," he cried, "save my life, I pray you !"

"Why should I ?" I answered.   "Just now you deserted me and my people, so that my two brave hunters are dead.   Had you with the bearers stayed behind to fight with us, I think that they would not have been dead—but this you can talk over with them in that land whither you are going.   Again, you tried to murder the white lord for reasons which I do not understand, and after you had sworn to me that you would not harm him. By his strength he overthrew you, and now your life is justly forfeit to him.   Yet out of the greatness of his heart he offers to spare you if you will swear a certain oath to him upon a certain name.   You refuse to swear that oath upon that name.   So what more is there to be said ?"

By this time, although he had not seen them, for his back was towards them and they remained silent, watching these proceedings with a kind of fascinated stare, evidently Kaneke remembered that Arkle had addressed some of the Dabanda people, who must therefore be present.   To these he made his next appeal, calling out :

"Help me, O my brothers, you over whom I have been appointed to rule.   Would you see me done to death by this white wanderer who comes to our land for no good purpose ? Help me, O Guardians of the Holy Lake and of the Shadow that rests upon the lake."

"Yes," said Arkle.   "Come forward, you Dabanda, laying down your spears, for know that he who first lifts a spear shall be dealt with by the Lord Macumazahn.   Come forward, I say, and judge between me and this man."

To my astonishment those Dabanda obeyed.   They laid down their spears, every one of them, and advanced to within a few paces of us, led by the little withered old man with keen eyes, who moved as lightly and silently as does a cat, the same man who had whispered into Arkle's ear.   Arkle looked at this man and said :

"Greeting, Kumpana, my friend and guide.   I thank you for the counsel you gave to me but now, for I know you to be wise and great among your people and it was you who taught me all that I have learned of them and of this Kaneke.   Judge now between me and him.   You have heard the story.   According to your custom, is not this man's life forfeit to me whom he strove to murder ?"

"It is forfeit," answered Kumpana, "unless he buys it back with the oath which you have demanded of him."

"And if he swears that oath, must he not, under it, become my servant and give to me his place, his power, and his rights among the Dabanda ?"

"That is so, White Lord."

"And if he swears it and breaks the oath, what then, Kumpana ?"

"Then, Lord, you can loose upon him the curse of the Engoi, and it will surely be fulfilled.   Is it not so, Dabanda ?"

"It is so," they assented.

"You have heard, Kaneke ;   yes, out of the lips of your own people you have learned their law.   Choose now.   Will you swear, or will you die ?"

"I swear," said Kaneke hoarsely, as the sharp knife—his own—approached his neck.   "I swear," and slowly he repeated those words which before he had refused to speak, transferring all his rights and privileges to Arkle and calling down upon his own head the curse of the Engoi if he should break the oath.   I noticed that as he invoked this fate upon himself, the man shivered, and reflected that after all there might be something in the curse of the Engoi, or that he believed there was.   Indeed, sceptical as I am, I began to feel that all this queer story had more in it than I had hitherto imagined, and that I was coming to the heart of one of those Central African mysteries of which most white men only learn in the vaguest fashion, perhaps from prejudiced and unsympathetic sources, and then often enough but by obscure hints and symbolical fables.

F

The oath finished, Kaneke kissed the white man's foot, which I suppose was part of the ceremony, and strove to rise. But forcing him to his knees again, Arkle addressed the little withered old man who stood watching all.

"Tell me," he said, "who and what are you, Kumpana?"

"Lord, though I until now have hid it from you, I am the head of the Council of the Shadow, he who rules in this land when the Shadow has passed from the world and before she returns again."

"Are you then he who weds the Shadow, Kumpana?"

"Nay, Lord. He who is called Shield of the Shadow dies when the Shadow passes. I am but a minister, an executor of decrees. As such I led you to this land, whence you were hunted because you would not be obedient, but broke the law. Mighty must be the strength that guards you, or by now you would be dead."

"If I have erred, O Kumpana, I have paid the price of error. Am I, then, forgiven?"

"Lord, I think that you are forgiven, as this Kaneke, who also erred in his youth in a worse fashion, was forgiven, or rather," he added, correcting himself, "suffered to go unpunished."

"Who and what is Kaneke?" Arkle asked again.

"Kaneke is he who was destined to be the Shield of the Shadow when she appears to rule for her appointed day. For his sin against the Engoi he was driven from the land and lived far off, where the white lord who is called Watcher-by-Night found him. At the proper time he was ordered back that his fate might be fulfilled, and returned bringing the white lord, Watcher-by-Night, with him, as also was decreed. The rest you know."

"Kaneke tried to murder me and bought his life by a certain oath, selling to me his place and rights. Shall I then be known and named Shield of the Shadow in place of this Kaneke?"

"It would seem so, Lord," answered Kumpana, a little doubtfully as I thought. "But first the matter must be submitted to the Council of the Shadow, of which I am only one. It may be," he added after a pause, "that the Council will call upon you to buy the Shadow at a great price."

Then I, Allan, took up my parable, saying:

"Kumpana and men of the Dabanda, I, a white hunter, have been led, or trapped, into a land that is full of mysteries which as yet I do not understand. I have rescued this white lord when he was about to be killed. I have brought him here, fighting my way through warriors who seemed to be your enemies. In so doing I have lost two servants of mine, brave men whom I loved, who came to their deaths by the treachery of yonder Kaneke and therefore my heart is sore. He deserted us, hoping that in like fashion I should desert the other white lord who is lame, that thereby I might save my life. I did not desert him, and you have seen the end of that story. Now we are all weary, and sad because of the death of the two hunters who sacrificed themselves for us; hungry also, needing food and rest and sleep. The white lord whom you name Wanderer has made his bargain with you, a strange bargain which bewilders me. I would make mine, which is simpler. If I and my servant here, the yellow man, come on into your country, have we peace? Do you swear by the Engoi, who seems to be your goddess, and by the Shadow her priestess, that no harm shall come to us and that when I desire it in the future, I shall be helped to leave your country again, you giving me all that I may need for my journey? If you do not swear, then I turn and go back whence I came, if Heaven permits me to do so."

Kumpana spoke with some of his companions. Then he said:

"O Macumazahn, Watcher-by-Night, we swear these things to you by the Engoi. At least we swear that after you have finished the service, to work which we caused you to be brought hither, then you shall be sent hence in safety as you demand."

I reflected to myself that this promise was vague and qualified. Yet remembering that I should certainly extract none more favourable and being thoroughly worn out and quite unfit to face the Abanda who probably were waiting outside, I accepted it for what it was worth, and requested Kumpana to lead us to where we could eat and rest in safety.

CHAPTER XIII

BEFORE THE ALTAR

BY the time that we emerged from the pass, that really was nothing but a cleft or crack zig-zagging through the lava rock of the volcano's lips, which we did in complete safety, seeing no more of the Abanda, it was drawing towards evening and the plain beneath us was flooded with the light of the westering sun. It was a very wonderful plain, though, except for its size, of a sort not uncommon in the immense wilds of Africa. Looking at it stretching away for miles and miles, it was difficult to realize that it was nothing but the crater of some huge volcano, or group of volcanoes, which millions of years ago had been a lake of seething fire. Yet undoubtedly this was the case, for all round ran the precipice of rock that once had formed the wall of the outer crater. Now this wall enclosed a vast expanse of fertile land that sloped gently down to the confines of a forest.

Nor was that all, for from this height we could see that within the ring of forest, at the bottom of the crater-pit as it were, lay a great sheet of water, the holy lake that was named Mone. It looked handsome and terrifying enough at this hour when the tall forest trees that grew around cut off from its surface the light of the sinking sun, such a place as might well be the home of mysteries.

At that time, however, I was too tired to study scenery or indulge in speculations, and glad enough I felt when we were led to a kind of rest-house, or perhaps it was a watchman's shelter, that was hidden away in a grove of mountain palms. This place consisted of a thatched roof supported upon tree-trunks and enclosed with a fence of what looked like dried bulrushes, which formed the walls of the house. It was clean, comfortable, and airy ; moreover there must have been a cooking-place outside, for hot food was brought to us, of which I ate thankfully, being too exhausted to inquire its nature or whence it came.

Only one thing did I ask of Kumpana—whether it was necessary to set a guard. When he assured me that we were absolutely safe, I took him at his word and went to sleep, hoping for the best. I remember reflecting as my eyes closed that for some reason or other, humble individual as I was, I seemed too valuable to these people for them to wish to make away with me. So having ascertained that Kaneke was elsewhere, I just turned in and slept like a dog that has hunted all day, and I believe that Arkle did likewise.

When I woke the sun was high and Arkle had gone. I asked Hans what had become of him, saying that I feared foul play.

"Oh no, Baas," answered Hans. "You see that Baas Red-Bull, having conquered Kaneke, and bought his birthright from him in exchange for not sticking him like a pig—just like the man in the Bible, Baas—is now a great chief. So because he is lame those Dabanda brought a litter in which they set him and have carried him off. He told me to tell you that he did not wake you up because you were so tired, but that you would meet again at their head place, which is called Dabanda-town, Baas. Meanwhile you were to fear nothing."

"Which means that he has deserted us," I said.

"Oh no, Baas, I think not ; I think he went because he was obliged, and that we shall find him later on. You see, Baas, the Baas Red-Bull has become a priest and a chief, and such people are never their own masters. They seem to rule spirits and men, but really these rule them and order them about as they like. For the rest, Kumpana stays here to guard us, and breakfast is coming, so let us eat and be happy while we may, Baas."

The advice was good and I acted upon it at once. After a wash at the spring by which the rest-house was built, I ate an excellent breakfast, a stew of kid's flesh with quails in it, I remember it was, made memorable by the fact that after it Hans produced a skin bag full of excellent tobacco. On inquiry it appeared that the Dabanda grew this herb, and what is more, smoked it in cigarettes made of the soft sheath which covers the mealie cobs. Also, like the Bantu, they took it in the form of snuff.

By the way, what an interesting study would be that of the history of tobacco in Africa. Is it indigenous there, or was it perhaps introduced from some other land by the Arabs, or later by the Portuguese ? I don't know, but I remember how delighted I was to see it upon this occasion, when ours was exhausted and the spare supply a bearer carried in a box was discovered to have got wet in crossing a river and to be nothing but a mass of stinking mould. Some people inveigh against the use of tobacco, but to my mind it is one of the best gifts that Heaven has given to man.

Just as I had lit my pipe with delight and was testing the sample, which proved to be sweet and cool though rather strong, Kumpana arrived and asked if I was ready to start. I said yes, and off we went with a guard of ten Dabandas, marching downhill in the direction of the forest.

Now I saw that this vast crater was a wondrous and a most beautiful place, though it is true that its climate is hot. For the most part it was lightly timbered with large trees, a species of mahogany, many of them, mixed with cedars, growing in groups or singly, and interspersed with grassy glades after the fashion of some enormous park. Among these trees wandered great quantities of game ; thus I saw eland, koodoo, sable-antelope of a very large variety, and blue wildebeest, to mention a few of them, also bush-buck of a bigger kind than I had ever found anywhere in Africa.

It seemed, however, that the elephant and the rhinoceros did not live here ; nor, strange to say, were there any lions, which perhaps accounted for the great number of the various species of buck.   The birds, too, were numerous and beautiful ; and everywhere I noted lovely butterflies, some of which, of a brilliant blue colour, were of great size and flew high and as fast as swallows. In short, so far as its natural conditions were concerned, after the arid plains beyond the mountains, the place was a kind of earthly paradise ; well watered, also, by little streams that came from springs and ran down fern-clad ravines towards the lake.

As we went I talked with Kumpana, who, outwardly at any rate, proved to be a most agreeable and candid old gentleman. From him I gathered much information, true or false.   Thus I learned that his people were really star-worshippers, as were the Abanda who lived without the mountain, and knew a good deal of crude astronomy.

It seemed that originally the Abanda and the Dabanda were one race, but that "thousands of years ago", as he put it, they were ruled by two brothers, twins, who quarrelled.   Then ensued a civil war, in the course of which one brother murdered the other treacherously.   This angered the Engoi of that day, whom both of them aspired to wed ;   indeed, this was the cause of their difference.   She called down the curse of heaven upon the murderer and those who clung to him, divorcing them from her worship and causing them to be driven (whether by force of arms or by supernatural means, I could not discover) out of the earthly paradise of the crater on to the mountain slopes and plains beyond.

From that time forward, Kumpana explained, the Abanda had sought reunion with the goddess, both because of the material benefits they believed to be in her gift, such as rain and plenty, and for some spiritual reason that had to do with the fate of their souls after death.   This, however, they had never achieved, since the curse upon them continued from age to age.   Indeed, the prophecy was that their desire could not be fulfilled until a high priest of the Engoi, the husband or the affianced of the Shadow, she who was also called "the Treasure of the Lake" came to lead them back into the land of the Dabanda and made peace between them and the Engoi incarnate in the priestess known from generation to generation by the name of "Shadow", who, from birth till death, dwelt on the island in the holy Lake Mone. Until that hour, went on Kumpana, none of the Abanda dared to attempt to re-enter Mone-land, as the country encircled by the crater's walls was called.

"Why not, if they are so brave and numerous ?" I asked, astonished.

"Because, Lord, if they did the curse would fall upon them and they would perish miserably, I know not how. At least, so they believe, as we do ; and it is for this reason that from the moment you entered the pass of the cliff yesterday, you were safe. Had it been otherwise the Abanda would have followed you and killed you in the pass, for they were many and you were few. For this reason, too, we do not so much as guard that path and certain others."

Hearing this I reflected, first that I liked not the security. For what was the sum of it ? That a vast horde of savages, or semi-savages, who believed themselves to have been driven out of a kind of Garden of Eden by the flaming sword of a heavenly curse, although they were much more numerous and stronger than those who still dwelt in the Garden, and although the gates of that garden stood open, dared not enter them because they were sure that if they did so, the invisible sword of the curse that always hung over them would smite and destroy them.

Still, there seemed to be truth in the story, for otherwise why were we not followed into the unguarded cleft ? Doubtless the Abanda were frightened of our firearms, but seeing that we were but three men against hundreds, this was not enough to have held them back. No, the mighty hand which restrained them must, as Kumpana declared, have been that of spiritual fear.

Oh, what a force is superstition ; as I sometimes think, the greatest in the whole world, or at any rate in Africa. So mighty is it that when I contemplate its amazing power, at times I wonder whether in many of its developments it is not rooted deep in the soil of unappreciated and unknown truths.

Of these reflections of mine, however, I said nothing to my companion, because I thought it wiser to be silent. Yet I did ask him—if he felt at liberty to tell me and had the necessary knowledge—what part I and Arkle, whom he called "The Wanderer", had in all this business.

To my astonishment, instead of refusing to answer the question or thrusting it aside as natives can, he replied quite frankly that he did not know, or at any rate knew very little.

"The stars guide us, Lord," he said. "We consult them, as our fathers have done from the beginning ; we read their messages and obey their commands. Long ago the stars told us, speaking through the mouth of her who is named Shadow, not she who rules today, but she who went before her and has been gathered to the heavens, that in this year a great war would fall upon us—we do not know what war. More recently we were told, through the mouth of that Shadow who has faded, to call back Kaneke from the land where he dwelt because of his crime against her, that he might bring with him a certain white man whose name was your name, namely Watcher-by-Night. This command was sent to Kaneke and he obeyed it, as he must do or die ; for if he disobeyed, the messenger was commanded to bring death upon him, as she was commanded, if he obeyed, to protect him from all dangers. That is all we know of the reason of your coming, though now I see that if you had not come the other white lord would have been killed."

Reflecting that this tale about myself was, with variations, much the same as that told by Kaneke, something real enough to these people, but to me a mystery, and wondering if by any chance this fate-dealing messenger was White-Mouse, I left the subject and attacked one of more immediate interest, namely that of Arkle, saying outright :

"The white lord Wanderer told me that you, Kumpana, met him beyond the country of the Abanda and guided him into your own land. Why did you do this ?"

Kumpana's face changed ; it was as though a veil fell over his eyes and mild, intelligent features, a veil of secrecy.

"Lord," he answered, "there are matters of which it is scarcely lawful that I should speak, even to you who have come here to be our friend. I would have you understand that we Dabanda are not as other folk. We are a small people and an ancient who live by wisdom, not by strength, and this wisdom comes to us from heaven. We worship the stars, or rather the Strength beyond the stars, and from them come spirits who teach us through the mouth of the Lake-Dweller, Shadow, or otherwise, much that is not known even to the wise of the earth, such as yourself, Lord. They give us gifts of vision also, so that at times we can see into the darkness of the past, and even look beneath its curtain into the light of the future that blinds the eyes of other men.

"Moreover we, or some of us, have certain powers over Nature. Death indeed we must suffer like all who live. Yet we know that it is not death ; that it is but a door of darkness through which we pass to another house of flesh, a better or a worse house according to our deserts, that is yet inhabited by the same spirit. So, too, we have strength over beasts" (here I bethought me of Kaneke and the elephants), "which we can cause to obey us as though they were our dogs. You smile. Then, look upon those buck," and he pointed to a bunch of blue wildebeests, which I have always found wild and savage creatures, that were staring at us from among some trees about a hundred and fifty yards away. "Now I will call them, that you may believe."

Well, stepping a few paces to my right, call them he did, uttering cries in a kind of sing-song voice. The wildebeests seemed to listen. Then presently they moved slowly towards us, and soon were standing within a few yards of Kumpana, as cows might do that are waiting to be milked. There they stood, patient and submissive, until they caught my wind, when they snorted, whisked their tails, put down their heads and, to my great alarm, prepared to charge me. Just as Hans and I were about to fire to keep them off, Kumpana said something and waved his hands, as a beast-tamer does to his performing animals, whereon those gnus turned and gambolled off in their well-known lumbering fashion.

"They are no wildebeests, Baas," whispered Hans to me. "Like the elephants, they are men wearing the shape of brutes."

"Perhaps," I answered, for I was too mystified to argue ; also Kumpana was speaking again, saying :

"Now mayhap you will believe me when I tell you that we have power over the animals, who are as our brothers and not to be harmed by us ; so much power that we have driven those of them that can hurt men, such as lions, from our land ; yes, and evil reptiles also. Search where you will here, Lord, you will find no snakes," a statement which caused me to reflect that St. Patrick must have bequeathed his mantle to the Dabanda. "Thus, too," he went on, "we control sicknesses, summon rain, and hold off tempests, which is why we are reported to be a people of wizards."

"If so," I replied, "all this does not tell me why the white man Wanderer was guided by you and why afterwards he was driven away, as it seemed, to death."

"I guided him, Macumazahn, because I was so commanded, and because he is appointed to play a great part in our history, as once before he did in the past. He was driven away because he was disobedient and suffered folly to master him, for which

causes he must be punished and learn the taste of terror.   Ask
me no more concerning this lord, for I cannot answer you.   Yet
it may happen that before all is done you will learn the answer
for yourself."

Now I proposed, in my thirst for information, to put some
questions to him concerning the wondrous woman, or sacred
personage who was said to dwell in the lake, and who, as I
suspected, was an African version of the old legend of the
Water-Spirit which is to be found in many lands.   But when I
mentioned her name of Shadow, Kumpana turned upon me with
so fierce a look in his eyes, hitherto mild enough, that I grew
silent.

"Lord Macumazahn," he said, "I see that you do not believe
in our priestess, the Shadow of the Engoi whom we worship.
Though you have never said so to me, it is written on your face.
That is to be understood, for white men, I have heard, can be
very ignorant and scornful of faiths that are not their own.   Yet
I pray you do not make a mock of her to me, as I am sure you
were about to do.   I have answered all your other questions as
best I might, but as to her I answer none.   Nay, of her you must
learn for yourself" ;   and before I could reply or explain, he
departed to join the guard, leaving me alone with Hans.

"Baas," said that worthy, "you are always seeking new
adventures and strange peoples, and this time I think you have
found both.   These folk are all wizards, Baas, like Kaneke, and
we are caught in their web, where I expect they will suck us dry.
I think the Baas Red-Bull is a wizard also, for otherwise why was
he not killed ; and unless he is one of their brothers, why are these
Dabandas so glad to see him ?   Also, how did he learn so quickly
all that oath which he made Kaneke swear ?   Then there was
White-Mouse who, I am sure, was a witch, though a very pretty
one, for otherwise how could she have deceived *me*, Hans, as she
did, making me believe all sorts of things that were not true,
such as that she was a jealous wife of Kaneke who liked me for
myself ?   Oh, we have come into a land of spells where the
fierce wildebeests are as dogs and the passes are held by ghosts,
and I do not think we shall ever get out of it alive, Baas, unless
indeed, for their sport they turn us into animals, like elephants
and the wildebeests and hunt us hence."

Now I remembered that Tom and Jerry had talked in this
fashion, with good reason in their case ;   and looked at Hans
doubtfully, fearing lest he might have caught the infection.
However, this was not so, for as is common with primitive men

of mercurial nature, suddenly his mood changed, and, grinning, he said :

"Yet, Baas, though White-Mouse did blind me for a little while, these wizards will have to be very clever if they hope to deceive Hans, who is such a good Christian that he can defy the devil and who, moreover, has the reverend predicant, your father, for his friend and guide. Cheer up, Baas, for I think I shall bring you through safely, if only you will be guided by me and not let that Shadow woman make a fool of you, as White-Mouse did. Yes, yes, everything may still be well, and after all, perhaps those wildebeests were just tame buck like some that the Scotchman kept on his farm near Durban which used to come and feed out of his hand."

"Yes," I said, "no doubt they were tame, and I don't believe in the magic. Still, I should like to know what has become of the Baas Arkle."

Well, we walked on all day through that most lovely land, until towards evening we came upon patches of cultivated ground and drew near to the edge of the forest, where I saw that there was a town.

It was a straggling place and quite unprotected ; just a number of neat houses built of whitened clay and thatched with palm-leaves, or in some cases, having flat roofs of lime cement, standing, each of them, in a garden of its own on the borders of wide roads or streets. In short, this Dabanda town had nothing in common with the crowded cities, if they may be so called, which exist in Nigeria and elsewhere. It was just a sparsely populated village, such as may be seen by scores in certain districts of Eastern and Central Africa.

"If this is their big kraal, these Dabanda are but a little people, Baas," said the observant Hans.

I agreed with him. As I had noted during our march, their crater-land was wide and most fertile, but until we approached the town I saw few signs of cultivation. Here and there on the track that ran to the pass were two or three huts surrounded by gardens. Nor in these outlying districts were there many domestic animals ; they were almost entirely occupied by wild game. Near the town, however, we did see herds of cattle of a small breed, also flocks of long-haired goats. Clearly the Dabanda, so far as numbers were concerned, must have been but an insignificant tribe, relying for their protection upon moral forces rather than those of arms, a fact that seemed to bear out some of

Kumpana's statements as to the reason why the passes were left unfortified.

We entered the main street of the town which began nowhere in particular, and walked down it without exciting much attention. Occasionally a woman stared at us from the door-way of her house, or an old man stopped his work in a garden to see who the passers-by might be. Also from time to time a few grave-faced children, three or four perhaps, followed us for a little way, then stopped and returned whence they came. This I thought strange, for they could never before have seen a white man, except perhaps Arkle. But then everything about the Dabanda was strange ; evidently they were a folk apart, one of whose characteristics was a lack of curiosity.

To tell the truth, they gave me the impression of people living in a dream, or under a spell, human in form and mind, yet lacking some of the human attributes ; lotus-eaters who felt no need for energy or effort, because Nature fed them and they were, or considered themselves to be, god-guarded. Such was my first impression of these Dabanda, which in the main was confirmed by what I saw and learned of them in after days. I should add that they were all extremely good-looking, men and women together, but very like one another, as though from continual in-breeding ; remarkable, too, for their fine-cut features, light-coloured skin like to that of half-castes or Persians, straight hair and large, sleepy, owl-like eyes, of which I observed the pupils seemed to grow bigger after nightfall, as do those of certain animals that seek their food by night.

The long, wide street ended in an open area that for want of a better name I will call a market-place, where the ground was levelled and trodden hard. At intervals round half this area stood houses of a larger size than those that we had passed, occupied, as I guessed rightly, by the chief men of the tribe, with their wives and children, if they had any. The other half of the area was bounded by a dense forest formed of tall and solemn trees, which forest ran down to the borders of the lake that, as I had judged from my view of it from the higher land, lay at a distance of several miles from the town. In the centre of this open space stood three curious erections ; two pointed towers of rough stone, fifty or sixty feet high perhaps, with spiral stairways winding round them to their tops, and between these a large platform twenty feet or so in height, that looked like the base of an uncompleted pyramid, on which platform burned a fire.

"What are those, Baas ?" asked Hans.

"Watch-towers," I answered.

"What is the good of towers whence one can see nothing except the sky ?" asked Hans again.

Then I guessed their real object. They were observatories, and the truncated pyramid was a great altar where priests gathered and offered sacrifices. Of this I had little doubt, though I wondered what they sacrificed.

At the moment I had no time to make further observations, for just then we reached a house where Kumpana, who had rejoined us on the outskirts of the town, informed me I was to lodge. Though flat-roofed and somewhat larger than the rest, except one adjoining which I took to be that of the chief, like the others it was situated in a garden and had a veranda, from which a door-way led into the building. It consisted of one big, white-washed room, without windows. Such light as there was came through the open door-way, over which a mat was hung, to be used at night, for there was no door. Like the passes, the houses were undefended against attack or thieves ; indeed I learned afterwards that such a crime as theft was quite unknown in Mone-land.

In this room, to my delight, I found all our goods which had been carried by the Dabanda porters for so many weary marches. There were the spare rifles, the ammunition, the medicines, the cooking-pots, the clothes, the beads and cloth for presents— everything ; even the suspicious Hans could not discover that a single article was missing. While we were checking them, food that had been prepared in a cook-hut in the garden at the back of the house, was brought to us by a decently clothed old woman, who seemed to accept our presence without curiosity, also earthenware jars full of water and a tub burnt out of a block of wood in which to wash. This we did on the veranda, for the surrounding fence made the place quite private, and afterwards sat ourselves upon wooden stools which we found in the room, and ate a good meal.

By the time we had finished our food it was dark, and the old woman appeared again carrying two lighted earthenware lamps of an elegant boat-shaped pattern, filled with some kind of sweet-smelling vegetable oil in which floated wicks made of pith or fibre.

As there seemed nothing else to do and no one came near us, I began to take off my clothes in order to turn in upon one of the very comfortable-looking wooden bedsteads that had been provided for us.   This bedstead was of the kind that is common in Eastern Africa, having a cartel, as the Boers call it, strung with green hide and a mattress stiffed with dried grasses that gave a scent of hay.   Already my boots were off when Kumpana appeared and said that he had come to conduct us to a ceremony where we should see the other white lord who was called Wanderer.   This being what I most desired, I put them on again in a hurry and away we went.

Kumpana led us to the market- or gathering-place that I have described.   Here we found what I suppose was the entire adult population of the town, seated on the ground in front of the truncated pyramid of which I have spoken, the men upon one side and the women upon the other, as they might be in some high churches.   They were very quiet and orderly and for the most part engaged in smoking their native cigarettes.   We were conducted along a broad passage which was left between the men and the women, to the foot of the pyramid and up some twenty rough steps to the platform that proved to be quite a large place.

Here in front of a low altar, a primitive erection about twelve feet square built of blocks of black lava, upon which altar burned the fire that I have mentioned, stood three white-robed men facing the fire, whom I took to be priests, for their heads were shaved and they seemed to be engaged in prayer.   To the right of this altar, seated on a stool and clothed in a white robe like a Dabanda, was none other than Arkle, who, I am bound to say, so far as the firelight revealed him to me, looked very imposing in this costume.   Opposite to him, also clad in white and seated on a stool, was his enemy Kaneke.   Very fierce and sullen did he appear as he glowed at Arkle with his great, round eyes.   I noted at once that he was guarded, probably to prevent him from making another attack upon his rival, for behind him stood three tall men armed with spears.

A second stool was set by that of Arkle and to this I was conducted, Hans, who seemed rather uncomfortable and kept his hand upon the hilt of his revolver, being directed to stand behind me.   Then Kumpana left us and took up a position facing the audience midway between Arkle and Kaneke, with his back to the altar and the priests.   Here he stood silent ;   indeed, everyone was silent, and when I tried to whisper something to Arkle, he shook his head and laid his finger on his lips.

Very impressive was that silence.   Never shall I forget the scene as I saw it by the light of the young moon which changed its quarter that day, and of the bright stars burning in the deep-blue sky.   Not a breath of air was stirring.   To my left the great trees of the forest stood motionless in endless rows. To my right were the dim grey roofs of the town, and between them the crouching audience of robed Dabandas, looking few and small upon that wide expanse, the glowing tips of their cigarettes marking the ordered lines in which they sat, like men and women stricken with dumbness.   Then, within a few paces, the primeval altar upon which even the fire seemed to be subject to the general spell, for it burned brightly without a sound, and the three shaven priests bowing and waving their hands, but uttering no word.

I felt like one under a charm, which was not strange ; for so deep was this quiet that when I shifted my foot, causing the nails in my boot to grate upon the stone platform, the noise seemed quite loud, so loud that all turned their heads and looked at me as though I had done something outrageous and indecorous. This went on for quite a long time, till at length I felt an hysterical desire to rise and make a speech, just to show that I was still alive.   Indeed, I think that very soon our strained nerves would have caused either Hans or me to commit some indiscretion involving sound, when suddenly the chain of silence was broken by a melodious voice above us.

I stared to see whence it came, and for the first time observed that on the top of each of the tall columns which rose in front of the platform stood a white-robed figure, evidently engaged in observing the stars.   Instantly the chanting voice on the right-hand column was answered by a similar voice upon the left-hand column.   Then both of them sang something in unison, something sweet and solemn, though what it meant I could not understand, and as they sang, pointed with wands they held upwards to the heavens.

At this signal all present seemed to come to life, as in the story did the Sleeping Beauty and her court at the kiss of the Fairy Prince.   The audience or congregation below us began to talk with some eagerness, men calling across the passage to women, and *vice versa*.   Evidently they were discussing the message conveyed to them in the chant of the astrologers on the towers, telling them, I suppose, what those astrologers had read in the stars.   In the same way the three priests, ceasing from dumb show, broke into open prayer, which again I could not understand, because the language was probably archaic.   At any rate it differed so much from the dialect of Arabic used by these people that I could only distinguish one word, "Engoi", which was their name for the Divine.

Encouraged by this change of demeanour, I asked Arkle in English what it all meant and what he was doing there dressed up like a Dabanda.

"You forget, Quatermain," he answered, "that I have become a chief or a priest, or both, by virtue of what happened yesterday between me and the gentleman opposite. At least, I fill these offices on probation, for my true position is about to be settled at this meeting. For the rest, those men on the towers have been reading omens in the stars, though exactly what they read I cannot tell you. Now I think that they are about to make prayers or offerings to the planet Venus, which you can see blazing away up there near the moon, after which my case will be tried."

He was right. Having thrown something on to the fire, what it was I could not see, the three priests turned so as to face the congregation below and, pointing to Venus, began a hymn in which the whole audience joined, also pointing at the planet with their right hands. Even the astrologers on the towers pointed with their wands and took part in this chant, which was really very fine and moving, a great volume of rhythmical sound.

Presently Kumpana, who now stood in front of the three priests, acting apparently as a master of ceremonies, waved his arms, whereon the song ceased with a crash of sound. In the silence that ensued he began to speak, but so rapidly that I could make out very little of what he said. He may have been reciting ritual, as was suggested by the strange words and forms he used. Or perhaps he was repeating passages from ancient history. At length his address became less impetuous. He spoke more slowly, and in language that was easier to understand, so that I had no difficulty in discovering that he was telling the story of what had happened between Arkle and Kaneke in the pass ; of the attempted assassination of Arkle, of the overthrow of Kaneke, and of the oath that he had sworn to the victor. Finally he said :

"The stars, having been consulted by those who can read them, declare that Kaneke, who by the choice of that chief who went before him, was appointed to follow him as Chief of the Dabanda, the Holy People of the Lake and the Guardian of the Treasure of the Lake, and, after long punishment and exile, was named to be the Lord and Shield of the Shadow, is rejected from his place and stripped of his offices. They declare also that the stranger, who in this land is named Wanderer, he whom Kaneke tried to murder and to whom he swore the oath of submission and fidelity, giving up to him all rights and power in exchange for life, henceforward stands where Kaneke stood. Do you, O People of the Dabanda, to whom is revealed the secret mystery of the stranger that for ages has been hidden, accept the decree of the stars and depose Kaneke, setting up in his place the white lord, his conqueror?"

"We do," answered the audience, with such singular unanimity that I guessed all this scene to be formal and arranged.

"Kaneke," cried Kumpana, "you have heard the decrees of the stars and of the Holy People confirming your own oath. Do you obey?"

Now Kaneke sprang to his feet and answered in a great voice that seemed alive with rage:

"I do not obey. What I swore was to save my life and such oaths are binding upon no man. As for the decrees of the stars and of the people of the Dabanda, these are but tricks. I, too, am a master of the stars, and I read their writing otherwise, while the people are in the hands of the priests, who in their turn are in the hands of Kumpana and the Council who plot against me. The sin that I sinned in my youth against the Shadow, who has passed back to the Light which cast it, is purged by punishment. Moreover, was it half as great as that of this white thief, whom most justly I would have killed, he who, as I have heard, strove to do violence to the Treasure of the Lake, and for that cause was hunted from the land? But let that matter be. Who is this foreign man that you name Wanderer? What does he in our country? I know what the magicians declare, namely that, like myself, he is one long dead who has returned again; that he is the very king who fought with his brother to win the Treasure of the Lake, and drove his brother and those who clung to him over the mountain edge, where they became exiles and the fathers of the people of the Abanda. Yes, that king who, being wed to the Treasure of the Lake, was so beloved of her that when she knew death was near to her, she killed him that he might accompany her to heaven, a crime for which heaven brought woe upon her.

"So runs the tale, but I say that it is a lie told by the Council of the Shadow to favour this white wanderer, who has made great promises to them if they will give the Shadow into his keeping that he may steal her away, leaving them to rule the land."

This statement, I noticed, seemed to disturb the audience below, among whom, it appeared afterwards, Kaneke had many friends, members of his family and others who desired that he should be chief and wed the Shadow. These stirred impatiently as the meaning of the sacrilege came home to them and whispered to one another.

"Yes," went on Kaneke, "such is the accursed plot of the white stranger who is named Wanderer which has been revealed to me, a plot so wicked that the guardian spirits of the Lake and Forest cast him from our land that he might die by the spears of the Abanda. Yet he did not die, because he was saved by the other white man, the Lord Macumazahn whom I was commanded to lead to our country, doubtless that he might play his part in the plot and be rewarded of the thief his friend."

Here I remarked in a loud voice to Kaneke that he was a liar as well as a traitor, for I knew nothing of any plots, but he took no heed of me and continued :

"Therefore it was that I sought to execute justice upon this red-bearded lord who had escaped from the Abanda. Yet I was overcome not by strength, but by evil magic, and swore an oath to save my life who desired to live on that I might avenge you, the Holy People, upon him who would rob you of your Treasure and your Oracle."

At this point Arkle intervened in a businesslike and British fashion.

"You dirty dog !" he said. "You snake who spits poison at me whom you have failed to reach with your fangs. You traitor who deserted the lord Watcher-by-Night and brought about the death of his servants, because you hoped that it would mean my own death also, and afterwards tried to stab me whom you had sworn not to harm. You oath-breaker. I will not reason with you as to your falsehoods, but I am ready to fight you again, here and now and to the death. Yes, weary and lame as I am, I am ready to fight you under the stars you worship, before their altar and in the presence of your people and thus let Fate judge between us. Answer. Will you fight me again ?"

"I will not fight you, Red Wanderer, that I may once more be overcome by magic and butchered," shouted Kaneke. "Nay, I appeal from you and from your fellow plotters to our Lady, the Voice of the Engoi. If I am justly judged, if I have spoken what is not true, let her appear here and now and pass sentence on me with her own lips. Ay, Kumpana, chief of the Council of the

Shadow, summon the Shadow if you can, and let the people see her and hear her voice."

Thus he spoke in tones of triumph who, as I learned afterwards, knew well that never in their history had the Lake-dweller who was named Shadow come from the lake to the town to judge of any matter, and having spoken, sat himself down and waited.

Then in quiet tones Kumpana answered :

"O Kaneke, I will make prayer to the Shadow. Perchance she may be pleased to do as you desire, and come hither to give judgment in this cause in the presence of her people."

CHAPTER XIV

SHADOW

"WILL she come ?" I whispered to Arkle.

"Yes, I think so—that is, I hope so," he replied.

Then I guessed it was arranged that on one pretext or another the holy personage called Shadow or the Lake-Dweller, should make a public appearance that night. It might well be, and indeed probably was the case, that Kaneke's appeal to the head and source of the local law was but a happy accident which chanced to fit in with a preconceived plan. But, putting two and two together, that such a plan existed seemed to me more probable. After all there might be something in Arkle's story, which up till now I had held to spring from the illusions of a man who had suffered great hardships and had been hunted almost to death. I allude not to his dreams of a twin-soul awaiting him in some far-off place, which were of a character that has been heard of before in the case of young men and women of strong imagination and romantic nature, but to his tale of having actually met this lady on the shore of the sacred lake, after which he remembered no more until he found himself running for dear life from the spears of the Abanda.

According to this tale on that occasion his love-affair had made most satisfactory progress. The lady, it seemed, was a thorough convert to the twin-soul theory and alleged that what he had experienced were no myths but spiritual realities, or in other words that for years the two of them had been in some kind of mystical communion. Moreover the not unnatural conclusion of the matter was that he had embraced her. It was true that she protested, yet why ? Not because she was personally offended, and much less shocked or pained ; but for the reason that he was violating the sacred law of her country and thereby exposing himself, and possibly her also, to very terrible risks and danger, even of death—which in fact, whether from this or some other cause, nearly overtook him.

Well, always presuming that some such event took place, what was more natural than that these two young people should wish to meet again and to, so to speak, regularize their relationship ? Nothing can be more dangerous to either party among savage or semi-savage peoples, than that a stranger should become extremely intimate with a sanctified lady who by the custom of ages is vowed and sealed to the ruler of her tribe. But if that stranger himself becomes the ruler, the face of the problem changes.

Now it appeared that, for reasons which I could not pretend to fathom, this was exactly what was desired by the priestess herself and by some of her most important adherents. Otherwise why did Kumpana, the Prime Minister or head of the Council of the Shadow, go to meet Arkle far away and guide him through the Abanda and into the hidden country at great risk to himself ? And having done this and other things, would it be surprising if he had arranged a dramatic public appearance of that priestess, at which she was to recognize the stranger as the man of the prophecy, as chief, too, in place of one who had been given his life in exchange for his abdication of that and other offices, and consequently as her future husband ? Oh, the whole business was as clear as the tall observation tower in front of me ; such obvious manœuvres could not deceive a person of my acumen for a moment—or so I thought.

Now while I was reflecting thus, Kumpana had passed between the priests and, standing with his face to the fire upon the altar, was engaged in uttering some petition in a voice which I could not hear because he spoke very low and his back was towards me. Nor could I see much of him or anything else, for the reason that the observation tower I have just spoken of as so plainly visible, vanished from my sight, being suddenly obscured by clouds which appeared upon the face of the sky. They were thick tempest clouds, for I heard the muttering of distant thunder, and a breath of cold wind passed through the forest with a moaning noise. Indeed, everything became so dark that I whispered to Arkle to look out lest Kaneke should take advantage of the gloom to attack him. He made no answer ; his attention was so fixed upon other matters that he did not seem to hear me. He leaned forward, breathing heavily like a man under the stress of emotion, and stared at the fire upon the altar. I, too, stared at this fire, because in that gloom I could see little else except figures moving dimly against the background of the fire, which I took to be those of Kumpana and the priests.

The heart of the distant storm rolled away over the western cliffs of the crater, drawing the clouds after it and the half-moon appeared again. Its light falling direct upon the platform revealed a single figure standing in front of the altar, the tall figure of a woman arrayed in glittering robes, green they seemed to be, sewn with silver. Of her face I could only see that it was young, and fair-skinned like to that of a white woman, for it was shadowed by a dark veil which hung from her head, unless indeed what I took to be a veil was the mass of her black hair flowing over her shoulders. Her arms were bare except for bracelets of what looked like pearls fastened upon the wrists and above the elbows, and on her head she wore some kind of crown or fillet which added to her height and shone, but of what it was made I do not know.

The whole effect of this figure seen thus in the half-light and against a background of the altar with its flickering fire, was strangely impressive, mystic, and beautiful ; so much so that I remember catching my breath at its first appearance. If I had any doubt as to who this woman might be, it was removed by the audience on the plain who, with one voice cried :

"*Engoi ! Engoi !*" (a word that among them means, it seems, "Spirit" as well as "Divinity") and prostrated themselves.

Arkle, too, muttered something about "Shadow" and half rose as though to go to her, when an instinct warned me to catch him by the arm, whereon he sat down again and waited.

She fixed her fine eyes upon the face of old Kumpana, who stood in front of her but to her left, and began to speak in a very sweet low voice, that gave the suggestion of a chant learnt by heart rather than of ordinary talk, for in it was something dreamlike and rather unearthly. Indeed, it was unlike the voice and speech of any woman that I had ever heard, except one—and she was in an hypnotic trance. In fact, it reminded me forcibly of what the prophet Isaiah describes as the voice "of one that hath a familiar spirit" speaking "low out of the dust". Hearing it for the first time I felt rather frightened, because it suggested to my mind that this fair creature might be under an unholy spell, or even something more or less than mortal. Evidently Hans thought the same, for he muttered into my ear :

"Keep clear of that one, Baas, or she will bewitch you worse than White-Mouse. She is not a maiden but a spook. Yes, she is the queen of the spooks."

I hit him in the face with my elbow as a sign to be silent, though the thought did pass through my mind that there was an air about this lady which reminded me of White-Mouse, White-Mouse grown taller and more imposing. To my fancy they might well have been sisters.

Then in the midst of the deep quiet she spoke, or chanted as an oracle might do.

"I have been called. I come from where I dwell upon the water. In my secret place where I dwell with my maidens and no man may set his foot save he who is appointed to be my lord ; yes, there in the ancient halls built by a people that is no more, the swift messenger has brought me the message of my priests, and I have considered of their riddle. To it I, the Oracle inspired, give answer in the hearing of my people that all may learn my will and the will of That I serve :

"One," and she pointed to Kaneke with something in her hand, it looked like a little wand or sceptre of ivory, "who sinned against the Shadow that has faded, and was driven from the land, has returned again to take the place that was sworn to him according to the ancient law and to wed the Shadow that has risen from the House of Shadows. One," and she pointed to Arkle, "called hither by the decree of Fate, a wanderer from far, has come to the hidden land and suffered many things because in ignorance he broke its customs. One," and she pointed to me, "who, like the Wanderer also called hither by the decree of Fate, rescued him, the Wanderer, from death at the hands of the Abanda, my enemies. He who should be chief of the people and Shelter of the Shadow, foully strove to murder the white Wanderer, but was overthrown of him, and to save his life swore an oath upon my name and upon that whereof I am the Voice, that in return for breath he would sell his lordship and its rights. So he was spared and not slain, and became the servant of the Wanderer whom he would have murdered. Now, the message tells me, he takes back his oath and claims the chieftain-ship that was his heritage, and with it the Holy Bride. Is the case thus, O Priests and Ministers and People ?"

"It is thus," all answered with one voice, for even Kaneke attempted no denial.

Now she stared hard at Kumpana, as an actor might at the prompter in the wings, then seemed to catch her cue and went on :

"I, the Voice, speak the judgment that is set within my lips. Hearken. It is told, ay, and written in the secret records which are hidden yonder where I dwell, that once in a far age it chanced that he who was appointed to be the Shield of the Shadow, sought to slay another foully. But this other conquered that murderer, and in exchange for the gift of life bought from him his place and power and the Shadow of his day herself. Thence came a great war and the division of the people which endures until this hour. As it was, so let it be. I, the Voice, decree and declare that Kaneke, the murderer at heart and the oath-breaker, is no longer chief of the Dabanda and that never shall he be the Shield of the Shadow and her spouse. I decree and declare that his chieftainship has passed to the Wanderer lord whom he would have slain, and that with it passes the Shadow herself, should the Wanderer desire to clasp her for his hour. The Voice has spoken. Is the decree accepted, O Priests and Ministers and People ?"

The dreamy, mysterious tones died in the silence and again in a great volume of sound came the answer :

"It is accepted !" and a priest speaking out of the darkness added, "Kaneke called upon the Shadow to appear and give the judgment of the Engoi. The judgment has been given ; the Engoi has spoken by its oracle ; it is finished."

"It is not finished ; it is but begun," shouted Kaneke. "You who have bewitched the Shadow, call down a curse upon your souls and on her the curse of war."

Here his words came to a sudden end, for what reason I could not see, but I think that the guards threatened him with their spears, commanding his silence. Nor did she who was called Shadow seem to hear them, for once more she spoke in her cold, chirping voice like one who repeats a lesson in her sleep.

"Come hither, O Wanderer," she said, "to do me homage, and take from me the lordship of the Land of the Holy Lake, and if it be your pleasure, swear yourself to me, as I will swear myself to you. Or, do not come, if such be your will. For know, O

Wanderer, that with this rule goes trouble and the dread of death. Yonder man who would have murdered you spoke truth. War is at hand, and of that war the end is not shown to me. Mayhap in it you will find nothing save doom and loss. Choose, then."

"I have chosen," said Arkle, and rising, strove to walk to her, only to find that his hurts had stiffened so that now he could scarcely stand unaided.

"Help me !" he said, and a few seconds later was limping towards the altar supporting himself upon my shoulder. It was but a little way, yet that journey seemed long to me, perhaps because of its strangeness, perhaps because the concentrated interest of every watching man and woman beat upon me with such intensity that it hampered my physical powers. At length we reached the altar and the big, golden-bearded Arkle sank on to his knees before the goddess, for so they held her.

For the first time I could see her face, though even now not too clearly because her back was to the fire. Certainly it was beautiful ; the fine features, the curving lips, the large eyes, dark and tender, shining under the ivory pallor of her brows the masses of the black hair flowing from beneath her coronal —all were beautiful, as were her arms and shapely, tapering hands. Her tall figure, too, was full of girlish grace and yet of dignity, that of one born to command, while her shimmering robes, how fashioned or of what stuff I know not, were such as might have been worn by the creature of a dream and even suggested something unfamiliar to our world.

What could this woman be, I wondered, and from what blood did she spring ? Arab, Egyptian, Eastern ? I never learned the answer. One thing, however, I did learn then and there, namely that when the shell was off her, at heart she was very human. Her face showed it as she bent down over this man whom in some strange fashion she had drawn to her from half across the world. It was not the face of the priestess of some ancient, secret faith welcoming a worshipper, but rather that of a woman greeting her lover won at last. The lips trembled, the eyes filled with happy tears, her figure drooped ; she grew languid as though with an access of passion, her arms opened as if they would clasp him, then fell again when she remembered that eyes were on her—oh, that this man was everything to her I could not doubt !

With an evident effort of the will she recovered herself and began to speak again, but in a fuller and more natural voice than she had used when she played her part of cracle. Indeed it was so different that if her face had been hidden from me, I should not have thought the speaker to be the same.

"Wilt thou serve my people and accept lordship over them, O Wanderer?" she asked, probably in the adapted words of some ancient ritual.

"The lordship I have bought already, and I will serve them as best I may," he answered.

"Wilt thou do homage, O Wanderer, to me, Shadow, the Dweller in the Lake, the Oracle, the Priestess of the Engoi?"

"I will do you homage, O Shadow," he answered, and bent his head as though to kiss her sandalled feet or the hem of her robe.

She saw it and swiftly stretched out her arm, murmuring so low that only he and I could hear.

"Not my foot, my hand."

He took it and pressed it to his lips. Then with her little ivory sceptre she touched him on the brow twice, once to accept the homage, and next to give him all authority. Now she spoke for a third time, asking.

"Wilt thou swear thyself to me, that at the time appointed thou mayest take the Shadow to thee and for thine hour protect her on the path of Fate?"

This she said out loud so that all should hear, then before he could answer, made a sign to him to be silent, and added in a whisper,

"Bethink thee, O Beloved, before thou dost answer. Thou knowest the mystery and that our hearts have spoken together across the empty air, as once they spoke in an age bygone. Yet remember that I am not of thy land and race, that I am strange and secret, full of a wisdom that thou dost not understand, that my day is short and that when I die it is the law that thou diest also, so that together we may pass to another home of which thou dost not know and in which thou mayest not believe. Remember also that dangers are many, and it may be that never wilt thou hold me to thy heart. Therefore be warned ere thou tiest a cord that cannot be undone save by the sword of death. Dost thou understand?"

"I understand," he whispered back, "and on the chance that thou mayest be mine if only for an hour, I, who have risked much already, will risk the rest, I who love thee, and if need be, for love will die."

She sighed, so deeply that her whole frame shook as though with the joy of an intense relief, saying, still beneath her breath,

"So be it.   Now take the oath."

Then in a loud voice he said.

"I swear myself to thee, O Shadow.   Dost thou swear thyself to me ?"

"I swear myself," she began, but said no more, for at that moment Kaneke leapt upon her, swiftly as a leopard leaps upon a buck.   I suppose that while all watched the remarkable scene I have described, he had slipped from his guards.   What he meant to do I am not sure, but I imagine that trusting to his great strength, he intended to carry her off with the help of confederates among the people.   Or perhaps it was in his mind to kill her out of jealousy rather than see her give herself to another man.

The sequel was both swift and most amazing.   I did nothing, to my shame be it said ;   I was taken too much by surprise, and before I recovered myself that sequel was accomplished.   The priests did nothing either, being like myself overcome with astonishment.   Arkle was on his knees and even if he understood what was passing, being lame and stiff, could not rise from them without assistance.   Only from either side of the altar, or from behind it, white-draped figures seemed to flit forward.   I suppose these were the virgins of the Shadow, but really I cannot say, for their appearance was so quick, so mysterious and so vague that in that light they might quite well have been shades born of imagination, or even large white-winged birds seen for a moment in the light of the fire.   Nor, whatever they were, did they take any action that I could discern ;   they just came and presently were gone again.   Further, my attention was not fixed upon these appearances which I only saw out of the corner of my eye, as it were, but on the central figures, the lady called Shadow, and on her assailant, the owl-eyed Kaneke.

Evidently she saw him come, for her face grew frightened and she uttered a little cry.   Then in a twinkling her aspect changed, or so I fancied.   She drew herself up to her full height, her face hardened and became stern, the fear passed from it and was replaced by a cold anger.   As the man leapt on her she stretched out her arm, that in which she held the little sceptre and exclaimed.

"Be accursed !"

The effect upon Kaneke of these words, or of her mien, or of both, or of something that I could not see or appreciate, unless it were the flitting white figures, was wonderful.   I have compared his rush with that of a leopard.   Well, have you ever seen such a beast stopped by a bullet, not a bullet that killed it dead, but one that paralysed its nervous system with the shock of its impact, taking all the courage out of it, causing it to stop, to tremble, and finally to turn and flee for shelter ? If so, you will understand what happened to Kaneke better than I can describe it in writing.

He came to a standstill, so sudden that the weight of his charge caused him to slide forward for a foot or two upon the pavement. Then he appeared to collapse ; at least to my sight he looked actually smaller, I suppose because his breath left him, causing his body to shrink. Next he uttered a low cry of fear and, turning, fled like a flash, bounding down the steps that led to the altar and vanishing into the gloom.

I think that some ran after him, but of this I am not sure. If so, perhaps it was the faint indefinite figures that I have described, for I lost him in a kind of white mist that may of course have been an effect caused by the robes of those who followed.

To tell the truth I did not look long, because Arkle, who was struggling to his feet, uttered an exclamation which caused me to turn my head and perceive that the Shadow lady was no longer there.

"Where is she ?" I asked.

"I don't know," he answered. "I think women came and took her away, but it was all so confused I cannot swear."

Then the gathering broke up in tumult. Kumpana and others escorted us down the steps, Arkle still leaning on my shoulder and expostulating, for naturally enough he wished to follow the Shadow, which he was not allowed to do. At the foot of the steps we were separated, he being helped off I knew not where, while I was taken back to the guest-house.

"We will meet tomorrow," he called after me, and I replied that I hoped so. Then he and his escort vanished into the darkness.

"Baas," said Hans, as I began to undress, "it is almost a pity that those Abanda did not catch the Baas Red-Bull."

"Why ?" I asked wearily.

"For two reasons, Baas. If he had been killed he would have been saved a great deal of trouble, who now is caught like a fly in a spider's web. You know the sort of spider, Baas, which bites the fly and sends it to sleep for days or weeks, until it wants to eat it. The fly looks quite happy and so it is until the eating begins, when it wakes up and kicks because it can't buzz as its wings have been pulled off. Well, that is what will happen to the Red Baas. The pretty-painted spider has got him and made him drunk and he will be quite happy, not knowing that his wings have been pulled off until the time comes when he wakes up to be sacrificed, or something of that sort, Baas. That's the first reason."

Now I bethought me that as usual there was wisdom in Hans' cynical remarks and metaphors. Undoubtedly Arkle was entangled in an evil web, and what was the fate which lay before him, a white man of good birth and education and presumably a Christian? He was beloved of a beautiful and mystic woman whom he in turn adored and probably in due course would marry.

This seemed pleasant enough, and natural—if bizarre. Could he have taken the lady away to his own land perhaps the adventure might even have proved successful in a matrimonial sense. But what were the facts? Departure was impossible for her and for him also. Once he was wed to her, here he must remain to the end of the chapter.

Moreover for a bridal dower he took with her a mass of obscure and dangerous superstitions, as to which only one thing was clear, namely that, as I had heard her declare with her own lips, these would involve the pair of them in certain death, possibly quite soon, and surely at no very distant date. Of course he might maintain that he had been given fair warning and that the price he must pay was not too high for what he won. But then he was not in a state to judge with an even mind, and as an individual of his own race and standing with some experience of the world, I could not agree with this view of his case.

Such were some of the thoughts that passed through my mind, but of these I said nothing to Hans, contenting myself with asking his second reason.

"Oh, Baas, it is this," he answered. "If the Red Baas were out of the way, you would have been put in his place, as I dare say will happen after all if Kaneke manages to murder him, or those priests change their minds about him."

"Thank you," I said, "and what then?"

"Then, Baas, as happy married pair always does, you would set up house on that island, which otherwise we shall never see, and find out where they keep their gold and other things that are worth money, of which I learn they have plenty hidden away on the island, although this silly people does not use them because they are a holy, ancient treasure, Baas, that has been there for hundreds or thousands of years."

"And if this treasure exists and I found it, what next, Hans?"

"Why, then, Baas, of course you would steal it and get away, leaving the lady to look at the empty boxes, Baas. Perhaps you think it would be difficult, but Hans would manage it all for you. Priests can always be bought, Baas, and as for oaths and the rest," he added, springing to a very pinnacle of immorality, "good Christians like you and me wouldn't need to bother about *them*, Baas, because you see they have all to do with the devil. So we should get away very rich and be happy to the end of our lives. But," he went on with a sigh, "it is nothing but a nice dream, because the Red Baas stands in our way, Unless indeed"— here he brightened up—"we can make a bargain with him and go shares in everything that he gets."

I did not try to argue with Hans because his lack of moral sense, real or assumed, was, so to speak, quite out of shot of argument. So I only said :

"I should be glad enough to get out of this place without any treasure, if only I could do so with a whole skin. Did you hear all the talk about war?"

"Oh yes, Baas. From the beginning that owl-man Kaneke has said that there would be war, which was why he brought you here."

"Well, Hans, if it is to be with the Abanda, I don't see what chance these Dabanda will have, for they are but a handful."

"None, Baas, if the fight were with spears. But they don't trust to spears ; they trust to magic of which there is plenty in this land. Didn't you see when the Engoi woman cursed Kaneke, how he curled up, just as though she had kicked him in the stomach, Baas, and ran away, although a minute before he had meant to carry her off with the help of his friends, of whom no doubt he has plenty? That was magic, Baas."

I shrugged my shoulders and answered :

"I think it was scare and a guilty conscience. But I don't understand about this Kaneke. Why, if they don't like him, was he ever brought away from the place where he was living? Why did White-Mouse insist upon our rescuing him, and a dozen other things?"

"Oh, for lots of reasons, Baas. While he was named as the Chief-to-be, no one else could take his place according to their law. That is one. Also no one else could guide you to this country. That is another. Also he had to come because the Shadow Lady said so, something to do with their fetish business,

or prophecies, Baas ; you will never learn what makes the minds
of spook-people like these Dabanda turn this way or that."

"I dare say not. What I should like to learn is whether our
friend Kaneke is alive or dead."

"Alive, I think, Baas ; yes, I am almost sure that he got
away by the help of his friends in the crowd below, though I
dare say that the curses of the Shadow Queen went with him ;
indeed I thought I saw them following him like white owls. I
expect we shall see and hear plenty more of Kaneke, Baas."

As usual Hans was quite right ; we did.

CHAPTER XV

LAKE MONE AND THE FOREST

AFTER this tumultuous and exciting night I spent a very quiet
time at Dabanda-town, where for the next ten days or so nothing
happened that could be called remarkable.

Grateful enough I was to rest thus awhile, because our long
journey had tired me out and I found it delightful to enjoy repose
and leisure in a climate which although hot, was on the whole
delicious. Still as I am an active-minded person, I took advantage of this pause to learn all I could about the Dabanda and their
enemies, the Abanda, only to find that in the end I had really
learned very little. Kumpana and other members of the Council
came to see me frequently and talked with great openness upon
many matters, but when I came to boil down their conversation,
the residium was small enough.

I was told that Kaneke had escaped, as they said, "by
making himself invisible", a feat in which no doubt the darkness
helped him. Where he had gone, they were not sure. Possibly,
they said, he had turned traitor and run away to the Abanda,
though such a crime had never been heard of in their history. Or
he might have returned towards the country where I had met him.
Or possibly he was dead, killed by the curse of the Engoi, though
they did not think this probable, for being himself a magician
and one of the initiated, he knew how to fashion shields which
would turn aside or delay the deadliest curses.

My inquiries upon other matters were almost equally unfruitful. I asked when the promised war would come and was informed that they did not know, but that no doubt it "would happen at the time appointed".

Nor would they tell me anything definite about the lady called Shadow, whom I had seen upon the altar platform. They were, they asserted, ignorant of what caused her to be fairer-skinned and more beautiful than other women ; they only knew that for many generations the Lake-Dweller always had been so ; it was a family gift. They admitted that she lived upon an island in the waters of Mone, in the company of certain virgins who dwelt with her in ancient buildings erected by an unknown and forgotten people, but of these buildings and the fashion of her life there they could say nothing, as none of them had ever visited the place, upon which it was unlawful for any man to set foot except the husband of the Engoi after marriage, and so on.

Thus it came about that at last I abandoned inquiries, which led to no result, for the very good reason that those whom I questioned were determined to tell me nothing, and fell back upon my own powers of observation, assisted by those of Hans. Being allowed to do so with an escort, I walked about the country, but saw nothing worthy of note.

Here and there were little villages inhabited by a handful of people, and round these some cultivated fields, also grazing grounds on which were herded cattle of a small breed and goats, but no true woolled sheep, creatures that would not thrive in so hot a district. The rest of the land, which was of extraordinary richness and could have supported ten times as many people, was given up to game of every variety except, as I have said, those that are harmful to man, which did not exist there.

The animals were wonderfully tame ; indeed one could walk among them as Adam and Eve are reported to have done in the Garden of Eden. Again I asked Kumpana and others how this came about and was answered—because of the spell laid upon them, also because they were never molested or killed for food. I inquired why and was informed because they were holy, taboo in short, as Father Ambrose had heard from the slave in bygone years. Then for the first time I discovered that the Dabanda believed that after death the spirits of men, or those of certain men of their race, passed into the bodies of animals ; also that sometimes this happened before birth.

It was for this reason that the beasts were not touched, since nobody likes to put a spear through his grandmother or his future child.

Next I referred to the elephants we had met outside their country, over which Kaneke seemed to have control, and inquired how this happened. The reply was that these beasts or their progenitors had once lived in Mone-land, whence they were driven, or "requested to leave" as Kumpana put it, because they did so much mischief, which accounted for the mystery.

My own view, of course, is (or, perhaps I should say, was) that the creatures were tame because no man ever harmed them, but I quote the story as an example of the superstitions of these star-worshippers. To many African tribes certain creatures are taboo, but never before or since have I heard of one to which all game was sacred, perchance because no other of small numbers has so rich a food supply that it needs to be supplemented by the flesh of wild animals. Among the Dabanda, however, this was so.

Their fertile soil, amply watered by rain and streams, needed but to be scratched to yield abundantly of corn and various roots and vegetables, while their numerous flocks and herds furnished all the milk and meat they required. Therefore there was no necessity for them to undertake the risk and toil of hunting, with the result that those beasts which they never killed, in the course of time naturally became both tame and sacred.

Having finished such investigation of the country as I was allowed to make—all approach to the lip of the crater was, I should explain, forbidden to me—I was seized with a great desire to explore the forest land and to look upon the sacred waters of the Lake Mone.

At first, when I mentioned this matter, Kumpana always turned the subject, but ultimately on the day of full moon, he said that if I so desired, he was ready to conduct me through the forest so that I might look upon the lake by moonlight, adding that it was not lawful for any man to enter this forest, much less to see the lake, in the daytime.

Of course I jumped at the offer, and shortly after moonrise we started, three of us, Kumpana, I, and Hans, whom at first Kumpana wished to leave behind. Indeed he only gave way on the point when I refused to go without him, while Hans on his part remarked, in infamous Arabic, that it has always been his custom to shoot anyone who tried to separate him from his master.

Within five minutes we found ourselves in a pit of blackness. That forest must have been dark at noonday, and at night, even when there was a full moon, it was like a coal-mine. We could only get along at all by help of some yards of the stem of a creeper of which Kumpana held one end. Then I grasped it at a distance of a few feet, and lastly came Hans holding to the other end.

It may be asked how Kumpana could see his way.

The answer is—that I do not know, but he led us quite briskly along some path that I was unable to perceive, which wound in and out through the trunks of giant trees, and skirted some that had fallen. Thus we walked for some hours, only seeing a ray of light now and then where a tree, dead and devoid of leaf, allowed it to reach the ground.

At length this forest ceased as suddenly as it had begun, and we stood upon the broad beach of the lake, most of which doubtless was covered in times of heavy rain.

Oh, how desolate was that great sheet of water glimmering in the bright moonlight, and yet how beautiful, set in its ring of forest land. Save for the soughing sound of wildfowl flighting far out of sight, and the occasional croak of a frog, it was utterly silent. Its lonesomeness was oppressive, almost terrible, for no beasts seemed to frequent it ; nor did I see or hear so much as a fish stirring ; well could I understand that a semi-savage race should deem it to be holy and haunted. Far away I could see the island on which the priestess Shadow was said to dwell, and noted that it was large, over a mile long as I judged, though how wide it may have been of course I did not know. What is more, I could distinguish buildings amidst the palms which grew upon this island.

Taking my glasses, very good ones of a German make which were fitted with a lens for use at night, I studied the place and saw at once that these building were large, massive, and apparently covered with sculpture. They seemed to be constructed of lime-stone or alabaster, or some other white rock such as marble, and before them stood gateways and towers, certain of which looked as though they were half in ruins. In architecture and style they were totally different from any that I knew of in Africa, not excepting the Zimbabwe ruins.

They had, however, a distinct resemblance to the remains of the temples of Old Egypt which at that time I had never seen except in pictures. There were what might be pylon gates ; there were walls covered with great carvings ; there were courts with pillars in them, for the end of one of these had fallen down or never been completed, and with the glasses I could see the columns.

G

The sight thrilled me.   Was it possible that these mysterious buildings had been erected by people from Ancient Egypt, or even by some race that afterwards had migrated to Egypt, taking their architecture with them ?   Now that I come to think of it, the truncated-pyramid outside the town where stood the stone altar upon which the fire burned, suggested that this might be so.

I turned to Kumpana and questioned him closely, but he could, or would, tell me very little. He repeated that he had never been on the island "in the flesh" for the reasons that he had already explained, but that he understood the buildings there to be tremendous, of a sort indeed to defy time for thousands upon thousands of years.   There was no record of their construction, or of the people who had accomplished this mighty work and dwelt there.   Not so much as a tradition survived.   Time had eaten up their name and race, though perhaps the sculptures might tell something to anyone who learned enough to understand them.   For the rest from generation to generation they had always been sacred to the Engoi and the home of her who for her day was known as Shadow, and her virgins.

"Can I not visit them ?" I asked.

I saw a sarcastic smile upon Kumpana's wrinkled old face as he answered.

"Oh yes, Lord, if you are a very good swimmer.   Only should you live to reach the island the women there will tear you to pieces."

Now since then I have often thought that this was rubbish, for surely women who lived in such an unnatural state would be glad to satisfy their curiosity by inspecting even so unfavourable a specimen of the male sex as myself, that is, if there were any truth at all in this tale of an African nunnery or Order of Virgins, like those of the Sun in Old Peru or the Vestals of Rome.   At the time, however, all I thought of was the fate of the men who intruded upon the women's mysteries in ancient Greece, which was not one that I wished to share.

Today I am sorry that I did not show more pluck and have a try to reach that island, but then the adventure appalled me and our lost chances never return again.   Not that I believed the story about the nuns, for I felt quite sure that if no one ever visited the island, these sometimes made a trip to the lake shore, as, according to Arkle, the Shadow herself had done. Kumpana's tale, however, was that their numbers were kept up by votaries who joined them every year from the mainland, picked girls of the age of twelve who were called "slaves of the Engoi".

While I was talking to him Hans, who had the sight of a vulture, said in Dutch.

"Look, Baas. The women are coming out of that big house."

Raising my glasses I saw that he was right, for a procession of white-robed figures emerged from under a gateway and walked in procession down to the water's edge. Here they must have entered boats, though, owing to the shadow of palms which grew upon the island shore, I could not see them do so, for presently three large canoes, each containing five or six women, appeared upon the tranquil bosom of the lake and were paddled slowly towards us. (Who made the canoes if no man ever visited the island? I wondered.) In much excitement I asked if they were coming to see me as I might not go to see them; but again Kumpana smiled and shook his head.

On they glided till they were within about two hundred yards from where we stood. Then they halted in a line and began a sweet and plaintive chant, of which in that great stillness the sound reached us clearly.

"What are they doing?" I asked. "Making an offering to the full moon?"

"Yes, Lord," Kumpana answered, "and I think something more."

He was right. There was "something more", for presently the women in the central canoe bent down and lifted a white draped form which they cast over the prow, so that it fell into the water with a large splash and vanished there.

"Is it a funeral?" I asked again.

"No doubt, Lord. See, they throw flowers on to the water where the body sank."

That was his reply, but something in his tone caused uncomfortable doubts to rise in my mind. What if the form wrapped in those white veils was quick—not dead? What if this rite was not one of burial but of sacrifice or execution? Here I may state that afterwards Hans swore that he saw the draped shape struggle, but as I did not, this may have been his imagination.

Still the business was eerie and made me shiver; so much so that I was not sorry when the women turned the canoe-heads islandwards, and departed still singing, or even when Kumpana said it was time for us to follow their example and go home. To my mind there was something weird, even unholy, about this sacred lake and island, where rose fantastic buildings of unknown age inhabited by night-haunting women who made offerings to the full moon, as the old Egyptians might have done, and I believe did to Nut or Hathor, ominous offerings shaped like a human corpse.   And if this was so with these, the forest was even worse, as I have now to tell.

We entered its shapes guided as before by Kumpana with the help of the creeper-stem.   Somehow it depressed me more even than it had done upon our journey lakewards, perhaps because my nerves were jangled by all that I have described.   At any rate, I suppose in an instinctive endeavour to keep up my spirits, I entered into conversation with Hans behind me, speaking perhaps rather more loudly than was necessary as a kind of challenge to that overpowering silence.

I need not repeat our conversation in detail, or further than to say that it had to do with the Dabandas, their superstitions, and their pretentions to magical powers.   Speaking in Dutch, and sometimes in English, so that Kumpana might not understand me, I criticized these in no measured terms, announcing my belief that they were rubbish and that the Dabanda priests and magicians were a set of infernal humbugs.   Hans, always argumentative, combated this view and gave it as his opinion that the Dabanda, from Kaneke and Kumpana down, were particular favourites of the devil.

At this point Kumpana looked back and remarked somewhat sternly that it was well not to talk so loudly in the forest lest the spirits who had their home there should be angered.

Then I lost my temper and expressed entire disbelief in these spirits, asking him too well what he meant by trying to fool a white man with talk of tree-dwelling spirits, and whether he was referring to monkeys which we knew lived in such places and were reported sometimes to pelt travellers through them with sticks or nuts.

Apparently Kumpana did not appreciate the joke, for he looked back at me (I could see him because at the moment we were wading through a little swamp where no trees grew), with an expression on his face that I thought threatening, and said with cold courtesy :

"I pray you to be silent, Lord Macumazahn, and above all not to offer insults to the masters of this place."

This made me angrier than ever.   Was I, a more or less educated Christian man, to have my mouth stopped with the mud of such heathen mumbo-jumbo stuff ?   Certainly not.   Therefore

I continued my argument with Hans, speaking more loudly than before. Hans replied with sarcasm which was the more irritating because it contained a grain of truth, that the real reason I talked thus was that I was afraid and therefore made a noise to shout down my fear, as children do. Then he went on with a garbled version of the story of the Witch of Endor who, he declared, I think erroneously, also lived in a wood, and to quote absurd remarks about witchcraft, which he attributed to my poor old father, adding his devout hope that he, "the reverend Predikant" as he called him, was keeping an eye upon us at that moment.

Truly I believe that there must have been some exciting quality in the air of that forest, exhaled perhaps by the foliage or flowers of certain trees or creepers that grew there, for at this point a kind of rage possessed me which caused me to rate and objurgate Hans, begging him to be good enough not to take my father's name in vain and put words in his mouth that he had never spoken, in order to justify his low, savage beliefs in ghosts and magic.

Just then we came to a spot where a great tree had fallen, breaking down others in its descent and allowing the moonlight to reach us for a few paces. As we went round the stump of this prostrate tree Kumpana turned again, saying :

"I have warned you and you will not listen. White stranger, I shall warn you no more."

I looked at the man and it struck me that his aspect had changed. No longer did he seem the little withered old fellow with shrewd eyes and a wrinkled, rather kindly, if cunning, face to whom I was accustomed. He apperaed to have grown taller and to have acquired a fierce cast of countenance, while his eyes glowed like those of a lion in a cave.

Remembering that moonlight plays strange tricks and that his added height must be due to the fact that he was standing on a root of the fallen tree, I took no heed, but continued to wrangle with Hans like one who has had too much to drink, or is half under the influence of laughing-gas. Then we proceeded as before and presently were again enveloped in the utter gloom of the forest. Suddenly I was brought to a standstill by butting into the trunk of a tree, while Hans behind ran the muzzle of his rifle into my back.

"Where are you going, Kumpana ?" I asked indignantly, but there was no answer.

Then to call his attention I pulled at the vine-like creeper that

served us as a rope. It flew back and flicked me in the face ;
no one was holding it !

"Hans !" I exclaimed. "Kumpana has given us the slip."

"Yes, Baas," he answered. "I thought something of that
sort would happen, Baas, if you would keep on spitting in the
faces of the forest spirits, of which probably he is one himself."

I reflected a while and had an idea.

"Let us get back to the place where there is light, and think
things over," I said.

"Yes, Baas," he answered. "Lead on, Baas, for I don't
know the way and can't see our spoor in the dark."

I turned and started, with the most disastrous results. Before
we had gone ten paces I crashed into another tree-trunk and
hurt myself considerably. Circumventing this, presently I
plunged into a piece of swampy ground and sank over my knees
in tenacious mud, out of which Hans pulled me with difficulty.
Once more we started with my boots full of water, but before I
had taken five steps I became entangled in some thorny creeper
which pricked me horribly. Freeing myself at length I stepped
forward again, only to catch my foot in a root and fall on my
face. Then I sat down and said things which I prefer not to
record.

"It is very difficult, Baas, to find one's way in a big wood
when it is quite dark," remarked Hans blandly. "What does
the Baas wish to do now ?"

"Stop here till it grows lighter, I suppose, if it ever does in
this infernal place," I answered. Then I filled my pipe and finding
that I had lost my matches, probably when I fell, I asked Hans
for one.

He produced his cherished box, of which we had not too many
left, and having first filled his own pipe, struck a match and handed
it to me. As I took it I remembered noticing how steadily the
flame burned in that utterly still air. Then I lifted the match
to my pipe and as I did so something blew it out.

"Why did you do that ?" I asked angrily of Hans. "Are
you afraid of setting the forest on fire ?"

"Yes, Baas—I mean no, Baas. I mean I didn't blow it out,
Baas. A monkey blew it out ; I saw its ugly face," replied Hans
in a voice that suggested to me that he was frightened.

"Rubbish !" I exclaimed. "Give me another match."

He obeyed rather unwillingly and the same thing happened,
no doubt because there was a current of air which passed between
the tree-trunks in puffs.

Well, my desire to smoke suddenly departed and I told Hans that we must not waste any more matches in such a draughty spot. He agreed and set his back firmly against mine, explaining that he was cold, a palpable lie as the heat in that stifling place was so great that we both ran with perspiration.

"Now be still and don't talk ; I am going to sleep. You can wake me up at dawn." I said.

Scarcely were the words out of my mouth, when distinctly I heard laughter, of a queer sort it is true, for it was singularly mirthless, but still eerie laughter which appeared to come first from one quarter and then another.

"That old fool, Kumpana, is making fun of us all the time," I said. "He shall laugh the wrong side of his mouth—if I catch him."

"Yes, Baas, only now he seems to be laughing on all sides of his face and from everywhere at once——" Hans began, but the rest of his remarks were lost in a peal of unholy merriment.

It came, as he said, "from everywhere at once", and seemingly even from above our heads.

"What the deuce is it—hyenas ?" I asked.

"No, Baas, it's spooks, very bad spooks. Oh, Baas, why would you come into this accursed forest to look at a lake where they drown people at midnight, and then sneer at the devils of the place and call them monkeys ? I am going to pray to your reverend father, Baas, hoping that he will hear me in the Place of Fires. For if he can't help us, no one can."

I did not answer him, for when Hans was in this superstitious mood argument was useless. Moreover I was trying to remember a very interesting lecture I had once heard about echoes and how these are multiplied by natural causes. The laughter had died away and I was just recovering the thread of the lecture when something else happened. A great stone or clod of earth fell with a thud close to me, and was followed presently by scores of similar missiles. None of these touched us, it is true, but they struck everywhere around and even against the trees above our heads.

After that I really cannot recall what followed, for between weariness, bewilderment, and exhaustion I grew confused, so that my mind became torpid. I remember all kinds of sounds, some of them very loud as though trees were crashing at a distance, and some of them small and sharp and close at hand, like the agonizing squeals idle children can produce with a slate-pencil. I remember a feeling on my face which suggested that my ears and nose were being pulled by tiny hands.

I remember, too, Hans announcing in a voice which was full of fear that gorillas with eyes of fire were dancing round us, though if so I never saw them. Lastly I remember that he fired his rifle, I suppose at one of the nightmare gorillas, or some other dream-beast, for the sound of it reverberated through the forest as though it had been a cannon-shot. Also in its blinding flash I thought I saw queer figures round us with fantastic faces.

Then I remember nothing more of all those noises and visions, which were more appropriate to a victim of *delirium tremens*, than to a strictly sober man lost in a wood, till at length I heard a gentle voice say in Arabic:

"Rise, Macumazahn. You have wandered from your path and the air beneath these trees is poisonous and gives bad dreams. I have been sent to guide you and your servant back to Dabanda-town."

I obeyed in a great hurry and presently felt a soft hand leading me I knew not where. Or perhaps I should say that I thought I felt it, for I dare say this was part of the nightmare from which doubtless I was suffering, and seemed to be led forward, Hans clinging to my coat-tails like a child to its mother's skirts, for how long I cannot tell. All I know is that just as the dawn was breaking we found ourselves upon the edge of the forest, for there in front of us was the truncated pyramid upon which burned the altar fire, and beyond it the town. Here in the shadow of the last trees our guide departed, or seemed to depart. I noted vaguely in the gloom that she was a woman wrapped in white and of a graceful figure.

"Farewell," she said with a suspicion of mockery in her voice that somehow I thought familiar, adding:

"You are very wise, Macumazahn, yet, I pray you, grow a little wiser, for then you will not mock at what you do not understand, and will learn that there are powers in the world known to its ancient peoples of which even white men have not heard."

As she spoke she stepped backwards and before I could answer her had vanished, although still out of the darkness of that accursed forest I could hear her musical voice repeating:

"Farewell, Macumazahn, and mock no more at the powers of the ancient peoples."

"Baas," said Hans as we staggered into our house, "I

think that missie must have been White-Mouse come to life again."

"I don't want to know if she was White-Mouse, or Black-Mouse, or Piebald-Mouse, or no Mouse at all. What I want is to get out of this accursed country," I replied savagely, as I kicked off my boots and threw myself down upon the bed.

CHAPTER XVI

KANEKE'S MESSAGE

IT may be wondered why I have said so little about Arkle, the real hero of this story, whom Hans and the natives named Red-Bull because of his taurine build and great strength. The reason is that I saw little of the man. After the appearance of Shadow, "the Treasure of the Lake", that night before the altar and the disappearance of Kaneke laden with curses like the scapegoat of the ancient Jews, he was laid up for a while in the Chief's big house or hut with a sore heel. Notwithstanding their alleged mastery over diseases, this heel, which resulted from his race for life before the Abanda and his subsequent tramp to the Lake-town, defied all the skill and spells of the Dabanda doctors or magicians, for they had but one word to describe the followers of both these trades.

So I was called in and tackled the case with the help of a pot of antiseptic ointment bought originally in some chemist's shop, and lint that I made by picking a rag of linen to pieces. While visiting him for this purpose of course I talked to him, but even then with a sense of restraint. The truth was that already the man was hedged round with ceremonial. Yes, this English gentleman was, as it were, guarded by a pack of heathen priests; white-robed mystics who never left us alone. Of course they could not understand our language, but on the other hand they were preternaturally shrewd at reading our faces and what was passing in our minds, as I found out from remarks that they made now and again.

Thus I always had a sense of being spied on, and so, I think, did Arkle. If I tried to talk to him about the lady Shadow,

I saw their large eyes fixed upon me and their ears, as it were, stretched out towards me, till at length I came almost to believe that after all they understood or guessed the meaning of every word I uttered. This did not tend to promote candid conversation, indeed it was paralysing, and at last reduced me to prattling about the weather or other trivial subjects.

At last I cóuld bear no more, and taking advantage of the temporary absence of the priest on guard, for I guessed that he had only retired behind a mat curtain, I said outright, "Tell me, Mr. Arkle, if you like this kind of life. You seem to me to be a prisoner in all except name, though they call you a chief. Do you think such a position right for a white man of your upbringing ?"

"No, I don't, Quatermain," he answered with vigour. "I hate the business, but I tell you that I am a man under a spell. I see you smile, yet it is true. Years ago it began with those dreams in London. Then I kissed, you know whom, down by that lake, and the spell became a madness. Lastly I swore allegiance to her and all the rest of it that night upon the platform yonder, and the madness became a fate. I am bound by chains that cannot be broken, this chieftainship is one that you can see ; but there are others—and that's the end—or the beginning."

"Do you wish to break them ?" I asked.

"My reason does, but my spirit, or my heart, or whatever you choose to call it, does not. I must win that woman, even if it costs me my life ; if I do not I shall go mad."

"Forgive me," I answered, "but don't you think that in a way it may cost you more than your life: that is, your honour ?"

"What do you mean ?" he asked.

"I mean that like all of us you were brought up with certain traditions and, as you have told me, in a certain faith; in short, you are a white man. Now a love-affair with a woman who has other traditions and who is of another faith, or even a marriage is well enough sometimes—as Saint Paul points out. But this business is bigger than that, for in practice you must adopt *her* traditions and *her* faith and give the lie to your own. Further, you don't know what these are or where they will lead you. Remember, she warned you herself, for I heard her before that altar."

"No, Quatermain, I don't know, and she did warn me. But I took the oath all the same and I've got to keep it ; moreover, I wish to keep it, for love sanctifies everything, doesn't it ? And if ever a man was in love, I am."

"That's an old argument," I said, "and I am not sure. For love means passion and passion is a blind leader of the blind."

Here my wise remarks were cut short by the re-entry of the priest, who I was quite sure had been listening through the mat curtain and making out all he could from the tone of our voices. He was accompanied by Kumpana whom I had not seen since we parted in the forest. Remembering the trick he had played me there, and all that followed, the sight of this old fellow looking more bland and amiable than usual made me indignant, especially when he asked me how I was and if I and my servant had been taking any more walks in the dark.

"Listen, Kumpana," I said. "You played me an evil trick when you left us alone the other night in that thick wood, and still worse ones afterwards, of which I will not speak. You should be ashamed of yourself, Kumpana, seeing that I am a stranger whom you are bound to help and not to desert as you did."

"I ask your pardon," he replied very courteously, "if I say that I think it is you who should be ashamed, Lord Macumazahn, for although I prayed you not to do so, you reviled what I hold to be holy until I was forced to leave you to your punishment, which might have ended worse than it did. However, you are not at all to blame, because the air of that forest sometimes goes to the head, like strong drink, and takes away the judgment. Therefore let us forgive each other and say no more."

He spoke so courteously that I felt abashed and even humbled, for after all he had some reason on his side ; acting under influences which I did not understand, I *had* offered insult to the spirits or elementals, or natural forces, which he revered. So I turned the subject by saying that Hans and I were now rested from our journey and should be glad to say good-bye to him as soon as possible, if the Council of the Shadow would be so kind as to help us to leave the country.

"You are free to go when you will, Macumazahn," he answered, "but if you attempt to do so before the time appointed, I warn you that it will be at great risk to yourself."

"I am not afraid of risks——!" I exclaimed, and that moment Arkle broke in, saying:

"For God's sake don't go, Quatermain. Stop here as long as you can, that is, until I vanish from your sight, I mean until we are separated, as I gather that we must be. For when this business is finished I have to begin a new life, but until then, don't leave me to deal with war and trouble alone."

Anxious as I had become now that my curiosity about Lake Mone was satisfied by an actual sight of its waters, to get clear of these eerie people who depressed me and of the land where even the air was so strange and unnatural that it affected the nerves and made one behave like a drunkard, I was touched by this appeal.   I felt that there was a struggle in the heart of Arkle between his inherited convictions, or perhaps I should say all the impulses and associations of a man of his race and class, and the devouring passion which possessed him for a lovely and mystical woman, a priestess of some faith with which it was not healthy for one of white blood to have to do.

Perhaps if I stayed I might yet be able to save him from this snare ; or circumstances might arise which would cut its claims. Whereas if I went his fate was sure.   One by one the barriers of civilization and Christianity, which protected him from the inroads of primeval instincts and engulfment in the dark super-stitions surviving from the ancient world that flourished here untouched by time, would be broken down.   He would become in fact what already he was in name, the chief of these star-worshipping Dabanda.   He would dwell upon the island with their priestess, his country would see him no more, and at last, when his part was played, there would be some unholy scene of sacrifice, mayhap such a one, if Hans were right, as we had been shown beneath the midnight moon on the waters of that lone-some mere beyond the forest.

I shuddered as a vision of it rose in my mind : the drugged man, helpless in his encircling cerements, being cast with songs and offerings of flowers into the bottomless crater-lake, there to seek the woman who, her day of power done, had preceded him to doom.   Or there might be other fates yet more awful, such as madness induced by disillusionment, despair, and the impossibility of escape, or even by long-continued terrors like those of which we had tasted in the forest.   Oh, the bait was rose-scented and set with jewels, but what of the hook within, I wondered, I before whose eyes it did not dangle.

All this and more that I do not remember passed swiftly through my mind with the result that I was about to say that I would stop and see the business through, when suddenly the mat which hung in the door-way of the room was thrust aside and there entered a priest conducting two men.   These men, whom I recognized at once as belonging to the farming class of the Dabanda, prostrated themselves before Arkle, showing me that he was now acknowledged as Chief by all the people.   Then the priest, bowing, informed him that they had a tale to tell and a message to deliver.

He bade them speak, whereon the elder of the two husband-men said :

"Last evening towards sunset, O Chief and Father of the Dabanda, to whom it is promised that he shall be the Shield of the holy Shadow and father of the Shadow that is to be, I and my son here were tracking a lost goat. We followed this goat into the western pass that leads through the lip of the mountain from the holy Land to that of the Abanda on the slopes and plains beyond.

"At length we caught sight of the goat near to the farther mouth of the cleft, and ran fast to catch it before it strayed into the country of the Abanda, whither we might not follow. The goat heard us and, being wilful, leaped ahead, so that before we could reach it, it was out of the mouth of the pass and into Abanda-land.

"Here, then, we sat on the border line, since we dared not pursue farther, and called to the goat to return to us. It knew our voices and was coming, when suddenly between us and it appeared armed men out of the bushes, and at the head of them no other than Kaneke, he who has forfeited the chieftainship and been cursed of the Engoi.

"'Stay still and listen,' he said, 'for if you stir we will throw spears and kill you.' So we stood still and he went on :

"'I, Kaneke, of the pure blood, the Chief of the Dabanda and the Shield of the Shadow, am now Chief of the Abanda also. Yes, I have brought together under one rule the two peoples who were divided long ago. Go you therefore to Kumpana, the first of the Council of the Shadow, and say to him that he may tell it to the Shadow, that the Abanda perish for the want of rain, which is withheld from them by the witchcraft of the priests and Council of the Dabanda. Their crops wither, their cows and goats give no milk, their springs dry up, and their children are in want and like to die.

"'Therefore if within six days no rain falls upon their land, I, their chief and yours, will lead them in their thousands through the passes of the mountain-lip, fearing no curses such as of old have held them back, now that I, Shield to be of the Shadow, am their captain. We will kill any that oppose us ; we will kill Kumpana and the Council of the Shadow who guide her ill ; we will kill the priests of the Shadow who are evil wizards, practisers of black magic ; we will pass the forest, not fearing the wood-dwellers ; we will cross the lake, and I will take the Shadow and make her mine, and thenceforward rule over the two people become one again. Lastly, we will kill the white thief who is named Wanderer, and by the people Red-Bull. Yes, we will kill him by torture as an offering to the moon and the host of heaven, that henceforth rain may fall without the mountain as well as within its circle, giving plenty, so that all the people may increase and grow fat.

"'With him we will kill the white hunter name Macuma-zahn, because now I know that I was made to buy him to come to this land, not to give me help as I believed, but to work me evil and to set in my place the thief Red-Bull; and the yellow man his servant we will also kill, burying them alive or burning them upon the altar. None of them shall escape us, for night and day all the passes are watched and any that set foot outside of them shall be hunted to death for our sport, as the thief Red-Bull would have been, had he not been saved by Macumazahn. Now go and at this same hour on the second day return with the answer to my message.'

"Then, Lords, Kaneke and those with him went away laughing together, killing our goat as they went, and my son and I came here to deliver the message."

For a while there was silence in that room. Kumpana seemed to be perplexed; the priests were speechless with indignation; I was horribly frightened at the prospect of the fate promised to me, and so was Hans who all this while had been sitting on the ground behind me, smoking and pretending to hear nothing, for he whispered:

"Oh, Baas, why did you ever come to this land of spooks? Why did you not run away after you had got Kaneke's ivory? Now we shall be buried alive. Or be grilled on that altar fire—just like buck's flesh, Baas."

"If so, it won't be Kaneke who will do the grilling, that is if ever he comes within three hundred yards of me," I answered savagely in Dutch.

Then I stopped short to consider Arkle in whom I noticed a curious change. A few minutes before he was looking troubled and unhappy, for reasons that may be guessed. Now he had brisked up and seemed quite cheerful, as is the way of some Anglo-Saxons (I am not one of them) when there is the prospect of a fight.

"When did you say I should be able to get about as usual, Quatermain? Was it tomorrow?"

"Yes, I think so, if you will keep a bandage on your heel,"

I said, then was silent, for Kumpana was speaking to the peasants, telling them to go away and rest until he sent for them.

When they had departed he bade the priests summon the Council of the Shadow, which they did with marvellous rapidity, for within five minutes they arrived in the room, six or seven old fellows. I suppose they were hanging about outside, having scented trouble. At any rate they appeared, bowed to Arkle and to me and sat down upon the ground. Kumpana repeated to them the tale of the two peasants which did not seem to surprise them ; indeed they appeared to know it already. Next he asked them what they thought should be done, and they gave various replies which I scarcely understood, because they all talked together and very fast, using terms that were not familiar to me. Nor in fact did Kumpana appear to pay much attention to what they said, which gave me the idea that this asking of their advice was more or less of a formality. When they had finished he turned to Arkle and with much deference inquired his views.

"Oh, fight the beast—I mean Kaneke," answered Arkle with emphasis, adding, "but first ask Macumazahn there ; he is a wise man and has seen many things."

So Kumpana repeated his question, inquiring of me whether I also held that we should fight.

"Certainly not, if you can do anything else," I replied, "for you are few and the Abanda are many. They say that they want rain and I have heard you declare that you, or some of you, can cause rain to fall. If this is true, do so. Give the Abanda as much water as they want and there will be no war."

This I said not because I believed that the priests or the Shadow, or anyone else, could break the drought and bring rain from the heavens upon the parched fields of the Abanda, but because I wanted to hear Kumpana's views upon the suggestion. To my surprise he accepted it with great respect, saying that the plan was good and worthy of consideration and that it should be submitted to the Engoi—that is to the Lady Shadow—for her decision.

"Do you mean that she can give the Abanda rain if she chooses ?"

"Certainly," he answered with an air of mild astonishment, "at any time and in any quantity."

Then I collapsed, for what is the use of arguing with cranks or lunatics, although of course I knew that many natives hold similar beliefs as to the powers of their rain-makers.

Now, to my surprise Hans took up his parable. Squatted there upon the floor, he said in a brazen fashion :

"The Baas thinks himself wise, you all think yourselves wise, but Hans is much wiser than any of you. This is what you should do. Kaneke is the post that holds up the roof of the Abanda house. They dare to offer to fight you and to say that they will take away your priestess who lives in the lake, because Kaneke, whom they believe to be your real chief and high-priest with a right to the Lake Lady, has become their captain, so they are no longer afraid of you or of the curses of your Engoi. Kill Kaneke and once more they will be afraid of you, for without him they dare not invade your land which they have always held to be holy."

"And how are we to kill Kaneke ?" asked Kumpana.

"Oh, that is easy. When those two men take your answer —unless the Baas would rather do it himself—I will go with them and hide behind a stone, or disguise myself as a Dabanda . . ."

Here Kumpana looked at Hans and shook his head.

". . . then when Kaneke comes to listen I will shoot him dead ; that is all and there will be no more trouble."

On hearing this cold-blooded proposition Kumpana expressed doubts as to whether Kaneke could be disposed of in this way. It seemed to be his idea that a priest of the Engoi could only meet his end in certain fashions which he did not specify, and he added that had it been possible for him to die otherwise, Kaneke would have done so before, especially not long ago when he had tried to seize the Shadow, and afterwards. However, he was prepared to consider Hans' suggestion which did not seem to shock him in the least.

Having collected all our views Kumpana announced coolly that he would now lay them before the Engoi and learn that celestial potentate's will through the mouth of its earthly incarnation and minister, the Shadow. Of course, I thought that he meant to pay a visit to the island in the lake and remembering the riddle of those ancient buildings which I yearned to explore, I began to wonder if I could not persuade him to allow me to be his companion on the trip, though it is true that I had no liking for another midnight journey through that forest.

But not a bit of it. His methods were very different. Suddenly he commanded silence and ordered extra mats to be hung over the door-way and window-places, so that the room became almost dark. Then he sat down on the floor, the two priests kneeling on either side of him, while the Council of the Shadow, also sitting on the ground and holding one another's hands, made a circle round the three of them. Hans, who, scenting spooks, showed a strong disposition to bolt. I and—as I was relieved to observe—Arkle remained outside this circle playing the part for audience.

"By Jove," thought I to myself, for I did not dare open my lips, "we are in for a seance."

A seance it was. Yes, there in Central Africa a seance, or something uncommonly like it, which once more caused me to remember the saying of wise old Solomon, that there is no new thing under the sun. Doubtless for tens of thousands of years there have been seances among almost every people of the earth, civilized and savage, or at any rate similar gatherings having for their object consultation with spirits or other powers of which ordinary men know nothing.

The priests said some prayer in archaic language which I did not understand, if indeed they understood it themselves. I gathered, however, that it was an invocation. Then the circle began to sing a low and solemn hymn, Kumpana seated in the centre keeping time to the chant with motions of his hands and head. By degrees these motions grew fainter, till at last his chin sank upon his breast and he went into a deep trance or sleep.

Then I understood. Kumpana was what in spiritualistic parlance is called a medium. Doubtless, I reflected, it was because of this gift of his which enabled him to put himself in communication, real or fancied, with intelligences that are not of the earth and with human beings at a distance, also to exercise clairvoyant faculties, that he had risen to the high estate of President of the Council of the Shadow, the real governing body of the land. Afterwards I found that I was quite right in this supposition, for Kumpana was humble by birth and not a member of one of the priestly families ; yet owing to his uncanny powers he outdistanced them all and in fact was the ruler of the Dabanda. The chief of the tribe was but an executive officer who acted upon the advice of the Council and in due course became the husband of the Shadow of the day, destined to the dreadful fate of dying with her when the Council so decreed.

As for the Shadow herself, she was nothing but an oracle, the Voice of some dim divinity through whom the commands of that divinity were made known to the Council, which interpreted them as it pleased, if indeed it did not inspire them as even then I suspected. The priests, by comparison, played a small part in the constitution of this State.   For it was a State in miniature, the survival and remnant, I imagine, of what once had been a strong and in its way highly civilized community, whose principal gods were the moon and the planets (not the sun, so far as I could learn), one that had owed any greatness it might possess to its religious reputation and alleged magical powers, rather than to strength in war.

Therefore in the end it had gone down before the fighting peoples, as in this carnal world the spirit so often does in its struggle with the flesh, for as someone remarked, I think it was Napoleon, Providence is, or seems to be, on the side of the big battalions. These priests, I should add, in addition to attending to the religious rites and offerings before the altar, were the learned men and doctors of the tribe.   It was they who studied the stars, drawing horoscopes and reading omens in them, not without some knowledge ; for I have reason to believe that they could predict eclipses with tolerable accuracy.   Also they kept records, though whether these were in any kind of writing, or merely by means of signs, I am sorry to say I was never able to ascertain, because on this point their secrecy was strict.

This is all I could discover, during my brief sojourn among them, as to the mystical religion of the Dabanda, if religion it can be called, of which I was now witnessing one of the manifestations.

After Kumpana had sunk into his trace the chant continued for a considerable time, growing fainter by degrees till at length it seemed to come from very far away like distant music heard across the sea.   At least that was the effect it produced upon me, one as I think, of a semi-hypnotic character, for undoubtedly this hymn had a mesmeric power.   At any rate, either owing to it or to the gloom and closeness of that room, I fell into a kind of bodily torpor which left my mind extremely active, as happens to us when we dream.

In my imagination I seemed to see a shadowy Kumpana standing before the beautiful woman upon whom I had looked on the altar platform, and speaking to her in some great dim hall.

She listened ;   then stood a while with outstretched hands and upturned eyes, like one who waits for inspiration.   At last it came, for tremblings ran up and down her limbs, a slight convulsion shook her face, her eyes rolled and grew wild ;   the pythoness was possessed of her spirit or familiar.   Then her lips moved rapidly as though from them were pouring a flood of words, and the fancy faded.

Of course it was nothing but a dream induced by my surroundings and some heavy perfume, which I forgot to say, unseen by me, evidently the priests had sprinkled or scattered about the room. Yet probably this dream represented faithfully enough what took place when the oracle was consulted, for whether such ceremonies occurred in ancient Greece or are practised by the witch-doctors or diviners of Africa, there is much similarity in their methods.

I woke up, Kumpana woke up, everybody woke up. (Both Arkle and Hans told me afterwards that, like myself, they went to sleep and dreamed dreams.) The old seer yawned, rubbed his eyes, stretched himself and said quietly that he had received full directions from the Engoi as to what was to be done to meet the danger which threatened the Dabanda, but what those directions might be he declined to reveal. Then he sent for the two husbandmen and, pointing to one of the priests, said to them:

"Return to the Western pass with this man, and tomorrow at sunset, be at that spot where Kaneke spoke with you. If he comes again or sends messengers, as he will, say that his words have been delivered to the Engoi, and that this is the answer: 'Remember that you are accursed, O traitor Kaneke. Take what road you will, but learn that every one of them leads you to the grave.' Say also that the rain which the people of the Abanda demand shall fall upon them in plenty, for the time of drought is done. Let them be content therewith and know that if any of them dare to follow Kaneke into the land of the Holy Lake, a curse shall fall upon them also, such a curse as has not been told of among them or their fathers. Add these words: 'O Kaneke, the Engoi reads your heart. You do not seek rain to make fruitful the fields of the Abanda. You seek the Shadow. Kaneke, for you that Shadow has faded; for you she is dead. She whom you strove to bear away is dead and there awaits you only the fate of one who has slain the Shadow.'"

This cryptic message Kumpana caused the two peasants, also the priest who was to accompany them, to repeat twice. When he was sure that they had it by heart to the last word, he sent them away without any ceremony, as though he attached no particular importance to their mission.

Now I could no longer suppress my irritation, or rather my wrath. I was most heartily sick of the whole affair. I saw that there was going to be fighting of some sort in which no doubt I should be expected to take part, and I did not want to fight. What had I to do with this ancient quarrel between two long-separated sections of a tribe, who were at loggerheads over the possession of a priestess supposed to be gifted with powers as a rainmaker?

Moreover, the moral atmosphere of the place was unwholesome and jarred upon me. African customs of the more recondite sort and ancient superstitions are very interesting, but I could have too much of them, especially if certain, as I was, that behind their outward harmlessness, lies hid some red heart of secret cruelty. I wanted to get out of the place before that cruelty became manifest, or before something horrible happened to me —with Arkle if possible, but if he would not come, without him.

To tell the truth I was frightened. I suppose that my dreams in the forest and the occurrences of this seance, if I may so call it, had got upon my nerves, just as old Zikali used to do in the Black Kloof. I have always believed that there are forces round us which our senses do not appreciate, secret doors in the natural boundary wall of life that most of us never find, though to them some may have the key. But I also believe that it is most dangerous and unwholesome to come into touch with those forces, or to peep through those doors when they are opened by others. Here in Dabanda-land, however, they always stood ajar, or so I imagined, and through them came experiences and what Hans called "spooks", which thrust themselves upon the attention of those who did not desire their company. In short I wished to be gone back to a wholesome, everyday existence and never to see or hear anything more of Lake Mone, its priestess, or her votaries.

"Kumpana," I said, "is there to be a war between your people and the Abanda?"

"Yes," he answered with a slow and rather creepy smile, "there is to be war—of a sort."

"Then I want to have nothing to do with it. Kumpana, I want to get out of your country at once; risks or no risks, I wish to be off."

"I fear that is impossible, Lord Macumazahn," he answered. "Have you not heard the word of the Engoi that the drought which has endured beyond the mountain for three years is at an end? That word is true; great storms are coming up through which you could not travel. The rain would stop you even if you escaped the spears of the Abanda. Moreover," he added quickly before I could express disbelief in the arrival of these storms, and with a faint sneer, "we have been told that the Lord Macumazahn is a very brave man, one who loves fighting."

"Then you have been told a lie. Also, who told you?"

"That does not matter. We know more about you than you think, Macumazahn. Also we have been told that you accepted payment from Kaneke to come to this country and not to leave it until the object of your coming was accomplished, payment in ivory and gold; and we believed, Lord Macumazahn, that you were a very honest man who always fulfilled your promises, especially when your services had been bought."

Here Arkle, to his credit, intervened sharply, saying:

"Be silent, Kumpana. Would you insult your guest——?"

"Thank you, Arkle," I broke in in English, "but I can look after myself. He will only tell you that you are now the Chief of his people and that I am your guest, not his."

Then addressing Kumpana in his own language, I went on.

"You have been misinformed. I never pretended to great courage, especially in wars that do not concern me. For the rest my bargain was to accompany Kaneke to his country, not to fight battles there, as I could prove to you if you were able to read my language. This Kaneke who was to be your chief, said that he could not travel here without me, which is true, for had it not been for me and Hans he would never have started. Further, had it not been for us he would have been killed by the Abanda who were hunting the white lord who is now your chief. So I came, not for that reason but because he paid me, for in such fashions I earn my living. Yet I should not have come for this cause alone. I had another. It was that I had heard of your holy lake and a little of your people and their customs, and being curious in such matters I desired to look upon the one and to study the others for myself——"

"Which things you have done to your heart's content," broke in Kumpana.

"Still," I went on not heeding him, "never shall it be said that I, Macumazahn, took pay that I did not earn to the full. Therefore I will take my share in your war, doing all that is asked of me as best I can, especially as I have a score to settle with this Kaneke, who by his treachery brought my two servants to their death. Only I demand your promise and that of the Council of the Shadow and that of the white lord who has now become your chief against my counsel, that when this war is finished, I and my servant shall be allowed to depart at once in peace and with such help as you can give me."

"It is yours, Lord, we swear it by the Engoi!" exclaimed

Kumpana in a humble voice and with the air of one who is ashamed of himself. "Pardon my words if they offended you, for know that as to your love of fighting I have but repeated what your servant Hans told me, and for the rest I learned it from Kaneke."

"Whom you have proved to be a traitor and a liar," I said angrily.

Then I turned to Arkle and asked him whether he also gave me his promise that I should be allowed to go when the war was ended.

"Of course, if you wish it," he answered in English, "though I hoped that you would stop here with us a while. The truth is, Quatermain, that I shall be very lonely without you," he added with a sigh, which I thought pathetic, knowing all it meant.

"Then why do you stay here ?" I asked bluntly.

"Because I must ; because it is my fate ; because I am under a charm that may not be broken. Also, Quatermain, do you not understand" (this he said rapidly and in a low voice) "that if I were to break my oaths, or try to—which I cannot— I should not live another day ?"

"Yes, Arkle, I understand and I am sorry," I replied, and, bowing to them all, left the house.

"Baas," said Hans outside, "do you remember that trap of willow-rods I made once to catch eels" (he meant barbel mud-fish) "down on the Tugela when we could get nothing else to eat ? It was a very good trap, Baas, for when the eel had pushed its way in, the willow rods shut up behind it, so that it could not get out again, and afterwards we ate it. This land is a trap like that, and the Baas Red-Bull is the eel and the Shadow lady is the bait, and by and by I think these spook people will cook and eat him."

I shivered at Hans' suggestive illustrations, and answered :

"Look out that they do not cook and eat us too."

"Oh no, Baas, they won't do that because they haven't found the right bait to catch you. Luckily there are not two Shadow-ladies, Baas, and the trap is no good without the right bait."

CHAPTER XVII

THE GREAT STORM

THAT evening clouds like to those of a monsoon began to bank up over lake-land and all the country round so far as the eye could see.

"That Shadow-lady is a very good rain-doctoress, Baas," said Hans. "You remember Kumpana said that she promised rain to those Abanda who have had none for three years, or very little. Now I think that they are going to get plenty."

"Then perhaps they won't make war," I answered indifferently.

Certainly the weather was very peculiar. The heat, which had been considerable for some days before, now grew intense ; I should imagine that on this particular evening it must have risen to 108 or 110 degrees in the shade. Moreover it was of a most oppressive character ; the air was so thick that I felt as though I were breathing cream and I could not make the slightest effort without bursting into profuse perspiration.

There I lay upon my bed stripped to the shirt in the best draught that I could find, which was none at all, and gasped like a fish out of water, praying that the storm would burst and bring coolness. In the lady Shadow's powers I had no faith. I was quite certain, however, that Kumpana and the other old men were well acquainted with the signs of the local weather, and knew that it was about to undergo a general break after the long drought. Hence the prophecy so confidently announced by the Council. This drought, for some reason which I cannot explain, never affected the crater area unduly, for the Dabanda had just gathered in an excellent harvest.

Hans, who like most Hottentots was quite indifferent to heat, went out into the town to prospect and returned saying that the people showed considerable alarm. Some were looking to the roofs of their houses, while others were driving their stock into caves and sheltered places, or carrying home the last of the harvest in baskets, even the children, of whom there were not many, being pressed into this service. The priests, too, he said, were engaged in building a kind of palm-leaf tent over the altar on the stone platform, presumably to prevent the rain from putting out the fire, which it seemed had always burned there from time immemorial.

The night came, a night of dreadful heat in which I could not sleep a wink, or do anything except swallow quantities of water mixed with the juice of a sub-acid, plum-like fruit that grew wild in the crater, which made an astringent and most refreshing drink. The dawn that followed was as dark as that of a November day in London, but as yet there was no rain nor any lifting of the heavy silence.

After eating, or pretending to eat, I crept across to the Chief's house, to be informed by a priest outside that I could not be admitted, as the lord Wanderer was engaged with the Council. I took the hint and went home again, feeling sure that the plan was to cut me off from Arkle over whom my influence was feared. It almost seemed as though Kumpana and his companions were psychological experts, if that is the right description, who could read what was passing in the minds of others. Indeed, I began to believe that although they could not understand our words when we spoke in English in their presence, they understood the drift of them, also that I wished to persuade him to shake off their shackles and get out of their clutches.

Why were they so anxious to keep him here ? I wondered. I wonder still. Doubtless there was some overwhelming reason which they would not reveal. As I do today, I inclined to the view that mainly they were actuated by ambition. They, a dwindling, superstition-ridden race, desired once more to become a power in their world. To accomplish this they must add to their number, which could only be done by incorporating the thousands of the virile Abanda under the rule of a man of force and ability who understood the arts of civilization. This to my mind is why Arkle was brought to Mone-land, tempted by the bait of the beautiful woman called Shadow to whom he had been so mysteriously drawn.

That is the best explanation which I can offer ; not a very satisfactory one, I admit, because it presupposes that this lady Shadow could impress her personality upon him from a great distance, as he alleged that she had done, and also some knowledge of the future on the part of her priests and advisers. Or mayhap these were only acting upon the dictates of some ancient prophecy of a sort that is common enough among the more mystical of the African peoples, although such prophecies rarely come to the knowledge of Europeans, save in forms too obscure and tangled to be understood by them. The same reason, if to a

less degree, made them so anxious that I should visit their
country for a while. They wanted to pick my brains as to our
system of government and the rest, which indeed they did
upon every opportunity, although I have not recorded their
questions. They were a little, buried folk, which its astute
rulers, especially that very clever man Kumpana, desired to build
up again into a nation. This, I believe, was the true key to the
secret of all their plottings.

When I got back I found men strengthening the roof of my
house and others digging a trench round it, connecting it with a
sluice or water-course not far away, which showed me what they
expected in the way of a storm. I went indoors and tried to take
a nap, but could not because of curious noises that I was unable to
explain and felt too languid to investigate.

Towards sunset Kumpana came to see me. Although I
received him somewhat coldly he was very polite. Having
inspected the arrangements for the protection of the house, he
apologized for having sneered at me on the previous day, saying
that he did it for a reason and not because he believed that I was
a coward or had taken pay for which I did not intend to give
consideration. This reason, he explained frankly, was that he
knew I should get angry and promise to stop with them till the
end of the war, and that having once given my word I should
not break it.

I sat amazed at his cunning, which showed so deep a knowledge of human nature and such insight into my character, but
I really was too hot to argue with him. Then, leaving the subject
quickly, he begged me not to go out, as the storm might begin
at any minute, and also for another cause.

"You are wondering what the strange sounds you hear may
mean," he said. "Come up to the roof of the house and I will
show you."

As I have said I had heard such sounds, which I thought were
like to those of the galloping of herds of cattle, mixed with
grunts and bellowings. When I reached the roof I saw whence
they came. On either side of the town enormous numbers of
every kind of game were rushing towards the forest, doubtless to
shelter there from the approaching tempest. There were elands,
hartebeest, gnus, sable-antelope, oryx, buffaloes, quaggas, and a
host of smaller animals, all possessed by fear and all galloping
towards the trees.

"These beasts understand what is coming," said Kumpana,
"and are mad with terror. They will not hurt us Dabanda

because they know us, and, as you have seen, we have power over them; but if they smelt you, a stranger, they would toss and trample you."

I admitted that it was very probable, and stood a while staring at this, the strangest sight, perhaps, that I have seen in all my experience as a hunter. Presently I turned to descend, but Kumpana bade me wait a while if I would see something still more strange.

As he spoke I heard a sound which I could not mistake: that of an elephant trumpeting shrilly.

"I thought you told me that all the elephants had been driven out of Mone-land," I said, astonished.

"So I did, Lord," answered Kumpana, "but it seems that they have come back again, flying before the great storm or earth-quakes for shelter to the country where some of them were bred generations ago, before we sent them away."

As he spoke, emerging from a cloud of dust to the right of the town there appeared an enormous bull elephant running rapidly, and behind it many others. I knew the beast at once by its size, the grey markings on its trunk and forehead, and certain pecu-liarities of its huge tusks. It was the king-elephant with which we had experienced so curious an adventure upon the mound in the midst of the plain that Kaneke had called the gathering-place of elephants; the very beast which we had seen being greeted by the countless company of its fellows, which, too, with them, had afterwards pursued us back to our camp. Its appearance here was so marvellous, so utterly unexpected even in that eerie land of strange happenings, that really I turned quite faint. As for Hans, who was beside me, he sank down in a heap, muttering:

"*Allemagter!* Baas, here is that ugly old devil which threw Little Holes and Jerry into the pool and nearly blew my stomach out. He has come after us, Baas, and all is finished."

"Not yet," I answered as quietly as I could. "Also perhaps he has come after someone else."

Then I turned and watched the majestic creature rush past the town, followed by a great number of others, between fifty and seventy, I should say; all of them, I noted, mature bulls, for not a cow or a half-grown beast could I see among them.

Kumpana seemed to understand my wonder at this circum-stance and without its being explained to him, for he said:

"These elephants are the bulls that were bred in this country long years ago in our fathers' days, and have now returned to their home. The cows and all their progeny have gone else-where, and indeed we did not need them."

"What do you mean by that?" I asked sharply, but he pretended not to hear me, or at any rate he made no answer.

When the herd of elephants had thundered past and, following all the other creatures, had vanished into the forest, we descended from the roof into the house, where Kumpana began to say fare-well, cautioning me not to leave its shelter until the coming storm was over.

"Wait a minute," I said. "Where is the white lord, your new Chief?"

"In his own place where he must stay, Macumazahn," he answered.

"I perceive that you wish to separate us," I said again.

"Perhaps for a while, Macumazahn, for the good of both of you. You, for your part, wish to separate him from us which, though it is natural enough, may not be. The white lord has sworn himself to the Dweller in the Lake and must abide with her and us. Should he try to break his oath, he would be slain; and should you tempt him to do so, you would be slain also. Therefore it is best that you should remain apart till this war is accomplished."

"Is it certain that there will be a war?" I asked, "and, if so, when?"

"Yes, Lord, I think there will be a war of men after that of heaven is finished," and he pointed towards the sky, "for Kaneke will surely strive to win back all that he has lost. In that war, Lord, you will be called upon to take your share, though perhaps it will not be such a one as you expect. When the time comes I will wait upon you, and now farewell, for the great storm is at hand and I must seek shelter while it rages."

When he had gone I talked to Hans about the arrival of the mysterious old elephant and its herd, which upset him very much, for he answered:

"I tell you, Baas, that these beasts are not elephants; they are men bewitched by the Dabanda wizards, and, Baas, there is something terrible going to happen in this accursed land."

As he spoke "something terrible" began to happen, for the dense air was filled with a moaning sound, the exact like of which I had never heard before, caused, I suppose, by wind that as yet we did not feel, stirring in the tops of the trees of the vast forest. It was as though all the misery in the wide world had gathered and was giving utterance to its pain and sorrows in prolonged, half-stifled groans.

"The ghosts are flying over us, Baas," began Hans, but he did not finish his sentence, for at that moment the solid ground began to heave beneath our feet. It heaved slowly in a sickening fashion that made my vitals writhe within me and threw to the floor articles from some rough shelves which Hans had made.

"Earthquake! Out you go before the roof comes down!" I exclaimed to Hans, quite unnecessary advice in his case, for he was already through the door-way. I followed, running across the little garden to the open space where there was nothing to fall upon us. Here I was brought to a standstill, for another prolonged heave threw me to the ground where I thought it safer to remain, praying that it would not open and swallow me.

"Look!" said Hans at my side, pointing to one of the two column-like towers whence the Dabanda astrologers observed the stars, or rather at what had been the tower, for as he spoke it bowed gracefully towards us, as did the forest trees, as though they were making an obeisance. Then down it fell with a crash —which, however, we could not hear because of the moaning sound that I have described.

The heaving ceased; that earthquake went by, and with it the moaning, which was succeeded by an intense and awful silence. It was now the hour of sunset and the air seemed to be alight with a red glow like to that of molten iron, though the sun itself could not be seen. This glow, in which everything appeared monstrous and distorted, suddenly broke up into great flakes of furious colour, which to my fancy resembled wide-winged and fantastic creatures, such as haunted the earth in the reptile age, only infinitely larger, flitting away into the darkness overhead.

These shapes departed on rainbow-tinted wings and the darkness fell, a palpable thing, a mass of solid night stretching from earth to heaven. A minute later this inky blackness ceased to be, for it was changed to fire. All space was filled with lightnings, not here and there only, but everywhere those lightnings blazed, and in the glare of them we could see for miles and miles. They seemed to be striking all about us. Thus I saw trees collapse and vanish in clouds of dust, and a great rock that lay not far off shatter to pieces. By common consent we rose and ran back to the house, and as we passed its door came the thunder.

I have listened to much thunder of the African brand during my roving life, but over it all that of Lake Mone can claim supremacy. Never have I heard its equal. Some thunder cracks, like a million rifle shots, some roars like the greatest guns, and some rolls and mutters. This did all three, and at once; moreover, the cliffs of the huge crater in which the Dabanda lived caused it to echo backwards and forwards, multiplying the volume of its sound. The general effect was fearsome and overwhelming; combined with that of simultaneous and continual lightnings it crushed the mind.

Through the tumult I was aware of Hans staring at me with a terrified countenance which the blue gleam of the flashes had turned livid, and heard him shouting out something about Judgment Day, a quite unnecessary reminder, as my own thoughts were already fixed upon that event, which almost I believed to be at hand. I do not know for how long we endured this awful demonstration of Nature at her worst, because I grew bewildered and could take no count of time, but at length the turmoil lessened somewhat and the flashes blazed at longer intervals. Then, just as I hoped that the storm was passing, the rain, or rather the water-spout, began. Seldom have I seen such rain; it fell in a sheet and with an incessant roar for hours.

Our house had stood the shakings of the earthquake, which still continued at intervals, because its walls were made of tree-trunks plastered over, and therefore being non-rigid, gave to the shock. But these had cracked the roof in two places, with the result, of course, that the water poured into the building, so that soon we were half flooded. Indeed had not the cement-like mixture, as yet not firmly set, which had been poured on to the roof that day to strengthen it, been driven into those cracks, and closed them, I think that we should have been washed out of the house. But luckily this happened and we only experienced great discomfort. Luckily, too, our beds stood upon a kind of raised platform, so that the water did not reach them and we were able to lie down, and after the earth-tremors ceased, at last to sleep.

When I woke daylight, of a sort, had come and it was raining less heavily. Throwing a skin rug over my head, I climbed to the roof, and beheld a scene of desolation. All the country was more or less under water, some of the houses of the town had been shaken down by the earthquake or washed away, and many of the forest trees were shattered by lightning.

The open place on which stood the stone platform was a lake, and the shelter which had been erected to protect the fire upon the altar was crushed or shaken flat, having as we learned afterwards, extinguished the fire, to the great consternation of the

Dabanda people and especially of their priests. Moreover, although there was less rain falling within the crater-ring, over the country beyond, as the sky there showed, it was pouring as heavily as ever. Also new thunderstorms were in progress far away.

For three days this miserable weather continued, marked by constantly recurring tempests beyond the borders of Mone-land, and a few more slight shocks of earthquake. During all this time Hans and I scarcely left the house, nor were we visited by anyone, except the women who waited on us and brought us food. With great courage these women stuck to their duty through everything, and from them we learned that all the people were terrified, for no such tempest was told of in their annals.

On the fourth morning old Kumpana appeared, looking as calm as ever. He told us that, so far as they could learn, no one had been killed in Mone-land which, as the crops had been harvested, had taken little harm. Reports reached them, however, that the Abanda who lived on the outer slopes of the mountains and plains beyond had suffered terribly. Some had been drowned by the torrents which rushed down the hillsides, and some crushed in their houses that, owing to their lack of timber, were largely built of stone, and therefore were overthrown by the earthquake. Also such crops as they had, which ripened later than those in Moneland, were flattened and destroyed.

I remarked that all these misfortunes must have taken the heart out of them, with the result that they would probably give up the idea of making war, especially as they had now got all the rain they wanted.

"Not so," answered Kumpana, "for they need food of which they know there is plenty in our country and nowhere else. Tomorrow, Lord, we shall ask you to march with us to fight them."

"Where ?" I inquired.

"I am not sure, Lord. The order that we have received is that we should march to the western pass. Doubtless when we come to it, other orders will reach us, telling us what we must do "

"Whose orders ?" I asked, exasperated. "Those of your new Chief ?"

"No, Lord, those of the Engoi which come to us through the air."

"Oh," I exclaimed, "do they ? And does your Chief, the Wanderer, come with us to this battle ?"

"No, Lord, he stays to guard the town. Now I must bid you

farewell as there is much to do. Tomorrow, when it is time to march, I will send for you."

"Well, I'm blessed !" I said as the door closed behind him.

"No, Baas," said Hans, "not blessed ; another word, Baas, which your reverend father would never let me speak. As he used to say, Baas, the world is full of wonders and it is nice to see as many of them as one can before we go to the place where there is nothing but fire, like there was here the other night when the storm burst. This will be a very funny war, Baas, in which the orders reach the generals through the air and they don't know what they are going to do until they get them. That war will be a fine thing to think about afterwards, Baas, when we are back in Durban or in the Place of Fires, whichever it may be."

"Stop your ugly mouth and listen," I said. "I mean to get out of this hole. We are going to march to the western pass ; well, I shall run through it and desert."

"Yes, Baas, and leave the guns and everything else behind, and be killed by the Abanda on the other side, or lose our way and starve if we escape them. Well, it will be soon over, Baas, and we shan't have a long journey to make this time."

So he went on, talking sound enough sense in his silly, topsy-turvy idioms, but I paid no more heed to him.

So sick and tired was I of the whole business that I did not care what happened. I would just go as the wind took me, hoping that it would blow me out of Mone-land as soon as possible. If it were fated otherwise I could not help it and there was nothing more to be said.

That day I made yet another effort to see Arkle, but when we had tramped through the mud to the Chief's house, it was only to find it guarded by soldiers, who politely turned us back. Then understanding that a wall had been built between him and me which I could not climb, I returned and wrote up my diary. Those pages of smudged pencil, by help of which I indite this record, are before me now and their language is so lurid that it is difficult to believe they were written by a man as temperate in all things, and especially on paper, as myself.

That night some solemn ceremony took place on the altar platform, to which I was not asked and, I think, should not have attended if I had been. I believe that it had to do with the relighting of the fire, for from our roof we saw this blaze up suddenly. It was witnessed by a great number of people, Arkle among them, for Hans caught sight of him arrayed in Dabanda dress and escorted by priests with torches.

It distressed me to think of him playing the part of a high-priest among these uncanny other-world kind of folk, but like the rest, there it was and could not be helped.

The religious function, for I supposed it to be religious, was accompanied by much melancholy music and many songs, also by drum-beating, which I had not heard before. It went on for a long while and ended with a torchlight procession back to the town.

After we had breakfasted next morning, Kumpana arrived, accompanied by a guard of thirty spearmen, and remarked casually, just as though an evening party were concerned, that if we were ready, it was time to start to the war. I replied in an airy fashion that, being impatient for battle, I had been waiting for him, for I wished to give him the impression that I was pawing the ground with eagerness, like the warhorse in the Book of Job.

He smiled and said he was glad to hear it and that he hoped I should remain in the same mind, adding that he knew I could run fast from the rate at which I entered Mone-land.

I reflected to myself that this would be nothing compared with the rate at which I should leave it, if I got the chance, but contented myself with inquiring who would look after our possessions while we were away. He replied that they would be removed to a hiding-place and well cared for ; which left me wondering whether they would ever come out of it again.

So off we went, closely surrounded by the guard, two soldiers carrying our spare rifles, ammunition, and necessary kit. As we marched through the town where I saw women, but no men, repairing the damage done to the houses and gardens by the storm, a girl pushed through the soldiers and gave me a note. It was from Arkle and read :

My Dear Quatermain,
          Don't misjudge me, as I fear you must. I cannot go with you. It is impossible, for reasons you would scarcely under-stand. Also if I could, my foot is not well enough yet. Whatever you see, do not be astonished, for these Dabanda are not as other people and play their own game, which is dark and difficult to follow. Above all, don't try to escape. It would only mean your death and that of Hans.

That was all, except his initials, and quite enough too, as I thought. Evidently Arkle was an eel in a trap, as Hans put it, or a bull in a net, a better simile in his case. Also he or some of his confounded councillors had guessed my desire to escape, for in this country a bird of the air seemed to carry the matter even faster than it does in others, and he warned me against it, having been told what the result would be. Well, the idea must be abandoned ; from the first it was madness to think that such an attempt could succeed.

About three miles away at a village, or what remained of it after the storm, we met the "army", to give it Kumpana's imposing name. It consisted of some two hundred and fifty spearmen ! I asked him where the rest of it was and he replied, with his odd little smile, that it did not exist, for all the other able-bodied men had been left to defend the town and the Chief. Then I asked him what strength the Abanda could put into the field. He replied that he was not sure, but he thought from ten to twelve thousand warriors, for they were a large people accustomed to the use of arms, and sometimes they warred with other tribes and, always conquering, absorbed those who were left of them.

Lastly I inquired in mild exasperation how he expected to fight ten thousand men with two hundred and fifty. He replied blandly that he did not know, being himself a councillor and seer, not a soldier, but that doubtless it would be done somehow according to the directions he might receive ; adding, I presume in a sarcastic spirit, that my presence would be worth many regiments, because Kaneke and the Abanda were afraid of me and my white man's wisdom and weapons. Then I gave up, fearing lest more of such gibes should cause me to lose my temper and say things I might regret.

We marched on for the most of that day through the beautiful crater country where flooded rivulets—for it had no large streams, some of which we forded with difficulty—gave evidence of the great tempest, as did landslides on the slopes and lightning-shattered trees. But not one soul did we meet, although I saw a few cattle grazing, apparently unherded. The land seemed to be quite deserted, even by the game which I presumed was still hiding in the forest, and when I asked Kumpana where the people had gone, he said he did not know, but he supposed that they were in hiding fearing a return of the storm. Or perhaps, he added, as though by an after-thought, it was the Abanda that they feared, knowing that now they were under the command of Kaneke who might dare to enter the land.

At length in the afternoon we came to a village, to reach which we had to march round some deep clefts that, from their

H

fresh appearance and great depth must, I saw, have been caused by the recent earthquakes. Here a few old men, and some women, also old, were engaged in cooking large quantities of food, evidently in preparation for our arrival.

We were now within five or six miles of the wall of cliff which surrounded the whole crater, although we could scarcely see this cliff, because the village lay in a hollow and for some time we had been passing through park-like country where tall trees grew so thickly that they cut off the view.

We ate of the food, which was excellent, and rested, because Kumpana told us that we should remain at this place until far on into the night, when we must march again, so as to reach the cliff by dawn. I asked what we were to do when we did reach it. Again he replied that he did not know; perhaps we should go through the pass and attack the Abanda, or perhaps we should wait for them to attack us, or perhaps we should retire. Then he hurried off before I could put more questions.

The last thing I saw as the sun set was the party of old men and women who had cooked the food tramping off eastwards with their bundles on their backs, which suggested that they did not mean to return. Then, in order that I might be fresh in the face of emergencies, I went to sleep, and so remained till about three on the following morning when Kumpana woke us and suggested that we should breakfast, as the army was about to start.

Having swallowed something, presently off we went, travelling by the light of the waning moon and the stars. It was so dark among those trees that had not a man led me by the hand I should not have been able to see where to go, but the gloom did not seem to incommode the Dabanda, a people who must have had the eyes of cats. On we travelled, always uphill, for we were now climbing the slope of the cliff, till at length the sky grew grey with dawn. Then we halted, waiting for the sun.

Presently with startling suddenness it appeared over the eastern edge of the crater far away, its level beams striking upon the western cliffs, although the crater itself was still shrouded in mist and gloom. Or rather, immediately in front of us, they struck upon where the cliff should have been and showed us a strange and terrible sight, which caused a gasp of astonishment to burst from the lips of even those cold, silent men. For behold, it was riven from crest to foot by the shock of earthquake, and in place of the narrow pass a few yards wide, was a vast gulf that could not have measured less than a quarter of a mile across!

The great mass of the precipice was torn asunder and hurled,

I suppose, down the outer slopes ; at any rate there was but little debris in the cleft itself, which suggested that the earth-waves that did the damage must have rolled from within the crater outwards towards the plain. Why it should have concentrated its terrific strength and centre of disturbance upon this particular spot I cannot say who am ignorant of the ways of earthquakes, unless it was because here the wall of cliff was thinner and weaker than elsewhere ; also it may have been destroyed in other sections of the gigantic ring of precipice upon which I never looked.

The result of the cataclysm, so far as the Dabanda and their country were concerned, was obvious. They were no longer protected by a mighty natural wall pierced only with a few narrow clefts that could be held by a handful of men, for there was now, as Hans remarked, a fine open road between them and the rest of Africa, on which an army could march in safety without breaking its ranks. Their seclusion was gone and their secret land lay open to the world.

Did Kumpana understand this and all it meant ? I wondered as I gazed at his impassive face. More, did he know what had happened before we reached the place, and, if so, why did he come there with his beggarly little force ? Was it with some subtle hidden object ? I cannot tell, though in view of what happened afterwards I have my own opinion of the matter.

CHAPTER XVIII

ALLAN RUNS AWAY

"IF you intended to hold the pass with these, Kumpana," I said, pointing to the redoubtable two hundred and fifty, "now that it has grown so wide, that cannot be done."

"No, Lord," he answered, "it is not possible by strength alone ; even charging cattle could sweep us away with their horns if there were enough of them."

"Then what do you mean to do, Kumpana ? Return home again ?"

"I cannot say, Lord. Let us go forward and look through the

gap in the cliff, for then perhaps we shall learn what we must do. It may be that the Abanda, frightened by its fall, have run away, or that they are afraid to enter lest another earthquake should come out of Mone-land and swallow them up living."

"Perhaps," I answered, but to myself I thought that unless I were mistaken, it would take more than this to frighten the furious and desperate Kaneke.

Kumpana issued an order to his men who, with a kind of stolid indifference which suggested fatalism or a knowledge that they were protected by unseen forces, instantly marched forward towards the new pass.

"Baas," said Hans to me, "we are not captains here, but only 'luck-charms', so let us keep behind. I don't like the look of that place, Baas."

As usual there was practical wisdom in Han's suggestion, for if there should happen to be an ambush, or anything of the sort, I did not see why we should be its first victims. So, taking my chance of again being sneered at by Kumpana, I kept well to the rear of the little column, among the carriers indeed.

Well, there *was* an ambush, in fact a first-class specimen of that stratagem of war. In one of Scott's poems I remember a description of how a highland hillside which seemed to be quite deserted, suddenly bristled with men springing up from behind every bush and fern-brake. Substituting rocks, of which thousands lay about in the newly opened pass, for bushes and bracken, the scene repeated itself in that Central African gorge.

Indeed, unless their Engoi had developed wonderful spiritual activity for their protection, I suppose that every Dabanda spears-man would have been killed, had not some donkey among their enemies made the mistake of blowing a horn before they had advanced into the mouth of the pass, thereby giving a premature signal to attack. At the sound of this horn the rocks became alive with Abanda warriors who rushed to the onslaught with a savage yell. Our heroes gave one look, then turned and bolted in a solid mass, I presume without waiting for orders. Or perhaps their orders were to bolt at this critical moment, which had been foreseen. Really I neither know nor care.

"Run, Baas," said Hans, wheeling round and giving me the example, and off I went back upon our spoor. Never a shot did I fire, or do anything except foot it as hard as I was able.

I think I have told how Kumpana remarked at the beginning of this expedition that he believed I was a good runner, which is, or was, true, for in those days I was very light and wiry with an excellent pair of lungs. Now I determined to show him that he had not over-estimated my powers. In fact, for quite a long way I led the field with Hans, who also knew how to step out when needful, immediately at my heels.

"Baas," puffed that worthy when we had done a mile or two down the slope, "if we did not lead these dogs to battle, at least we are leading them out of it."

So we were, but just then some of the most active of them got ahead of us.

Well, to cut a long story short, we ran all day, with short intervals for repose and refreshment. Looking back just as we entered the more densely wooded country where we had camped the night before, I saw that this strategical retreat was quite necessary, for at a distance followed the Abanda army by the hundred, or, unless my fears multiplied their number, by the thousand. But they could not run as we did, though once they made a spurt and pressed us hard. Or perhaps they feared lest they too were being led into an ambush and therefore advanced with caution, sending scouts ahead. At any rate, after this rush from which we escaped with difficulty, they fell back again, and when we reached Dabanda-town, which we did before evening, for we returned at about twice the rate of our outward journey, they were not in sight.

Some of the Council and a few others were waiting for us in the town. Evidently they knew we were coming, how I cannot say, but there they were with watchmen set upon the altar platform. Also most fortunately they had prepared food and native beer for the consumption of their retiring heroes. Good heavens ! how we fell upon it, especially upon the drink, of which Hans swallowed so much that at last I was obliged to knock the pot out of his hand.

Whilst we were devouring this meal, with anxious eyes fixed upon the route we had followed, I realized the fact that except for the few people I have mentioned, the town was quite deserted ; nobody could be seen.

"Where have they gone ?" I said to Hans.

"Into the forest to join the spook-elephants, I expect, Baas," he replied, stuffing a lump of meat into his mouth, "and that is where we shall have to follow them."

So it was, for just then Kumpana arrived, quite calm but looking a little the worse for wear. Having congratulated me upon "the strength of my legs", he remarked that we must take refuge by the lake at once, and that as the forest was a difficult place in which to find one's way, we should do well to keep close to him."

"Certainly," I replied, "and I hope that this time you, Kumpana, will keep close to us."

So we started, wearily enough, and without an opportunity being given to us to visit our house, as I wished to do. As we reached the first of the trees, looking back I saw the Abanda hordes running into the town, which was quite undefended. They did not stay to plunder or to burn it ; they simply ran through it on our tracks. When they reached the stone platform, however, they stopped, and one of them, I think it was Kaneke himself, rushed up the steps followed by some others, and scattered the sacred fire, extinguishing it for the second time.

Kumpana, at my side, shuddered at the sight.

"He shall pay. Oh, certainly he shall pay !" he muttered, adding, "Come on, you fools, come on. The Engoi awaits you !"

Then we plunged into the thick of the forest and lost sight of them.

This happened while it was still afternoon, some time before night-fall, so that light of a sort befriended us until we were well into the wood. Just before the perennial gloom of the place, deepened by the advance of evening, turned to darkness, we reached a spot where few trees grew because of the swampy nature of the soil. Here, on the shore of a shallow lake formed by flood water, Kumpana announced that we must camp till the following morning, as so many men ignorant of its paths could not travel through the forest before the sun rose.

"What if the Abanda overtake us here ?" I asked.

"They will not overtake us," he answered. "They dare not enter the trees until there is light, and then I think that only the boldest will come, because they know this place to be holy, one forbidden to them."

As I was too tired to inquire further about this or any other matter, I accepted the explanation and just lay down to sleep, hoping that Kumpana would not give us the slip for the second time. To tell the truth I was so exhausted after racing along all day in a hot climate, that I was ready to trust to luck, not caring much what happened.

On the whole I rested well, which is not always the case when one is over-weary with mental and physical exertion, and without suffering from any of the unpleasant experiences which had afflicted Hans and myself on our return from our visit to the lake. Once I did wake up, however ; I think it was after midnight, for the moon, now in its last quarter, shone brightly overhead and was reflected in the flood-water. By its light I saw a long line of shadowy and gigantic forms marching between the trees upon the farther side of this water, and for a moment wondered what they were, or whether I was dreaming. Then I remembered the elephants that we had seen fleeing before the storm and earth-tremblings to refuge in this forest, where doubtless they still remained with the other wild beasts.

After this I went to sleep again, nor did I wake until the sun was up. We rose and ate of food that was given to us. Whether the soldiers carried it with them from the town, or whether it was brought to them during the night, I do not know, but both then and afterwards there was plenty for us all.

Our meal finished, Kumpana gave the order to march, and off we went, walking slowly round the stretch of flood-water which I have mentioned into the dense woodland beyond. While we crossed this patch of comparatively open ground, I observed that our numbers were now much diminished. We had entered the forest over two hundred and fifty strong. Now I could not count more than five and twenty men, the rest had vanished.

I asked Kumpana where they had gone.

"Oh," he answered, "this way and that to talk to the wild beasts, of which the wood is full after the storm, and tell them that we are friends whom they must not harm," a reply I thought so crazy that I did not continue the conversation.

When I discussed the matter with Hans, however, he took another view.

"They are spook-beasts, as I have told you before, Baas," he said, "especially the elephants. These wizards have command over them, as we have seen with our eyes, and doubtless have gone to order them out of our path, as Kumpana says. It is as well, Baas," he added meaningly, "seeing that we are without rifles."

"Have you not been able to find that man to whom I gave mine to carry?" I asked, colouring.

"No, Baas. He is not to be found ; perhaps he is dead or perhaps he has stolen it, or hidden it away. Nor are those who carried the spare guns to be found."

"And where is yours?" I asked sharply.

"Baas," he answered in a dejected voice, "I threw it away. Yes, when I thought those Abanda were going to catch us, I threw it away that I might run the faster."

We looked at each other.

"Hans," I said, "do you remember that Tom and Jerry did this same thing when we were hunted by the elephants, and how I told them that this *we* should never do, whereon they said that if they were not Christians they would hang themselves for very shame ? And do you remember that only just before they died so bravely to save us, you taunted them about that business, bidding them throw away their guns again if they were too heavy to carry ?"

"Yes, Baas, I have been thinking of it all night."

"And yet, Hans, we have done worse than they did, for they were only being hunted by beasts, while we fled from men, so that now when presently we may have to fight, we have no rifles."

"I know it all, Baas, and I am so ashamed that almost I could hang myself as Little Holes and Jerry wished to do."

"Then we ought to hang together, for what you did I did. At least I gave my rifle to a savage, knowing that very likely I should never see it again, so that we shall be defenceless before the enemy and these Dabanda will make a mock of me, the white man who has promised to serve them."

Here Hans became so deeply affected that I saw him draw the back of his hand over his flat little face to wipe away the tears of shame.

For a while we trudged on in silence, then he said in a broken voice :

"Baas, it was quite right of you to give your rifle to a black man to carry, as it is the custom of white masters to do, and if he stole it or was killed, it cannot be helped. But it is different with me. Baas, I am a yellow cur, but even curs can learn a lesson, as I have."

"What lesson, Hans ?"

"That we shouldn't judge each other, Baas, as I did when I mocked Tom and Jerry, because you see we may always do the same things or worse ones. Baas, if ever we get back to Zanzibar I will give all the money I earn upon this journey to Jerry's daughter, who is in a school ; yes, and my share of that which Kaneke gave you, and not spend one shilling upon gin or new clothes."

"That shows a good spirit," I said, "but what should I do ?"

Now all this requires a little explanation. When writing about our flight before the Abanda hordes, I was ashamed to tell what after all I have been obliged to record because of this talk between Hans and myself, and what happened afterwards. As I have said, there was a time during that flight when the Abanda,

rushing forward, pressed us very hard, and because of the heavy
rifles and ammunition which we carried, Hans and I were dropping
behind and likely to be speared.   Then it was that I gave my gun
and cartridges to a long-legged soldier who bore nothing except
his spear, and Hans, seeing me do so, bettered my bad example
by throwing his away, which enabled us to put on the pace and
again draw out of danger.

It may be argued that we were justified by the circumstances,
and, so far as Hans was concerned, doubtless this is true.   But
I was not justified, I, the white man to whom all these people
looked up as one braver and superior to themselves, and at whom
now doubtless they jeered as Hans had done at Tom and Jerry.
There is nothing more to say, except that I look upon this incident
as one of the greatest humiliations of my career.   Not only to
Hans did it teach a lesson as too loose and easy criticism of others,
for from it I learned one which I shall never forget throughout my
life.

For most of that day, stopping now and again at the command of Kumpana, we marched on slowly and with caution
through the forest, of which the dense gloom did not tend to
raise our spirits, that were already low enough.   From time to
time I caught sight of elephants and other wild game, which
stared at us as we went by, but neither ran away nor attempted
to attack.   It was as though they knew these Dabanda, to whom
they were taboo, to be their friends.   Indeed, during that march
I grew quite convinced that Kumpana's story as to the mastery
of his people over the beasts of the field was true, for, as will be
seen, they were savage enough where others were concerned,
whom, I suppose, they recognized to be different by their smell.
Of course, as I have said, Hans had another explanation, for he
was, and always remained, convinced that these animals had the
spirits of men in them, which is absurd.

At length towards evening we emerged from the forest and
saw the great lake in front of us.   Also we saw that on its shores
were gathered several hundreds of the Dabanda, a sight that
gladdened my eyes, and in the midst of them Arkle himself, easy
to recognize by his great height and size and red beard, although
he wore Dabanda dress and carried a long spear.

Presently we were among them and I was shaking Arkle by
the hand.

"I see that you look depressed," he said, "and I fear that
you have had a bad time."

"Very bad," I answered.   "I have run from enemies faster

than ever I ran before, and I have lost my arms, which a soldier should not do—they were heavy to carry, you see. Nor indeed did I want to shoot people with whom I had no quarrel."

"I don't wonder you threw them away, Quatermain. I did the same when the Abanda hunted me. I had rather live without a rifle than stick to it and die."

"The point could be argued," I answered, "but there isn't time. Tell me, what the devil does all this play-acting mean ? Why was I dragged out with two hundred and fifty men to fight thousands of Abanda, which, of course, was impossible ?"

"I am not sure. You see, Quatermain, I am only a figurehead in this country, and figureheads are not told everything. But if you ask me, I believe you were sent to be a bait. You see, Kaneke thinks you a very great man, and it seems he had announced that if he could capture you, or, failing this, if he could kill you, the Abandas must win, he would get all he wanted—you know what it is—and they would grow into a mighty people, never lacking rain or anything else. Also the Dabanda would become their slaves and the power and wisdom of the Engoi would go with them ever more."

"Still I don't understand why we went out to fight," I said, "without the ghost of a chance of winning, or doing anything except run away."

"Because you were meant to run away, Quatermain, in order that you might draw the Abanda after you. Unless you had run they would not have followed, for not even Kaneke could make them enter the Land of the Holy Lake. You see the ruse has succeeded, for presently they will be here. Don't look at me angrily, for on my honour I had nothing to do with the business."

"I should hope not !" I exclaimed. "For if I thought you could play such a trick upon a white man who has done his best to help you, I would never speak to you again. Besides, what is the object of it all ? Why have the Abanda been tempted to take possession of this country, from which you will never be able to drive them out again ?"

"I cannot tell you," he answered in a low voice, "but I think in order that their fighting men may be destroyed. Quatermain, I believe that something terrible awaits those unfortunate people, but I swear to you that I do not know what it is ; those priests will not tell me."

At this moment Hans nudged me.

"Look," he said, pointing towards the edge of the forest.

I did so and perceived a great body of men, a thousand or

more of them, emerging from its shadows, drawn up in companies. The Abanda were upon us with Kaneke at the head of them. Arkle saw them also, for I heard him utter an exclamation.

"Well," I said, "we can't run away this time, so I suppose that we must fight until we are killed. Have you your rifle? If so, give it me and I will shoot that Kaneke."

"It has been taken from me," he answered, shaking his head. "When I protested they told me that the white man's weapons were unlawful for me, and would not be needed."

As he spoke a number of Dabanda priests ran up and surrounded Arkle, so that for the time I saw no more of him. Confusion ensued while Kumpana and other officers tried to marshal their men into a double rank. Hans and I found ourselves pushed into a place in the centre of the first line. There we stood, unarmed, except for our revolvers and a few cartridges, which fortunately we had preserved. Arkle, still surrounded by priests and others, was kept at the back of the second rank in such a position and with such precautions as to give me the idea that the business of this force was to act as a bodyguard and safeguard him, rather than to fight the Abanda. Yet it seemed that fight it must, for the lake, into which retreat was impossible, was behind it and the enemy was in front.

The Abanda marched on. Scrutinizing their faces as they came, it struck me that there was something the matter with these men. Of course they were tired, which was not strange, seeing that after enduring the terror of the earthquake and the storm, they had pursued us all the way from their own boundary and through the forest. But their aspect suggested more than weariness; terror was written on their faces. Why? I wondered; since although they must have left most of their army behind, perhaps in occupation of Dabanda-town, they still outnumbered our force by three or four to one.

Had they perhaps met with strange adventures in the forest, as once Hans and I had done? Or were they overcome by a sense of their sacrilege in violating the forbidden land, upon whose soil for generations none of them had set a foot, except their leader, the renegade Kaneke, and were fearful of some supernatural vengeance? I could not tell, but certainly they had a frightened air, very different from that of the bold fellows whom we had met hunting Arkle and who had tried to cut us off from the mountain pass.

Still they advanced in good order, as I supposed to attack and make an end of us. Yet this was not so, for at a little distance they formed themselves into three sides of a square and halted. Now, while I marvelled what was going to happen (had I been in command of the Dabanda I should have rushed at them), Kaneke emerged from their ranks and walked to within fifty paces of us, which he was quite safe in doing, for the Dabanda had no bows, being armed only with long and heavy spears that could not be thrown.

"Men of the Dabanda," he cried in his big voice, "though you ran fast, I have caught you at length, and with nothing but water behind you, you are in my power, for I see that the white man, Macumazahn, has lost the weapon with which he is so skilled." (Here I was minded to see whether I could not reach him with a pistol shot, but remembering that the quarrel was none of mine and that I had very few cartridges, I refrained from trying.)

"Yet, men of the Dabanda," went on Kaneke, "I do not wish to kill you among whom I was bred and who I hope will live on to be my subjects. I do not even wish to kill Macumazahn and his servant, because once they saved me from murderers, and we have been companions upon a long journey. There is only one whom I will kill, and that is the white thief, whom I see skulking yonder behind your lines, who has stolen my place and heritage, and would steal the Shadow, my appointed wife. Therefore give him up to me that I may make an end of him before your faces and submit yourselves to me, who will harm no other man among you ; no, not even that cunning jackal, Kumpana."

Now Kumpana stepped forward and said clearly but quietly :

"Cease from your boastful talk, Kaneke, wizard and traitor, who sold your birthright to save your life, you who did violence to the Engoi before her altar, you who but yesterday scattered the holy fire of the altar and stamped it out, you who are accursed. Hear me, men of the Abanda," he went on, raising his voice, "what is the quarrel with us ? You asked for rain. Has not rain been sent to you in plenty ? Do not your lands run with water ? Give us this man who has beguiled you and depart in peace—or keep him and be destroyed.

"Has not the ancient prophecy been handed down to you by your fathers, that the very rocks will hurl themselves upon those of your people who dare to set foot within the forest and to look upon the holy lake, and that the wild beasts will rend them, and that those who escape the rocks and the beasts will be seized with madness ? And have not the rocks already hurled themselves upon you, killing many who dwelt beneath them ? Will you wait till all the curse fulfils itself, or will you give up this man and depart in peace unharmed ? Answer while you may, for by sunset it will be too late."

Now I could see that the Abanda soldiers were much disturbed. They whispered one to another, and some of their captains began to consult together. How it would have ended I do not know, though I doubt whether these Abanda, who seemed to me to be brave and loyal savages, would have consented to surrender the man whom they had chosen as their general in the attempt to possess themselves of Dabanda-land, with its material riches and the boon of what they believed to be an especial spiritual protection. This matter, however, remained undecided, for Kaneke, who doubtless feared the worst, cried out :

"Men of the Abanda, am I not the appointed Shield of the Shadow, a greater wizard than yonder low-born Kumpana, the son of a slave ? When the mountain heaved did I not open a roadway through it, making the two lands one, and as for the beasts, are they not also at my command ? If you doubt it, ask the white lord, Watcher-by-Night, and the yellow man, his servant, to whom I showed my power over them. And remember that but now I have led you unharmed through a host of elephants that fled at my word. Ho ! you white thief"—and he pointed at Arkle with his spear—"I have an offer to make to you. If you are not a coward, come out and fight me man to man, and let the conqueror take the Shadow. Come out and fight me, I say ! Or go tell the Shadow that he who woos her and has come from far to win her, is but a coward with a heart whiter than his face."

Arkle heard him ; with a roar of rage he shook off the priests who held him and charged through our lines straight at Kaneke. To my horror I saw as he passed me that he was quite unarmed, for either he had dropped his spear or it had been taken from him by the priests ; yes, he was attacking the man with nothing but his naked hands.

"Let none come between us !" he shouted as he went.

Kaneke lifted his spear to pierce him, but somehow Arkle avoided the thrust and, rushing in, gripped its haft and snapped it like a twig, so that the broad blade fell between them. Then he threw his arms round Kaneke and they wrestled. They were mighty men, both of them, but once that spear was gone I had little doubt of the issue. Still, the end came sooner than I expected, for Arkle seemed to lift Kaneke from his feet and dash

him to the ground, where he lay half stunned. Then, before
the Abanda could come to the help of their captain, he picked him
up as though he were a child, carried him to the ranks of the
Dabanda and through them, and cast him down at the feet of the
priests !

CHAPTER XIX

THE BRIDAL AND THE CURSE

THE torrential rains which fell during the storm had reached the
lake by many streams, with the result that its waters had en-
larged themselves. The old shore-line, fringed with tall reeds,
where I had stood on my first visit, was quite a hundred yards
away. Thus the reeds, or rather the upper halves of them, now
stood like a thicket at that distance from the shore, cutting off
the view from the stretch of water that was beyond but near to
them, while the rest of the lake and the distant island were turned
to a dazzle of gold by the fierce rays of the sinking sun.

Out of these reeds, at the exact moment when Arkle cast down
the great form of Kaneke before the priests, suddenly emerged
a large canoe, or rather a barge, for its stern was square. It
was paddled by white-robed women, quite thirty of them, I
should say, seated upon either side of the craft, which had a
gangway running down its centre. Upon the broad poop was a
curious carved seat, large enough, I noted, to accommodate two
persons, and in the centre of this seat sat a woman whom I knew
must be she who was called the Engoi, or Shadow, a tall and
beautiful young woman whose gauzy robes glittered in the sunlight as though they were sewn with gold and gems, which perhaps
they were. She wore a high head-dress with wings, not unlike
to those of a viking's helm, from which, half hiding her face,
flowed down a veil spangled with stars.

On came the boat, so gently that one could not hear the
paddles' dip, and as its prow touched the shore, priests sprang
forward and held it fast. The regal-looking woman rose to her
feet, while there went up a great shout of :

"Engoi ! Engoi !"

Clothed, as it were, with burning light, she stood above us on the high poop, gazing at the prostrate form of Kaneke, at the man who had cast him there, at the tall, white-robed, large-eyed Dabanda spearsmen, and at the Abanda warriors beyond. Then she spoke in a clear, flute-like voice, which in that silence could be heard by all.

"I, the Treasure of the Lake, greet you, servants of the Engoi ; I greet you, White Lord from far away" (this was addressed to Arkle ; of me she took no notice). "I greet you all. Tell me, O Kumpana, Father of my Council, what host is this that threatens you with spears ?"

"That of the Abanda, O Engoi, who, breaking the oath sworn by their forefathers and braving the curse, have dared to enter the holy land of Mone to slay us and to give you, the divine Shadow, to be the wife of this dog." Here he pointed to Kaneke, who, I noted, had recovered his senses, for he raised himself upon his arm and listened.

"Take him and judge him, the accursed, according to your law," she said, "for on him I will never look again." Then added in louder tones that trembled with cold anger : "Men of the Abanda, the curse with which Kaneke is cursed, clings to you also and the mercy that you would not take departs from you. *Begone to the beasts for judgment and become as beasts*, till Heaven lifts its wrath from off you and creep to my feet as slaves to pray pardon for your sins."

The Abanda heard. They stared at the priestess clothed with light, they spoke together, as I supposed making ready to attack us. But it was not so, for, of a sudden, panic seemed to seize them. I saw it pass from face to face, I saw them tremble and cover their eyes with their hands. Then without a word they turned and ran back to the shelter of the forest, an army that had become a terror-stricken mob.

They were gone, the thunder of a thousand feet died away into silence ; not one of them could be seen ; they were lost among the darksome trees.

The beautiful maiden called Shadow, whose eyes had been fixed upon the water, lifted her head and looked at Arkle, saying softly :

"White Lord from afar, our dream is fulfilled and once more we meet, as was foretold, and I am yours and you are mine. Yet if you would depart with your companion"—here for the first time she glanced at me—"still the road lies open. Go, then, if it pleases you ; only if you go, learn that henceforth for this life and all that are to come we separate for ever.   Learn, too, that if you stay, there is no power in heaven or in earth that shall part us while time endures and the star we follow shines in the sky. Choose, then, and have done."

Arkle stared at the ground, like to one who is lost in doubt. Then he lifted his eyes and met hers that were fixed upon him, till the radiance which shone upon her face seemed to pass to his, and I knew that she had conquered.   He turned and spoke to me, saying :

"Farewell, my friend whom I shall see no more.   I know you believe me mad, even wicked perhaps, and so I am according to your judgment and that of the world we know.   Yet my heart tells me that love can do no wrong and that in my madness is the truest wisdom, for yonder stands my destiny, she whom I was born to win, she who was lost and is found again.   Farewell once more, and think of me at times as we shall of you, until perchance elsewhere"—and he pointed upwards—"we meet again, and you too understand all that I cannot speak."

He took my hand and pressed it, then very slowly stepped on to the prow of the boat, and passing down its length between the two lines of women who sat like statues, came to her who stood upon its poop.   As he came she opened her arms and received him in her arms, and there they kissed before us all.   For thus was the shadow wed in the presence of her people.

Side by side they sat themselves upon the throne-like seat. The priests thrust the boat out into the water, the paddlers turned its prow towards the reeds and the island that lay beyond them, and the sun sank.

The sun sank, the waters of the holy lake grew dark, and these strange travellers departed into gloom.   Once more only did I see them after they had passed through the reeds out on to the darkened bosom of the lake.   Some cloud above caught the last rays of the sun that had vanished behind the crater cliffs, and reflected them in a shaft of light on to the water and the boat that floated there, turning those it bore to shapes of glory.   Then the ray passed and the shadows hid them.

"That's a good omen for the Red Baas and the pretty spook-lady who has carried him off," remarked Hans reflectively, "for you see after the sun seemed to be dead, it came to life again to wish them luck, Baas."

"I hope so," I replied, turning my back upon that melancholy lake and not in the best of spirits.   Arkle at least had won the lady whom he so passionately desired, but I, who had won nothing and nobody, felt very much alone.   My part in all this business had been to do everybody's dirty work—that of White-Mouse, of Kaneke, of Arkle, and of Kumpana—and to tell the truth I did not like it.   No one really enjoys the humble office of a tool which is thrown aside when done with.

That night we camped by the lake, and I have seldom passed one that was more disturbed.   From its solemn and mysterious depths came the mournful cries of wildfowl and the drear sighing of the wind among the reeds.   But these were as nothing compared with the sounds which proceeded from the forest. Fierce trumpeting of infuriated elephants, bellowing of other beasts, and, worst of all, what sounded like the screams of terrified and tortured men, which were so loud and persistent that if I had known where he was sleeping I would have gone to Kumpana and asked their cause.   But I did not know and probably if I had found him he would have told me nothing.   At length, too, these noises ceased, and I got some rest.

Before sunrise, when the sky grew grey and the night mist still hid the face of the lonesome lake, Kumpana appeared, bringing us some food and saying that we must eat it as we marched, because it was time to be gone.   So off we went, and entered that hateful forest just as the sun rose.   Before I had gone three hundred paces between the trees, I stumbled over something soft and, looking down, to my horror discovered that it was the mutilated body of an Abanda warrior, who from various signs I knew must have been killed by an elephant.

"See here, Hans !" I said, pointing to the dreadful thing.

"I have seen, Baas," he answered, "and there are plenty more of them about.   Didn't you hear those spook elephants hunting them last night as the Dabanda wizards brought them here to do ?"

"I heard something," I answered faintly, remembering as I spoke the words of Shadow when she told the Abanda "to begone to the beasts for judgment" !   Great God, this was the judgment !

Hans was quite right.   There were plenty more of the poor creatures lying about, indeed I imagine that some hundreds of them must have been killed.   What an end !   To be hunted in the darkness of night and when caught, stamped flat or torn to pieces by these maddened animals which probably tracked them by their scent.   If this were the fate of his tools, what, I wondered, was that reserved for Kaneke, who by the way, as I supposed, had been taken on ahead of us for I saw nothing of him?

Until then I had merely disliked the Dabanda, now I hated them and desired nothing so much as to get out of this land of cruelty and African witchcraft. For although I had tried to find other explanations, such as the fact that all game was taboo to them, what but witchcraft or some force which we white men do not understand, could account for the dominion of these people over wild animals? It may be thought that the attack upon these Abanda by the elephants was an accident resulting from their breaking into the herd in their terrified retreat after they fled from the presence of one whom they believed to be almost a goddess. But this could scarcely be so seeing that when, following on our footsteps, the Abanda passed through the forest to the lake, the elephants must have been all round them, for as I have said, I saw the great beasts watching us from between the trees.

Why, then, were they not attacked upon this outward journey? I can only suggest one explanation. At that time Kaneke was with them whom the beasts knew and obeyed, as they did other leaders of his tribe, for had he not shown his power over these very elephants long before we entered Dabanda-land? When the Abanda soldiers were deprived of his protection the case was different, for then they were fallen upon, trampled and torn to pieces as Hans and I should have been if we had been alone.

As a matter of fact, however, we should have had nothing to fear on this return journey, for we never saw these beasts again. Indeed, I heard afterwards that when they had wreaked vengeance on the Abanda, led by the ancient bull, they marched solemnly out of the forest and across the crater-land to the pass through which they had appeared. What became of them I do not know, but I suppose that they departed back to their own haunts where we had first met them.

After sundry halts, of which I was not told the reason, towards evening we emerged from that awful forest, only to be confronted with more terrors. On the open space which surrounded the altar platform and in the streets of the town beyond, hundreds of men of the Abanda army were running to and fro, some with torn robes and some stark naked, shrieking and staring about them with eyes that were full of fear. A mob of raving maniacs who seemed hardly human, they foamed at the mouth, they rolled upon the ground, they tore their hair and bit each other's flesh.

"They are all mad, Baas," said Hans, getting behind me, for as is common with African natives, he had a great horror of the insane and supposed them to be inspired by heaven. "Don't touch them, Baas, or we shall go mad too."

His exhortation was needless, for my one desire was to get as far as possible from the hideous sight of these poor creatures. What could have brought them to such a pass, I marvelled, as I do today. I can only suppose that when the survivors of the regiments which had followed us to the lake arrived among the army that awaited them at the town, they communicated to their brothers the terror which had driven them crazy.

Or perhaps now that Kaneke had disappeared, the superstitions he had kept in check broke out among them with a force so irresistible that they lost their minds, remembering the ancient curse which was said to overtake any of their people who set foot in the land of Lake Mone, whence they had been driven in past ages. I cannot tell, but certainly they had "become as beasts", as the priestess Shadow foretold. It was shocking, it was terrible, and thankful indeed was I when, on catching sight of us, with howls and lamentations they drew together and fled away, I suppose back to their own land.

Soon they were gone into the gathering darkness, thousands of them, and quiet fell upon the town, which was quite unharmed. Hans and I made our way to our own house where we found a lamp lit and food prepared, I presume by the women who waited upon us, who all this while had remained faithfully at their post. The first thing that we saw were our lost rifles and ammunition, carefully laid upon our beds.

"*Allemagter!*" exclaimed Hans, pointing first to the lamp and food next to the rifles. "We have met many strange peoples in our journeys, Baas, but never any like these. But, Baas, they are not men and women, they are witches and wizards, every one of them, whose master is the devil, as those Abanda will think when they get their minds again."

Then, quite overcome, he sank on to a stool and began to devour his meal in silence. I, too, collapsed ; no other word describes my state, brought about by physical fatigue and mental astonishment. At that moment I was almost inclined to agree with Hans, though now of course I know that these events which at the time seemed so strange were quite susceptible of a natural interpretation. It was not wonderful that the Abanda soldier should have been attacked in the forest by a herd of elephants whose tempers were upset by storm and earthquake, or that the survivors of them and their fellows should have been crazed by the experience, added to the effect of their inherited superstitions.

Nor was it wonderful that an ardent man like Arkle should have succumbed to the charm of a beautiful priestess, whose personal attractions were enhanced by the mystery with which she was surrounded, though I admit that I do not understand the tale of his previous telepathic intercourse with her, if it may be so described. Very possibly, however, this existed only in his imagination, and the real romance began, on his part at any rate, when he first saw her upon the borders of the lake.

Still, the cumulative effect of so many eerie happenings, reinforced by the legends with which my ears were filled, and the constant ceremonies and experiences of an abnormal and unwholesome nature in which I had been forced to take a part, together with the vanishing away of Arkle into what I understood to be a kind of Eastern *houri* paradise, was crushing ; at least this was its effect upon a tired and puzzled man.

So I went to bed with an attack of fever and low spirits that kept me there for a week, after which I took another week to recover my strength.

During all this time very little happened, for Hans reported that everything in the town went on as it used to do before the great storm. The people were cultivating their gardens ; the sacred fire was re-lit upon the altar and the priests had rebuilt their fallen observation tower, whence they watched the stars nightly as of old. To judge from the aspect of the people, indeed one might have thought that nothing unusual had occurred, or at any rate that it was quite forgotten.

Now, being filled with nervous apprehensions and extremely anxious to escape from this country as soon as I was well enough to face the journey, I tried several times to get into touch with Kumpana, the only man in the place who seemed to have any real authority, but was always told that he was absent.

At length he came, bland and smiling as ever, and apologized for not having done so before, "For then," he added, "I, who am a doctor, should have been able to cure you more quickly."

I replied that it did not matter, as I was now quite recovered who never suffered from serious illness. Then I asked him the news.

"There is little, Lord," he answered. "From the lake we hear that the Engoi and her husband, the Shield of the Shadow, are well and most happy. The Abanda, now that they have reached their own land and found their wits again—for only about two hundred of them were killed by the elephants—are very humble and have sent to make their submission, promising henceforth to be our faithful servants and to live with us as one people."

"So you have got what you want," I said.

"Yes, Lord, for now we shall become a great tribe, a nation, indeed, as once we were hundreds of years ago, because these Abanda are brave fighting men and their women have many children, whereas ours bear few or none at all. Never again will they threaten us, but, directed by our wisdom, will do all that we command."

"Which was your object throughout, I suppose, Kumpana?"

"Yes, Lord, it was our object, which explains much that you have never been able to understand, amongst other things, why you were brought to Mone-land. Without you Kaneke could not have been saved from the Arabs, and the White Lord, Shield of the Shadow, could not have been saved from the Abanda after his madness had caused him to be cast out of our country, which even I was unable to prevent."

"But why did you want Kaneke back, Kumpana, seeing that at once you took away his chieftainship and made him an outlaw?"

"Because, amongst other reasons, if he had not returned and been driven out again, he would not have fled to the Abanda and led them to attack us, as we wished that he should do, knowing the fate that would overtake them. Even then I do not think that the Abanda, who fear the Engoi and her servants, would have followed him, had they not seen you, the great white lord whose fame is everywhere, running before them like a hunted jackal, which was why we took you with us to the pass, telling you that it was to fight them."

Now controlling my wrath as best I could, for it was useless to argue with Kumpana about this disgraceful episode of my career, I said with sarcasm:

"So you foresaw all these things, Kumpana, and arranged accordingly?"

"Of course, Lord, for we have that gift," he replied in the mild, protesting voice of one who humours an ignorant fool.

This amazing lie took away my breath, but again feeling it useless to argue, I changed the subject, by asking:

"And why did you bring him who is now her husband here to marry the Shadow, instead of giving her to Kaneke, to whom she was promised, or to some other man of your people?"

"Because, Lord, our men are——" and he used an Arabic word which I can only translate by the English phrase 'played out', "The race has grown too ancient and too interbred. Therefore it was necessary that she who is now the Engoi upon earth should wed one of a different stock who has knowledge of the arts and laws of the great white races. For, Lord, from this marriage will spring a woman, the Engoi to be, who will be very great of heart. It is she," he went on with a ring of triumph in his voice, "who will once more make the Dabanda mighty among the peoples of Africa, not the lady who now rules over us, or the white wanderer who is her spouse."

"So that is another of your prophecies, Kumpana?"

"Yes, Lord, and one which most certainly will be fulfilled," he answered in the same triumphant tone. Then, as though the matter were one which he declined to discuss, he said in his ordinary voice:

"This is the night of full moon, and there is a ceremony before the altar which we pray you to attend. For tomorrow doubtless you will wish to bid us farewell as it has been arranged that you should do."

"I am glad to hear that," I exclaimed, "but I don't want to be present at any more of your ceremonies."

"Yet, Lord," he answered with his queer little smile, "I am sure you will do what we wish, now, as always before."

"Which means that I must come."

"Oh, Lord, I never said so. Still I am certain that you will come and shall send an escort to attend upon you, that you may fear no harm."

Then he rose and bowed himself out.

Not until he was gone did I remember that I had never asked him what had become of Kaneke.

"Baas," said Hans, "I always thought you clever in your way, but this Kumpana is much cleverer than you, or even than I am, because you see in the end he always makes us do, not what we want but what he wants, and then laughs at us about it afterwards. We shall have to go to that fetish business tonight, because if we won't walk, we shall be carried there, quite nicely, of course, by the men he is sending to protect us. I wonder what we shall see, Baas."

"How do I know?" I snapped, for the gibes of Hans irritated

me. "Perhaps the lady Shadow and her husband will come to visit us."

"I don't think so, Baas. I think that they are sitting holding each other's hands and making faces at each other, and saying silly things about the moon. If it were six months later when they want to hold other people's hands and to look into new faces and have forgotten all about the moon, then they would come, Baas, but not now. But perhaps Kaneke will visit us, unless he is dead, which we haven't heard, and I'd much rather see him, Baas, than two people who keep saying 'Sweetie-Sweet' and 'there's no one else in the world, Pretty'."

"Would you, you ugly little sinner?" I replied, and walked away.

As it happened, Hans, who could smell out the truth like any witch-doctor, had made no mistake, for when, conducted by our promised escort, a strong one by the way, we reached the altar platform that night, it was to find that the centre of interest proved to be Kaneke and no one else, and that for the second time it was our lot to see him tried for his life. What is more, even among that undemonstrative people, made apathetic by the passage of many ages of plenty, and by iron priestly rule, the event excited keen and universal interest.

This might be seen from the fact that every creature from the town who could walk or be carried, was gathered upon the market-place beneath the platform, and with them a great number of people from the villages and farms beyond its borders. The priests too were present in force ; the astrologers watched the heavens from their towers and shouted out the messages of the stars ; a choir hidden behind the altar sang solemn chants at intervals ; and the sacred fire blazed like a signal beacon upon a mountain, as though to make up for the fact that very recently it had twice been extinguished. Indeed it was a veritable furnace.

In front of it, its fierce light playing on him, stood Kaneke, bound and closely guarded, while on either side sat the white-robed Council of the Shadow, whose office seemed to be that of judge or jury, or both. Near to them, so placed that he could be heard from the audience below as well as by all upon the platform, stood Kumpana, who in this drama played the part of the prosecuting counsel.

When I arrived with Hans and had been given a seat not far from Kumpana and facing Kaneke, the proceedings began. I need not detail them further than to say that they consisted of a recitation of all his crimes, starting with a long account of the act of sacrilege he had committed in his youth against a former Engoi, that apparently was much worse than he had intimated to me, and had resulted in his banishment or flight, and going on to those offences with which I had some acquaintance.

At length the tale was finished, and Kaneke was called upon to answer. This he did with a certain dignity, pleading that his judges had no jurisdiction over him, that he was their lawful chief and could not be tried by any court. The crimes alleged against him he made no attempt to deny or explain, perhaps because they were too flagrant to admit of defence.

When he had finished speaking, Kumpana said to the Council and the priests :

"What say you ?"

Whereupon they answered all together :

"We say that he is guilty !" and the people gathered in the market-place beneath echoed the words in a roar of sounds.

Then Kumpana cried aloud to the astrologers upon their towers, asking :

"What reward is appointed to this traitor Kaneke, the accursed of the Engoi, for his sins against the Shadow and against the people ?"

The diviners on the towers stared at the stars, making a pretence of consulting them, then spoke together in a secret language I did not understand. At last one of them, he on the right, called out :

"Hear the voice of Heaven ! Let him who quenched the fire, feed the fire."

I contemplated the leaping flames upon which the priests had just hurled more wood, and not understanding all that these words meant, remarked to Hans that it did not seem to want feeding.

"Oh, Baas," he replied, "why are you so stupid ? Don't you see that they are going to burn this owl-man as an offering ? The woman in the hut told me that it is what they always do to anyone who has tried to lay hands upon the Shadow of the Engoi, and sometimes to her husband also if she gets tired of him."

"Great heavens !" I exclaimed, turning quite faint. Then, before I could get out another word, Kaneke, who was a coward at heart, as he had shown when he bartered his birthright to Arkle in exchange for his life, with ashen face and bulging eyes began an impassioned appeal to me to save him.

I did try to say something on his behalf, I forget what it was, but at once Kumpana cut me short with the remark that there was plenty of room for two upon that altar. He added in explanation that in his country under an ancient law, he who tried to save a criminal condemned to death must share his punishment.

Hearing this, as I was helpless and could not stop there to see a man burned alive, however great a blackguard he might be, I rose and with the best dignity I could command, walked down the platform steps and through the people at the foot of them, back to our house. As I passed him Kaneke shouted out :

"Farewell, Macumazahn, whom I met in an evil hour. If, before you leave this land, you see your friend, the white thief who has stolen her that was mine, tell him that in a day to come, instead of her lips he too shall kiss the altar flames."

Now all my pity departed, for I knew well that these cruel words had been spoken to create baseless fears and doubts in my mind and in that of Arkle also, should they reach him.

"Cease from lying and die like a man," I said.

If he answered me I did not hear him, for just then the priests set up a song, a very savage song, which prevented his words from reaching me. At the edge of the market-place some impulse caused me to look back, just in time to see the great shape of Kaneke outlined against the flames into which he was being tossed whilst the people around, who till now had remained silent, uttered a shout of joy.

A while later Hans joined me.

"Baas," he said, "I am glad they burned that beast Kaneke."

"Why ?" I asked, for I thought the remark pitiless.

"For two reasons, Baas. First because he left Little Holes and Jerry to be killed when we were running for the pass, being a coward who could desert his friends ; and secondly because he called out after you that if he had won, he would have burned you and the Red Baas and me, Hans, as well. That is why I stopped to see the end of him, Baas."

"Let us pack up," I said, "for tomorrow we start."

"Yes, Baas, but where to, Baas ?"

"I don't know and I don't care," I answered, "so long as it is out of this accursed country. Why on earth they ever brought me into it I can't understand even now."

"That you might bring Kaneke, Baas."

"But why did they want Kaneke ? They would have got on quite as well without him."

"To burn him, Baas. He had sinned against another Shadow

who is dead and ran away, and the priests, who never forget, brought him back that he might be killed for his sin. That is why White-Mouse was sent to tempt him from home, telling him that he was to marry the new Shadow, and that is why she was so much afraid lest he should be killed by the Arabs and cheat the fire on the altar. Oh, they had thought it all out quite nicely, Baas, as Kaneke has learned."

"Perhaps. Well, they won't tempt *me* back," I said.

CHAPTER XX

FAREWELL

Now with the execution of Kaneke in the savage fashion that I have described, the story of my visit to the sacred lake called Mone, and the people who dwelt there comes to an end. Perhaps, however, there are one or two things that I should mention.

All the day following the horrible scene upon the altar platform, Hans and I spent in getting ready, tying up loads for the bearers who, we were informed, would be provided on the next morning, superintending the cooking of food to take with us, seeing to our boots that were much the worse for wear, and so forth. In our spare time I tried also to think out the great problem as to the route that we should take. Were we to return by that which we had followed into the Lake-country, or to strike out on a desperate journey for the West Coast? Upon my soul I did not know, and all that Hans would do was to point out the difficulties and dangers of either course.

When I lay down that night I was still quite unable to make up my mind, and went to sleep determined to postpone further consideration till the morrow, hoping that meanwhile some inspiration might come to me. As a matter of fact it did, and in a curious fashion.

About midnight I woke up and saw, by the light of the lamp which I kept burning, the white-draped form of a woman, standing at the foot of the bed, who appeared to be looking at me.

"What the dickens——" I began in a hurry, when she stopped me with a motion of her hand.

Then she drew her veil aside so that I could see her face. It was that of White-Mouse!

Surely I could not be mistaken, although I had only seen her twice or thrice upon a single night. There was the same delicate shape, the same pleading, dark eyes, the same curling hair, and the same sweet, plaintive face so suggestive of mystery and acquaintance with secret things.

"White-Mouse!" I murmured beneath my breath, for to tell the truth I was half afraid to speak aloud, fearing lest what I saw before me was a ghost, or at the best a dream.

"Yes, Lord Macumazahn; at least once I bore that name far away among the Arabs."

"But you are dead! They killed you there in the courtyard of Kaneke's house."

"No, Lord, they could not kill me. I escaped out of their hands and returned to this country before you, making your road smooth and easy."

"Before us! How did you do that?"

"It is one of the secrets which I may not reveal, Lord, nor does it matter. Also we have met since then when you were in trouble yonder with the 'dwellers in the forest' and one came to guide you."

"I thought it!" I exclaimed; "but before I could make sure you were gone, so that almost I believed you to be—not a woman but—well—one of the dwellers in the forest."

"I knew it," she replied with a sweet little smile, "and for the rest, even now are you sure that I am a woman?"

"No, I am not," I answered.

"Nor am I quite sure, Lord Macumazahn, but that is another of the secrets, and it does not matter. See, I am a messenger tonight whatever else I may be and I have brought you a letter which you can read when I am gone, for I think that to it there is no answer. Or if there should be an answer, shape it in your mind and I shall learn it there and deliver it word for word."

"Again I begin to think that you are a ghost, White-Mouse, for women do not talk thus," I said as I took the little roll of paper which she handed to me and laid it down upon the bed.

The truth was that at the moment I was more interested in White-Mouse than in what might be written in the roll.

"Although some do not know it, we are all of us ghosts, are we not, Lord Macumazahn? Though often if the veil of flesh be gross, the light of the ghost-lamp that shines within you cannot be seen. Lord, my time is short and I have something to say to you. Will it please you to listen ?"

"When you speak, what could please me better, especially in this land, White-Mouse ?"

Again there flitted across her face a quick smile so strangely sweet that it thrilled the nerves, as do certain notes of music we hear upon a violin. At least for some indefinable reason I always connect that smile of hers with such vibrating notes.

"Yet it would not please you in other lands, Lord, for there among your own people nothing would delight you less than to hear the voice of a ghost-woman, the dweller in a spell-bound, haunted place. Were it otherwise, perchance I should accompany you, as, although you will not see me, I may do yet."

"What do you mean ?" I asked rather anxiously.

"Nothing that you need fear, Lord, except that I like you well, and both ghosts and women are pleased to be with those whom they like. Oh, I have watched you from the first and noted how you have borne many troubles that were not of your seeking, and read your heart and found it worthy to be praised. In this land, Lord, such are not found."

"I am glad to hear it," I said, who had little admiration for the Dabanda. Then to change the subject which I found somewhat personal and embarrassing, especially to a modest man who could neither rise nor escape, I added, "Will you do something for me, White-Mouse, and before you go ? Tell me, why I was ever brought to your land ?"

"You wished to come, Lord ; and if they be real, wishes always fulfil themselves soon or late. Moreover, besides those you know which Kumpana has set out to you, there are other reasons, which, even if I might explain them, you would not understand."

"Why not ?"

"Because they have to do with things which you have forgotten ; yes, with other lives that lie buried in the past, when you and I and two great ones who dwell in the midst of Lake Mone, and Kumpana and Kaneke knew each other, as we do today. Man's life is a long story, Lord, of which we read but one mad chapter at a time, thinking that it is all the book, and not knowing what went before, nor what shall follow after."

Now I reflected that many wise men, of all epochs, such as Plato and others, as I have heard, were of this opinion—one that it is not impossible though difficult to accept at any rate in the West, whatever the East may hold. Not wishing, however, to enter upon so vast a subject, I merely said :

"And do *you* know, White-Mouse?"

"I know something, Lord, and I guess more. For the Dwellers in the Lake, whom doubtless you believe to be savages blinded by the teachings of a false faith, yet have the wisdom of our race."

"Yes," I answered sharply, "wisdom of which I saw the fruits last night when a man was burned living upon your altar fire."

"You are wrong, Lord. In our wisdom of the Lake, cruelty has no place, and with it she who rules the Lake has naught to do, though the Dabanda be given to her for servants, and in a fashion, for masters. When she learned what had chanced to Kaneke and to those whom he led astray, she wept, though she knew that these things must come and uttered the decree of death. Yes, we women of the Lake renounce the world and fix our thoughts on heaven, which is our home. Therefore do not judge us hardly, Lord, or measure us with the Dabanda rule. Now I have done, who may say no more, save this : Have no fear upon your journey, for we know that you will accomplish it safely and live on for many years. Go where fortune seems to lead you and all will succeed with you. So farewell, Lord Macumazahn. Think kindly of us of the Lake, although we be women, for as you have learned, or will learn, women, with all their faults, are better and wiser than men, for sometimes to them is shown the light that is hidden from the eyes of men."

Then she bent down, took my hand, kissed it, and turning lifted the curtain of the door-way of the house and glided away into the darkness, leaving me glad that I had found one person whom I could like in Mone-land, one, too, who liked me !

From the bed on the other side of the room came the stifled voice of Hans, whom all this while I had quite forgotten, saying :

"Is that the last kiss, Baas, and if so, may I put out my head ? It is very hot here under this skin rug, where I have hidden my eyes for so long without being able to breathe, Baas."

"Well, you haven't hidden your ears," I said, "so stop talking rubbish and tell me what you think of White-Mouse."

"Oh, Baas," he said, sitting up, "I think that she is a spook, more so than all the rest of them. But I think also that she is a nice spook, although she did deceive me yonder in the Arab town, making me believe that she was a jealous wife of the Owl-man Kaneke, and that she liked me much more than she did him. Also I am happy now, Baas, because she, who being a spook knows all about it, said that we shall come safely to the end of our

journey.   But of course you are very unhappy because you have
seen the last of one of whom you think so much, that you have
even forgotten to read the letter she brought you, for reading
letters is much duller than being kissed, Baas."

"Bring me the lamp," I said as I loosened the string of
scented grass with which it was bound and undid the little
roll.

It was of paper cut from a note-book, and, as I expected, from
Arkle.   It ran thus :

Dear Quatermain,

*We know that you are going, and I send you this by a
sure hand to bid you farewell.   Do not think badly of me, Quatermain, because I have forsaken my country and put aside all the
traditions in which I was brought up, in order to marry the priestess
of a strange faith, here in Central Africa.   Love is stronger than
are the ties of country or of tradition, and in our case it is a force which
will not be denied : a destiny indeed.   Probably you put little faith in
the stories I have told you of how I came to be drawn to my wife,
thinking them the harmless imaginations of a romantic mind.
Therefore of them I will only say that to me they seemed real enough
and to be justified by the event, though of course here coincidence
might have played its part.   Probably, too, you set little store by the
occult powers and supersitions of this secret and ancient people,
finding for all, or most of them, a natural explanation.*

*For many reasons I wish that I could share this view, but
alas ! I believe those powers to be very real.   And here I want
to make one thing clear : they do not reside in the spirit of her
who amongst other titles is given that of the Engoi or rather of
the Shadow of the Engoi !   She is but the medium.   The strength
lies with others, in the present case principally with the head of
the Council, Kumpana.*

*Did you notice the voice with which she spoke when first you
saw her upon the altar platform, and again in the boat on the day
of our marriage, and that it was not natural ?   At least to me it
seemed very different from that which she used when addressing
me directly, as a woman addresses the man she loves.   For example
she seemed to pass sentence upor the Abanda giving them into the
power of the beasts, over which undoubtedly the Dabanda have command, and to the fate of madness, which I learn fell upon them
afterwards.*

*Yet I assure you that she never knew she had spoken these words,
any more than she knew that the rascal, Kaneke, was doomed to be*

burned alive ; in short they were uttered by her under an obscure, hypnotic influence. Further, it seems that these mediumistic gifts pass away in the course of years, and that is why the Dabanda priests kill their Engoi at a certain age, and her husband with her and choose another Shadow to fill her place.

You will say that for her and for me the prospect therefore is terrible enough. But I want you to understand, Quatermain, that I have no intention of sitting still and allowing such a fate to overtake us. I mean to match myself against those priests and the Council and to overthrow them—how I do not know—and to establish in their place a pure and kindly rule. If I find that this is not possible, then I mean to escape from this country with my wife. So do not look upon us as lost, or on me as wholly a renegade and an apostate, but rather as one who is hidden for awhile.

Meanwhile, I assure you that I am intensely happy and that the book of an ancient wisdom which I thought lost to the world, is being opened to my eyes. I would that you could see this place and the buildings on it, and the old writings it contains in a language I have not yet learned to decipher. But that cannot be, for any such attempt would certainly cost you your life. So you must go your way while I go mine, hoping that our paths may cross again, even in this world.

Meanwhile, I thank you for all you have done for me, and trust that your strange experiences may bring you some reward for your work and the dangers you have run. God bless you, my friend, if I may call you so, and farewell ! I beg you and Hans to talk as little as possible about me or the Dabanda and Mone, the Holy Lake. Above all, do not try to return, or to send other white men to explore, or to search me out, for such attempts would certainly end in death. Let me vanish away as many a white man does in Africa, and my story with me.

Again farewell,

J. T. Arkle.

P.S.—I enclose a note addressed to the captain of the hunters whom I left in charge of stores and equipment at a place to which you will be guided. He can read more or less, and it commands him to hand these over to you absolutely, and with them a sealed box that contains a sum in gold, which I hope you will find useful. I recommend you to head for the West Coast, as the hunters can guide you on that road, at any rate for part of the way till you come into touch with white men.

J. T. A.

Such was this strange letter, which I was most glad to receive. For did it not give me hope that one day Arkle would escape from this accursed country, either with or without the woman whom fate had appointed to him as his wife ? Further, did it not explain much, or at any rate something, of mysteries that hitherto had been as black as night to me ? I think so.

Here I will stop this tale, for to describe all my adventures and experiences on my way to the West Coast would take another book, which I have neither the time nor the inclination to write. Suffice it to say that all went well. I was guided to Arkle's camp, and by help of the outfit I found there, to say nothing of the money, of which there was much, ultimately I came to the sea and took ship back to South Africa, where I gave it out that I had been for a long hunting-trip in Portuguese territory.

"Baas," said Hans to me one day when we had been talking over Arkle and his great passion, "what are the 'twin hearts' of which you talk ?"

I explained as best I could, and he replied :

"Baas, you remember that Kaneke said just before they put him on the fire, that the Red Baas would follow him there one day. If that is what must be paid for having a 'twin heart', I am glad I haven't got one—unless it is for you, Baas !"

I should add that of Arkle, if this was his real name (which I doubt), I have heard no more. Nor until now, when after many years I write it down, have I ever told his story.

THE END